By Z. ALLORA

Illusions & Dreams
Lock and Key

Published by DREAMSPINNER PRESS
www.dreamspinnerpress.com

Lock and Key

Z. ALLORA

Published by
DREAMSPINNER PRESS

5032 Capital Circle SW, Suite 2, PMB# 279, Tallahassee, FL 32305-7886 USA
www.dreamspinnerpress.com

This is a work of fiction. Names, characters, places, and incidents either are the product of author imagination or are used fictitiously, and any resemblance to actual persons, living or dead, business establishments, events, or locales is entirely coincidental.

Lock and Key
© 2016 Z. Allora.

Cover Art
© 2016 K-Koji.
Cover Design
© 2016 Paul Richmond.
http://www.paulrichmondstudio.com
Cover content is for illustrative purposes only and any person depicted on the cover is a model.

ISBN: 978-1-63477-168-9
Digital ISBN: 978-1-63477-169-6
Library of Congress Control Number: 2015920901
Published July 2016
v. 1.0

Printed in the United States of America
∞
This paper meets the requirements of
ANSI/NISO Z39.48-1992 (Permanence of Paper).

To my love.

ACKNOWLEDGMENTS

To My Pretties: Thank you for sharing yourselves with me every day.

I want to thank all my critique partners and betas for helping me through the many versions of this work: Eden, Doug, Danny, Carla, Val, Laura, Andrew, Becky, and several others who helped untangle Z. speak.

Dreamspinner: I'm proud to be part of Dreamspinner Press. Thank you for polishing my story. (Lynn West: Best no EVER! I am indebted to you.)

CHAPTER ONE

FADING INTO the shadows and hiding was second nature to Zack Davis. People didn't notice him. His older brother was a drummer in a wildly popular rock band, and his younger brother was a talented, outgoing artist. Zack was easily overlooked between the two of them.

Probably a good thing since he was nothing but a twisted fuck. Invisibility had been his shield of choice, his only way of masking how much he didn't belong… anywhere.

Now, at least, he had a job that utilized his skills of stealth. He was a roadie for his brother's rock band, the Dark Angels, a job whose main objective was to get things done while drawing no attention.

His boss told him his duties during this afternoon's sound check were to be ready for anything the band needed and to stay out of sight. Zack stood behind the curtain, comfortably hidden while the band checked their equipment. He focused on his assignment of waiting around and staring at the stage, or at least he tried.

Who is that?

Need slashed through Zack. He attempted for the millionth time not to stare at the man in leather who paced back and forth, speaking in hushed tones into a cell phone. That wasn't a unique scenario backstage. But the way the leather clung held Zack's attention hostage.

He'd always found the sight and smell of leather a turn-on. Images from the latest BDSM website he'd joined danced through his head. Not even being kicked out of his mother's home for his "perversity" drove him to control his need to explore his dark desires.

Damn, why wouldn't Sex-in-Leather turn around? The way he faced the opposite direction made it too easy for Zack to drool over how the black leather cupped the guy's ass to perfection. Wow, his jacket must have been tailored to fit the expanse of his broad shoulders and narrow hips.

Zack memorized the enticing image for use at a more appropriate time.

Getting hard at work might violate his contract, so he redirected his attention to the sound check. It appeared to be going well, but what the hell did he know? This was his first concert working as a roadie.

Dusty finished his solo on the drums. His voice echoed a bit through the sound system as he said, "Your turn, Josh and Dare."

The bass and lead guitar players tested their equipment by plucking their strings in a duel between the instruments. Josh switched out his bass halfway through the song to check his guitar. Damn, they should do that during a concert. The crowd would love it.

"Charlie, I just don't understand…." The leather man's exasperation carried across the backstage area.

Zack turned and caught sight of the man's chiseled movie-star profile, which was marred by a frown.

The guy ran his fingers through his dark brown hair and asked into the cell, "What do you mean you're not going to make it?"

Zack shouldn't be listening, so he pulled out his own phone. He'd gotten one text from his little brother, Jordon, stating, *Late*, signed with a little artist emoji.

Zack quickly texted back, *Why? Justin still with you?*
Traffic. Yes.

Zack released the breath he'd been holding. *OK*, he typed back. His kid brother might very well be the death of him.

His phone buzzed with another text. *Stop worrying. Fine.*

He shouldn't worry. His older brother's boyfriend, Justin, was good with Jordon, but some habits didn't die.

Another text followed. *B there in 20.*

He slipped his phone into his pocket as the makeup artist darted past him and then rushed over to him. "Zack, honey, did you see Augusto?"

"Um, who?" He tried to remember her name. Carla? Cindy? Celia? Casey? It was something with a *C*.

She sighed with a touch of "I'm going to strangle you" and said, "Oh right, you're new. He's the hairdresser. The bastard's late again."

How would that impact the show? "Oh, Augusto. No, I haven't seen him. Sorry."

"If you see the fucker, tell him to get his ass to the dressing room pronto," she called over her shoulder as she jogged off in the opposite direction.

Should Zack look for him? He glanced down the hallway she'd run. No, the stage manager told him to be here and help with the sound check. That's what he'd do. Besides, Zack wouldn't know the hairdresser in question if he walked right past him.

Zack glanced back in the direction of the sexy man milling around with his phone to his ear. His tone tense, Sex-in-Leather asked, "You're going to *whose* party? But I thought—I'm not forcing you to do anything…. Okay, I'll s—" He pulled the cell away from his ear and stared down at the device. Shaking his head, he said, "See you later."

With liquid movements, Sex-in-Leather pushed his cell back into his jacket pocket. How was such a simple action so alluring? What would he be like in the dark? Or better yet, the light, so Zack could see Sex-in-Leather's excitement twist into satisfaction.

Lost in fascinated lust, he stared for a second too long.

Shit! The guy caught him midgawk.

Zack spun toward the progress on stage. He edged deeper into the curtains, hoping to camo himself into invisibility.

On stage, Angel Luv, the lead singer of the Dark Angels, was testing his microphone by singing nursery rhymes. Zack had never thought of *The Three Little Pigs* as a ménage story, but with a few word changes, the plot was right there.

A deep, rich laugh rang out and warmed Zack's insides.

Curiosity made him glance over his shoulder. Leather's mesmerizing blue eyes stared at him from only a few feet away.

All blood, sense, and reason left Zack's head.

Kneel. Serve. His.

"Um… hi." Zack's voice picked a shitty time to crack.

Lame. Lame. Lame.

The most exquisite man he'd ever seen, and all Zack came up with was "um hi." He should have gone to college; he'd have made a stunning communications major.

"I'm Andrew Nikeman."

Kneel. Serve. Wait!

"Nikeman?" He repeated the word as if it tasted funny in his mouth. *Nikeman.* Well, that was shitastic! He'd filled his spank bank with images of—"Justin's brother?"

"Yeah. Oh wait, are you one of Dusty's brothers?"

"Zack Davis. Um, our brothers are dating, er, well, now I guess they're living together."

Fuckety fuck fuck.

"Indeed." Andrew gave him a million-dollar smile that made Zack want to drop to his knees.

Managing to stay on his feet but with a dry mouth, sweaty hands, and the beginning of an erection, Zack prayed for something not completely stupid to come out of his mouth.

Andrew's brilliant blue T-shirt matched his eyes, but that wasn't really a conversation starter. Clearly, the deity in charge of lust had better things to do other than throw him a bone.

Why did their brothers have to be dating? Zack could… do nothing. This guy was way out of his league. Fantasies and dreams were the only option left, but even those bordered on wrong.

A voice from the stage broke the spell. "Zack Davis? Zack Davis. Please report to the stage with a new set of drumsticks. Your dumbass brother managed to break all of his. Ow! Don't throw your broken sticks at me!" Angel tapped the microphone, making everyone wince. "Is this thing on? Oh Zackery? Zack?"

"Oh, I should…." He gestured toward the stage but didn't want to go. "I'll, um, see you soon."

Proud he'd managed words, Zack smiled, spun on his heel, and slammed right into the wall behind the curtain.

Ow!

He crashed backward.

Strong arms caught him, preventing his ass from hitting the floor.

Oh God! Mmmm, *oh God*…. He wanted to stay right there forever in Andrew's embrace. Damn, the body he reclined against was as hard as it appeared under the leather. The scent of leather and man and….

His rescuer steadied him and stepped back. Maybe it had become clear Zack wasn't making any attempt to stand on his own two feet.

"You okay?"

Dazed, Zack muttered, "Yeah. Thanks."

He grabbed several spare sets of sticks off the table. Shoving aside the curtain that betrayed him, he used his hand to find the moving wall before he escaped to the stage.

Angel chuckled. "Zack, did you whittle those?"

"No, sorry, I was…" *making an idiot out of myself backstage.*

Zack handed the drumsticks off to his brother. Then, darting to Angel, he plucked a piece of the broken stick out of the singer's hair.

Elsewhere on stage, Josh made his guitar sing before swapping the instrument out for the bass.

Dusty busted on the bass player, "You can front all you want, Josh. Just remember, The Doors made it without a bass player so... how relevant are you?"

Josh winked at Zack and hid his grin as he turned toward the drummer. He fluttered his fingers. "You know what this is, Dust?"

Zack bit back his smile as he worked on gathering the rest of the wood shards scattered across the stage.

"You trying to find the strings of your bass?" Dusty stared across the stage with a confused expression.

"No? A flock of these," Josh said as he flipped him the middle finger times two.

No one would ever guess this bunch of misbehaving adolescents were actually famous rockers. Though the true delinquents were the two that had started the band, his brother and Dusty's best friend, Angel Luv. Angel shouldn't ever be without adult supervision, and while Dusty might have raised Zack and their younger brother, Jordon, Angel seemed to bring out Dusty's immature side.

Zack bit back his chuckle and scurried off the stage, which now roared with the band's laughter. He envied the band, not their rock-star status, but their camaraderie. One of the drawbacks of being invisible was that he didn't have many friends.

Where was—oh.

Andrew leaned against the back wall like a model at a photo shoot. Phone in hand, he glanced up and smiled at Zack. "Crisis averted?"

"Yeah." Someone must have rolled in the rack of costumes for the show, and Zack busied himself with adjusting the hangers. He shifted the rod to a diagonal position, which allowed him to watch Andrew without being obvious.

Andrew peered at him. "Being the drummer's brother, you've probably been backstage a lot."

"Yeah, some." Not this past year, though. His mother had decided the Dark Angels' concerts were sinful, so he and Jordon hadn't been allowed to go. In her divine wisdom, she tried to stop them from seeing Dusty altogether a few months ago. But that had the opposite effect, because now they were both living with Dusty... well, were on tour with him.

The makeup artist came rushing back through. "No Augusto, right?"

"Nope, sorry." Zack stopped fussing with the clothing.

"Son of a bitch! That little prick!" rang through the backstage a moment before Megan, the group's manager, stomped in, waving her cell. "Fucking cocksucker!" She looked up and realized she wasn't alone. "Oh, sorry. No offense. I love sucking cock too."

Was she referring to Zack? If so, damn way to out him. *Wait!* Was she referring to both him and Andrew? Was Andrew gay?

He dared a peek at Andrew and got caught up in his dreamy gaze.

Andrew gave Zack a small nod.

Was that a nod of confirmation? An indication of solidarity from a member of the cocksuckers union he'd yet to join? What did the nod mean? Did he want his cock sucked? Did he want to suck cock? 'Cause Zack would be up for any of that! He nodded at Megan.

Megan handed her phone to the makeup artist. "Here, Cindy. Read this."

She looked down, handed the phone back, and flapped her hands. "So now what?"

Megan put her hands up. "I've got to make calls. Have faith."

Zack whispered to Cindy, "What happened?"

"Augusto was arrested for DUI and possession... again. I hope he goes to jail this time." She shook her head and frowned. "The band put him in rehab twice."

The members of the band flooded backstage.

Dusty and Josh danced past the curtain, bobbing and darting around. They both tried to avoid being whacked themselves while attempting to smack the other in the head.

Darius and Robin were speaking in whispers.

Angel meandered in last as he sipped from a mug.

Dusty put Josh in a headlock. Josh did a quick spin, and somehow the move ended with Dusty's arms being secured behind his back.

Damn! Good move! Josh needed to teach Zack how to execute that.

Dusty reminded him, "Drumming tonight."

Josh released him but smacked him in the head and ducked to miss Dusty's retaliation swat.

Angel stopped drinking. He glanced around, cocked his head, and squinted at Cindy.

She ran down the hall, telling him, "Ask Megan."

Instead of asking Megan, the singer's attention fell onto Zack. "Spill."

It wasn't his place to say anything, but Megan appeared to be busy swearing into the phone. "Um, well, I think Augusto... he won't make it tonight."

"My hair!" Robin, the blue-and-green-haired keyboard player, wailed, looking as if the plague had broken out.

Josh told him, "You look fine."

"It's flat!" Robin was trying to fluff out his lion's mane of hair. He had terrible stage fright and was only able to perform when hidden behind his impressive hairstyle, Robin's own brand of duck and cover while under the spotlight. "I don't even have a hat!"

The other roadies filtered back in from the smoking area and the tour buses. The news of Augusto's arrest spread like wildfire. They guessed at the details and filled the gaps where necessary.

There were so many people backstage Zack couldn't see Andrew. Not that he looked. The guy probably thought Zack was a complete tool.

A roadie, whose name Zack didn't want to remember because he was a dick, asked, "Are they still going out there without their hair all prettied up? Will the music even sound as good?"

Dusty got into the guy's face. "Problem?"

People seemed to forget Dusty was tall and had major arm power from drumming for hours at a time. Dust was a placid kind of a guy, but you didn't fuck with Justin, Dusty's brothers, or the band, especially this close to showtime, unless you had a death wish.

"Um... no." The guy backed down.

Angel clapped and got everyone's attention. "Okay, Pretties. Let's get to our battle stations and get ready for the show."

Zack glanced over at his supervisor for direction, but he got an index finger telling him to wait.

Angel danced to Megan as if there wasn't an issue. "So, Megan, solutions?"

She ended her call with a loud "Fuck you!" and plastered on a big smile. "How are you guys at doing your own hair?" The lilt in her voice suggested they should be excited about the opportunity.

Robin groaned like he'd been shot.

Dusty shrugged. He ran fingers through his long hair and said, "Done."

Angel moved his hands toward his head. He stopped and dropped his hands to his sides. "Why mess with the perfection that is Angel Luv?"

Darius snorted.

Andrew stepped forward and cleared his throat. "I'd be happy to offer my services."

Angel took a step back and shook his head. "Thanks. You're handsome and all that, but I'm taken. Darius is my one and only fluffer."

Darius whacked him.

"Careful you don't hurt anything you'll want later."

Darius gave him the evil eye.

Everyone laughed except for Angel.

Andrew put his hands out and clarified, "Um, no. I have a hair salon, and I'm happy to assist you with your emergency *styling* needs."

Dusty stepped up and said, "Andrew, I didn't even see you there. Let me introduce my band of idiots. This is Angel Luv. He thinks everyone wants to blow him."

Angel shrugged. "They do!"

Ignoring the singer, Dusty continued, "This is Darius or Dare Stone. No one knows how or why he puts up with Angel. And this is Josh and Robin Strider…. This is Justin's brother, Andrew Nikeman."

Andrew nodded to the band. "Nice to meet all of you. I enjoy your music. Dusty, it's good to see you again, man."

"Good to see you," Dusty said as he gave him a shoulder-clap-man-hug that Zack was not jealous of at all. "Oh, hey, have you met Zack?"

Zack's invisibility skill failed to melt him into the floor.

Andrew's gaze seemed glued on him. There was no hiding from this guy. Andrew *saw* Zack.

Kneel. Serve….

"Yeah, I've met your kid brother," Andrew admitted with a smile.

What?

"Emphasis on *kid*," Dusty growled.

"I'm eighteen," Zack snarled. He hated being referred to as a kid. Eighteen meant being of legal age. Okay, he couldn't drink, but he was legal for all the things that mattered to him at that moment in time.

Andrew held up his hand. "Sorry, I got your ages mixed up with… um, with Jordon, your little brother."

Mollified slightly, Zack still needed him to be clear. "Jordon's only sixteen. I'm eighteen."

"Sorry, man." Andrew appeared sincere, but probably still thought of him as a kid. After all, the guy owned a salon and was in his midtwenties.

What had Zack done? His big accomplishment was to graduate from high school this past month and land his first job.

Andrew cleared his throat and turned toward the band members. "If I can help with your hair, I'd be happy to."

Dusty waved him off. "You don't have to do that. I'm sure we can manage."

Robin rushed forward, knocking both Dusty and Angel aside. "Oh, sorry, guys. But no, I certainly can't. Andrew, please! Look at me. I can't go out there looking like this."

Andrew grabbed his bag from a shelf. "I have a new wax that you'll love."

Robin squealed and dragged him off toward the dressing room.

Josh tripped after his lover, and the rest of the band followed.

Zack looked over to the stage manager, hoping for an assignment.

The asshole roadie grabbed his arm and sneered, "I don't care who your fucking brother is, *you* won't make it as a roadie."

Fuck that! Zack tugged his arm back. "I wouldn't put bets on that."

The stage manager turned and pretended he hadn't heard the threat.

Zack marched over to his unsupportive supervisor and asked, "What can I do?"

"Just stay out of *our* way." The incompetent man waved him away.

He could do that, but he refused to be treated differently. "Joe, I'm one of *you*. Tell me what needs to be done."

"Okay, okay, fine. Sweep the stage, clean the buses, and empty the trash."

"Yes, sir." He took pleasure at how his words gave the stage manager an expression of constipation. His boss needed to dole out much worse if he planned on making Zack give up or give in.

THE OPENING act took the stage. Zack had cleaned the buses, emptied the trash, and swept up the stage and smoking areas.

The supervisor must have run out of the worst type of meaningless jobs he could think of because the man grumbled, "Take your break."

Zack slipped into the band's crowded dressing room to check on Jordon.

The band had huddled around their manager on one side of the room.

On the other side, his little brother held court with Dusty's boyfriend Justin and… Andrew. The kid swung his arms around as he described the exhibition he and Justin had visited at the museum.

Andrew appeared at home chatting about art. Zack had to give him points for being engaged and not condescending like other people were with Jordon.

"Zack!" Jordon called him out of the shadows. He wished he had the kid's outgoing personality. Jordon asked, "You've met Justin's brother, Andrew, right?"

Without a glance in the man's direction, Zack nodded.

"Good. So, I was telling Andrew about the exhibition Justin and I went to. Here are the pictures." Jordon thrust his phone into Zack's hand. "How's your first day going?"

"Fine." Zack kept his head down and lasered in on the pictures and not the man in leather. He scrolled past the modern art quicker than Jordon probably wanted him to and slowed down on the Impressionists. "I like this one."

Jordon nodded eagerly. "Aw, yeah. The light was wicked in that. Remember this one, Justin?" His little brother nabbed his phone back and shoved it in Justin's face.

Justin stared at it for a moment. "Yeah, one of my favorites. I love Renoir."

Jordon shoulder-bumped Zack and asked, "So what's it like being a roadie?"

"Living the dream." Zack got the reaction he hoped for when Jordon busted out laughing. When Andrew's deep chuckle joined in the melody, Zack said, "I should, um… go."

"What? You just got here," Jordon complained.

"I'm working." Zack didn't know how long he could manage to stay this close to Andrew and not say or do something idiotic.

"Just five more minutes. I miss you," his little brother pleaded, giving him puppy-dog eyes.

Powerless, Zack agreed. For Jordon he'd suffer much worse than the strain of keeping his foot out of his mouth.

Andrew cleared his throat. "Justin said being a roadie is your first job, Zack?"

He nodded. Shit, he did a lot of that, so he threw in a quick word. "Yeah." But he couldn't meet Andrew's gaze, even as it burned through him.

Jordon leaned into the center of the group as if to reveal a secret. "That's 'cause he was keeping me out of trouble. Apparently, I'm a handful." His little brother giggled and snorted. "That's what *he* said."

Zack chuckled. "That *Office* quote never gets old, does it?"

Justin fist-bumped Jordon and spread his fingers in the "blow it up" gesture. He asked Zack, "I convinced Andrew to hang out with us after the show. Can you join us?"

"Not sure how long the breakdown takes." Zack said it like he wouldn't love to spend more time with Andrew. He allowed his gaze to meet Andrew's.

Kneel. Serve. His.

Justin stage-whispered to Andrew, "Is it bad I'm happy Charlie's not coming?"

"Who's Charlie?" The question spilled out of Zack's mouth before he thought about whether he wanted the answer.

Justin rolled his eyes and grimaced.

"My boyfriend," Andrew said.

Of course! Charlie was his boyfriend. Someone like Andrew wouldn't be unattached. Did Zack need a neon light flashing "Bad Idea" above Andrew's head to get the message?

Kneeling, serving, or being his wouldn't be happening in this lifetime. Even if he could circumvent dating brothers and the whole totally out-of-his-league concept, a boyfriend landmined any hope.

"I'll see what time it is when I'm done. If not, I'll catch you guys in the morning before we head out." Zack hesitated. Sparkling dialogue not within his grasp, he settled for saying, "Nice to meet you, Andrew."

He was grateful there had been no hidden wall for him to slam into this time as he left.

CHAPTER TWO

Seven months later

ZACK WIPED his palms on his pants and got out of his car.

Damn! Upstate New York winters sucked. The frigid air punched him in the face, and a gust of wind ripped the air from his lungs.

He zipped his leather jacket and hurried into the entranceway of the club.

Putting his shoulder against the door, he pushed it shut. He hadn't been aware he had an audience.

A woman perched on a stool eyed him with an amused smile. She wore thigh-high shiny purple boots, a black skirt, and a jam-packed purple leather corset. When she finished giving him the once-over, she said, "Welcome to Entwined."

"Um, thanks." He unzipped his jacket, straightened his hair, and tried to peer through the cloudy window of the door in front of him to see into the club.

She pressed her glossy lips together and then asked, "You do know we're a BDSM club, right?"

"Yes." Did he look like he wouldn't know that? He'd done extensive research. Entwined was a network of luxury BDSM clubs across North America.

Her stare intensified. "Are you here for the class?"

Zack nodded.

She pulled her purple specs down on her nose to stare over the rim at him. "Are you a member?"

Entwined catered to the BDSM crowd who could afford their exorbitant membership price. Zack had saved almost all the money he'd made on the tour and now had enough for the initial membership. "Um, not yet."

"Let's see your identification." Her long purple nails clicked against his driver's license. "Okay. I keep this here, and you pick it up when you leave. You need to read these forms, ask any questions you have, and then sign at the bottom or leave. Admission is twenty bucks."

Zack nodded. He sat on the sofa she pointed to and read the paperwork.

The first page was comprised of extensive rules club visitors had to abide by, everything from not being allowed into the back rooms without a senior member being present to a rule about no fluid releases in the main area.

Two men entered the club. One of them stopped to show the lady in purple his membership card.

She smiled and squealed, "Welcome, Master Mark!"

"Everything good in your world, Audrey?" The speaker attached a leash to the man next to him.

"Always," she chirped.

Zack dropped his head to stare at the page. *Shit!* This was real. He was here. But if he didn't focus, he'd never make it into the club.

He read through the second page, which described the club and the small group of Doms and subs that owned and operated it. The club's mission was to provide a safe place to meet, play, learn, and enjoy the practice of BDSM. The rules were detailed and a clear warning given that anyone violating the strict code of conduct would be removed. There was a small note about the thorough vetting process each potential member underwent before membership was granted. The third page contained a basic confidentiality form.

The last page had a bunch of statistics on STD transmission and the spread of HIV. Thanks to his big brother's insistence, Zack and Jordon understood all the ins and out of sexually transmitted diseases, and that even oral sex had a potential risk. He wondered how the new preventive medication he was on would impact these numbers. There was also a signature line for agreeing to have bloodwork done quarterly and a pledge to share any important medical information with play partners where fluids might be exchanged, including but not limited to HIV status.

Zack went back to the woman in purple and asked, "Do you have a pen?"

She studied him. "No questions?"

"Nope. It's pretty straightforward." Most of it was exactly what the club had on their website.

She pulled a purple pen from her corset, twirling it between her fingers before handing it to him. "Here you go."

"Thanks." He signed the forms and handed the packet, pen, and twenty dollars to her.

She pointed across the alcove. "The lockers are over there for personal items you don't want to take into the club. Make sure to leave your phone in the locker if it has a camera on it because if you take it in with you, you'll be asked to leave per the confidentiality form you just signed. The demonstration will start in a few minutes. If you need anything, my name is Audrey."

"Thanks." He put his cell in the locker and pocketed the key.

Fuck! This was really going to happen. He finally could explore the side of himself he couldn't silence. His hand trembled just a little as he pushed open the door to what felt like the start of his life.

Entwined was like stepping into heaven.

Everyone there was into BDSM or at least explored the lifestyle. He didn't have to hide his interest in kinky play.

Two men without clothing knelt on a towel beside a woman who stroked their heads and whispered to them. A short man wearing only a thong scurried to a wall filled with paddles, retrieved one, and rushed off to join a man standing toward the back of the main room. Those who were dressed were predominantly dressed in leather. Some wore collars and leashes or carried whips and handcuffs, and all went about their business with a casual confidence that melted Zack's brain.

Zack tried to appreciate the opulent Renaissance style of the club's decor but failed. The artwork, the gilded tables, cushioned chairs, and fainting couches contributed to the atmosphere, but all were lost on him.

He zigzagged around the tables to read the club's schedule, which was posted in a golden frame. Monday and Thursday were men's night. Tuesday and Sunday were women only. Wednesday, Friday, and Saturday were open play for everyone. Information on how to reserve rooms was described at the bottom.

The fact that he was in a *real* BDSM club hit him again. This wasn't him stalking the Internet for BDSM forums, blog posts, or websites of kinky sex. Entwined would allow him to explore his interests in the real world.

He inhaled.

Leather, sweat, and pheromones assaulted his senses.

Shit, he needed to find a seat before he passed out from excitement. He slid into a chair in the back row.

The velvet curtains to the stage were parted. A simple padded bench with black restraints stood in the center. On the table a paddle, crop, fuzzy mitt, candle, and an ice bucket rested.

A bald bare-chested man with leather straps crisscrossing his torso jumped up onto the stage. He held out his hand to help a younger, shirtless man who had hair down to his waist up onto the stage.

One of the women standing off to the side, twirling a crop, yelled out, "Have fun, Orion."

The longhaired man glanced in her direction and eagerly nodded with a big smile.

The audience chuckled.

"I'm Jason, and this lovely man is Orion. He'll help me give a very basic introduction to BDSM." The room was large enough that both men were miked.

Zack joined in the applause.

"BDSM stands for bondage and discipline, dominance and submission, sadism and masochism. Some people believe it's taboo, but most people have at one time or another explored part of BDSM. A blindfold in the bedroom, a student-teacher role-play, or a little playful tickling all are facets of BDSM."

Jason paced across the stage. "I see many new faces in the audience. Everyone has different reasons for being here. Some of you want to explore what exchanging power means. Maybe your significant other dragged you here. Perhaps you came because you want to learn how to practice BDSM. By the way, just like with anything else, it takes time and effort to be good at it. Or maybe you're here because you're just curious. It doesn't matter, we're glad to have you."

Jason meandered to the other side of the stage. "Who can tell me the basic principles?"

Zack said the holy trinity in his head as someone in the front row called out, "Safe, sane, and consensual."

"Correct. Safe, sane, and consensual is the difference between abuse and BDSM. But we like to go a little further in Entwined. I want us to just touch on the RACK philosophy."

Orion peered up at the man as if he were waiting with the rest of the audience for the lecture to continue.

"RACK stands for risk-awareness and consensual kink. Usually this goes for more intense play called… anyone?"

"Edge play," the man Zack had seen in the alcove called out.

Jason chuckled. "Yes, Master Mark. Edge play." He looked out into the audience and shared, "Master Mark is one of the founding members of Entwined."

Everyone applauded.

Master Mark stood with hands up to quiet everyone down. "Education is important. I'm glad so many people are here tonight. Entwined is concerned for your well-being. Education is the best way to grow within the lifestyle or to spice it up in the bedroom."

"Thank you, Master Mark," Jason said as the man sat down and petted his sub.

Orion gave a small wave in the founder's direction.

Jason continued, "Since this is only the first half of BDSM 101, we won't go too much into RACK, but the basic philosophy is that there's inherent risk with everything we do, so nothing can be completely safe. However, we can make things safer, which is what we endeavor to do. We do this by understanding and studying what we will do in a scene and what we can do to make our activities as safe as possible. I know there are folks who believe if you walk out of a scene with all your body parts still attached, you aren't hardcore enough."

The audience chuckled.

Jason smiled and waited for everyone to quiet. "BDSM isn't a competition. Each person is seeking something unique, so by using measurements that may not or should not be applied does a disservice to us all. Let's not invalidate each other. Okay, getting off my soapbox."

He guided Orion over to the bench and asked the audience, "Can anyone tell me the reasons a sub might wear a collar?"

Someone called out, "They're collared."

Jason nodded. "Correct. That's a commitment between a Dom or Master and a sub, bottom, or slave. Or sometimes a collar means the submissive is under consideration to enter into that level of BDSM relationship. What other reasons?"

The audience got quiet.

Zack wished he had the guts to raise his hand. He could list them off. Instead he waited for Jason to answer his own question.

"A collar being put on can be part of the ritual indicating the scene has started. Wearing a collar can be used as a way of identification, meaning a person wearing a collar is sub and they might be looking for a Dominant or Master. Or it can be used as a sign the individual is under the protection of someone. It might be also used in pet play or fashion."

Orion touched his collar and whispered something to Jason, who nodded. Orion spoke, "I wanted to add that if the person wearing a collar is part of a couple, it's protocol here at Entwined to ask the Master or Dom or Owner if you can speak to their sub. If you're new, the Master may want to learn more about you before she or he allows interactions between you and their submissive."

Jason smiled. "Just be respectful. If you breach protocol, most people here will help you get back on the right track as long as you intended no offense."

Jason whispered to Orion.

Orion nodded and added, "And by the way, I wear my collar to identify myself as a submissive."

A voice in the audience cried out, "And he's available!"

Once the chuckles and laughter died down, Jason continued. "As you can see, we are pretty relaxed here. Still, Orion and I have talked about what we'll do tonight. We both worked out the expectations of this scene. He's shared with me his limits, and I've shared mine."

A murmur raced through the crowd.

Jason grinned. "Ah, I see. You don't think someone in the Dominant role has limits or should explain those to the sub?"

No one said anything.

"Orion?"

Orion shrugged and said, "I wanted more intensity with the impact play than Master Jason was willing to give me. He told me his limits, and I need to respect them or find a new play partner."

Zack understood that kind of raw had-to-have-it need.

Jason nodded. "Neither partner should be forced into a place they're not comfortable in. I'm not saying limits shouldn't be pushed and boundaries can't be adjusted, but there's a process... a negotiation for that."

Orion frowned but didn't say more.

Jason looked out to the audience. "What else do I need to do before we start?"

Someone in the third row raised their hand, and after Jason nodded at them, they said, "A safeword."

"Exactly. A thousand words can't stop abuse, but in BDSM a single word stops everything. I strongly advise you to have a safeword. Playing without a safeword, especially with a new partner, is not a badge of honor, but a potentially dangerous situation." Jason turned to Orion and asked, "Want to share yours?"

"Cancer." He stared out into the audience as if daring anyone to comment.

Jason reminded everyone, "The word needs to be something you wouldn't say in the scene and is something that stops everything."

He guided Orion onto his stomach over the bench. "Because we talked beforehand, I know Orion has no physical limitations that will prevent him from being in the positions I'll put him in tonight. Remember, if you're a sub, it's your responsibility to let your Dom know if you're in the wrong kind of pain." Jason knelt down in front of Orion and took his hand. "I'm going to secure his hands and ankles to the bench. Restraints shouldn't cut off circulation. With this type of padded restraints and this kind of play, I make sure I can get one finger underneath."

Jason secured Orion's hands, then his ankles. He touched Orion's back and asked, "You okay, Orion?"

Orion glanced up with a dreamy smile and said, "Yes, Master Jason."

Jealousy rushed through Zack. To be tied down and under someone else's control was Zack's number-one fantasy. Ah, if Andrew ever....

"BDSM is about feeling intense sensation." Jason ran an ice cube down the center of Orion's bare back without warning.

Orion shifted away from the cold as much as the bondage allowed and gasped, "Ohhhhh!"

Jason drew slow lines of cold across the sub's back in a lazy pattern, making Zack shiver and grow hard.

"Sensation play." He picked up a towel, dried Orion, and then slipped on the fur glove. Jason stroked up and down Orion's back with the mitt and over his jean-covered butt.

"Mmmm." Orion arched into the gloved hand doing the massaging.

"There are other things you can use to get the sub to focus on sensation. Vampire gloves, snapping rubber bands, bumpy balls, violet wands, pinwheels, feathers, and many other things that can all be found online and in Entwined's toy store."

Jason released Orion's restraints. "Orion, turn and lay on your back."

"Yes, Sir." Orion did as instructed with a guiding hand from Jason.

The Dom grabbed the candle and lit it. "This is a plain paraffin wax candle. You don't want to use beeswax candles because they burn at a much higher temperature. Unless you've worked with the candle before, test it." Jason dripped a bit of the black wax on his wrist.

Orion raised his head to peer in Jason's direction.

"Head back, Orion," Jason commanded as he peeled the wax off his wrist and set it aside. "If you touch where you're going to drip the wax, it allows the sub to focus on that spot. Vary your rhythm based on what you're trying to accomplish. Slow will allow most subs to go into an almost meditative state or into subspace, but others like it fast. Subspace is different for each submissive. It's a place of complete connection…."

Orion whispered into his mic, "Nirvana."

Jason touched a spot on Orion's stomach and dripped the wax. A deliberate pattern evolved.

Tap, drip, tap, drip.

Zack struggled not to pant. He swore the wax was dripping on his own skin. He imagined the touch, followed by the drip of an enticing burn. He tried to shift into a position that found more room in his pants.

"Ohhhhh, more," Orion groaned.

Tap, drip, tap, drip.

"Always have a fire extinguisher nearby."

Tap, drip, tap, drip.

Jason said, "We could go on for hours. The tapping can fade away as your sub gets into subspace."

Drip. Drip. Drip.

Jason glanced up as if just remembering the audience observing him. "Vary the height of the candle when the wax is dripping. It'll hit the skin at different temperatures. Higher up allows the wax to cool before contact." Jason demonstrated his point by releasing a drop from three feet away and then one from six inches.

Orion arched toward the searing wax.

"If you use different color candles, remember they burn at different temperatures. If your sub happens to be hairy, you might want mummify them in plastic wrap before you use the wax." Jason didn't look at the audience. His gaze remained glued to Orion.

Drip. Drip. Drip.

Orion gasped with what sounded like pleasure. His expression held an "on cloud nine" quality to it that made Zack jealous.

"We don't have time to discuss the use of votive candles. Nor will I show how to use knife play or whips to remove the wax. There are classes and demonstrations throughout the year that focus on candles, wax, and heat play if you want to know more."

Jason plucked a piece of ice from the bucket and allowed the cool water to drip on Orion's skin.

The sub stirred enough to whimper.

Jason knelt down next to Orion and whispered to him. He peeled off the wax one drop at a time with his fingernails. Jason spoke into the mic, "Orion's doing a great job, and now he's going to turn over."

Orion stirred and looked around the stage. He shifted to lie over the bench again with assistance from Jason. His long blond hair hung down and became a curtain of privacy, shielding his face.

"Now we're going to show you impact play." Jason spoke as he resecured Orion to the bench.

Zack tried to control his breathing as the restraints were locked around Orion's arms and legs, holding him in place. Oh to be in such a position—

"There are lots of different things one can use. I strongly encourage budding Masters and Dominants to use implements on your body before they ever touch a sub. You need to plan where to aim an item to best benefit both you and your sub. Understand how each implement you use will affect your sub." He picked up a crop and twirled it. "These impact toys happen to be mine. I know the feel of each one intimately."

He ran a hand over Orion's ass. "Impact is physical."

Whap!

Zack bit his lip and inhaled.

"Mmmm." Orion pushed his hips back.

"Impact play can also be very mental. If I had him pull down his jeans or took him over my knee, that's a whole different aspect, isn't it?"

"Yes, Sir," the prone man moaned.

Zack tried not to whimper at the suggestion.

"Giving a warm-up helps prepare the skin and the submissive for harder play." Jason proceeded to slap Orion's ass with his palm for about a minute.

Each sharp, crisp spank dug out the fantasies hiding in Zack's mind. An image came unbidden to the forefront: Andrew smacking him on the ass and Zack loving it. Again and again, his Master spanked him.

The sound of bare skin getting slapped dragged Zack out of the daydream. Orion's jeans were now down around his ankles. He wore a fancy pair of underwear with the rump cut out. His cheeks were a bright pink as the crop kissed him over and over, no spot ignored.

"Crops come in various lengths from sixteen inches to twenty-eight inches. A shorter pole allows greater control." Jason peppered Orion's ass. "Light taps give great stimulation right, Orion?"

Orion groaned and hitched his hips.

Zack recrossed his legs and tried to catch his breath.

"The smaller the surface of the leather, the more the sting. Remember, if the leather is flappy, it will wrap around the skin for a deeper bite." Jason smacked Orion to demonstrate this and to punctuate his words.

Jason caressed the crop's pole over Orion's punished skin.

Orion groaned, and his leg muscles tensed.

"The crop is great for versatility. You can also use the pole part as a cane." Jason held the crop on either end and bowed it. "For beginners, I'd recommend a more rigid crop, allowing for better control."

With a flick of Jason's wrist, Orion grunted and a red line developed. "The crop can be used anywhere on the body. Before you do use one, I suggest attending our class on cropping. The crop is an amazing instrument, but it can also do a lot of unexpected damage. I advise beginners to stick with the butt. Now, Orion, are you ready?"

Orion whimpered and said, "Yes, Sir."

Jason gave him four more strikes, all with astounding precision. Each line stacked over the last an equal distance apart and appeared to have been drawn with a ruler.

Jason caressed his hand over the heated cheeks and exchanged the crop for a paddle with holes in it. He spun the paddle in his hand and then rubbed the wood over Orion's ass, raised the implement, and tapped him.

"More, Sir," Orion demanded.

"Ah, as tempting as it might be to give in to that request, never let your sub control the scene. The Dom or Master always needs to be the manager of the action. This isn't to say that the sub's reactions shouldn't guide or modify the Dominant's behavior, but at no time should they be allowed to control it. They surrender their power over to you for safekeeping. The sub isn't in the right frame of mind to judge anything other than using their safeword to stop the scene."

"Please, Master Jason." Orion's begging touched Zack.

Jason shook his head and continued to give light taps. When Orion stopped pleading, Jason gave him three rapid smacks that left defined red rectangles, darker than the shade already coloring his lined ass.

Zack wiggled in his seat, along with most of the audience.

Orion remained silent except for the occasional gasp at a particularly hard swat.

"Of course, you can have the sub count the swats, tell them to say thank you after each, or have them ask for another." Jason whapped Orion's presented ass with enough impact to make the onlookers jump.

Orion moaned and arched back.

Jason rubbed the paddle against the punished skin and said, "These are the last five, Orion. Are you ready?"

"Yes, Master Jason." Orion panted out the words.

Jason took his time and applied them over the course of a minute, leaving Zack as winded as Orion.

After the last smack, Orion groaned out, "Thank you, Master Jason."

Jason rubbed Orion's butt. "Always check the impacted area to ensure no unexpected injury occurred. Ah, Orion will be as right as rain by tomorrow. Though he may be sitting on a pillow." He smacked Orion's red butt one more time with his hand.

Jason unbuckled the restraints and gathered Orion in his arms. A woman handed him a blanket, and someone else had put a large chair on stage.

Orion kicked off his pants and allowed Jason to swaddle him in the blanket.

Jason guided Orion into his lap and murmured to him a bit before looking out to the audience. "Aftercare is extremely important. It reconnects the sub back to earth and allows the Dominant to come down from the rush one can feel when the gift of surrender is given. Keep in mind every sub responds differently. Some don't want to be touched. Others want sex. Sometimes it's another scene. I know Orion from previous sessions, and he needs to be held. Talk to the sub and see what's needed. Remember the sub's temperature might drop, so a blanket is good to have handy, and water."

He accepted the fresh bottle of water from someone and opened it. Jason held it while Orion drank. Jason petted him. "Aftercare depends on you and your partner's needs."

Jason cuddled Orion until he started to stir. "You doing okay?"

Orion smiled and kissed his cheek. "Yes, thank you, Master Jason. As you said, I'm right as rain." He turned to the audience and grinned. "And perhaps someone can translate that for me later."

Jason chuckled. "The imp is back to earth."

Someone grabbed the pants Orion had stepped out of when he curled up in Jason's lap and handed them back to him. He wiggled into them while under the blanket.

Jason helped Orion to his feet. "Also, if the scene is intense, it's always a good idea to touch base a few days later to see if anything came up that the person needs to process. Remember, BDSM involves a power exchange and trust. Whips, ropes, toys, and leather are all pathways to get to that transcendental space where nothing else matters. Many people enjoy the ritual or require it to reach that place. Others don't. Find out what works for you and your partners. Allow yourself to grow and change as you develop."

Jason guided Orion to the middle of the stage. "Well, we barely scratched the surface. I didn't talk about suspension, bondage, knife play, whips, fetishes, roleplay, or a host of other things you can look into. You'll find a list of classes on Entwined's website and in the front with Audrey. I believe the second half of BDSM 101 is next week at this time. Always play as safe as possible. Thank you."

Applause rippled through the room.

Zack couldn't move.

Shit! It was too much and yet not enough. His body felt hypersensitive, as if he had done more than watch.

The crowd swallowed up Jason and Orion. Eventually, though, the adoring fans dissipated. The submissive man hugged Jason and then joined a group of people who waved him over. They squealed when he sat down with them.

People were shuffling the chairs back to their original locations all around Zack. He jumped up and pushed his chair under the closest table.

Now what? He meandered over to the juice bar, took a seat, and ordered a cranberry spritzer. Jason sat right next to him.

"Um, that was... um, good, Jason." Words were never Zack's friend.

"Thank you. I hope people learned a little something."

"I'm Zack. Yeah, I'm sure they did. I mean... I did."

Jason asked with a warm smile, "First time?"

A lie wouldn't form in his mouth, so Zack nodded.

"It's a lot different from what people usually see on the Internet." Jason took a sip of whatever the bartender had put in front of him.

"Porn." Hardcore scenes danced through Zack's head.

"There's typically a lot of focus on a clear-cut defined world, sub-Dom or Top-bottom. And while that is the preference for many people, in my humble opinion, some of us have the potential to be anywhere on the spectrum, and that can alter over time. See that couple of over there?"

Zack tracked the direction of Jason's gaze and nodded.

"The collared one used to be the Top, and over the years, they, as a couple, have transitioned into different roles," Jason said.

"Switches?" Zack lowered his voice. In some circles switches were seen as being indecisive, having sub shame or being unable to grasp their own dominance.

"It's okay, you don't have to whisper. In Entwined, everyone accepts where you are and who you are. Some people need to be on both sides of the whip, and that's okay. Others don't."

Zack shook his head. "I've been on a few BDSM forums that have kicked switches out."

"It's unfortunate and limiting. I find what's between the defined lines and on the fringes most fascinating—"

A tall man with salt-and-pepper hair tugged Jason into a passionate lip-lock that left both men laughing and gasping for breath.

"So, what fascinating things are you talking about, my love?" the kisser asked.

Jason beamed up at the man like he was the answer to every question ever asked. "Zack, this is my heart, Gene."

Zack shook the man's hand.

"Good to meet you, Zack. Did you enjoy the demonstration?"

"Informative." Zack was satisfied he sounded normal.

"Jason's a wonderful teacher," Gene said.

Jason bumped Gene with his elbow. "Hey, put it back on?"

"Of course." Gene pulled a collar out from his waistband and fastened the leather around Jason's neck.

The Dom from the stage disappeared, and the man with the collar on sighed, "Thank you, Master."

Zack tried not to react, but holy fuck he hadn't seen that coming.

"You're surprised," Jason stated more than asked.

"Um, yeah. I guess. I mean there's nothing wrong with... um, but on stage...."

"On stage, I was a Dom to a wonderful sub and now—"

Gene touched Jason's face and said, "Now, you're *my* wonderful sub."

Jason leaned into the touch as if to absorb all the love the man offered.

An ache of want crashed through Zack. He yearned for that kind of connection.

"People assume submissives are fragile, broken, or weak." Jason spoke with vehemence. "That's not the case. It's really based on the individual."

"My partner of twenty-six years is the strongest person I know." Gene beamed with pride. He turned to Zack. "Are you just curious, or a budding sub or Master?"

"Or both," Jason added.

"I-I'm not sure." Not completely true, but it was as far as Zack would commit to at this time.

"If you'd like to go in the back, we can explore with you...." Gene made the offer, and Jason nodded with enthusiasm.

Zack scratched his head. They were looking for a threesome? Or? How would that—?

A figure across the room caught Zack's eye. Was that?

Shit! What was *he* doing here?

Andrew strolled out from the back of the club. Another man scuttled along next to him, chattering to him.

Holy fuck! He'd been in the back room of Entwined… playing with a sub? Being a sub? No, if Andrew was into the scene, he'd be a Dom. Andrew must be into the lifestyle?

Kneel. Serve. His.

"Oh? Oh! Um, I'm sorry. I have to go. I'll be back."

"Famous last words." Gene smiled, and both he and Jason waved as Zack escaped out the door.

CHAPTER THREE

ANDREW STOOD alone on his balcony and sipped the bubbly champagne. His iPhone played "Auld Lang Syne," the traditional New Year's Eve song.

Staring at the stars, he pondered the question the song asked. "Should auld acquaintance be forgot?"

What an interesting query.

Andrew's year had been one of upheaval and change. Everything that had been a certainty at the beginning of this year... now was no longer.

Some distant cheering made him glance at the time. It was odd not to kiss Charlie Happy New Year. Though if he were honest, Charlie hadn't been around much to kiss recently... or was that ever?

Andrew suspected his live-in partner, who he'd been with since high school, had been hooking up with randoms for several years. Andrew had even broached the subject of having an open relationship. Hell, if that's what Charlie needed, Andrew could have figured out how to make it work, but his lover had refused to even entertain the thought.

Charlie had denied his affairs until Andrew found proof in the shape of a sleeping male in his bed. The other men hadn't devastated Andrew, but the lies had. Sex was just getting off. Unfortunately, the man he'd intended on spending forever with wasn't playing on an Andrew-Charlie team, but his own.

God, Andrew had been such a fool.

He'd like to forget how the relationship ended, but he had a feeling the day after the discovery would be emblazoned in his mind forever. Charlie had sat on the uncomfortable sofa he'd demanded they buy, with his bags packed. There was no discussion, no fight, just a peck on the cheek before Andrew's lover of a decade waltzed out the door. The void and confusion that overwhelmed Andrew swallowed his heart.

He poured a little more Pierre-Jouët Belle Époque. He'd gotten the bottle to celebrate their anniversary.

No more anniversaries.

Andrew raised his crystal flute and toasted the stars.

His phone buzzed with yet another text from Megan. The powerhouse behind the Dark Angels' success reminded him, *It's the new year. You owe me a yes!*

What a year!

He hadn't planned on going on tour with a rock band as their stylist, but with a bit of juggling at his salon, the staff had managed without him. Megan was being tenacious in her insistence he take the position permanently.

He'd figured out how to keep his salon running while on tour, and he could do it again. He texted her back. *Yes.*

She responded. *Good. I'll send your schedule for the magazine interviews tomorrow.*

He sipped at the cool fizz, resulting in an increased warm buzz.

Entwined should not be forgotten in this year. With Charlie exiting, there was no one to impede his exploration of that side of himself. No more burying his desires because his lover didn't want to experiment. There were plenty of men who did. He was learning to put his need for control and order to good use.

His phone buzzed with a call. He glanced at the screen, and a picture of his brother sticking his tongue out filled it.

He answered and hit Speaker. "Hey, Justin."

Justin shouted, "Happy New Year!" and rattled a noisemaker. Other hoots and hollering competed with his voice.

Andrew smiled. "It sounds like your party is a success."

"I wish you were here. Come over," Justin begged.

Glancing at the bottle he'd half emptied, he shook his head. "Not tonight, but have fun."

"Jordon, get off your brother's back." Justin snorted, sounding a bit tipsy. "Literally, the kid is on his brother's back. Angel's just as bad by encouraging him."

"Go rescue Dusty." Andrew chuckled at the image of the rambunctious teen riding Justin's boyfriend's back.

"No, he's on Zack."

Well, that gave Andrew a whole different image of riding, and Jordon was nowhere in that picture. Zack bent over whatever flat surface was available and—

"Happy New Year, Justin. I'll see you tomorrow around 2:00 p.m." He ended the call.

Whenever something was excluded from one's diet, it became a craving. Andrew was sure that's all his interest in Zack could be. After all, almost seven years separated them. What could they possibly have in common?

The night had grown frigid.

He stepped into his condo and slid the balcony door shut behind him.

"I GOT it," Jordon's scream accompanied stomping footsteps. The door flung open.

"Happy New Year," Andrew exclaimed to the grinning teen.

"Back at you. Come in." Jordon yanked him in and snatched his coat. "Everyone's in the kitchen."

Andrew's heart beat a little faster. *Everyone?* That would include Zack. He trailed after Jordon's bouncing stride.

"Andrew!" Justin gave him a big hug. "I just hung up with Mom. She said they pulled into port this morning and she'd already talked to you."

"Yeah, sounds like she's having fun on the cruise." Andrew scanned the room.

Where was—oh.... Zack stood between the kitchen and the breakfast room. A plant helped him in his attempt to disappear.

"Hey, Dusty. Happy New Year." Andrew clapped him on the back during their man-hug.

"It's going to be a great year." Dusty squeezed his shoulder, then went back to banging the pots around the stove.

Jordon rolled his eyes. "He says that every year."

Andrew meandered closer to where Zack touched the plant's leaves. "Hey, Zack. Happy New Year."

Zack stopped petting the houseplant and peeked around. "Happy New Year. Um, it's good to see you."

Andrew came prepared with small talk. That should put Zack at ease. "Well, I—"

"I should go make sure the table's set." Zack darted into the dining room.

Jordon scrunched up his face and called out, "We just set the table ten minutes ago."

Zack appeared in the doorway. "I was double-checking."

"How can I be of use?" Andrew asked Justin, who was pulling the roast out of the oven.

"You can mash the potatoes."

Andrew saluted and rooted around the refrigerator, trying to locate the butter.

Zack came over and found the stick. "I try to keep it organized, but no one puts things back." He raised his voice on the last part of his sentence so the guilty parties might be included in the conversation.

Justin apologized. "You're right. It's my fault. I throw things in there. You should see Andrew's refrigerator."

Andrew smiled. "Order is a good thing."

Zack peeked through the shagginess of his god-awful haircut and nodded eagerly. His cheeks tinted with an alluring blush, and he looked away.

That simple grin shouldn't have Andrew silently spelling the ingredients in most shampoos to avoid an erection. Damn, but Zack was cute… and young. *Must remember he is only eighteen.*

Andrew mashed the potatoes and helped get the massive feast on the table. "Um, Justin, how many people are you expecting?"

"Just us." Justin stopped and surveyed the enormous amount of food. "Eh, leftovers are always good."

Jordon rushed in and frowned. "Did you touch the name cards, Zack?"

Justin asked, "Name cards?" He stared at Jordon. "We have name cards?"

"Yes, Andrew is a guest, therefore Japanese etiquette requires he sit with his back to the best view in the room."

"We're not Japanese," Zack pointed out. "Is that even the right custom? I thought—"

"By sitting him here, we can look at him and appreciate my painting right behind him." The littlest Davis snatched up an intricately painted card with Andrew's name on it. The card had been placed next to Zack's seat, but now his name card sat across the table.

Zack brushed past Andrew and sat at the far end of the table where his brother had put him.

Everyone sat. The pork roast, potatoes, and three kinds of vegetables were passed around. Talk was at a minimum, limited to comments about the food.

During second helpings, the conversation turned tense.

Dusty beat a rhythm with his fingers on the placemats. "Zack, I think you should just let *me* tell Joe we need to use your recommendations. It makes sense."

"No! Dusty, no! That's all I need, for my big brother to force the stage manager to listen to my ideas."

Dusty stopped the drumming to focus on Zack. "Joe's not doing his job. You didn't have to tell me. Anyone can see there's chaos between the local arena crews and our guys. Hell, you guys barely got it together the last few shows, and sound check started late more than once on this past tour."

Zack groaned. "Just let me deal. I've got most of our guys convinced to break up into groups and work as team leads so the local guys will have a clue what we need them to do. I can handle this."

Justin leaned over to Andrew and explained, "Zack did these chart and flow lists. Gantt charts, I think he calls them. He developed a process that cut the time to set up and break down the stage for shows."

"Impressive." Andrew had tried to do a flowchart for his salon, but it never quite worked out.

Zack's cheeks flushed. "Not really. I developed a Gantt chart and put everything on a timeline. Developing a process was pretty much a no-brainer. What I'm proposing is something anyone could do."

Dusty shook his head and drummed with his silverware. "But no one has."

"Look, I only read a few books; what do I know?"

"The definition of insanity is doing the same thing over and over and expecting a different result each time," Dusty said as his tapping increased in volume.

Justin put a hand over Dusty's, and the rap-tap-tapping stopped.

Andrew asked, "What books?"

Zack shook his head. "Just *Lean Thinking* by James Womack. That type of thing."

"I'm telling you, Zack, no kid your age reads these books for fun and then puts a process together." Dusty exhaled, making the flame on the tapers in the center of the table flicker.

"I'm not a *kid*!" Zack shouted as his gaze drifted in Andrew's direction.

"Certainly doesn't sound like a kid's book." Andrew wanted to support him without undermining Dusty.

"I wish you'd reconsider applying to college." Dusty's tone of voice made it apparent this was an old argument between the brothers.

Justin cleared his throat. "Zack may still apply, but right now it sounds like he can make a difference for the Dark Angels' road crew."

Zack nodded. "Right, see? Justin gets it."

Jordon dismissed Dusty with a wave. "Yeah, let us stay on tour with you. I mean, really, how much longer do the Dark Angels have?"

"What?" Dusty swiveled his head around to stare openmouthed at Jordon. "We don't have an expiration date!"

The little defector asked, "Are you sure?"

"The Rolling Stones have been together over fifty years!"

Justin asked, "Dusty, do you want another roll?"

Dusty shook his head and frowned. "I'd better not. I don't know if I have the time to squander on eating it. After all, the band's only got a few more years."

Jordon snorted. "Few more years... that's optimistic of you."

Andrew laughed. He couldn't help it. Jordon was a puppet master extraordinaire. "I'll have another roll, Justin. Thanks."

Zack jumped out of his chair, grabbed the basket from Justin, and hurried around the table to present the baked goods to Andrew.

"Er, thank you, Zack." Andrew accepted the butter Zack provided after the roll. "Such service."

Zack opened his mouth, but nothing came out. He slid back into his chair, but his gaze remained glued to Andrew's.

Jordon stared at Andrew, then Zack, and then back to him, probably trying to figure out if what passed between them would ignite the tablecloth.

The youngest member of the dinner party cocked his head and asked, "Zack, pass the rolls?"

Without breaking eye contact with Andrew, Zack picked a roll out of the basket and tossed it in Jordon's direction.

The poppin' fresh goodness hit Jordon on the forehead and fell into his gravy. Jordon picked the roll up, said, "Thanks," and ate it without missing a beat.

Zack blinked and glanced down at his plate of uneaten food.

The spell had been broken.

Relief and disappointment coursed through Andrew in equal parts. *Too young* echoed through the rational side of his brain while a competing voice sang, *He's delicious.*

Justin mentioned a new museum exhibition, and Jordon dominated the rest of the dinner conversation, allowing Andrew to study Zack.

Apart from a horrid haircut given to him by someone unaware of how to texture, Zack was captivating. Golden blond waves, peridot-green eyes, a body built from hard work, and a cute face made him compelling. However, it was the hidden depths that screamed at Andrew to investigate further.

Zack never said much, but when he did, it was accurate, and people, including Dusty, listened to him. He was smart, and he got along with everyone.

Andrew had to remind himself that however mature Zack was, he *was* still a kid. Maybe that's what the appeal was: young, new, and inexperienced. Ha, if he could convince himself that was the sole attraction, he wouldn't have gone hard by simply watching him not eat his dinner.

After the dishes were cleared and the kitchen returned to its reasonably pristine condition, Zack milled around the outskirts.

Andrew mentioned, "You know, I tried to do a flowchart for the salon."

"Really?" Zack stepped closer.

"It didn't work at all," Andrew confessed.

"Why not?" Zack sat in one the chairs at the small table Andrew and Justin were sitting at to watch the birds outside.

Andrew shrugged. "No clue."

Justin snapped his fingers. "Hey, maybe before the next tour, you could stop by his salon and see what you can do."

A bad idea never sounded so appealing. Andrew shushed his conscience and said, "I'd be happy to pay you in haircuts."

Justin snorted. "Be forewarned: he only wants to get his scissors in your hair."

Zack ran his fingers through his shaggy blond waves, making Andrew's fingers itch. He wouldn't deny it.

"I doubt I'd be much help, but I'd be happy to take a look, give my opinion, and offer suggestions. Remember, though, I don't know what I'm doing."

"Great." What had Andrew done?

Dusty poked his head in from the kitchen. He didn't say a word, but he had "big brother on alert" written all over him.

Justin wandered out of the room, checking his phone. Dusty followed him, and Jordon was nowhere in sight.

He sat alone with Zack in the plant-filled room as the sun set. Birds hopped from feeder to feeder. Maybe he should—

"Look. A cardinal." Zack pointed out the bright red bird.

"Gorgeous." Andrew dragged his gaze away from Zack's glowing face to look at the bird. It plucked seeds and flicked its tail about before flying away.

"The hummingbirds come back in early May." Zack turned his head, still wearing his big heart-melting smile. He glanced at Andrew, and his cheeks tinted pink.

That was not sexy. It was a blush. Andrew did not find Zack's innocence enticing. He should—

"So, um, do you know of any good clubs in the area?" Zack stared at him.

Not ones you should be at! Andrew jumped up and went over to the refrigerator as if the images of Zack tied up wouldn't come with him. "I'm not really much of a club person."

"Oh." The disappointment in Zack's voice made Andrew want to fix it. Made him want to take Zack to a club… not Entwined, but a regular club. Instead he focused on restacking the leftovers properly so his brother would be able to locate the basics when needed.

A chair scraped against the floor, and Zack scuffed over to the sink and grabbed a towel. He cleared his throat several times as he ran the towel over the counter. "So, um, Drew, what do you do for *fun*?"

Wait…. "You called me Drew."

Those big green eyes got bigger. "Oh, I'm sorry, I didn't mean—"

"No, it's okay. I kind of like it." No one had ever called him that.

Zack gave him the tiniest smile, only barely perceptible, but it made Andrew want things he shouldn't want… especially not from Justin's boyfriend's brother.

CHAPTER FOUR

THIS WAS a mistake! What had Andrew been thinking last week at the New Year's dinner?

Zack stood in the front of the salon with his hands stuffed into his leather jacket pockets, ready to make good on his promise of helping Andrew. He shifted from foot to foot as the troublesome twosome, Phillip and Monique, budding hairstylists, chatted with him.

Hating himself for the possessiveness he had no right to feel, Andrew hurried to the front. He opened the door and waved Zack safely away from the blowjob Phillip was likely getting ready to offer.

"Zack, thanks for coming. Come on in out of the cold."

"Oh. Um… yeah." He gave Phillip and Monique a half nod and trudged inside.

Andrew asked his two workers, in his practiced supervisory tone, "Did you two finish doing the inventory?"

"Almost." Phillip lied through his teeth, if Monique's openmouthed, wide-eyed expression was to be believed.

"My first appointment isn't until this afternoon, so if you two would finish inventory, I could place an order before that." Andrew left them to finish washing the windows.

Zack stared at the hair products by the door as if they were alien to him.

Andrew bit his tongue to stop the offer of several concoctions that would work wonders on Zack's hair. "Let's go to my office."

"Andrew! Andrew!" Mrs. Harris was seated at Patrick's station and waved him over.

"Hello, Mrs. Harris. You look well."

"I am. I turned eighty-six last week, and I got the salon's card. Thank you."

He hoped he was half as spry at her age. "Wonderful. I hope you're using your birthday discount today."

"Of course, dear boy, at my age you never save things for tomorrow. Sale is one of my favorite four-letter words."

Andrew chuckled and redirected the conversation, hoping he could avoid her listing the others. "Are you having Patrick put in a stripe of color?"

"Oh, yes. I'm visiting my niece in New Mexico, so we were discussing a stripe of teal."

He asked, "Were you thinking of the usual place?"

"We were considering here or here and here." Patrick gestured down one side of her hair, then on both sides.

Andrew hesitated, but if anyone could carry the color off, it was Mrs. Harris. "If it were me, if you're going bold… go all the way."

"Absolutely right, dear. Patrick, triple-stripe me. We're going all the way." Her eyes sparkled.

"Good choice." Andrew patted her shoulder.

He paused to greet two other clients before finally getting Zack into his office.

Alone.

Andrew veered away from sitting on the comfy leather love seat. The image of Zack lying back on the leather taunted him with ideas outside the realm of possibility. He took the chair behind his black-lacquer desk, forcing a barrier between them.

Zack slid into one of the two armchairs in front of the desk and glanced around the space. "Nice office."

"Thanks." Andrew hadn't realized how private his office was until he'd shut the door.

One wall of the office had a large picture window that looked out onto a small garden, now buried in a foot of snow.

"Wait. You collect hairstylist art?" Zack stared at the wall with floor-to-ceiling black-lacquered shelves.

Andrew was careful not to let his staff fill the horizontal surfaces with clutter. Some wicker baskets stored the nonsense he wasn't able to file or toss, but the real threat didn't come from his staff.

"Yeah, my mom and stepfather insist on gifting me these hairdressing wonders from every art fair they've ever attended." Andrew shrugged. "What would Jordon think?"

Zack's laughter was music Andrew feared he'd never grow tired of hearing. He shook his head, making his poorly cut waves dance, and said, "I won't be sharing this with Jordon."

Brothers. Their brothers were dating. Justin was finally happy. Andrew would not create any discord. He'd focus on why Zack was here and not how stunning he'd look straining to orgasm… or not to climax.

"So, where do we begin in this streamlining process?"

"Why don't you walk me through the different things you do in the salon. We can make notes, and then we can start looking for ways to make things more efficient. Let's start with an easy one. Haircuts. What are all the steps involved in a haircut?" Zack handed him a spiral notebook and a pen.

"Wash and cut the hair," he wrote as he spoke.

Zack shook his head. "That's not the beginning of the process."

"It's not?"

"Nope. First the client is greeted at the front."

"Okay, so you want from the time they arrive until they leave." Andrew started to realize why his first attempt at doing this hadn't worked.

"Yup. If you make a list for haircuts, I'm sure parts of that list can be used for, say, I don't know… color."

"Right, because each time the client is greeted, coat taken, settled in the lobby or walked to the hairdresser's station, caped, shampooed…. Wow, there's a lot of things that don't have to be done by the stylist, per se," Andrew realized. But knowing something and internalizing a concept were two different things.

"Exactly. A greeter doesn't need the same skill set as a stylist. Megan calls it 'saving the talent.'"

Andrew chuckled. "I can't tell Phillip that."

"Having everyone's job clear will help get the entire task done faster and with more precision, allowing the talent—I mean the stylist, to focus on… um, styling." Zack peeked up at Andrew in that adorably uncertain way of his and stared.

God, if only….

A minute passed, and Zack cleared his throat. "Drew, so, um, if you want to make a list of all the things that go into a client getting a haircut, that would be helpful."

Andrew got enough of a grip to nod and wrote down everything he did and what he expected the other stylists to do. He handed the long list to Zack.

"Thanks." Zack reviewed the list. "Do you have any haircuts later? If so, I can watch so I can compare this list to the actual process."

"Why wait? I promised payment in haircuts. Let me cut your hair." *What the hell?* Was he that desperate to get his hands on the kid?

"Oh, um… yeah. Okay, that, um, makes sense." Zack ran his hands over his jean-covered thighs and pinned Andrew with a stare.

The heat that flashed from his peridot-colored eyes reminded Andrew that, while Zack might be shy and a tad awkward at times, he was *not* a kid.

"We can skip the greeting. Just take me to your chair."

Andrew guided Zack to his chair, caped him, and finally got his fingers into the wealth of gold. "What a color!"

Zack blushed.

Andrew glanced in the mirror. Good, he wasn't drooling and might pass as a professional and not someone with trichophilia. Though touching Zack's hair might give him reason to develop a hair fetish.

Zack's long eyelashes rested on his cheeks with his lips pressed together.

Andrew would like to press his—"So, what are you thinking?"

Zack blinked his eyes open. "Um…," he said, his voice soft.

"Your hair?" Andrew took comfort that it appeared he wasn't alone in this whirlpool of wants and can't haves.

"Oh, Drew, whatever you think. Just not too short."

Zack had only surrendered to Andrew's expertise, but it felt like so much more.

Andrew dropped Zack's shoulder-length hair and rested his palms on Zack's shoulders. "Of course not. You need to be able to pull it into a tail while you're working. I'm going to add some texture, and I'll shape up the ends."

Zack bit his lip, and the trust Andrew found in his eyes shouldn't be affecting him…. It was just a haircut.

"Come on, let me shampoo you." Andrew led a docile Zack to the sink. He settled him into the chair and tipped him back so his head was in the sink. He adjusted the water temperature and asked, "Is this good?"

"Mmmm." Zack stiffened in the chair. "I mean yeah, it's fine."

Andrew wet Zack's hair, then pumped a rich lavender shampoo into his hand and spread it through Zack's hair. He massaged Zack's scalp in unhurried, circular motions.

Zack squirmed a little in the chair.

Perhaps Andrew was a sadist, because he tormented them both by giving Zack a longer than necessary shampoo. He rinsed and repeated the process until Zack almost panted.

"Conditioner." His Dom voice fell out of his mouth. Where had that come from?

Zack hissed out, "Yes, please, Drew," to a question Andrew hadn't asked.

Focus!

Andrew spread the conditioner by raking his fingers through Zack's hair, stimulating Zack's scalp as he dragged his fingers down to the ends. Again and again Andrew repeated the movements until each strand was coated in the nurturing cream. He indulged in another languorous scalp massage.

He rinsed and guided a wrung-out Zack back to his station. He combed, clipped, and razor-textured a style into the gorgeous head of hair in front of him. Adding a touch of product and a bit of time with a hairdryer and Zack looked stunning.

Zack's gaze locked on to his. Lurking in the depth of Zack's eyes was a pleading challenge that Andrew felt compelled to answer.

"I—"

Monique cleared her throat. "Andrew, your two o'clock is here."

Andrew looked at her. How did that happen? "Thank you, Monique. I'll be right there."

She stared at him for a few seconds before she wiggled back out front.

Andrew shouldn't be disappointed. "I'm afraid we won't finish the task list."

"That's okay. I can work on this and come back in a couple of days."

Yes. No. "You don't have to—"

Zack jumped out of the chair and said, "No, it's good. It will give me something to work on before the next tour starts."

"YOU WERE right. The Chinese Garden does make a better sauce than Hunan Palace." Andrew finished the last of the beef with broccoli Zack had brought for their lunch. For a number of weeks, they'd been comparing foods from their favorite Chinese places since they'd already determined the best Thai came from Bangkok Bistro.

"Most of the services you offer at the salon have the standard process figured out. Now you need to determine how long each task should take, so I can put it into a Gantt chart." Zack collected the empty Chinese food containers, plates, and chopsticks, then tossed them into the trash.

Andrew pulled out a bottle of spray cleaner and wiped down his desk. He ran the paper towel over the only other thing on his desk, his computer.

"You sure it's not too much trouble?" They'd been spending several days a week together for the past couple of months. Other than Justin, he'd never enjoyed someone as much as he enjoyed Zack... as friends.

"None at all, Drew." Zack's words were accompanied by that dreamy expression he wore sometimes.

Andrew needed to go back to Entwined, or maybe just get laid, so he didn't liquefy every time those striking green eyes gazed in his direction.

"Patrick is doing a color. You can watch to double-check the task list, and I can put the time in for each activity."

Zack's expression snapped from wistful lust to business within seconds. "Sure," he said as he slipped out the door.

Andrew slumped into his chair. He spun toward the window and stared out. Spring was trying to break through the frost, and though the snow had melted, it was still cold.

He twisted the chair back to his desk, opened the list of tasks on the computer, and went through it, adding the time to each activity.

That took longer than he expected. Was Zack still even there?

Andrew rushed out to find Phillip leaning on a broom chatting Zack up.

It wasn't jealousy that spread through him. No, it couldn't be. It was his duty to protect Justin's boyfriend's brother....

"Ah, speak of the devil and you manifest him. Hey, boss man." Phillip smirked in Andrew's direction.

"Were you?" Andrew kept his tone professional.

"Yeah, I just said how cute you two were together." Phillip drew in a deep breath as if he were telling Andrew something he didn't know. "And he said you're *not* together."

Zack kept his gaze glued on Phillip. Only his telltale pink cheeks said he was flustered.

"Our brothers are dating, and we're just friends." Andrew was pleased at his measured tone.

"Yeah, I guess he doesn't want someone *your* age." Phillip batted his eyelashes with an innocence he'd probably lost at eleven.

Andrew opened his mouth to say he wasn't ancient, but there was no point. One didn't have to attend every argument one was invited to.

Zack peeked at Andrew. "Twenty-six isn't old."

Phillip asked, "Yes, but you're what? Seventeen?"

Anger crossed Zack's face. "I'm almost twenty."

In another thirteen or so months, but Andrew wasn't adding that. They would celebrate his nineteenth birthday in a couple of weeks.

Phillip changed gears quickly. "Great, so you can come out clubbing with me."

"Nah, I really don't do dance clubs."

Andrew released the breath that got stuck in his lungs with the images of what Phillip would do to Zack, and dancing wasn't among them.

Looking perplexed at Zack's rejection, Phillip suggested, "We can go to a movie, then."

"Usually I see movies with my kid brother."

"Oh, I see." Phillip glanced between Andrew and Zack. "Well, if you change your mind, I'd be happy to go out with you." He pushed the broom and actually swept up after the last haircut.

MONIQUE KNOCKED on the door, then poked her head in and looked around Andrew's office. "Lunch."

"Thanks, Monique."

Zack jumped up and took the bag from her. "Thank you."

She cast one last squinty-eyed glance at Andrew before she left.

Andrew said, "Let's eat outside. I think it's warm enough." He opened his door to the private garden off his office.

"Cool. I never noticed the table and chairs out here before."

"Yeah, I picked the set up this weekend. I figured we—I eat at the salon a lot, and it might be nice."

Zack sat down, wearing a big smile. "It's really great. I love it out here."

The birds chirped and hopped around the branches of the tree that overhung the cement wall surrounding the garden.

They divided the food and ate.

Andrew surveyed the space. "Every year I promise myself I'll do something with the garden, but I never get to it."

"If you ever want help, I'd be happy to sort the weeds from the overgrown bushes. I just finished outside the morning room at Dusty and Justin's yesterday."

"No! This garden would be way too much work."

"Nah...." Zack stood and stepped around the riot of weeds no one could claim were wildflowers. He paced the fifteen by eighteen plot of land. "Okay, so it would be some work, but it's your building, right?"

"Almost." Andrew had worked like a dog to prepay the mortgage on the building, and now he had less than a year of payments before he owned it outright.

"After lunch, I'll grab tools from the house and come back," Zack told him.

"Oh—"

"I'll clear the weeds and cut back the bushes. Do you want them squared or rounded?"

"Squared."

Zack nodded his approval. "You might lose that one, but it shouldn't be too expensive to replace and then we—I mean *you* can see what you have left."

"Okay." Andrew let his eyes shut and enjoyed the sunshine on his face. When he opened his eyes, he caught the reason for his contentment staring at him.

Zack started gathering their lunch trash.

"I'll get this. I have appointments until 6:30 p.m. so I won't be able to help you out here."

"No worries. I got it." Zack took the trash and headed out.

Within an hour, Zack whisked through the salon with a number of shovels, rakes, clippers, and gardening tools.

Andrew had fifteen minutes between clients. He went into his office to check... e-mails.

What— The vision through the window stopped him in his tracks.

Zack had his shirt off, and the hint of a tan made his body glow. His toned muscles glistened as he strained to pull the rake through the weeds. Sunlight dappled through the trees, making his golden hair shine. Andrew should call *Sexy Gardeners Monthly,* because one of their pinups escaped.

"Yum!" Phillip startled Andrew.

Andrew glared, wishing the man would stop looking at Zack like he was candy. "Phillip, are the birthday cards done?"

"Yes, and don't get testy, boss man," Phillip said in his sugar-sweetened voice.

"I'm not testy," Andrew growled.

His worker and sometimes friend said, "That boy is ripe for the picking. Whatever are you waiting on?"

"He's too young." Andrew stated the obvious. He was so beautiful it hurt.

"Bullshit," Phillip said.

Andrew shook his head, not sure why he wanted someone to understand his position. "Our brothers are living together."

"So what?"

"I can't. My brother's boyfriend would kill me. I don't want to put any stress on Justin. You know he's had a tough time and has enough issues to get past. Now that he's finally happy, I can't risk doing anything that would jeopardize that."

"Wow."

"What?"

Phillip chuckled. "You say that shit like you believe those excuses."

"It's true." Before Dusty, Justin hadn't had a relationship since he'd been brutally raped. Andrew wouldn't do anything to screw this up for his brother now that he was content.

"Justin wouldn't want you to put your life on hold for him," Phillip pointed out.

"You don't understand." How could anyone understand? Andrew wanted nothing more than to see where the sparks with Zack led—

"No, what's true is that little bitch Charlie hurt you. And the boss man doesn't want to go through that shit again. So, you'll avoid what you want."

"I have a client." Andrew reached down and grabbed a bottle of water out of his mini fridge.

Phillip smirked and held his hand out as he said, "Oh, is that for Zack? I'll take it to him. You go to your client."

"I'm sure something needs to be cleaned," Andrew suggested as he walked through the door to the garden.

Zack paused mid-tug and leaned on the rake. "Hey, Drew."

The way his name was caressed by Zack's tongue…. He ignored the clenching of his heart and said, "I'm amazed at how much you've accomplished. It's starting to look like there's a garden here."

Accepting the water, Zack beamed and said, "Thanks."

Andrew looked away from Zack's working throat muscles as he chugged the water. "You used sunscreen, right?"

"Yup. Hundred SPF." Zack gestured to the spray can on the bistro table.

He swallowed his disappointment at not being able to act out the start of many porn fantasies by applying sunscreen to the nubile young man. What was wrong with him?

Monique called from the doorway, "Your next client is here."

He waved, but she didn't leave. Did she think he needed another chaperone?

"I'll catch you in a bit." Andrew stomped over to the doorway. He didn't miss Phillip's smirk or Monique's expression littered with questions.

ANDREW STARED out at the garden. He and Zack had finished the area that weekend. The cement wall was edged with shrubs that went up half its height. In a few summers, they would reach the top, creating a wall of green.

Zack had hung a hummingbird feeder on one of the lower branches that draped over the wall. Two hummingbirds drank their fill before flitting away.

The bronze table and chairs sat off to the right, so they didn't mar the view from his office chair. Zack's suggestions spoke of an attention to detail that made Andrew's world tick.

They talked about planting a Japanese maple and possibly adding a little pond.

How did Zack get so intertwined with Andrew's life? When had it happened? He shouldn't be thinking about him all the time, and he certainly shouldn't miss him the days they didn't see each other. They weren't dating.

The work they'd done on streamlining Andrew's salon in preparation for the next tour with the Dark Angels was complete. So what if they hung out and enjoyed comparing ethnic food restaurants? People needed to eat. And it wasn't a crime that Andrew, who despised yardwork, relished gardening with him. They were good friends, and it was nice to be outside.

Though he certainly couldn't have anticipated doing Zack's hair would be something akin to erotic edging.

His cell buzzed with a text from Zack. *Drew?*

That happy pleasure he got every single time Zack called him "Drew" should have been a warning bell. One he shouldn't have ignored for this long.

He texted back, *Zack?*

Con't w/ Japanese or do U concede Tokio Road is the best?

Andrew shouldn't keep doing this. Where was this going? A better question was, where did he want it to go? Space. He needed some so he typed, *Sorry. Can't today.*

You ok?

Andrew typed, *fine*, but deleted it. *Sick*, he texted. The nauseous feeling in his gut prevented the text from being a total lie.

An immediate *Can I get U anything?* buzzed his cell.

Andrew closed his eyes. He wanted too many things, none of which could ever happen in this lifetime. *No. Thanx.*

He turned off his phone, grabbed his keys, and walked out of his office. After checking the appointment book, he asked, "Monique, could you please reschedule Ms. Shuber for tomorrow?"

With her hands on her hips, she asked, "Why?"

"I need to leave. I'll be back tomorrow," he reassured her before he made his escape.

He drove around a bit with the radio blasting. At a red light, a man with kids in the back of his beat-up SUV glared at him.

Andrew lowered the angsty beats and headed home.

He straightened his doormat, pulled his toaster two inches away from the wall, and shifted the angle of his coffeemaker just a tad to the right. The cleaning service had come today. At least everything was dust-free.

The doorbell rang, halting his adjustment of his things. Hopefully, UPS was at the door and not the members of the church down the street wanting to recruit him.

He opened the door, and there stood what had driven him out of his salon.

Zack held up a plastic bag. "Drew, I brought you some wonton soup. Miso doesn't always make people feel better."

In all the time he and Charlie were together, not once had his self-centered ex ever attempted to make Andrew feel better. He needed to get a grip on his emotions. It wasn't a big deal. Zack was only being a good friend.

Andrew chuckled and said, "That's your dislike of tofu talking." He shouldn't invite Zack inside. If he did... no. "I'd ask you in, but I don't want you to get sick."

"Oh... um, yeah, sure. I just wanted to drop this by." Zack handed off the soup and waved as he loped down the front stairs.

Andrew shut the door and slid the bolt lock in place.

Entwined. He needed to go tonight.

CHAPTER FIVE

TIME WAS slipping away. It was already the end of June. Tonight was the night. Zack didn't want to let another opportunity slip through his fingers. Carpe diem and all that shit.

Finally he'd go for what he wanted… Andrew Nikeman.

Zack was ready. He'd attended every BDSM class Entwined offered in the past six months. He had half hoped he'd run into Drew at the club, but he hadn't. That exchange might have moved him out of the friend zone.

He hadn't seen much of Andrew since mid-May. Getting the salon ready for his absence must have taken all of Drew's time.

Zack missed spending time with him, but he had focused on his own work. There had been a lot of preparation for the Dark Angels tour. He'd presented his new process for setup and breakdown. The initial resistance from the stage manager and a few dickwads was overruled. The mass majority of crew wanted to do a good job minus the chaos. In the end, his process had been accepted and implemented. The teams and the new procedures shaved an hour off setup and about forty-five minutes off breakdown. He'd gained credibility. Zack had proved he wasn't on the road crew just because of who played drums.

Now the tour was underway, and things had settled down into a routine. It was time to explore the sparks that ignited almost every time Andrew's intense blue eyes gazed his way. Zack's subby side ached to kneel and serve Drew. He was ready to learn how to be Drew's perfect submissive. Every cell in his body demanded he follow that single desire. More than needing air to breathe, Zack yearned to fulfill Drew's every wish.

The fact that their brothers were dating each other had put a crimp in fulfilling his craving thus far. Though Zack's experience might have been limited to a few backroom hookups, there was no denying Andrew wanted him. He couldn't have been this far off base.

Zack couldn't risk waiting any longer. The Dark Angels had played another great show. He might have only been a lowly roadie, but he flew high from the success. Tonight all the snags backstage that might have become huge deals went unnoticed because he'd caught them.

He was celebrating at the after-party with his brothers when he spied Andrew across the room. He rarely attended these gatherings. It was as if he'd been avoiding Zack.

The euphoria must have increased Zack's confidence, because when his wet dream left the table he'd been sitting at, Zack decided he couldn't throw away the chance to speak with Andrew. He tried to play it cool, even though his heart jumped into his throat, and waited a whole ten seconds to follow.

Zack meandered in the general direction Andrew's path had taken him, nodding to the other roadies and his friends as he zigzagged toward the back.

Shit! He needed to slip past the stage manager. The guy was a talker and appeared drunker than usual. Damn, he didn't make it. Why did the guy have to be alert now?

His incompetent boss waved him over. "Zack, Zack. Come over here, my good buddy."

"Hey." Zack tried to keep his gaze on the men's room without being rude.

Joe stood and stumbled as he shook Zack's hand. "I need to buy you a drink, my man. You really saved my ass tonight. Thank you."

Granted, a stage manager who stayed sober until the end of the show would have eliminated most of the issues that arose during that night's performance, but Zack simply said, "You're welcome."

"Well, I want you to be my assistant. I called payroll, and you'll get a bump in your salary. It's not much, but it's something."

Wow, a promotion to assistant stage manager.

"You deserve this," Joe slurred a bit.

Zack agreed but said, "I won't let you down."

"What about that drink?" The guy tripped as he tried to pull Zack toward the bar.

"I'm still underage, but thanks." Zack escaped.

Luck seemed to be on his side; Andrew hadn't left the bathroom. Zack's invincibility allowed him the additional confidence he required to wait outside the restrooms for Andrew.

Drawing a deep breath, Zack gathered his courage as he prepared to lay his heart on the line. The time was now.

Zack had been in lust from the first time he'd seen Andrew. His older brother and his friends assumed he had a simple crush. But after he'd gotten to know Drew, no doubt remained; this was a once-in-a-lifetime feeling. He might be younger and less experienced, but he wasn't stupid enough to toss what they could have.

He paced in the little alcove outside the restrooms, rubbing his sweaty palms against his jeans. Finally, the door opened, and Zack's heart all but stopped.

Andrew stopped dead and stared at him with wide eyes. He pushed a hand through his long, lush dark brown waves, which fell right back into place, as if his hair knew better than to look messy.

"Hey, Zack."

Breathe. Talk. Tell him.

"Um, hi, Drew." Zack froze and simply gawked. Did they turn the heat up in the club? Andrew's attention focusing on him made his temperature skyrocket. His body broke out in a sheen of sweat.

"Good show tonight." Andrew gave him a guarded smile.

Fuck the small talk! Zack sucked in a deep breath, held it, and tried to quell the writhing of the snakes in his stomach. What had morphed their friendship into something uncomfortable again?

Zack nodded, realizing he should speak. "Yeah." Damn, his voice had cracked.

Somehow their time apart made his internal monologue, which played on an eternal loop in his mind, louder and harder to think past.

Kneel. Serve. His. Kneel. Serve. His.

The inner demands made Zack a little insane. "So, um, are you seeing anyone?"

Andrew shifted away instantly. He swept moisture over his lower lip before he answered in his deep voice, "No. You know how it is… I'm not ready for anything yet." He swiveled his head to the right, then to the left as if he were looking for an escape path.

Zack ignored Andrew's clear message and forged ahead with his plan.

Kneel. Serve. His.

He'd spent days at Andrew's salon, and he hated himself for never being brave enough to ask him out. Zack had to do this right now.

Andrew attempted to step around him.

Zack leaned in, and their bodies brushed against each other's. He shifted to block Andrew's path of retreat.

Andrew's body heat added to the inferno burning Zack. His intoxicating cologne mixed with the scent of leather. The heady fragrance forced the words out. "Drew, would you consider going out for dinner sometime?"

"Of course…. We never fully addressed the Japanese cuisine question." Andrew stepped backed again, hitting a wall.

Zack stepped forward and peered up at the man, who was about a head taller. "No, not just as friends… as possibly more." Friends didn't lay their heads at their Master's feet waiting for permission to move.

Kneel. Serve. His.

Andrew's firm hand at Zack's shoulder held him back from making further progress. "Zack, that's impossible."

The word "impossible" rained down like a cold shower, dashing his dreams and expectations. He needed to form the words and make Drew understand.

"I *really* like you, Drew." Zack didn't care if he begged. Maybe if Andrew understood how much, it would make a difference.

Kneel. Serve. His.

"Zack, you're too young to know what you like," Andrew said in a kind but firm tone.

Andrew combed his skilled fingers through Zack's hair, adjusting the style. The stimulation shouldn't have been so erotic, but he was primed.

No! He had to stop Drew's rejection. It wasn't supposed to go this way. Drew needed to agree to at least a date!

"But, Drew, I know what you *like*. I saw you. I go to Entwined too. I want that too. I *am* that. Please." Desperation washed through him, ending as moisture formed in his eyes. Maybe if Andrew comprehended that Zack could not only accommodate his needs, but also satisfy them completely. He'd be everything Andrew wanted and more.

Kneel. Serve. His.

"You're too young to be in places like that." Andrew shook his head, reinforcing his deceptive words.

Zack wasn't too young. "I'm a member."

Andrew traced his fingers softly down Zack's face as he spoke. "You're sweet, but we can't. It's not that I don't think you're beautiful."

Kneel. Serve. His.

The only thing Zack had ever really wanted was being snatched away from him.

No! No! No!

His heart shattered.

No words left. He let his body speak when his mouth wouldn't work. He pressed in and pushed Andrew against the wall. The man refusing him was hard too. Shouldn't that prove they should be together, or at least go out on a date? Andrew's rejection made no sense.

Kneel. Serve. His.

Andrew swallowed and cleared his throat. He narrowed his eyes and focused on Zack. "You should be playing the field. You're young. Go experience the world. Explore."

"It's just a date." Zack grasped at straws.

Kneel. Serve. His.

Andrew stared at him. "I don't want you to have regrets."

"Drew, I'm not Charlie. I'm talking about one date," Zack lied through his teeth. He didn't want *just* one date… he wanted everything.

Andrew shook his head the same way the lecturer who taught BDSM and Codependency did. The class asked the submissives in the group to examine why they wanted to exchange power. Zack had. What had started out as simple kinky insta-lust had grown into wanting to share everything he was with Drew.

Zack couldn't hide from Andrew, and he didn't want to try. "I don't want to play the field."

"You say that now." Andrew stopped short of referring to his age, but Zack heard the implication.

"I'll always want you, Drew." Zack tried to entice the man into reconsidering his offer by rubbing his lower body against Andrew's, grinding against Andrew's cock through their clothing.

Andrew didn't move. His mouth dropped open.

Zack begged, "I'd be such a good sub for you. Really. I would do anything you told me to do. Anything. Everything."

Kneel. Serve. His.

Andrew exhaled hard and stared at Zack for a second. Measuring the truth in his words, maybe?

Please!

Andrew's resolve wavered. All those small moments for the last few months, Zack hadn't imagined the energy and connection between them. It was there.

He rocked his lower body harder against Andrew's, making their cocks slide against each other. The hardness of Andrew pressing against Zack sparked stars of pleasure, encouraging Zack to surge forward for a kiss.

He pushed his lips onto Andrew's. His heart sang with joy. *Finally!*

He kissed the man of his dreams with all the love and passion he carried in his heart. Zack ran his hands along powerful abs, slipping up to appreciate Andrew's chest and skimming along to rest his hands on broad shoulders. Hope grew when Andrew's lips parted.

Kneel. Serve. HIS!

Drew secured Zack by the nape of his neck. He slid his tongue along Zack's. A hint of spearmint danced over his taste buds as Drew thoroughly kissed him.

His body molded to Drew's perfectly as if they'd been carved from the same piece of wood. He squeezed Andrew's shoulders to remain standing on legs that had grown weak, and continued grinding their lower halves together.

Kneel. Serve. His.

YES! YES! HIS!

Andrew ended the kiss and set Zack gently away from him. He shook his head.

NO! Kneel. Serve.

"We can't," Andrew whispered.

His. His. His!

"Please. Drew, I know you want me." He could feel, see, and taste their shared desire.

"That's not even a question," Andrew confirmed.

"Please—"

Andrew exhaled loudly. "It wouldn't be right. Our brothers are dating, and you're not even twenty, Zack. Besides, imagine how weird holiday dinners would be when it ended."

NO! NO! NO! NO! NO!

"It doesn't have to end."

Andrew's bitter laugh stung.

Zack didn't have to be told most people didn't usually meet the love of their life at eighteen. He'd never harbored fantasies of fairy-tale endings until... Drew.

Andrew shook his head.

Zack's heart lurched. "I don't care. Please." Silent screams rang through his mind. Devastation overwhelmed him, but he pleaded his case one last time. "I'd do anything for you. I want you."

He should've accepted Andrew's rejection. Even a small measure of self-respect would help to soothe his pain later. But pride was nothing without the man he... loved. "Please!"

Kneel. Serve. His.

Andrew slouched and covered his eyes with his hands as he crushed Zack with rejection. "No." That little two-letter word echoed with crystal-clear clarity.

No forbade misinterpretation. *No!* The word was the proverbial line in the sand that couldn't be breached. *No* meant the end. *No* meant never getting what Zack needed.

No. No. No. No. No.

That simple word shattered every single hope and dream Zack had for a happily ever after. Why was he so shattered at losing everything he'd never had?

Kneel. Serve. His.

No. No. No. No. No.

Never.

Zack had to get the fuck out of there. His dreams were dying a painful death. He cut out through to the club's side door to disappear.

Humiliation along with overwhelming sadness accompanied Zack through the shadows of the darkened streets. The GPS on his phone led him to the local underground BDSM club, or maybe it was a leather club. It didn't matter.

If he couldn't have Andrew, at least he'd fall back on physical sensations to numb the devastation. The club wasn't a part of the Entwined network, but fuck if he gave a shit. Anything was better than nothing.

And right then, all he had was *no*.

Zack hesitated at the door of the club. His age allowed him to get in, though he wasn't old enough to drink... or for Andrew.

He sauntered toward the bar and was approached twice within the first thirty seconds. The initial attempt was an older man who gave him the creeps. He sidestepped him with a brief smile and bumped into an attractive middle-aged man in all leather.

"Well, hello, little sugar." The man wore a practiced smile, and his tone sounded overly friendly.

Zack gave the guy the benefit of the doubt. Perhaps he didn't mean the greeting to sound like a sleazy come-on. "Hi."

"First time to our little club?" The man's voice dripped with lustful promise.

Heat rushed over Zack's face, and he reluctantly nodded.

The man in leather cooed, "You're a pretty thing, ain't you?"

Men found Zack attractive. He'd been hit on enough to believe in his looks. This guy had Andrew's coloring and height.

Zack cringed. Was he destined to constantly make this comparison? He yearned to erase Andrew from his heart, the worthless feelings and the pain of Andrew's rejection from his mind.

A distraction. That's what Zack required. He tentatively smiled at the man.

The man didn't seem to need any further encouragement. "Mmmmm, sugar. I'm Master Louis. Let me buy you a drink before I make all of your dreams come true."

ONE THING led to another, and Zack found himself in a grungy semiprivate back room. Master Louis had him bent over a sticky workbench.

The guy simply beat the shit out of Zack with the buckle end of his belt. After the abuse, which had nothing to do with BDSM, he rolled on a lubed condom Zack had insisted upon and jammed his cock into Zack. The prick pounded into him like he was a blow-up doll.

This experience lacked any of the promised sexy power exchange they'd discussed during their short conversation. It was nothing like what he'd learned about at Entwined. This was simply about this fuck getting off.

Zack tried to focus on his dingy surroundings, but a grunt of pain escaped through his tightly pressed lips.

"Stop whining, kid. I'm giving it to you, just like you want." The bastard slammed into him harder. Every thrust ripped Zack open with fire. Thankfully, Louis lacked endowment, so it wasn't as bad as it could have been. "Take it like a man."

The moans of another couple made Zack berate himself. The asshole said whatever he thought Zack wanted to hear. Desperate enough to get away from his reality, he accepted the punishing onslaught.

Zack kept still. He let the guy do whatever he wanted, praying for it to end. He'd known the risks of doing a scene with a complete stranger without a safeword. Maybe he'd been aware he was courting trouble by playing outside of the vetted members of Entwined, but it hadn't stopped him.

This entire scene had been a huge mistake.

Zack hoped he wouldn't be torn by the careless prick.

The dismal experience hadn't even given him an erection, which the asshole misinterpreted. "Oh, you're a good little bottom. You don't even need a hard-on to enjoy my cock." The fucker stabbed himself in harder to emphasize his point. "That's right. Be a good boy. You don't need an erection to give me pleasure."

Zack's skin crawled. He didn't throw up, though he came close. *Argh. Dirty. Disgusting.*

When would this end? He tried to remain stoic. The lubricated condom wasn't enough, and the thrusting started to hurt like a hot poker. The guy hadn't even taken any time to even stretch him.

Never again. Never.

Finally, the asshole playing the part of a Master grunted. His fingers dug painfully into Zack's hips. More bruises.

The guy pulled out. The pig tossed the filled condom into the corner of the room, zipped up, slapped Zack on the ass, and left.

The couple across the room came to a noisy climax.

Zack collapsed across the table, totally numb. He wasn't waxing poetic about Drew. Hell, he wasn't thinking about anything other than getting the fuck out of this hellhole. Now.

Never again. Never.

Fuck! He might have been bleeding. He wasn't sure, but he grabbed his jeans, which had been bunched around his knees, and hauled them up.

He was one mass of pain back there. It hurt to move. The fucker used his belt rather carelessly. His skin was sliced into bruised ribbons.

He stumbled through the bar. Searching for the door, he limped past Master Louis, who stood with a group of men. The asshole pointed at him, and all of his friends raised a glass in a mock toast.

Zack died a little more inside. Their laughter urged him to hurry out the door.

Never again. Never.

He refused to hobble, but he definitely shuffled. Zack was on the street before he acknowledged the wetness on his cheeks. He swiped at the tears.

Never again. Never.

What a fool he was! He'd asked for it… no, he didn't, but he didn't try to stop it when everything took a wrong turn. What type of self-destructive asshole had he become? How could he have allowed someone to use him in such a way?

He put as much distance between him and the bar as he could manage. How could he have been so stupid? He tried to let his mind go blank as he trudged in the general direction of the hotel.

"Zack." A voice cut through his mental chastisement.

Kneel. Serve. His.

His heart jumped into his throat. He didn't turn toward the familiar voice.

No! Holy fuck! Did he do something bad in a past life to deserve this?

"Zack, get in." The red car rolled beside him slowly. The command floated out the passenger side window. "Get in the car, now."

Kneel. Serve. Never his. Never.

Fuck! Zack climbed into Andrew's rental. Goddamn, it hurt to sit. With no other sign to mark his defiance, he slammed the door as hard as possible. He hadn't thought this night could get any worse. Rejected by the love of his life, then stupidly allowing a stranger to use him should have been the limit.

Wrong! The fates dished out the cruel and undue punishment of Andrew witnessing the aftermath of his shame.

Andrew studied him with sympathetic eyes, making everything a hundredfold worse.

Zack didn't dare to glance up from his cold feet, grateful for the warmth of the car's heater.

Drive. Please. Drive.

Finally, Andrew touched his hand. Zack jumped and hit the passenger side door as he tried to escape. Avoidance of reality wasn't possible. He groaned at the impact.

"Are you okay?" There was too much concern in Andrew's voice, especially after he showed how little the connection they shared meant to him.

Never his.

Silence. Zack couldn't find the strength to lie. Instead, he buried the truth out of sheer stubborn will.

"Zack, answer me. Are you okay?" Andrew spoke slowly but did not broker room for misunderstanding, and he expected an answer.

Zack swallowed. He tried to open his mouth to obey, but the memory of rejection sliced a cut into his heart again. *Fuck him!* "After tonight, you don't have the right to ask me anything."

"I have every right." Andrew inhaled and exhaled. "You're… family."

Anger tore through Zack, startling him. Tonight, he'd lost all the silly fantasies he'd concocted about Drew. Now Andrew had the nerve to rescue him from a long painful walk back to the hotel and tell him they were family. *Family!*

Never again! Never his.

Hurt and venom bled together in Zack's voice, a foreign sound to his ears. "You gave up any rights tonight." Zack turned his head to frown at the dominant man he loved and said, "Though I appreciate the ride."

Andrew asked with far too much tenderness, "Were you hurt?"

Not being able to keep the bitterness out of his voice, Zack snarked, "And again, why do you give a shit?"

Would this night never end?

"You know…." Andrew didn't finish, nor would he. This might be the closest thing Zack would ever get to an admission that there was something between them. Andrew persisted and repeated, "Were you hurt?"

"What's the right answer?" Zack snorted at how stupid he'd been to commemorate the loss of his future aspirations with a humiliating fuck.

"How about the truth?" Andrew bit the words out.

Never his.

Why did the answer matter to him? "You want the truth, *Andrew*?"

The steering wheel squeaked as Andrew squeezed the leather tighter. "Yes, Zack. I want the truth."

Zack sensed he'd won a small victory. Maybe any emotion was better than nothing.

Andrew's voice lowered as he asked, "Do you need a hospital?"

"No." Zack croaked out the possible lie.

"I need you to tell me if you're okay." Andrew stopped at a stop sign and turned his head to study Zack's face.

Zack barked out a laugh. Was he kidding? "I'm fucking peachy."

"Language," Andrew chastised him, and he continued down the road. The car rolled to another stop at a red light.

"How's this for language? Fuck you," Zack whispered loud enough to be heard as he yanked at the door handle. It didn't budge. He tried again. No luck. "Let me out."

Goddammit! There went his dramatic exit.

The fucker smiled a little. The light turned green, and he proceeded down the empty street as if Zack hadn't just tried to pull one of Houdini's vanishing acts.

Open! Zack wrenched the handle again and again, not caring if he hit the street at the speed Andrew's car moved. Zack wanted out, but the asshole must have engaged the child locks. Who did that on a rental? He kept trying to open the door until he realized he was making an asshole out of himself.

Fuck this! He gave up, slamming himself back against the passenger seat. Ow.

"Done with your tantrum?" Andrew's soft voice carried no amusement. *Never his. Ever.*

Silence. What could he say? Zack had acted every bit like the child Andrew had implied he was earlier this evening. He turned his head to stare at Andrew while his dream crusher focused on the road in front of them.

Zack drank in the movie-star face, which made his heart hurt with want of things that would never be his.

"What happened to your knuckles?" Zack asked with more care than he wanted to reveal.

Andrew glanced down at his ripped-up and bloody knuckles. He lifted his right hand and examined the gashes closer, as if he hadn't noticed them before.

He shrugged, staring back out the windshield. "I used them."

He *used* them. Zack glared at him for a second. What the hell did that mean? He reached over to lift the man's hand off the wheel and inspect the damage. Zack barely resisted the urge to kiss the cuts. He wanted his lips to heal the lacerations and take away the pain.

"It doesn't look broken, but you should put ice on it when you get back to the hotel." Zack kept surveying Andrew's hand as if the examination would justify touching him longer. Holding his hand brought with it a peace that wasn't meant for him.

Kneel. Serve. NO! Never his.

Zack dropped Andrew's hand.

"I will." Andrew returned his hand to the steering wheel.

Curiosity had always been Zack's downfall. "So, how did you damage your hand?"

Andrew frowned, and his jaw clenched as he maneuvered around an idling car. "I told you, I used it."

"What? On someone's face?" Zack winced at the sarcasm in his voice, but Andrew's brows lifted, the corners of his mouth turning up just a little. Was that an admission? Mr. Control had gotten into a fight? "You punched someone in the face?"

The car rolled to a stop at another red light. Andrew turned to gaze at him. He nodded once and kept scrutinizing Zack. Why did he try to see past the front Zack wanted him to focus on?

"Why?" Zack blurted the question out in confusion.

He'd never even seen Andrew raise his voice in anger, let alone his fists. He was all about having complete restraint in all his actions.

Andrew closed his eyes for a moment and swallowed. In a very quiet voice, he said, "He hurt you."

The shame and humiliation of the bar washed over Zack anew. Andrew had not only guessed what happened to him, he'd witnessed the aftermath and attempted to avenge him. As if his night hadn't sucked enough, this turn of events made the whole tragic evening a thousand times worse.

Zack used his hands to cover his face to hide from Andrew's scrutiny. He pleaded for the only thing Andrew might be willing to give him. "Don't tell Dusty."

A honk of impatience made Zack drop his hands and brought Andrew's attention back to the road. The bright green light in front of them summoned the car to move. Andrew rolled through the light and turned down a residential street that would cut back across to their hotel. He pulled over to the curb and threw the car in park.

"I won't say anything." His voice held a gentle quality Zack had never heard before. "Tell me he used protection."

The demand for reassurance that Zack wasn't a total moron was a knife in the heart. "I'm not that stupid."

He almost shouted the denial, hurting his aching head in the process. Given how the evening unfolded, perhaps Andrew's question was understandable. Maybe Zack's intelligence *should* be called into question.

"You aren't stupid at all. It shouldn't have happened," Andrew said in a quiet voice.

Never again. Never his.

"Why should you care?" At that moment, Zack didn't give a shit if he sounded like a resentful child.

Andrew turned to meet Zack's eyes. Even though Andrew tried to block out the link connecting them, it was still tangible and couldn't be washed away with rejection.

No! No! No! No! No! But, never... his.

"Please." Andrew hesitated. After several moments, he said, "I need you to be careful."

CHAPTER SIX

Almost two years later

ZACK FOUND a spot in Entwined's nearly full parking lot and checked his phone. Damn, three texts from Megan. Did she think he needed reminding about the Monday morning meeting? Hell, he was the one who pushed for it! Just because he'd been off the road for a few months didn't mean he wasn't chomping at the bit for the next tour. Or that she hadn't kept him busy.

Who did she think had made the band's televised Christmas and New Year's appearances go without a hitch? Not to mention charity concerts in November and March.

But his off hours were spent right here at Entwined, his second home.

He got out of the car and grimaced. *Jesus!* It was only May and hot as hell already. It didn't bode well for the coming summer. He hurried inside.

Audrey gave him a smile. "Back again, Sir Zack?"

"Where else would I be?" Zack presented his membership card with its shiny embossed MASTER stamp. Yeah, he didn't feel like an imposter. Not much anyway. With enough classes, a person could bypass their true nature. Hell, he proved that every single night he'd been there.

She handed him back the card. "Any plans for next weekend?"

He tilted his head. "Next weekend? Oh, right, Memorial Day weekend? I'll be here. You?"

"My Master is taking me to the beach to teach me to surf. Thank you for introducing us. He's too perfect!" Audrey adjusted her purple stockings. "Oh and just so you know, I hear there's a number of subs here just hoping to play with you tonight. So have fun!"

Good to see her so happy. Like she could possibly be anything else with a Master like Jerome. Strike up another win to his awesome matchmaking skills. "Hmmm, okay, then. You too." Zack smiled and waltzed through the doors.

The St. Louis, Los Angeles, and Baton Rouge Entwined clubs rocked, but this was still his favorite one. Maybe because it was the first club he'd gone to, where he took most of his classes and knew the most people. Each time the scent of leather and lust hit him, it was like a coming home. His Entwined "family" understood him, didn't question his needs, and simply accepted him.

He pushed away the image of kneeling at Andrew's feet and focused on the night ahead. Whose submissive dreams would he bring to fruition? If he couldn't have what he craved, he'd bestow that gift on someone else.

His gaze fell on Xander and Orion, who waved and rushed over to him. Orion cried out, "We're so glad you're here!" Xander guided Zack into his usual chair while Orion hurried off as if on a mission.

"So…." Xander looked around. Zack followed Xander's line of vision to subs gathering around Orion.

Within a minute, a Dominant helped Orion hop up on stage. Orion grabbed the mic. "May I have everyone's attention?"

Everyone stopped what they were doing—except the collared submissives, who only responded to their Masters' directions—and looked up at the stage. The same Dominant began to help a line of subs jump on stage.

"Sir Zack has been generous to so many of us. So some of the subs wanted to give Sir Zack a birthday celebration."

What? Right, he was now twenty-one as of last Wednesday. His brothers had forced a party on him so he'd blocked it out.

Several members he'd become friends with tugged him out of his chair and shoved him toward the stage.

"Speech! Speech! Speech!"

Fuck! He held up his hands. "I want to thank everyone here. You've allowed me to explore a side of myself I've always kept hidden. You've given me a place where I belong. I'm indebted to all of you. Thank you."

There, that had to be good enough. He smiled at the subs and hoped to evaporate.

Holy hell! It was quite a lineup, a who's who of subs he'd done scenes with since joining. Images from the past few months flashed though Zack's brain.

Orion's best friend, Xander, nabbed the microphone with a grin and started to sing, "Happy Birthday to you!"

Everyone joined in the song.

When the song came to a close, someone in the crowd yelled, "It's birthday spanking time!"

Orion took the paddle Zack hadn't noticed Tony was holding and handed the wood to Zack, handle first. He returned to the line and pulled down his pants.

Fuck! A line of the twenty-one cutest butts he'd ever seen were de-pantsed and wiggling for him.

The crowd applauded, and someone shouted out, "Get to it!"

Each of the subs peeked over their shoulder and grinned at him.

Orion said, "Give us each two for your birthday, Sir," as if it weren't a flimsy excuse for staging an exhibition.

Fuck! Zack prayed he didn't stumble and face-plant on the stage. He focused on the handsome, giving subs rather than being the center of attention. He traced his hand over each sub's presented backside. Soft skin, various skin tones, different sizes... it was a veritable buffet of spankable bottoms.

When he reached the end of the line, the bent-over man re-arched his back to give Zack a perfect target, and with a wicked grin, he said, "Happy birthday, Sir."

Zack drew back the paddle and whacked the smooth surface across the rounded butt in front of him. The swat vibrated the handle.

"One more, Sir," the sub begged and twitched his butt, inviting the paddle.

Zack swung and connected.

"Umph! Thank you, Sir." The first sub jumped up and rubbed his ass with two hands.

Wow! Zack stared down the lineup of men stretching across the entire stage, amazed they all had bent over for him. *Focus!* He sidestepped to the next sub. He answered the "Happy birthday, Sir" with one good hard whack followed by a second.

"Thank you, Sir!"

The third sub turned with big blue eyes, biting his lower lip. Ah, Roberto didn't like a lot of pain and only enjoyed playful pats. It melted Zack's heart that he would participate in this celebration anyway.

"Happy birthday, Sir." His voice cracked.

Zack respected the bravery and tapped him twice with a light touch on the bottom.

The sub mouthed, "Thank you."

The next submissive liked it hard. Zack complied and slammed the paddle down on the pristine cheeks, leaving two red rectangles.

"Mmmmm, thank you, Sir."

Zack shuffled down the line, doling out the paddle smacks according to each sub's needs. Some he pulled back and stepped into the swing to add an extra wallop, and for others he barely touched the wood to their skin.

The surreal nature of this scene hit him as he glanced back down the line of the subs. Some were rubbing their butts, a few had other subs rub their asses for them, and others had their pants back up, arms folded, and watching the live action.

Tony jumped up as he squealed, "Thank you, Sir." The big man liked the afterglow and the sting but not the stroke it took to get there.

Zack didn't look out at the audience, but he couldn't help but wonder if Andrew had shown. They didn't see each other much at the club, though that didn't stop his stupid heart from racing when he caught a glimpse of him. Or the slice of inappropriate jealousy that stabbed him in the gut whenever Andrew went into or came out of the back rooms.

He continued down the line, slapping asses.

Xander winked at him. "Happy Birthday, Sir." He turned his head forward and twitched his ass back and forth, as if his ass alone wasn't enticing enough.

Zack smacked the twerkable backside with a good solid whack.

"Again, Sir!"

After pulling back, Zack connected with a loud pop.

Xander popped up and rubbed his ass. "Ow! Thank you, Sir."

Orion happened to be last in line.

Zack doubted he'd ever give Orion what he needed, but he'd try to come close. He pulled the paddle over his shoulder.

"Happy Birthday, Sir. Hard, please." Orion grunted at the impact. "Mmmm, thank you, Sir."

Zack rubbed the red outline of the paddle on Orion's ass. Damn, that would be painful.

The man pushed the curtain of hair out of his face and asked, "How about one for good luck, Sir?"

The audience laughed.

Zack shrugged and gave Orion what he asked for by putting his weight into the swing. The pop of the paddle echoed through the room. "And one for good luck."

Everyone applauded.

Zack surveyed the subs. No one appeared worse for the wear from the paddle kisses.

There. Done. Zack waved and yelled, "Thank you, everyone." He jumped off the stage.

Luck had never been on Zack's side. He landed right in front of Andrew.

Fuck!

"You did well up there. Glad to see you're having a *very* happy birthday." Andrew's voice shouldn't sound like an invitation.

Kneel. Serve. Never his.

Zack found his own voice. "Thanks."

He stuck out his hand as Andrew tried to man-hug him. Awkward. As if they needed more discomfort between them.

"Appears they appreciate you." Andrew nodded his head toward the stage.

He and Andrew never spoke of Zack begging to serve him. Shoving down the emotion that followed was becoming a ritual. At times, Zack wondered if it had ever truly happened.

Zack glanced back at the subs. Each one of them was sweet, intelligent, and nice. Why couldn't he find someone to appease the ache that continued to eat him up?

"So, um—"

Andrew spoke at the same time. "Oh, it—"

"Sorry, go ahead," Zack said, relieved Drew—Andrew had something to say.

Andrew pointed and said, "It looks like they're signing the paddle for you."

Zack watched a sub sign with a flourish, then kiss the wood.

A sub Zack found much too bossy and bratty to play with whined, "Andrew, I've been patient. I watched the birthday spanking. Can't *we* go in the back yet?"

A sickening feeling of loss rose, but Zack pasted on a smile. "Don't let me keep you."

Not his. Not ever.

"It looks like your adoration society isn't done worshiping you yet." A frown marred the face Zack shouldn't still find so appealing.

The subs had gathered and were gesturing for Zack to follow them.

Petty or not, it was good to be appreciated. It wasn't like Drew— Andrew planned to venerate him. Andrew didn't want him, so Zack would take the path available to him. He hoped someday he'd find a destination he liked. Until then he'd enjoy his travel companions.

Xander called over to him, "Zack, we aren't done celebrating!"

Andrew reminded Zack, "I'll see you at Sunday dinner."

"Yeah, I'll see you then." Zack didn't meet Andrew's gaze, but at least he left with his dignity intact as two subs dragged him to the back.

Xander grinned. "We've got plans for you."

Zack would just ignore the sensation of Andrew's stare on him, burning a hole in the place his heart used to be.

Orion and Xander opened the door to the largest of the back rooms in Entwined. They guided Zack to a chair. All the men from the stage were in the room, in various stages of undress.

Orion and Xander pressed on his shoulders, forcing him to sit in the chair.

"So, now that you gave us birthday paddle whacks, we thought you'd like birthday blowjobs," Orion announced.

Zack was glad he'd sat. "What?"

"Sir, we all want to suck on you for your birthday," Tony clarified. He leaned in and whispered, "No one expects you to pop with all of us, Sir."

Who in their right mind said no to twenty-one mouths?

Xander dropped to his knees and fluttered his eyelashes. "You know you can't say no to some of the most orally inclined men you've ever met." He moistened his plump lips with a swipe of his tongue.

Fuck. "Well, if you insist." Poor excuse or not, Zack hitched his hips forward in the chair and unbuttoned his fly. He wore jocks that covered his ass and circled his cock with stretchy fabric so when he shifted his leather pants out of the way, his dick jutted forward.

"Mmmm, looks like a fabric cock ring." Orion tossed a pedestal pillow on the floor and became the first to take up space between Zack's knees. He reached into Zack's pants and drew his balls out, making them accessible for the line of eager subs.

Orion licked his long tongue along Zack's dick.

Zack moaned.

Orion lowered his mouth to lash his tongue along Zack's sac. He made Zack shiny with spit. "To celebrate and make things interesting—"

What? Zack had to ask. "More interesting than twenty-one *gorgeous* subs sucking me?"

The subs chuckled.

"We're each going to suck you for a minute." Orion licked his dick between every word or two. "During those sixty seconds, another sub—" Words stopped in favor of Orion covering Zack's cock with his mouth.

Xander shook his head and accepted the paddle from Tony. "The sub behind the sucker will paddle him."

Whack! Smack! Pop!

Orion pushed out his ass.

Xander gave him a couple more and said, "Twenty-one smacks each to encourage us to do good job."

"Fuck," Zack gasped. The subs were lining up.

Someone asked, "Who's going to time the sucker?"

This glorious group of subs decided on a timer while Zack sat there like a sultan. The entire event had a surreal quality to it.

They turned their attention back to Zack.

Xander continued to whap Orion's butt.

Orion smiled up at him and said, "Okay, Xander, you can start counting now." He fluttered his eyelashes and closed his lips back over Zack. He pushed his mouth forward and his already red ass back.

Zack gulped. "Twenty-one times of this?" Maybe he should celebrate lesser birthdays as well?

Xander counted out the strokes as he roasted Orion's rump while he sucked.

Suck. Smack. Slurp. Whack.

The sweet suction pushed any lingering doubts right out of his head as to whether Zack should be doing this.

To be slurped on by a guy who got smacked for the privilege was a mind fuck. This scene was hot, dirty, and a great birthday present. There was no way a member would ever not cough up the membership fee after this experience.

He tried to maintain his composure by concentrating on the differences in blowjob techniques, but by minute fifteen, it got difficult to identify the qualities of the heated pulls other than that they were incredible.

Slap! Smack! Pop!

Wood being spanked down on a bare ass fueled the erotic atmosphere of the celebration.

Zack found his Dominant voice. "Wait," he demanded, though in truth it was more of a beg for mercy, but the subs respected his instruction.

Glancing around the room, Zack saw the subs had formed a semicircle. Most of them caressed the sub next to them. Several had another sub comforting their asses that had been reddened while they were sucking. Mmmm, some were even kissing.

"Okay." Zack allowed sucker number sixteen to continue.

Pop! Smack! Slap!

As the twentieth-first mouth descended, Zack was in doubt as to how long he'd be able to last given the circumstances.

Suck! Spank! Slurp! Pop!

Perhaps it was time for him to take control of this party, before he lost it.

He stopped number twenty-one midsuck while the sub wielding the paddle with too much enthusiasm continued to give the sucker swats. An arched eyebrow was all it took to freeze the birthday smacks.

Zack said, "Anyone have any issue putting on a bit of a show for my birthday?"

Tony asked, "How can we please you, Sir?"

"I want you to each pair up with another sub and suck each other off." Zack used his deep voice.

A murmur of anticipation swept through the room.

He glanced around to assess the comfort level. "Anyone safewording?"

Everyone shook their heads.

Xander chuckled. "Safewording or a blowjob.... Hmmmm. Decisions, decisions."

The break allowed Zack to get his excitement under control. Though his erection demanded he move the party along, edging an orgasm was half the fun.

"Pair up and sixty-nine," Zack ordered, hoping he sounded in control.

Everyone buddied up and dropped to the floor. The guy with the paddle looked around, found a partner. The paddle dropped to the floor, abandoned.

Orion and Xander were the only ones left. They shrugged, grinned, kissed each other, and got into position.

When everyone's mouth hovered over a cock, Zack said, "Ready... set... suck."

Muffled groans echoed off the walls.

Damn! He was conducting a fucking birthday orgy.

Fuck! The man on his knees in front of Zack stared up with big blue eyes and said, "Feed me, Sir."

Zack groaned.

He tangled his fingers into the short hair of the man who began sucking him for all he was worth. He tightened his grip and guided the mouth just a little bit faster.

The submissive took him deep. Vague memories of how much this man enjoyed deep-throating made Zack thrust.

The man made the most delicious sounds when Zack's cock lodged in his throat.

He held him there a few seconds before releasing him. Once the man had a breath of air, Zack pushed back in.

The sub curled his fingers into Zack's thighs, staring up at him like he was a god. He pushed in deep, triggering the sub's gag reflex, and moaned as the man's throat fluttered. Tears streamed down the sub's cheeks. He dragged his lips back up.

"You going to swallow for me?"

The sub nodded and dove down, swallowing around Zack.

Men writhed. Heads bobbed. Wet slurping sounds mixed with moans.

Orion whimpered. "Sir, permission to come?"

Fuck! Right! Should he deny them? That would set off a frenzy, so instead Zack said, "Come when you want to." He hoped to avoid giving permission numerous times.

Red asses twitched and humped quicker. Everyone seemed to be chasing his own fleeting slice of heaven.

Mumbles and groans swept through the room.

Zack couldn't hold out any longer.

His eyes slammed shut, and he grunted. Pleasure radiated from his core and spread outward. He shook as he came in the heated suction that vacuumed his cock. His orgasm crashed over him.

The sub swallowed and dutifully licked him clean. When he was done, he peeked at Zack.

"So good." Zack's throat barely allowed the words out.

The sucking sub beamed at Zack.

Shit! No one had taken care of this man. Before Zack implemented a plan of action, Orion and Xander tugged the guy down so he landed on his back.

Orion reminded the sucker, "Sir said to come when you want."

Xander and Orion slid their lips up and down on either side of his throbbing erection. They kissed each other over the tip.

Orion took the dick in his mouth and sucked for few seconds, then Xander deep-throated him. Orion licked the man's balls.

The guy shouted, "Yes!" and rocked up into Xander's mouth.

The room was silent. Relaxed. Zack rebuttoned his pants, as did most of the subs, though some stayed naked, and a few remained shirtless.

Zack glanced around. All the subs were smiling, laughing, or chatting with each other. He remained on the fringes, though he was the center of attention.

Tony opened the fridge and took out a sheet cake. Someone lit the candles. They all got on their knees and sang a breathy "Happy Birthday" that would have given Marilyn a run for her money.

Plates and plastic forks appeared along with bottles of sparkling apple cider. Everyone toasted him with birthday wishes.

But there had only been one wish he'd had, and unfortunately that would never come true.

ANY SECOND the doorbell would ring and another Sunday family dinner would begin. Zack would have to pretend Andrew hadn't seen him on stage paddling twenty-one subs.

Ding, dong.

Kneel. Serve. Damn.

"I got it." Jordon's shout reached Zack's room.

Zack pushed off the bed and headed downstairs.

Andrew was hustling around the kitchen with Justin and Dusty, putting things in serving bowls with the efficiency of a chef.

Jordon called out, "Don't forget the pepper."

Zack mumbled a "Hi" to Andrew as he carried the plate of chicken to the dining room.

When everything was on the table, they sat and passed around the chicken, vegetables, and jasmine rice. The silence was a blessing.

Zack wasn't looking in Andrew's direction. He simply focused on eating.

"So, I've got a brain giant." Dusty leaned on the dining table.

Oh God! Now what? What kind of idea does Dusty have now?

Justin stared at Dusty with such love and admiration it hurt Zack's heart. Why didn't he have that? Did Andrew have to stare at him?

"Who wants to go on a safari?"

"In Africa? Do you have any idea how many shots you'd need?" Jordon screwed up his face and stared openmouthed at Dusty, then shot a look at Zack, as if looking to him for information.

"No, in California. There's a reserve with animals, and you sleep in tented cabins."

"You mean sleeping outside. Like as in camping?" Jordon's expression alone told everyone he was not up for the adventure.

Rolling his eyes, Zack shoulder-bumped his little brother and bestowed Jordon's rightful title, "Diva."

Jordon shrugged. "Your point?"

Dusty ignored him. "Justin and I thought it would be a family thing to do on the band's hiatus around the Christmas holidays this year."

"Camping with animals?" Jordon seemed to be struggling to wrap his head around that idea.

"Weren't you looking at specialized classes at that fancy San Francisco art school?" Justin asked, pushing Jordon's *yes* button.

Jordon glared at Justin for a second before nodding. "Yeah, and there are some amazing museums out there."

Andrew cleared his throat and asked, "Where in California is the safari?"

Was he considering going?

Elation and pain ripped through Zack. Twenty-two months and ten days had passed since Andrew had told him no, but who was counting? Zack had moved on with his life. Or tried. Hopefully by the time this tour season ended, he'd have his feelings for the man he'd never have under wraps.

Dusty said, "The wine country. We thought all of us would go have some quality family time."

Andrew looked at Zack and said, "That sounds great. I'd like to go."

Kneel—

Fuck! He'd work on it. Zack's stomach did a triple backflip with a heart clench.

Three months later

THE DARK Angels tour was well underway. It didn't take much effort to avoid running into Andrew. Zack only saw him across the room and always found a reason to leave. The distance tricked Zack into believing he wouldn't drop to his knees if Andrew snapped his fingers.

The band was playing in the same city for a second night. No breakdown required and no setup tomorrow, so he had a few hours free. Luck was on his side; the city had an Entwined.

He flashed his membership creds at the door, stashed his stuff, and stepped into the club.

Inhale. Exhale. Relax.

It was the first time he'd been able to take a deep breath in weeks. He needed this. Hell, even if he didn't do a scene, just being with like-minded people allowed the tightness in him to unwind.

He trudged over to the bar and ordered cranberry juice. He swiveled his stool around to survey the room. This club's décor had a medieval dungeon theme. Unicorn and dragon tapestries graced the walls. Lush red velvet couches were scattered around the room. In the corner sat an iron maiden, and on the longest wall hung heavy iron shackles.

The gold curtains were drawn over the stage.

He turned to the bartender and asked, "Is there a demo tonight?"

"Yeah. A Master from the East Coast."

No. It couldn't be.

The curtains opened.

Of course! Who else would it be? Zack's life had turned into a Mongolian clusterfuck, so why wouldn't the man he tried not to think about be the center of attention?

And why did he have to look so fucking good, standing up there in his black leather?

Zack had to get the hell out of there, and he needed to purge this man from his system.

CHAPTER SEVEN

"SO ARE you going to Ma's for Thanksgiving?" Andrew sipped his tea and waited. He hoped the question would distract Justin, who appeared to be gearing up to question him.

"Yeah, you?"

Andrew shook his head. He'd stay away.

Justin sighed. "I don't want to pry—"

"So don't." Andrew shrugged. It was rather simple.

His brother's eyes went squinty. "Look, it's just that things have gotten tenser between you and Zack. You said nothing happened—"

"And nothing ever will." Andrew was careful to keep the disappointment out of his voice. The last tour seemed to have increased the distance between them. Zack could barely stand to be in the same room with him.

"I still don't get why. I mean he's a great guy… smart, hardworking, attractive, maybe a little quiet. Though after your ex, I'd think that would be a welcome change."

Andrew didn't have to be told Zack's attributes. He cataloged them on a daily basis, but it didn't change one simple fact. "You're with Dusty."

"Yes. I'm with Zack's older brother… so what?"

Was Justin being dense on purpose? Did he need Andrew to spell it out?

After his assault, Justin had stopped dating altogether. He had even tried to end his misery by attempting suicide. Andrew would be damned if he'd do something to mess up Justin's life, even at the cost of his own happiness. "I don't want to screw things up for you."

Justin blinked several times a la Mr. Magoo. "Excuse me?"

Time to backpedal. "Well, I mean—"

"You think Dusty would leave me if things didn't work out for you and Zack?"

Yeah! Choosing words carefully, Andrew said, "Well, I mean—"

Justin laughed. Not just a chuckle, but a big gleeful chortle directed at Andrew. "Let me save you the trouble. You and Zack could implode in a disastrous supernova of a relationship, and Dusty would still be mine. If you haven't noticed, we're in it for the long haul. Drama is going to happen, but we'd never dump each other for what our brothers did. We've both been through too much. And now that we found each other, there's no way we're letting go."

Andrew spit out, "I just can't—"

"Stop using *me* as an excuse! How do you think that makes me feel?"

"But, I—"

Justin glared and cut him off, "You do, and it makes me feel like I'm broken."

"I never want to do that to you." *God no.*

"Well, then stop being an idiot."

Andrew shrugged as he tried to process it. "Easier said than done."

"And you're going to Safari West, so deal with reality."

Geez, when had his baby brother gotten so bossy?

As ANDREW drove up to Safari West to spend time with his brother and the Davis clan, he made himself a promise. He'd figure out a way to get Zack alone so they could possibly hash things out. Regardless of everything else, he missed their friendship.

He hated that through the entire tour season, Zack had appeared determined to avoid him. When he did happen to run into him at the clubs, Zack had always had an adoring sub hanging all over him. He'd dodged Sunday dinners whenever possible, and he even ditched a holiday party with the band. Had Andrew lost his chance?

He arrived at the animal reserve and emptied his suitcase of the packing cubes. Each large mesh container held an entire outfit, which included his socks and underwear. When he rolled the clothing properly or folded as necessary, there were no wrinkles to deal with. He unpacked his sneakers, his boots, and the one pair of dress shoes he'd brought, in case Zack agreed to go out to dinner with him. He put his toiletries in the bathroom.

A scream ripped through his tented cabin. *Who was that?* Another howl. Was that Jordon?

Andrew raced over to the cabin next to his to save Jordon from whatever made him scream like a banshee. He bounded up the cabin steps, taking three at a time. *What the heck—?*

Zack and Jordon were rolling around on the floor wrestling. They were both trying to reach… a sex toy? Why were they tussling over a neon pink Rude-Boy?

Andrew cleared his throat since neither seemed to realize he stood there. "Um, sorry. I just, well, I'm in the tent next door, and I heard Jordon's shouting…."

"I'm fine," Jordon growled through clenched teeth. The kid's dislike for him grew as Zack's distance did.

"I see Zack's with you and you're fine, so…." Andrew words ground to a halt, but his feet didn't move.

It had been weeks since he'd actually seen Zack, and he looked good, even on the floor scuffling with his brother.

The only sound was the roar of distant lions and… what the heck? The whirring sound of the dying sex toy? Everyone's attention turned toward the quiet buzzing on the floor. The Rude-Boy continued to quiver in a slow circle.

Jordon said, "Yeah, well, come on in. Don't just stand there like a turtleneck with ears."

He wasn't positive, but was pretty sure that Jordon had called him a dick.

Zack jumped upright and gave Jordon a hand to haul him off the wooden floor.

Andrew opened the door, which pushed the Rude-Boy farther into the room.

Both he and Zack bent to pick the toy up at the same time. They rose, each holding an end of the vibrating Rude-Boy.

This was closer to Zack than he'd been in months, so there was no way in hell he'd step back or let go. He wanted to press forward, but he needed to advance at a reasonable pace.

Zack's long eyelashes fluttered down to block his stunning green eyes. How Andrew adored the fact Zack's lashes were black but the tips appeared dipped in gold.

They stood there together transfixed and holding a sex toy between them. Oddly enough, it reaffirmed they had a connection.

Zack peeked up, and Andrew was mesmerized by his heated stare. If Jordon hadn't been there, would they have fallen into bed?

"You do know that's been up my ass," Jordon sniped. Zack's kid brother pushed the button down, turning the toy off, and ripped the device out of their hands.

Andrew couldn't help but smile. Without taking his eyes off Zack, he said, "Well, I hope you cleaned it...."

"With a good toy cleaner," Zack finished while he gazed through his long lashes at Andrew. "*Classic Erotica Before and After* is a good product."

"It is...," Andrew fairly panted in agreement. He needed whatever was between them to happen.

"You two need to get a fucking room, and not this one," Jordon snarked.

The kid put the device into his suitcase and snapped the latches. "Stay out of my shit, Zack. If you want me to stay out of yours...." Jordon widened his eyes and tilted his head in Andrew's direction.

Zack nodded once.

Optimism invaded Andrew to the point he dared to wink at Zack, then smiled at Jordon.

Apparently the younger Davis wasn't in the mood. "Shut up, Andrew. Robin and Josh gave me a bunch of sex toys for my birthday."

"No judgment, Jordon." Andrew held up his hands in defense. He'd never criticize anyone for sexual exploration.

Jordon stomped over to hold the screen door open. "Justin and Dusty are waiting for us."

Andrew swore he heard Jordon mutter, "Hurry up, you sausage monks" but he wasn't positive.

Sure enough, Dusty and Justin stood next to a big green Jeep emblazoned with a Safari West logo on the side, chatting with the guide.

Jordon called "shotgun" and jumped into the front seat. He spun around to mouth, "Hottie alert" as he thumbed toward the driver.

It couldn't have worked out better. Dusty and Justin slid into the middle seat, probably to keep a short leash on the youngest Davis.

Andrew jumped into the raised backseat and reached a hand down to help Zack into the Jeep.

Zack stared at his offered hand before taking it.

Victory! He tugged Zack into the seat and got him as close as possible without pulling him right into his lap.

Zack didn't release Andrew's hand until Justin turned around and peered at them.

Even though Zack dropped his hand, Andrew allowed his hope to grow. Yes, Zack could still be his. He had to get him to admit that. Then they'd work out their issues.

The backseat happened to be a little smaller than the other two, so Zack was crushed up next to him. His warm thigh pressed against Andrew's.

Andrew spread his legs wider. It was a jackass move, but he craved more contact between them.

The roads were uneven and tossed Zack against him time and time again. Each time he'd mumble "Sorry" and shift away to his own side.

The Jeep powered into a big dip, and Zack was nearly bounced into Andrew's lap.

Andrew threw an arm around him under the guise of securing him. Goddamn, indulging in the feeling of Zack in his arms had to be as close to heaven as he'd ever ascend.

Although most of his focus remained on Zack, Andrew heard bits and pieces of the information about the animals and other conversations going on in the Jeep.

Jordon flirted heavily with the attractive dark-skinned driver in between the man's narrative on the animals, their habitats, and mating rituals. Dusty clearly disapproved of his littlest brother's attempted moves on the driver, who must have been about fifteen years his senior.

Andrew didn't notice many of the animals, but he loved Zack's excited reaction to each of them.

Zack snapped pictures as a courageous ostrich stepped closer to the Jeep.

The driver introduced the bird to them. "This is Norman. He was rescued as a baby and transported to us. Unfortunately, he refuses to eat unless he's hand fed. He can be a bit of a snapper, so keep your fingers out of his mouth."

Norman poked his head in.

The driver called him over. "Here you go, my friend."

The bird plucked the lettuce from the driver's fingers and munched while surveying who had his next treat.

When it was Zack's turn to offer a leaf to Norman, Andrew asked, "Look this way."

Zack obeyed, and Andrew captured a beautiful picture of him full of exhilaration and a fragment of trepidation. Zack squeaked when Norman snatched the lettuce.

"Great picture. Here, take my leaf."

"Really?" Zack asked.

Andrew would readily hand over anything to make him happy. This time he captured a picture of Zack in profile as he stared into Norman's eyes.

An hour into the trip, the driver started returning Jordon's witty comments with flirtation. Then, in a bid to win Jordon, the driver stood on a rock to sing in some African language.

The sun sank slowly behind the hills, casting shadows of dusk. The strong baritone, accompanied by an animal choir in the background, with Zack close to him made the moment just about perfect.

Zack relaxed against him during the driver's rendition of what sounded like a love song. Justin turned around to say something, but his mouth dropped opened and he swung back around.

After the song, the driver drove them to see a few other parts of the resort. They visited the meadow where the giraffes roamed and raced around the thorny acacia trees.

"Look!" Zack pointed out several rhinos meandering along the fence. His face glowed as he took pictures of zebras and bongos galloping through the open fields.

"And so we are back where we started," the driver said.

"Thank you." Dusty tried to tip him, which the driver refused.

"It has been my pleasure." The driver turned to Jordon and asked, "Would you like to grab dinner with me?"

After an hour and a half of pure flirting, the kid backed away like the offer was an invitation to his own execution.

Dusty's growl stopped the driver's attempt at encouraging the date and made him take off at a good clip.

Zack jumped out of the Jeep to catch Jordon, who was stomping away. He waved off Dusty to keep him out of the conversation. The two youngest Davis brothers spoke fast and soft so no one would know what was said.

Andrew didn't take his eyes off Zack. He was stunning when animated.

Jordon appeared distraught until Zack hugged him. They strolled back to the group. Zack gave Dusty a "shut the hell up" look, which proved surprisingly effective.

Justin broke the quiet. "Well, that tour was fun."

"Yeah," Andrew and Zack agreed while Dusty and Jordon tried to stare each other down.

"I want to go paint." Jordon made the announcement as if someone might try to stop him.

Dusty sighed. He glanced over at Zack and said, "So, if you guys are okay, we have to get back for a phone call."

"A phone call?" There, that showed Andrew had interest in someone other than Zack.

"Yeah, um, the band is going to call." Justin turned to Dusty with big eyes. "Let's head back."

Dusty's grin appeared a little too wide for a phone call, but that was none of Andrew's business. Justin bounced with happiness, so Andrew was good with whatever those two would be getting up to with the band.

Andrew asked Zack and Jordon, "Do you guys want to see the rhino?"

Jordon did a double take between Zack and him. The kid was astute enough to pick up on the chemistry rolling off them. "Nah, I'm going to go draw some of the toucans out front near the lobby." Before they could respond, he headed off in the exact opposite direction of where the driver went.

After Jordon left, Andrew asked Zack, "Everything okay with him?"

Zack groaned. "Yeah, he's dealing with some stuff, but he's okay. Though the kid's going to be the death of me."

"Oh, I truly hope not." Andrew flirted shamelessly and ran his fingers through Zack's golden strands under the guise of fixing his hair. He deserved a better haircut than this.

Zack snorted. "Really? And why's that?"

"I'd miss you terribly." Andrew made his voice go deep as the words danced off his tongue. He caught Zack's gaze and held the stare.

Zack blinked first and sniffed before turning away. "Shall we see the rhino? I hear his name is Bender."

As they approached the animal's enclosure, Zack remarked, "I can see where he got his name." It appeared he was named after his favorite pastime of misshaping things.

An attendant put down her book to greet them. "You guys here to visit Bender?" After they nodded, she gave them a lecture on their safety and Bender's, then handed them wire-bristled brushes. "He loves to be brushed."

They didn't need to have a map drawn; the animal, the size of a small car, moved his head to get them to scrape the brushes where he wanted them.

Zack's snicker rang through the barn. "I bet he doesn't even care that you're a world-famous hairstylist."

Andrew chuckled. Yes, a teasing Zack equated to a happy Zack. He prayed their interactions would go back to a comfortable level.

He whispered so the attendant didn't hear, "Bender might be more of a hair whore than Robin."

Zack chortled and said, "Now that's saying something."

Andrew rubbed the brush up to Bender's muscular shoulder. The animal shifted his backside, probably to give the brush access to some elusive itch.

"He's a good boy," Andrew purred and didn't forget how Zack might take the phrase coming from him.

Zack's eyes flashed with heat. "A very good boy."

Mmmm. Zack challenged him. Andrew liked that.

Everything compelled Andrew to take Zack behind the barn and show him exactly how things were, but he couldn't. They had issues to work out first.

After a few more minutes of brushing the sweet creature, Zack popped upright and turned away quickly. "*Achoo*! Achoo! Achoo!" He wiped his eyes.

When Andrew handed him a hankie, Zack said, "Thanks." Once he used it, he stared at it a moment before studying Andrew. He asked, "You carry hankies? What are you? A retired Englishman?"

Zack could mock Andrew all he wanted as long as he talked to him with the ease they used to enjoy.

Andrew handed him a bottle he kept in his satchel.

"What's this?" He tipped the bottle and stared at the label. "How did you know?" Zack scrunched his nose and squinted his eyes, making him look rather adorable.

"That you have allergies or that you'd forget your meds?" Andrew was proud of his knowledge of all things Zack.

"Thank you." After another sneeze, Zack popped a pill into his mouth and would have swallowed it dry if Andrew hadn't handed him a bottle of water.

The attendant flitted over. "Ah, good job, guys. Bender's all brushed and happy. I can finish in here if you want to feed the giraffes. The giraffes love acacia trees." She pushed a basket of leaves at them.

"Just make sure the one with the heart-shaped mark on his neck eats. If he doesn't, tell me."

"Sure. Okay." Zack accepted the basket. They navigated the pitted path uphill to the large fenced-in meadow where the giraffes roamed. He peeked over his shoulder to give Andrew an alluring smile. "Coming?"

"Almost." He winked at the very pink-cheeked Zack. It was time.

When they reached a white wooden fence, every giraffe in the field raced over the high grass for the delicacy of the special leaves.

Zack held a leaf out and squealed when a black tongue swiped his fingers.

Andrew managed not to let out an unmanly shriek when one of their long-necked friends licked his hand, but it was a close call. He pulled out his camera and snapped several spectacular pictures of Zack feeding the giraffes.

"Look." Andrew pointed out a male sniffing and licking another giraffe's backside. "That's the Flehmen response."

Zack laughed, "Are you talking dirty to me?"

Andrew shook his head. "I will if you want me to, but he's testing her urine to see if she's in heat."

Zack asked, "By…. Ew, did she pee?"

"Yup. Otherwise, he wouldn't be able to check her hormone levels," he answered, glad he'd googled information on the animals they'd visit.

Zack nodded at him. "Oh, is that the excuse he's giving her? Let me put my tongue here to check your levels, baby."

"Sticking your tongue inside is rather more direct than a pickup line."

Zack snickered and gave the giraffes the rest of the leaves. When the basket was empty, Andrew pushed him against the fence.

Zack inhaled sharply. He was striking in the twilight.

"Do you like direct?"

Zack gazed up through his long eyelashes, making Andrew's heart thump out of control. "I do."

The basket dropped. Zack pushed back against Andrew.

Visions of him bent over the fence evaporated with the high-pitched voice of the attendant. "Oh, you two are so cute. How long have you been together?"

Dammit! Andrew stepped back. "Not nearly long enough."

Zack's eyes widened when Andrew tugged him into his arms.

She smiled in that dreamy, approving way some women got when they saw two men together. He refused to let Zack pull away, and after the first failed attempt, Zack settled into his side like he belonged there.

The sun had set, and twilight gave way to dusk. They ambled together in silence back down the dirt path, stopping to stare at the stars every once in a while. Without the light pollution from the city, millions of sparkling lights dotted the sky.

Andrew kept his arm wrapped around Zack, and nothing had ever felt so perfect. He couldn't seem to stop himself from planning past working out their issues, which would begin right after Zack agreed to come into his cabin.

Zack hesitated at Andrew's door.

The waiting was over. Andrew needed to go for it.

Zack asked, "So, um, have you heard from Charlie?"

"Charlie?" His ex's name sounded completely foreign. "I saw him at the beginning of the year. Right after Valentine's Day, I think."

"*Saw* him?" Zack's tone suggested he understood exactly what Andrew meant by saw.

"Yeah…." Andrew got the sinking feeling this wasn't going to go well, but he wouldn't lie.

"So Charlie just *happened* to stop by your house?"

How does any ex-lover materialize for a bad idea? "He came for a visit."

Zack stepped away, putting distance between them. He studied Andrew, appearing to be trying to make puzzle pieces fall into place any other possible way. "So you were with him?" Anger tinted his words.

Andrew stepped forward to put his hands on Zack's shoulders, but Zack shrugged them off.

"It didn't mean anything." Damn, the admission felt as if he'd nailed his own coffin closed.

"Didn't mean anything? Didn't mean anything?" Zack repeating Andrew's words wasn't a good sign. "How could you go back to him after all he did to you?" His voice was laced with hurt.

Both he and Zack had been with a number of people at Entwined. Why would his being with his ex matter? "How could *I*? How could *you*?"

All his frustration of wanting to do the right thing, of having to hear subs wax poetic about Zack's skills, of having to watch Zack prance around as one of the favorite Doms at *his* club poured out. The conversations had almost driven him mad.

Zack donned indignation and wore it well. "How could I what? Not wither away and die because you didn't want me?"

How did Zack believe that? Andrew forced himself to stay calm and find his center. He steeled himself. Everything he'd hoped for crumbled. "You know that's not true."

"Not true, huh? Who were you with? 'Cause it sure as hell hasn't been me!"

Andrew reined in his voice. "No, you know that's not even close to reality."

"Good luck with Charlie. Maybe he'll take you back."

"Charlie is getting married." It was true, but that didn't come out right. That wasn't what he'd meant.

Zack's face crumpled for a second before he put on the mask of indifference he wore too well and too often. "Oh, I see the rumors were true. Is that why you finally decided to give me a try?"

Andrew reached for him.

Zack stepped beyond his reach. "Don't… ever." He stomped right past all the plans Andrew had for them and into his own cabin next door. The location might as well have been half a world away. The distance between them didn't have a bridge.

Andrew needed to get out of there. He'd leave in the morning so Zack could enjoy time with his brothers….

ANDREW LEFT Safari West before dawn. He texted Justin from the road.

He'd seen a tweet from Robin's private Twitter account about a club he and Josh were going to tonight. After a few texts, he pointed his rental to San Francisco to hang out with them.

Andrew had unpacked into his new room when there was a knock on the door.

When he opened the door, Robin pulled him into a big hug. "Hey!"

Andrew hugged him back and guided the gentle man into his room. "What's with the hat?"

"Bad hair day," Robin grumbled.

Andrew peeled determined fingers off the woolen cap and revealed Robin's issue. *Yikes.* The usually beautiful blue-green hair was flat and flew every which way. "It's the soft water of San Francisco. No worries. I have an extra bottle of volumizing shampoo to give your hair back its bounce. I have some products to replenish the oils that were stripped away."

Robin frowned. "But I used my own shampoo."

"There's less calcium in the water here, so your regular shampoo goes into overload and strips your hair."

"Is that why my hair looks bad when I visit my Uncle Leo?"

Andrew went to his bag of tricks. It paid to be prepared. He pulled out his magical potions. "Your hair never looks bad, Robin. But hard water versus soft can cause chaos when you're on tour, so I use a product that counterbalances it."

Within five minutes, Robin sighed contently as Andrew put his hair to rights.

"So, why did you leave Safari West early?"

Andrew wanted to pretend he didn't hear him.

Robin opened one eye and asked, "Zack?"

Was he that obvious? "I didn't want to ruin their time together." Retreat seemed to be the wisest alternative. Zack had been too angry to listen to anything he had to say.

"What happened?"

Andrew wanted to say he didn't know, but he did. "He misunderstood something I said."

"Which was…?"

"Zack thought I was trying to hook up with him since my ex is getting married."

"Ah." Robin nodded.

"And he was pissed that I'd gotten together with Charlie months ago." Andrew exhaled hard. That night had been a mistake. He'd accepted once they'd finished the second bottle of wine, remembering the good times…. Regrets were to be expected. The one-nighter had been a round of selfish vanilla sex. "The entire event just reminded me of all the reasons why we aren't together."

"A closure fuck?"

"Robin!" Andrew hated the use of foul words; it reflected a lack of creativity.

His friend rolled his eyes. "What? It was, wasn't it?"

"Yeah." It was definitely the conclusion of their stormy relationship. Andrew couldn't mourn his years with Charlie, because those experiences made Andrew the person he had become, but he'd never wanted to go back to his ex and all the lies.

"Good." Robin nodded again.

"Zack and I both played with scores of different subs at Entwined. Zack had no right to be upset by it. We've never been together."

Robin squinted at Andrew. "Exactly. Charlie's had what Zack's never gotten, and you went back for a second go-round."

"Maybe," Andrew agreed while he flat-ironed Robin's hair.

"So what's your plan?"

"Other than giving Zack some more time, I haven't thought of one."

Robin turned and gave him a look. "Okay, well, while you're here, maybe you'll help me with a project."

"Sure." Andrew was game. He turned Robin back around so he faced straight ahead.

"You know Jack?"

He was the man living with Robin and Josh's uncle. He'd gone through a rough patch with drugs, but now he was sober. "Of course. I saw him a few days ago at the holiday party."

"You know he likes Sean?"

"Uncle Leo's son, the doctor? Yeah, it was kind of obvious at the party." Painful might be a better word.

"I'd like you to help me do a makeover on Jack."

"Sure. When?" Andrew sprayed his masterpiece.

Robin looked at his phone. "Um, now."

Andrew chuckled. "Sure. If you can't help yourself, you should help someone else."

Robin checked the mirror. "Thank you. You're a genius."

"This is what you need to use on the West Coast." Andrew handed him a bottle of shampoo he grabbed out of his bag and scrawled down some other helpful products.

"Great, I'll pick them up while I'm getting Jack's clothing."

"So what do you need me to do?"

"Make sure he does the spa day I've set up for him and that he gets dressed."

"I SERIOUSLY can't believe Robin wants me to wear this?" Andrew could hear Jack's frown through the bathroom door.

"Let me see," Andrew commanded.

Jack tentatively opened the door and peeked out.

"Step out from behind the door." Andrew hoped the gentling of his voice would encourage Jack to participate in the big reveal.

Jack dragged his feet forward to obey.

Andrew whistled. "You're even hotter than I thought!"

"What? No." Jack tugged at his snug T-shirt.

"I have no need to concoct fairy tales for you. You're beautiful." Sadly, the man didn't believe that. Andrew fussed a little with Jack's hair. "The way he always stares at you isn't going to change, but I hope this will act like a cattle prod for him."

"Who?"

"Please! Do you think I'm blind? Dr. Perfect wants you bad, and this little makeover will blow him away."

"Sean wouldn't care."

He hauled Jack over to the largest mirror in the room. "Don't you see how hot you are? You're stunning. Inside and out." Andrew tangled his fingers through Jack's hair. Maybe....

Andrew tugged Jack into a kiss.

Bloody hell! It was sweet, but.... Andrew ended the lip-lock with a sigh. "If we both weren't hung up on someone else, this would so happen."

Jack blinked. "Who are you hung up on?"

Shaking his head, Andrew said, "It doesn't matter."

"But he does want you," Jack stated.

Andrew ran his fingers through his waves. He'd thought so, but now... "I don't know."

"Wait! It's not...."

"Don't," Andrew warned.

"Okay."

Andrew changed the subject and physically spun Jack. "Dr. Perfect will be flabbergasted when he sees you."

Jack blushed and bit his lower lip. "You think he'll even notice?"

"Lower lip bite. Sexy! Unless the bastard is blind, he'll notice," Andrew reassured him. "Now, add the double-lick lip press."

"The double what?" Jack chuckled.

"Watch." Andrew stuck his tongue out slightly between his top and bottom lips. Then he curled his top and bottom lip before ducking his tongue back inside his mouth. He ended by pressing his two lips together as if blotting lipstick. "Try it."

Jack did it once but started laughing halfway through. "Sorry." He attempted the move again.

"Once more."

He did the double lick twice more.

"You've got the lips down," Andrew proclaimed.

Jack frowned at Andrew and shook his head.

"Seriously, Jack. You're a vision. Walk like it. Act like it. Own it. If he can't see you, trust me, others will. Let's go." Andrew guided him out of the room.

In the lobby, as Andrew predicted, Sean noticed. It was a movie moment if ever there was one. Sean lifted his head, his mouth dropped open, and he stared at Jack.

Andrew took pride in the part he played in getting Sean to appreciate Jack.

Sean's eyes roamed up and down Jack twice, and he croaked out, "You look... nice."

Andrew stirred the pot a little. "Oh, that's an understatement. Jack's delicious. He's hot as hell. I'm going to have to beat the guys off him, and not in a way they'll enjoy."

Sean didn't say anything; he kept on staring at Jack.

Andrew tapped them both on the shoulder. "We should go. The car's here."

ANDREW SAT next to Josh in the club's VIP section.

"You look gorgeous! Dance with me, Jack," Robin shouted over the music.

"I'm not very good," Jack said before taking a sip of sparkling water.

Andrew encouraged him, "Oh, I bet you're *very* good."

He watched his latest creation spin between the curls of dry ice smoke with Robin. Satisfaction filled a small spot in his empty heart.

What was Zack doing? Was he enjoying his time now that Andrew had left? Why couldn't Andrew have who he wanted?

Josh interrupted his thoughts. "You did good with Jack. He deserves it. The guy's had a tough life."

Sean snorted in what sounded like disbelief. Andrew wasn't in the mood and would flatten Dr. Perfect.

"What's your problem?" Josh barked. "With your dad's help, that guy has turned his life around."

Sean had the good grace to look away, but he muttered, "Just waiting for him to screw up and break my father's heart… again."

Josh shook his head and said, "The only one who's breaking Uncle Leo's heart is you. Why can't you see that? Maybe if you stuck around long enough, you'd understand."

Sean pushed his fingers through his unruly hair and closed his eyes for a moment. Andrew really studied the guy and saw the attraction Jack found there. The doctor was classically handsome, when he wasn't sounding like a jackass. He was smart and, according to Robin, could be funny as hell. With a good conditioner and an attitude adjustment, Andrew might see the appeal.

Clearing his throat, Sean turned his attention to Josh. "You're right."

"Huh?" Josh appeared taken aback by the admission.

"I'm sticking around. My dad isn't getting any younger, and well, there's things that need to be done on the home front…." He stared out wistfully at the dance floor.

Perhaps he wasn't such a dick. Andrew asked the simple question that would point Dr. Perfect in the right direction. "Why don't you ask him to dance?"

"I don't dance."

And back to asshole. Rolling his eyes, Andrew said, "Dancing is swaying and holding on to someone else."

Jack and Robin were the main attraction, surrounded by men and women trying to get into their space.

Josh winked at Andrew and stood. "Well, if you'll excuse me, my baby needs a rescue." He swung Robin into his arms, which left Jack to the encroaching wolves.

Come on, be a man, Sean. "Here's your chance to have what you want. Jack's right there, he's beautiful, and he's yours."

No movement.

"You really aren't going to go stake your claim?" Andrew prodded. Men were beginning to rub against Jack, and he was getting buried deeper into the crowd.

Sean stared at the table and said, "He wouldn't want to dance with me. He hates me."

"Wow." Andrew rose. "Your dad told me you had a photographic memory, but your damn lens has the cover glued on."

"Huh?"

"I'm shocked someone who practices medicine can miss something that's right there in front of him. Does someone else diagnose your patients for you?" Andrew was done with the idiot and stalked to the dance floor.

He threw himself against the tide of bodies and grabbed Jack's wrist. Jack relaxed when he saw who reeled him in. As soon as they were close enough, Jack slipped into Andrew's arms and stayed there. They danced for several songs.

After several wistful looks were exchanged, he and Jack frowned at each other. *Dammit!* Andrew said what they both already knew. "It's a shame we're only meant to be friends."

Jack started laughing. "I know. I know." A fast song came on, and Andrew spun him. At least they could have a little bit of fun together.

Out of the corner of his eye, Andrew watched Sean rock back and forth in his seat. The fucker just wasn't getting it. He pulled Jack to the DJ booth, handed over a fifty, and made his last-ditch effort by shouting a request in the woman's ear.

Within a couple minutes, the music morphed into a throbbing backbeat and an electro-buzz of high notes from a guitar. Recognition of the late seventies hit was followed by a frown that marred Jack's handsome face.

"You did *not* just do that."

"You can't deny you've got a bad case of loving the doctor." Andrew turned his attention to Sean as if he could will the guy to get off his ass and take what he wanted.

Andrew chose to ignore the irony of him encouraging others to do what he hadn't done. What he should be doing himself.

Jack must have decided to fuck it all, because he danced to the beat and started mouthing the words with feeling. He bumped into Andrew a couple of times because his full attention was devoted to staring at Sean.

As the song went on, Jack shouted the words. Hell yeah, he even pointed at Sean as he sang to the doctor about how no pill could cure him.

Andrew admired the guy. Jack put his heart right out there. He truly did have a bad case.

Unfortunately, Andrew understood how that went.

Jack swung around Andrew, turning him into a human stripper pole. The shimmy twist ended with Jack's ass thrust out. He wiggled, challenged, and dared Sean to take what he offered. Finally, Jack did the double-lick lip press, and that was it.

Sean jumped to his feet and steamrolled everyone in his path to get to Jack. He twirled Jack off Andrew and into his embrace. They ground against each other, making Andrew question whether they were going to drop to the floor and have at each other right in the middle of the club.

Robin danced over to them. He handed Jack a keycard and shouted loud enough for them to hear, "Josh and I got everyone a hotel room next door. We figured you might not feel like driving back to the other hotel."

It wasn't like the other hotel was that far away, though maybe just enough distance to make someone overthink a decision. Damn, Robin appeared to be quite manipulative when he set his mind to it.

Andrew respected a puppet master as long as it was for the greater good and it wasn't his strings being pulled.

He pushed the image of Zack out of his head.

Jack shook his head, but Robin kissed his cheek and slipped back into Josh's arms. "Enjoy."

Sean stared down at the room key as if it would burst into flames.

Jack darted a glance to Andrew as if he were looking for advice.

Andrew mouthed, "Go for it" and danced to Robin and Josh. He kept one eye on Sean and Jack's short exchange. Sean grabbed Jack's hand and led him out of the club.

Robin shimmied around to Josh with a big smile and fist-bumped Andrew. "Finally, their happily ever after."

Andrew doubted that. "This is the quiet before the storm."

Robin sighed. "You're probably right."

Feeling philosophical, he asked, "What is a happily ever after anyway?"

Josh rubbed a hand over Robin's ass. "A bunch of little happy moments that, when put together, add up."

Andrew danced with them for a while longer before he said, "I'm going to call it a night."

Away from the dance floor's chaotic noise, he tried not to think of all the choices he had made that denied him happy moments.

Only one choice gave him true regret. He called up a picture of Zack on his phone.

CHAPTER EIGHT

ZACK HAD always hated how the snow seemed to turn a depressing gray right after Christmas. He wished they'd stayed in California for New Year's but Dusty wanted to start the new year at home.

He grabbed mail addressed to him and headed to his bedroom.

Shit! It was freezing. He stumbled over and checked the temperature. *Dammit!* Jordon must have fucked with his thermostat! Zack raised the temperature to seventy degrees.

He rubbed his hands together. Once he could feel his fingers, he ripped open the padded envelope that was in his pile of mail. A gold box and a folded-up piece of pink paper fell to his desk.

Unfolding the note, he reread the contents twice before setting the note aside. He stared at the paper. Entwined was having a fundraiser. The flyer informed him this year's theme was "Are You Dom Enough to Be a sub?"

He opened up the box and snapped the lid shut immediately.

Fuck! Who would send him this?

His heart was going to beat out of his chest. He drew in several calming breaths before he reopened the box.

He gently traced his fingers over the leather circle and silver buckle.

He'd be in town for the event this year. Could he volunteer to be auctioned off for a weekend of slavery to the highest bidder?

A weekend as a slave.... A whole weekend!

Zack allowed his fingers to worship the leather collar.

Kneel. Serve. His. No! Never his....

He snatched his hand back.

Sighing, he shoved the box away.

He studied the envelope. The handwriting looked like Robin Strider's. The keyboard player had hinted more than once that he understood Zack's BDSM leanings. But Zack gave only a vague acknowledgment of belonging to Entwined.

Zack couldn't stop himself. He grabbed the box and stumbled to his bathroom. Sliding the lock in place, he stared at the box. He should at least try on the collar?

He pulled off his T-shirt and tossed it toward the hamper. With shaking hands, he opened the box. He held the leather to his nose, and inhaled the delicious scent that never failed to give him wood. Closing his eyes, he wrapped the circlet around his neck, then buckled it.

Opening his eyes, Zack stared and whispered, "Fuck. This is… me."

Maybe he should participate…. After all, it was for charity.

"HAPPY NEW Year, Tony." Zack was happy to speak to the man he hadn't seen much of in the last couple of months. Tony had all but disappeared from Entwined. He probably spent most of his time happily nesting with his new Master.

"Happy New Year!" Tony shouted. "I'm happy to hear from you."

"I wondered if you wanted to join me and my family for dinner." According to the text he'd gotten from Tony's new Master, the poor man would be home alone, and his family was out of state.

"Oh, that's okay. I thought I'd go into the shop and get some extra work done."

"It's a holiday. I know your doc got called in on an emergency."

"I don't want to disrupt your family dinner." Tony was a worrier.

"Tony, your Master doesn't want you to be alone." Zack would play the Master card if he had to.

"Well no, my Master wants me happy," Tony concluded.

"So come over," Zack encouraged. He gave him the address and the time.

ZACK HADN'T quite imagined the ramifications of inviting Tony to dinner. He didn't want a good guy to be alone on a holiday, but his family and possibly even Andrew thought Zack and Tony were more.

Maybe Zack should have explained he and Tony were truly only friends, especially now that he had set Tony up with a Master perfect for him. Perhaps it was passive-aggressive not to clarify? *Fuck it!* He hated the sad looks his brothers or the band gave him whenever Andrew happened to be in the vicinity. Zack was tired of being cast into the role of a pathetic lovesick puppy. No more. It was a new year.

Though some things never changed. They stood around the table and waited for Jordon to tell them where to sit.

"I'm sorry, I didn't have time to paint place cards this year," Jordon said while he surveyed the table. "Dusty, sit at the head and Justin on his right."

Dusty humored Jordon and held out Justin's chair.

"Tony, you're the guest of honor, so you sit here," Jordon muttered. "Hopefully, you won't turn into a twit like our last guest of honor."

Andrew folded his arms and cleared his throat. Maybe he wanted to remind Jordon he stood right behind him.

"Oh. Yeah. You… you can go sit across the table." Jordon frowned and waved Andrew away.

Andrew smiled and took his seat. "Thank you, Jordon."

Jordon glared at him. "No problem. I have no issues telling *you* where to go."

Zack gasped. "Jordon!" *Fuck!* The kid needed to dial down his loathing.

His little brother made his eyes go big, as if he were trying to convey total innocence, and asked, "What? I'll be happy to tell *you* where to go too."

Zack glared at him.

Jordon pointed to the empty chair. "You sit between Dusty and your *hot* friend."

Fuck, this wasn't the best idea.

Dusty started passing the food. "I used Justin's mother's recipe for the pork roast. I'm sure it won't be as good, but—"

Justin passed the greens with garlic and interjected, "I'm sure it will be. Tony, my mother and stepfather take cruises over the holidays, but Dusty had her on Skype at 4:00 a.m., having her walk him through the prep."

Zack blocked out the deep, rich laugh coming from Andrew's direction. "I'm sure Mom was the one calling him to ensure he did it right."

"It smells delicious," Tony said with a smile as he filled his plate.

Jordon seemed to think silence should be something to rid any gathering of so he asked, "Tony, how do you know Zack?"

Damn, leave it to the kid to bring up the one thing best left out of the conversation.

Other than his dark coloring and olive skin tone, Tony had none of the macho tendencies his Italian heritage suggested. Not even the muscles he worked on conveyed anything other than doe-eyed sweetness. The cute sub's dark eyes flashed with terror from Zack to Andrew. He dropped his stare to his plate and waited for rescue.

Zack restrained a sigh. "I met Tony at a club." He patted him on the leg to reassure him. Tony's tight posture relaxed a little.

"What club?" his older brother questioned.

What was this? A cross-examination? Did Dusty want a signed confession? That technique might have worked when Zack was ten and Dusty had gotten the truth out of him about encouraging Jordon to eat all the Easter chocolate in one sitting. *Ha!* Jordon had literally bounced off the walls for hours and then fell asleep midhop, but Zack wasn't ten anymore.

Tony cringed at the question and pushed a small bite of food into his mouth to avoid answering.

Shrugging, Zack smiled. "Just a club."

A part of Zack wondered what his oldest brother would think if Dusty knew Zack and Tony had met at Entwined. Zack wasn't in people's face like his younger brother, who currently sported a T-shirt proclaiming *I LOVE Boys* in bright pink letters. Zack had always been low-key; he didn't wear T-shirts that said *Kinky and Proud.*

"How long have you known each other?" Dusty asked, focusing on Tony before turning his attention back to Zack.

Zack turned to Tony and smiled. "I don't know. I guess a couple of years. Right, sweetheart?"

Why did he add the endearment?

Andrew shifted in his seat and ran a hand through his perfectly styled hair. It might have been immature and petty, but there was a small piece of Zack that liked knowing his implied relationship with Tony might bug Andrew.

"Yes, Sir," Tony blurted and blushed bright pink. "I mean, yes, Zack." His correction made everything a hundred times more awkward.

There was a flash of understanding in Dusty's eyes. His older brother backed off. A few years ago, Zack had confessed his interest in BDSM to Dusty in a self-destructive effort to push him away. Unlike his mother, his big brother hugged him. He let him know Zack always had a place to stay and he was loved. BDSM wasn't something Zack spoke about to people outside the scene. He shut down every uncomfortable conversation Dusty tried to have about safe, sane, and consensual.

Jordon's mouth dropped open, and he stared as the drama played out. It was like watching a reality television show. *It's Dinner at The Davises', starring the Davis brothers, plus the guy that broke Zack's heart and his wonderful brother, Justin. Tonight's guest is Tony the sub. Tony likes to be tied up and spanked till he comes.*

"Tony's got his own body shop." Zack threw out the random piece of information, hoping someone would run with it.

Leave it to his little brother to find *that* amusing. The kid burst out laughing. Granted, Tony might have been of shorter stature than average, but he was built like a Mack truck. He had muscles on top of muscles, although he was a submissive through and through.

Tony's grin suggested he got why Jordon giggled like a loon, but he didn't address the unsaid joke. "Yeah, I took over when my dad retired."

"Have you been working on cars long?" Justin's effort to keep a straight face scored him points.

Now on a comfortable topic, Tony opened right up. "I was working on cars from the time I was three. My dad taught me." His handsome face beamed as he reminisced. "I learned all the names of the tools so I was able to hand them to him as he worked." Tony gave a deep chuckle that made Zack wistful that he could've seen Tony as more than a friend. "My ma was mad because I couldn't name animals but I knew what a twelve-millimeter gear wrench was and where to find it."

Tony's ramrod-stiff posture relaxed and more of his charming personality came out, which made the meal evolve into easier conversation.

Everyone joked and laughed except Andrew. The enjoyment Zack tried to access broke each time he cast his gaze across the table. Andrew sat there studying him with an intensity that would melt Zack if he'd let it.

The stare wasn't exactly an eye-fucking, but the gaze heated him. Oh dear Lord! Why did Drew—Andrew, his name was Andrew!—Why was he staring?

Zack wasn't going to play his childish gawking game. He jumped out of his chair. "Anyone want anything from the kitchen? I'm going to get some water."

After a round of negative responses, he escaped from the dining room. He opened the stainless-steel refrigerator and let the frigid air cool him. He snagged a bottle of water and took a deep swallow to try to wash the desires he'd never have fulfilled down his throat.

Wanting more cold, he opened the freezer, grabbed a piece of ice, and held the coolness against his neck. Jesus, he needed to get a grip. Every time Andrew appeared, he got whacked out of sorts. His skin was too tight for his body, and he wanted to tear at it. Zack wanted to run.

The doors of the refrigerator and freezer shut on their own.

Shit! Not on their own. One inhale confirmed that Andrew was behind him.

Zack spiked a fever, and his heart pounded harder. Should he turn and deal, or hightail it back to the dining room to hide out with his brothers? Fuck, he wasn't afraid of Andrew.

He spun toward the heat behind him.

Andrew stood inches away, invading his space. He stepped forward and pinned Zack against the cool surface of the refrigerator with his body.

Fuck! Yes! No!

He picked up a piece of Zack's hair and twirled it around his long fingers. Andrew had the nerve to whisper, "I love your golden hair. Not even I am able to create this color. Did you know the strands have a variance that shimmers according to the light?"

Zack's cock hardened as if hairdresser-speak was erotic poetry. Whether from the physical contact, the compliment delivered by Andrew, or his scent, Zack wasn't sure, but he couldn't let the man know the power he still held over him.

"Thanks."

Andrew pressed against him.

Zack kept his eyes fixed on the other man, waiting to see what he'd do. Zack forced himself to breathe.

Andrew's sexy grin made the bastard even more handsome as he took the cube from Zack's fingertips and painted the ice over Zack's lips.

Mmmm, damn the cocksucker. The ice slid along his mouth like a cool, wet kiss.

"You know what they say about people who chew ice?" Andrew's voice reached Zack's cock and seemed to give his shaft a firm stroke.

Kneel. Serve. FUCK NO!

Zack tried to prevent himself from falling under Andrew's spell, but at such close range, he was transfixed.

"So, do you know?" Andrew arched his eyebrow.

Zack couldn't think or speak, so he shook his head. Fuck, he didn't even remember the question.

"Chewing ice equates to a high level of sexual frustration." Andrew pulled the ice away from Zack's lips and popped the cube in his mouth. He bit down and chewed the cube.

Crunch. Crunch. Crunch.

Fuck! Fuck! Fuck!

Zack focused on those exquisite full lips. The pleasurable memory of indulging in Andrew's mouth crashed over him. Why wouldn't the memory fade? Why did he still taste Andrew's soft lips? The recollection was a harsh filter that always remained at the forefront of his mind, ruining any other kiss he'd ever received.

The unspoken message Andrew delivered by crunching the ice sent shivers through Zack's body, doing nothing to cool the energy sparking between them. Sexual frustration?

Kneel. NO!

Zack's body had a mind of its own. He thrust his hips out, seeking Andrew's body. His cock throbbed and pulsed against Andrew. He ached for some attention. Any attention Andrew would offer, he'd accept.

The intoxicating man ground his erection against Zack, stealing all the air in the room.

Zack's heart sang with anticipation.

Andrew's mouth was only a couple of inches from his. Their gazes were locked, and Andrew's breath whispered past Zack's lips. God help him, but he craved the press of Andrew's mouth against his own more than the necessity of taking his next breath.

Andrew was going to kiss him—

"Did you two get lost in there?" Dusty's yell broke them apart.

Fuck! Punch! Kick! Strangle!

Andrew groaned and closed his eyes. He moved his head an inch closer to Zack and inhaled before stepping back, allowing Zack to slip free.

Shit! He needed to get a grip on himself. Zack poked his head into the dining room. "You guys sure I can't get anyone anything?" he asked, trying to give his arousal time to fade.

Andrew glided past, putting a firm hand on his ass, and gave his butt a good squeeze.

What the fuck was that? The touch certainly didn't help his situation at all.

"Actually, you know what? Can you bring me in a soda? A Mirinda, please," Jordon asked him sweetly. Trust Jordon to know he needed more time.

Dusty teased, "Justin, you still spoiling the kid by going across town to the Asian market to get him that orange soda?"

Zack listened in as Jordon piped up. "Of course, he does. Justin's my bro." Zack came back into the room to Justin and Jordon fist-bumping.

"Here you are." Zack handed over the orange treasure to grabby hands.

"Thanks, Zack." Jordon continued to call attention to himself, taking Dusty's questioning gaze off Zack. "So, Justin and I think...." Zack glued his eyes on his younger brother. Though he couldn't follow the ins and outs of the new manga they were writing, it was impressive his little brother was a published artist. But right then all he could manage was faked interest.

What the fuck had happened in the kitchen?

Unfortunately, Zack allowed his gaze to drift once or twice to Andrew. Andrew wasn't even pretending to listen to Jordon. All of the man's focus was zoomed in on Zack, and the attention did nothing to calm Zack's erection.

The rest of the meal passed without a hitch, lulling Zack into a false sense of tranquility. He jumped when Dusty tapped him on the shoulder. "Zack, do you have a second?"

Dusty's question would get him out of cleanup duty. Tony chatted pleasantly with Justin as he helped; Zack's friend didn't need saving. Andrew talked on his phone while carrying leftovers into the kitchen to be wrapped up and stored—not that Zack noticed where Andrew happened to be and what he was doing, because he was over the man.

He shrugged and trailed after Dusty to the "formal living room." Hmmm, this room was never used except for uncomfortable discussions. No one wanted to go in there because they—meaning Justin—had decorated the room in white, and everyone was petrified of messing it up. Justin had convinced everyone white served as the perfect backdrop to highlight Jordon's paintings that hung on the walls.

Zack collapsed into the big puffy chair, and Dusty plopped down on the velvet sofa after he moved the fancy beaded pillow off to the side. Zack wasn't sure if he moved the cushion so he didn't crease the fabric or because the beads really did dig into his back. They stared at each other for a moment before his older brother cleared his throat and broke the silence.

Oh great! A throat clearing confirmed this private sit-down would involve an awkward topic. Dusty tapped his fingertips on his knees. He stopped and rubbed his hands on his pants. Oh hell, another bad sign. *Run!*

"What are you doing?" Dusty leaned forward.

"About?" Zack asked, cocking his head to the side. Did he look like a mind reader? He needed to keep a cool head. His big brother would be attacking his self-control soon enough.

Dusty shoved his long blond hair over his shoulder and eyed Zack. He made him feel like he was seven years old again and he'd been caught sword fighting with Dusty's drumsticks. "Are you serious about Tony? I mean, he seems nice enough, but...."

"But what?" Zack went on the offense immediately. He'd learned early on that he sucked at defense.

Dusty shrugged. "Don't get me wrong. He seems like a nice guy, but he doesn't seem... *right* for you."

Zack shrugged at his brother. No sense denying the obvious.

Dusty pinched the bridge of his nose. Wow, usually that move was reserved for Dusty's best friend. "Look, I don't know what happened between you and Andrew at Safari West, and I haven't asked."

"Which gives you points in the best-brother contest I'm running. You're in the lead by the way." Zack wished humor would change the topic.

Dusty shook his head as he exhaled in a huff. *Poor guy!* He believed he was responsible for his brothers. "I want you to be happy."

"I am. I'm thrilled." Zack pasted on his fake smile to provide evidence.

Dusty sighed and shook his head. "Look, Zack, you're great at your job. The road crew loves you. I just wish...."

Maybe acknowledging his brother's concern would stop him from salting Zack's gaping wounds. "Yeah. I know. Trust me. I know."

Zack stood and paced. This conversation was going nowhere.

Dusty rested his head on the high back of the sofa. "I want you content with your life."

He sat back down hard and glared at his brother. "I am."

Dammit! Dusty didn't have any more faith in Zack's words now than when he'd tried to plant Dusty's drumsticks to see if they would grow and blamed Jordon. If the kid had learned to walk a few months earlier, Zack might have gotten away with it.

Dusty tilted his head and scrunched up his nose. "Andrew—"

Never again....

"Hey, he said *no* to me. Not the other way around. I would've.... Dusty, it's old news that no longer matters."

What did people want from him? He'd have given his left nut to be with the fucker, but he'd crashed and burned. Zack moved on, or at least wanted to appear like he had. Fake it until you make it and all that good horseshit.

"Yeah, but at Safari West—"

"No!" Zack lowered his voice and peeked at the doorway to make sure they were alone. "The only reason why he was interested... was because Charlie's getting married."

Dusty folded his arms, "You believe that?"

"Well... yeah." He did. Zack paced back over to stare out the window. Why else would he finally decide— Another gray day that brought more snow. "Ha, so much for a gentle winter in Upstate New York this year."

The silence grew between them until Dusty said, "I'm going to help clean the kitchen."

"Okay." *Whew.* He'd survived.

Did anyone think it was easy for him to see everything he ever wanted but could never have? He didn't even want to think about when Andrew collared a sub and had someone with him full-time. Andrew's little forays into the back of Entwined were enough to break Zack's heart if he dwelled on it.

Zack blinked away his blurry vision. He schooled himself to avoid non-value-added thoughts as the snowflakes drifted down and piled onto the blanket of white.

Was Safari West the only shot he'd ever have at Drew? Well, he had no plans to be second best, so it was water under the proverbial bridge. Like hell would he let himself drown in said water.

Zack checked his appearance as he ambled past the mirror in the hallway. Hmmm, go figure. He didn't appear nearly as shitty as he felt, so he headed to the kitchen.

Justin washed the dishes, and Jordon dried them. They were lost in their own world, discussing their latest plot twist for the Dark Angels' manga.

Andrew and Tony were packing leftovers in different-sized containers on the black granite kitchen island.

Standing in the doorway, Zack overheard their conversation. It seemed that Tony had loose lips. "Yes, and Zack introduced me to my new Master. He's wonderful. I know we've only been together for a short time, but I think this is *it* for me. Or at least, I hope it is." Tony's eyelashes fluttered as he spoke of the man Zack had set him up with a couple months back. "He's a surgeon. Can you imagine me with a doctor?"

Andrew nodded. "I certainly can. You're delightful."

Tony blushed. "Thank you, Sir. I mean, Andrew."

"Where is your man?"

"He had to do an emergency surgery today, Sir, er, I mean, Andrew." He twittered happily like a big muscled bird.

Zack cleared his throat.

Tony lit up with a big smile when he spotted Zack leaning against the doorjamb. "I was telling *Andrew* about *my* doctor."

Shit! There went his lifeline to sanity. Zack couldn't be pissed because the guy beamed with complete joy. He was clueless that he'd spoiled the illusion Zack had allowed to develop.

Sighing, he glanced over to see Andrew's reaction to this little revelation and regretted it when the flash of triumph settled over his face.

Dusty cleared his throat and set the trash can down in the middle of the floor. He frowned at Zack. Fuck, his big brother overheard them and easily figured out the ruse.

Zack shrugged and pushed the trash can back into its place in the corner of the kitchen. After all, he hadn't said they were a couple. He'd said they were friends. He shouldn't be blamed for the assumptions other people made. Everyone believed what they wanted the truth to be. He wasn't responsible for other's thoughts, was he?

Tony gestured toward the domestic scene. "Shouldn't you guys have a maid or something?"

Zack found Andrew's gaze and shared a head shake of understanding. This was their brothers' attempt at normalcy, but to anyone else it appeared downright weird. Rock stars should not take out the trash.

Fuck! He turned away. What the hell was he doing, sharing a knowing look with the devil?

Zack focused on Tony and answered, "Dusty doesn't understand he's a big-time rock star."

Jordon and Justin snickered at the claim before Dusty shot them the evil eye.

Dusty stalked across the kitchen and hoisted Justin into a hug. "Hey, did you know? I'm a *big* rock star."

Justin grabbed an unused dishcloth and shoved the towel in his mouth. The proclamation appeared to be responsible for his silent laughter.

His brother swept Justin into his arms.

"Oh, Dusty."

Dusty marched out of the room and up the stairs with his man.

"Well, I guess they're done for the evening," Jordon commented. "I'm going upstairs to work. It was nice meeting you, Tony. I'll be down for dessert later." The youngest Davis left Zack to fend for himself with the two remaining men.

Andrew started piling food containers into the refrigerator in a methodical way to get maximum storage. The fucker kept smirking at Zack like he'd won some sort of bet. If only there had been a way to wipe the smug look off the fucker's gorgeous face. *Fuck!* And fuck him for having a movie-star-pretty face to begin with!

Tony, unaware of the tension flowing between Zack and Andrew, said, "I can't wait for the 'Are You Dom Enough to be a sub?' charity auction."

"Sounds like a good cause," Andrew said in that frustrating noncommittal way he used far too often.

Tony grinned and asked Andrew a question that unfortunately Zack was dying to know the answer to. "Will you be joining us at Entwined for the charity auction?"

"Us?" Andrew cocked his head to peer at Zack.

"Yes, I'm an organizer, and I'll be the MC. Sir, I mean, Zack will be participating...." The guy stopped rambling. Did he finally realize he blabbed Zack's business? "So, you'll be there, right?"

"Zack as a sub? I wouldn't miss it." Andrew's voice dropped, making Zack's insides clench with something between indigestion and excitement.

CHAPTER NINE

AH, IT was good to be back at Entwined! Zack needed to find his footing after that New Year's Day debacle. When two of his favorite subs asked to do a scene with him, he didn't refuse.

Even in their utter exhaustion, Timmy Moore and Sam Shorenday stared at Zack as if he'd invented BDSM. They were stunning men, probably in their midthirties, who gave with rare grace.

Timmy and Sam had been together for six years. However, both were very submissive. The two of them managed their relationship through a series of compromises and added a third from Entwined to dominate them when the mood struck. The sweet subs had yet to find a permanent Master, so when Zack happened to be back in Upstate New York, he played with them.

Zack had just finished a light scene with them. Timmy's creamy skin highlighted where the crop had bitten into his flesh, while Sam's darker complexion hid most of the evidence of their activities. Zack always used Timmy's fair skin as a meter so he didn't push any boundaries.

His quick popularity at Entwined was simply a consequence of being completely focused on fulfilling the sub's every need. He never lacked for a play partner. Sometimes he'd work two or three scenes into a night at the club.

"Please, Sir, let us satisfy you." Timmy's big blue eyes were framed by fluttering long lashes. He begged so prettily for the gratification of servicing Zack's cock.

Recently Zack's scenes had been devoid of physical fulfillment, but these two were indeed exquisite. He stood there pondering sexual release as he stared down at the enticing picture of servitude. His silence encouraged the men to shift closer together. Their bodies seemed to melt into each other. They gazed up at him while licking their parted lips in invitation.

"Yes, please, Sir," Sam purred and boldly nuzzled Zack's leg like a loving cat.

Just when Zack decided he should give in, he heard a familiar laugh from the main room. *Fuck!*

Never his.

The sound compromised their private sanctuary. All thoughts of indulging in these two sexy creatures were chased away. "Not tonight." He hurried over and got them each a bottle of water out of the refrigerator to avoid witnessing their disappointed pouts.

"Crawl to me." Zack sat on the fresh white towel. He put his arms on the back of the red leather sofa.

The naked men undulated across the room on all fours. Sam cuddled into his right side and Timmy snuggled into his left. He took a lightweight blanket from the arm of the sofa and pulled the cozy fabric around them.

"You were both very good. I was proud of how well you handled the crop," he murmured, handing them each a bottle of water. "Drink."

Zack smiled as they instantly did so. He fussed with their hair and petted them as they purred with contentment.

When their dazed sub expressions dialed down to a happy glow, Zack asked, "I heard you've met some potential Masters. No luck yet?" Might be a dumb question. If they had succeeded, they wouldn't be playing with him tonight.

Timmy shook his head with a big frown and stared at the floor like it was somehow his fault.

Sam reached over and laced their fingers together over Zack's lap when he answered, "Not yet. We're meeting another Master later on this week."

"I hope this Master works out for you." Zack truly meant it. Everyone should have someone who could meet all their needs.

Timmy sniffled. "No one wants us. We're too old."

Zack hugged the man closer. "You're not old. You're both exquisite, smart, and interesting."

Timmy asked in a pouty voice, "Yeah, right. If we're so great, why don't you want us, Sir?"

Sam's quick inhale spoke volumes of how scandalized he was over Timmy's bold words.

Zack slid his hands down the smooth skin of both their bodies. "It's no reflection on you."

"I'm sorry, Sir." Timmy wiped at his eyes.

"It's okay. I wish…." Zack let out a weary breath and buried the words. Sam's erection pushed into the side of his leg. "Would you two like to show me how lucky you are to have each other and how much you love each other?"

"Mmmmm, yes, Sir." Sam moaned and tugged his lover to the floor. He held Timmy's face in his hands like the man was a precious piece of spun glass. Sam tilted his head and leaned in.

Timmy whimpered, parting his lips to receive his lover's tongue. Minutes passed as the two men explored each other with kisses.

There was no stopping his stray wishes to have that kind of love and devotion.

Timmy and Sam exchanged wet, openmouthed kisses as eager hands traveled over each other's bodies. Neither competed for dominance or control. They appeared to drift on the passion of their love.

Their sweet gasps and tender touches made Zack yearn to experience this kind of connection.

Why couldn't Zack have that for himself? But no, love and submission were for others, not him. While he enjoyed providing for others, he gave and gave but never received what he truly desired.

Dammit! Where was his someone who was devoted to him?

When their caresses grew more heated, they turned to Zack for direction. He cleared his throat and hoped he had a voice left that didn't crack. "Suck each other for me."

They moaned at his command and hurried to wiggle into position. Deep groans filled the small room. They each swallowed their partner's eager arousal. Timmy's hand remained clasped tightly with Sam's as they both sucked.

Sam traced his fingers over his lover's welted bottom. Timmy moaned and thrust deeper into the suction Zack imagined Sam had created.

He envied them the movements honed over countless encounters with each other.

In unison, they swiveled their heads toward Zack to gain his permission.

"Wait." His voice had a rough-around-the-edges quality. Pathetic, but he wanted to share in a little of what they had.

Timmy whined and tried to push his cock back into Sam's mouth.

Sam pulled back to answer for them and panted, "Yes, Sir."

"Kiss." Was it perverse to want to see more of the love they exchanged in their kisses? Love he'd never….

Obeying, the two men sat up and pressed their lips together. The kisses were all open mouths and wild tongues. They moaned with unspent passion.

Zack's erection throbbed, begging for release. He rubbed his hand over the leather of his pants to cup and tease his dick through the fabric. A particularly sexy whimper from the two putting on the erotic show for him forced him to unzip and pull out his cock, which, despite his morose mood, ran rampant.

Fuck, he craved kisses with that much intensity and love.

Kneel. Serve. His.

The aborted kiss from New Year's Day still haunted him. The press of Andrew's body scorching his and those lips had been only a breath away. To part his mouth for Andrew's tongue and to experience the plush moist lips gliding over his....

Yes!

He grabbed one of the hand towels to catch his orgasm before his come stained his shirt. He stroked himself to satisfaction with the visual aid of the submissives at his feet. Slowly, his cock began to soften.

The poor subs looked like they might overheat.

"Finish." The regretful sighs from when they pulled away from each other's mouths were quickly replaced by appreciative groans as their lips wrapped around each other's shafts. Within thirty seconds, Timmy cried out around Sam's cock as he humped his cute ass more quickly. Another minute later, Sam grunted. Timmy's mouth overflowed, and come ran out past his lips to streak down his chin. They shifted and collapsed into each other's arms.

Pushing his spent cock back into his leather pants, Zack stood. The two subs barely noticed when he laid another blanket over them. Usually he stayed with the submissives until after they had come down, but he knew from experience these two liked to be alone after a scene ended with orgasm. If either experienced any sub drop, the other would be there to deal with it or would come get him, but the scene hadn't been that intense.

"You two okay?"

Grinning, Timmy said, "Very, Sir." The adorable sub snuggled against his lover with his little red butt sticking out of the blanket.

"Good. The room is yours until midnight. Behave." He tried hard to sound firm. His admiration for the sweet-natured subs came across loud and clear.

He'd address any top drop alone since he'd never felt comfortable seeking support if the BDSM energy turned itself on him. It had never been bad. A couple times he had extra tension that he burned off with a run. Only once had he gotten depressed, but it passed.

"Grrrrr!" Sam rolled over on top of a laughing Timmy as Zack strolled out into the main part of the club.

Zack could have used a drink, but Entwined had a strict no-alcohol policy. Alcohol and BDSM did not mix well. He wound his way over to the juice bar, stopping several times to talk to a number of couples, some fellow Masters, and a few of the subs he'd played with in the past.

"I'll have a cranberry," he told the handsome toga-wrapped bartender.

The man leaned in and batted his eyelashes. "Right away, *Sir*."

Zack turned away, not in the mood for any other offers tonight. He sagged against the bar in an effort to remain upright. Damn, he was weary right down to his soul.

He was tired of being someone he wasn't. Or maybe his real issue might be not ever having what he wanted. There was no denying he was exhausted and tired of being alone. Unfortunately, the shift in his position made his gaze land directly on Andrew, who happened to be surrounded by a group of Dominants, Tops, and their subs.

Fuck! He should have braced himself.

Andrew seemed to know exactly when Zack noticed him because he gave him a nod in acknowledgment.

Zack's toes curled in excitement. *Shit!* Why did just seeing this man across the room make his heart race?

"Zack! Zack! Come here." Another man sitting with the same crowd waved him over.

Dammit! He grabbed his drink, wishing like hell there was some alcohol in the glass as he dragged himself across the main room. He pasted on a smile. "Good to see you, Mike." He tolerated the handshakes and back pats. "You too, Ross." He glanced down at the smiling sub kneeling at Mike's feet.

Ross peeked up at Mike. "Permission to speak, Master?" Ross was more slave than sub because he required maximum effort on any Master's part, but Mike had retired last year and thrived on micromanaging. The match was perfect.

"Yes, love, you may." Mike petted the younger male's face and smiled indulgently down at him.

Ross nuzzled into his touch and glowed under the attention. His smile grew radiant before he turned his attention to Zack and said, "Thank you, Sir, for introducing Master to me."

Zack sensed he was being watched, so he chose to focus on Mike and Ross. "You don't have to thank me every time you see me. I'm glad it worked out." They had been his first attempt at matchmaking.

"It'll be two years this Sunday since I've been blessed with this beautiful boy." Mike beamed. "Have a seat."

Wishing he'd simply left after playing with Timmy and Sam, Zack took a sip of his juice and sat on the Italian-inspired gold velvet sofa. If Andrew hadn't been there, Zack would have enjoyed catching up with the guys, but Mr. Tall, Dark, and Way Too Sexy lurked. Somehow that made Zack the awkward kid who wanted a shadow to swallow him.

Joe filled Zack in on the conversation, so the chat continued. "So, we're harassing Andrew here about why he hasn't settled down with a sub of his own."

Fuck me! Just nod and smile. This too shall pass.

Zack couldn't help but glance over to see Andrew's reaction to the teasing.

The louse swept his perfect hand around the group. "You Masters took all the good subs." The subs on their knees straightened their backs, and the ones on the laps of their Masters murmured at the compliment.

Zack winced. Even if Andrew hadn't meant his comment as an insult, it stung nonetheless.

"Oh come, Andrew. There's no sub out there who appeals to you?"

Andrew darted his gaze to Zack's and back to the group. "I can honestly say there is no *available* submissive whom I am interested in making mine."

Those words burrowed deep inside of Zack. He tried to swallow past whatever got lodged into his throat.

Kneel. Serve. NO! Never his. Never.

When he took a quick sip of his cranberry juice to wash away the acid that crept into his throat, the tart drink went down the wrong way and he started to cough.

In a flash, Andrew appeared next to him and patted his back.

"Shhh, breathe slowly." Andrew's deep, liquid voice oozed sex and threatened to give Zack an erection.

The coughing subsided, but Andrew still rubbed circles on Zack's back. God, Andrew's hands on his body were too good to be soothing, so he pulled out of reach. "Thanks."

"Anytime." The word dripped with innuendo.

Zack crossed his legs before the arousal he sported became noticeable.

Mike cleared his throat and said, "So, Zack, I hear you're helping out with the auction."

Here we go. "Yeah, it's a good cause. How could I not?" Easily, but he wasn't going to give up the opportunity… the remote possibility.

No. Never his.

"All the proceeds go to the children's hospital." Mike filled in for the couple, who had just returned to the country. "Some of the Doms who have enough balls, like Zack here, are going to be auctioned off as slaves for the weekend."

"Ohhhhh," one of the older subs—Zack didn't remember his name—tittered.

Another laughed and said, "I hear some of the unattached subs are pooling their money to bid on you, Sir."

"What?" First he'd heard of such a plan. Just his luck, the subs would win him and he'd be forced to dominate all weekend.

Andrew asked, "What? Who?" All eyes turned to him. He shrugged. "Isn't that against the rules?"

Frances, a co-chair of the planning committee, spoke up, "No, Sir, it's not against any rule as far as I know." He searched the group, maybe for validation. The others nodded in agreement or shrugged in indifference.

"Don't you think it invalidates the intention of the auction?" Andrew pressed his point.

"Um…." Frances shook his head. "I don't think so…." He glanced around the group again.

Mike smirked. "Not against any of the rules that I know of, but perhaps you should join the planning committee next year, Andrew."

Andrew glared and stood. "Anyone want anything from the bar?"

Ten tequila shots!

Everyone declined.

Andrew stomped off. His clenched teeth must have scared people. The crowd parted like the Red Sea, and no one stopped him to chat.

As soon as he left the group, Joe looked at Mike. "What's up with him?"

Mike smirked and shook his head. He turned to Zack to ask the question that seemed to be on every Dominant's mind. "How can you do that?"

Zack's face felt hot. He hadn't anticipated the sensation of being exposed his participation had created. Had they figured out his secret? "What do you mean? We've all been trained on both sides of the collar... or at least we should have been. And it's for a good cause."

Joe shook his head, and his hands skimmed over his cute sub, also named Joseph, so everyone called him Joey Junior. "How can you give up this?" He pinched his sub's nipple, making Joey Junior cry out. His stunning brown eyes shuttered shut as he absorbed the pain.

"It's only a weekend." God, he needed the fantasy.

"You gonna let whoever wins you have sex with you?" Mike leaned forward like an old gossip.

Of course, Andrew reseated himself right when Mike asked his question, and glanced at Zack with a grimace.

"Well, that all depends on the situation, doesn't it?" Did Zack sound a tad pissy? He didn't want to be questioned because he really didn't want to deal with the answers. "It's not about the sex."

"It's always about the sex," Joe said with a grin, and for some reason everyone's gaze seemed to go back and forth between Zack and Andrew, as if they were waiting for one or the other to say something.

Andrew cleared his throat, making Zack's stomach flip in anticipation. Instead of making a bold pronouncement, he slapped his thighs and stood back up. "Well, on that note, gentlemen, I will take my leave."

"What already? You didn't even touch your drink." Joe pointed out the obvious.

Setting his untouched drink on the table, Andrew said, "Yeah, it's time."

Disappointment zipped through Zack, though he hadn't really expected Andrew to say anything or do anything. After all, he never did.

No. Never his.

CHAPTER TEN

ZACK TOOK off his leather coat and handed it to an Entwined staff sub. He nabbed his cell out of the pocket as the device started jingling one of the Dark Angels' recent releases. The picture ID showed the caller to be the soft-spoken keyboard player.

"Hey, Robin. What can I do for you?"

"Not a band-related call."

Okay, Zack did get a little intense and serious when work was involved.

"I don't want to bother you, but I wanted to wish you luck at tonight's fundraiser." Robin was one of the few people who knew Zack was into BDSM outside his friends at Entwined, but they'd never discussed their shared interest directly.

"Thanks, and thanks for the encouragement." Zack's hands began to sweat. He toyed with the leather circlet in his pocket.

"You're welcome. I didn't know if I should say anything and I thought sending you a collar might get you in the right frame of mind. Are you nervous?"

Terrified might be a more accurate description. Zack wiped one of his hands on his thigh and switched to do the same with the other. "Not really."

Robin sighed. "Oh, um, I guess Andrew's not going to make it."

Zack almost dropped the phone. "What?"

Not that he thought Andrew would, no, but he hadn't been able to eliminate the tiny kernel of hope that the man would win him. Silly.

"Justin said Andrew went to the doctor two days ago. So he must really be hurting if he's willing to go get checked out."

Huh, no shit. During the tail end of the last tour, the man refused to go to the doctor even when he had a fever of 104. When the show started, Angel and Megan insisted that Zack escort him to the medical staff. Fun times.

"He'll be okay, though, right?"

"Yeah, Justin thought he needed meds and rest. But I'm sure lots of men will bid on you."

Zack didn't want to think about serving someone else. He ran his fingers through his new style and confessed, "I dyed my hair… black."

Robin's harsh intake of breath shook Zack's belief that he had done the right thing. "Oh, but honey, your blond hair is gorgeous."

Zack paced over toward a quiet corner of the locker area. He needed to step away from the chaos of fluttering subs ushering whining Doms toward the staging area. "I cut it too."

Robin whistled. "Wow. Someone's making a change."

Why shouldn't he? He ran a hand through his hair, feeling the various lengths. His hair was past his shoulders, just with more layers. "The hair color will wash out." He needed to be someone else… or maybe he was just trying to be himself.

"I'm sure you look stunning with your black hair. You need to get ready, so good luck."

"Thanks, Robin. Say hi to Josh for me."

"Um, Zack? Have fun, okay? Just be. Let it happen. It can be… freeing."

Zack sighed. "I'll try."

And he would, too. But now that the possibility of Andrew bidding on him had plummeted to zero, he almost wanted to back out.

Ending his call, he checked his messages. Jordon had sent a picture of his latest creations, a bedazzled pair of sneakers and matching T-shirt. They were well done, but he hoped his brother wasn't planning on wearing them beyond the house. Dusty asked a question about the new drumheads he had ordered, so Zack texted him the information. He fielded several other requests for information from his friends before powering off his phone.

He set his phone in his locker and took a deep breath as he headed backstage. Entwined's stage's bloodred velvet curtains hid the harried drama.

The other Doms greeted him as he joined them.

One asked, "What's with the hair, Zack? Trying to do this incognito?"

Zack shrugged. "Just trying something different."

"I am only doing this for the charity" seemed to be the response when he asked how they were doing.

Zack wanted to tell them to suck it up, but sweet Joey Junior handed out gold lamé thongs that left little to the imagination. Fuck, these were tiny! Hot and cold washed over him. He wore more material to the pool.

Frank Lopez, a big burly guy who was probably a police officer, snorted as he examined the garment. "Let the humiliation begin." He twirled the scrap of fabric around his finger. He stripped and then slipped the thong on. The mountainous man told anyone who would listen, "I'm only doing this because I lost a bet."

Damn, Frank was hung, and his erection challenged the fabric and called him a liar. Zack pointed out, "I don't think you mind the loss."

Frank adjusted the front of his thong and laughed. "I can't confirm or deny that."

As the group shucked off their clothing, volunteer subs hung each item up on hangers with their locker keys pinned to their clothing. A staff sub would collect their personal items for the newly won. Masters would be given their personal effects so the sub would have them after the auction. They placed all their items into clothing bags with their names on the front.

The floor was cold on Zack's bare feet. He nabbed his collar out of his pocket and zipped up the bag.

He tugged at the clinging fabric he wore. Damn, there wasn't much of it. He knew from the breeze across his ass, the thong left little to the imagination. Catching sight of his image in the mirror, Zack blushed.

Wow. Um, how could such a tiny piece of material make him look like a slutty bottom in need of a Top?

Zack wrapped the leather around his neck.

Fuck. Fuck. Fuck!

His heartbeat thundered, and he was surprised no else heard it. He threaded the buckle and secured the collar. A shiver ran through him, and then a bit of calm washed over him.

The quiet, fragile-looking sub didn't quite meet Zack's eyes when he shuffled over to him with a pair of black shimmery wings. He was assisted into the feathers. Each of the "subs" would be wearing a different color.

Frank complained, "Goddamn Andrew Christian and Victoria's Secret for their underwear ads."

Everyone laughed, or tried to.

The wings might have been an attempt to recreate the popular lingerie ads, but Zack compared them to the ones used in the Dark Angels' shows. He touched the leather around his neck, and it was almost like turning on a switch that blocked out all the crazy of his life outside of Entwined.

The cute male flitted around him to adjust the wing fastener to his collar. He softly said, "The wings look great on you. Did you dye your hair to match?" The sub fluffed out his hair, and Zack couldn't help but wish those fingers belonged to….

Kneel. Serve….

"*No!*" He wasn't going there. His outburst made the sub jump away from him. "Sorry. I mean, no. I didn't know I'd get the black wings." He reached out to touch the now wary sub's cheek. "I'm a little tense. This makes me admire you and the other subs even more."

The delicate male batted his eyelashes at the compliment and leaned into Zack's palm. "Thank you, Sir."

"Just Zack today." There was a legion of striking men here tonight. Why couldn't he fixate on one of them?

"Okay…. Zack, when Tony announces each of subs, you'll move to the front, and he'll press this button on the wing fastening and ta-da." Zack's retracted wings spread out behind him.

A tad dramatic but he gave the sub a small smile. "Impressive."

The sub pushed the button again, and his wings pulled in and lay against his shoulders. The volunteer sub fussed a bit more before moving on to another temporary sub whose askew wings were in need of attention.

Zack shoved irrelevant thoughts aside and buried his need. Sometimes getting a little of what he required was better than getting none of what would never be his. Or, was that actually the case?

Shit! He had to get out of his fucking head. He assessed the other guys. They were an interesting mix.

John Delta and Si Taylor stood in front of the mirror and chuckled at their images. John turned and twerked his ass, which made Si burst out with a belly laugh. They were switches, and both were excited to play sub for a weekend.

Carl Mans was a full-on top with a collared sub. He'd told Zack earlier he was doing this for his sub's birthday.

Bob Mickoletti and Greg Wood were rivals who'd basically double-dog dared each other into participating. They'd been unable to prove who the better Dominant happened to be, so they were determined to find out who was the best submissive. Bizarre. They should have had the subs of the club settle the matter. Zack hoped they'd learn something from this experience.

Was he the only one harboring secret fantasies? Desires that he fulfilled for every other sub in the club while he went without? Perhaps this weekend would be enough to experience a little for himself.

Bob strolled over to him with a grimace. "So, Davis, I hear you have a bunch of fans who have pooled their money together for you."

Greg strutted over. "They only like him because he's easier than we are on them."

Damn, jealous much? Zack tried to steer clear of these guys whenever possible. They had never liked him. He hadn't figure out if their misplaced anger was because he happened to be related to a rock star or if his popularity with the subs meant he never lacked for a play partner. Whichever, the guys were jackasses.

Shrugging, Zack said, "I try to give them what they need."

"Right!" Bob chimed in. He glared at Zack, his hands tightened into fists. "All these little bitches would benefit from the bite of my whip."

John, Si, and Carl ambled over.

Si asked in his Boston accent, "Everything kosher here?"

Trying to come up with a quip might have taxed Bob, but Greg said, "It's fine. We were saying what the subs around here need is a real Dom, not some wannabe."

The implication made Zack clench his fists. "I can see how they flock to the two of you... the *real* Doms." He wasn't in the mood to let anyone get away with insulting him. He'd happily throat-punch them both and damn the consequences.

Bob growled, "At least Greg and I are man enough to discipline them."

What the fuck? Zack barely controlled his fury at that wild-assed assumption. "Not all subs are looking for the same thing. Each is an individual with very different wants and needs. BDSM isn't one size fits all."

"Oh, look at this, Bob. Zack thinks he should be teaching a Master class."

Slamming his fist into that mouth spewing stupidity would feel incredible. If Zack added a leg sweep, the moron would end up on his ass. "No, Greg, I simply think getting to know the people you have scenes with is vital. Otherwise, how do you know what they'd like to get out of it?"

Several subs within hearing distance nodded their agreement.

"Oh, please! These subs think they want a little spanky-spanky and an orgasm. You have to show them what—"

Frank stomped over from across the room as if he expected this interaction to come to blows. He put his huge mass of muscle a bit in front of Zack. "Problem?"

"Pushing limits should be done in a trusted relationship, not haphazardly." Zack stood his ground and stared at the stupid fuckers, daring them to make one more comment. Just a simple word would be all the excuse he needed.

Bob and Greg raised their hands and backed off.

"Relax, Zack." Si put his hands on Zack's neck and massaged him.

"I'm fine." Zack inhaled and exhaled as he counted in his head.

"Thank you," the sub that dressed him said as he glided past.

John grinned. "You're all twitchy, Zack." The change in John's persona was dramatic. He went from being a macho he-man to a more relaxed, laid-back version of himself. "It's cute when you get overly excited, and in these wings, you look like an avenging angel."

Zack snorted at the smartass. John was always quick with a joke; tonight was no different.

"Is this the first time you'll be switching since you've started?" Si asked.

"Yeah," Zack answered with caution.

"You'll do great. Just relax. Focus on what's asked of you. You don't have to think beyond that. Someone else will take care of the rest."

Zack drew in a deep breath. The liberation from responsibility appealed to him. If only the person taking care of the rest could be Drew. He released the air and the unfulfilled wish.

Roberto and Tony, the subs in charge, took an inventory of everything and everyone. The sounds of conversation grew in volume on the other side of the curtain, promising this event would raise a lot of money.

Fuck, did the band feel this way before every show? This shit was nerve-racking. He'd rather be behind the scenes, making everything seamless, not up on stage. What had he been thinking?

Tony reached into the back of Zack's thong and pulled to make sure the scrap of fabric disappeared into his ass.

"Hey! Don't floss my butt," he objected.

Tony snickered and went off to fix the next sub. Jeez, talk about a wedgie. Zack tried to wiggle the material out, then gave up.

Another sub skipped over and checked his collar. "This isn't the temporary one Entwined provided."

"No, it's mine." Zack ignored the cute sub, whose eyes popped open at his admission.

Zack hustled over to his bag and pulled out a blindfold he'd stuffed into his jacket pocket.

When he got himself under control, he meandered back to the group.

"What's up with that?" Si asked, pointing to the blindfold.

John smirked. "Afraid of what the Master who wins you will look like?"

Chuckling, Zack shook his head. "It will help me get into the right frame of mind." That didn't sound rehearsed at all.

Frank nodded. "Maybe I should get one."

Roberto fluttered up to him. "Oh, no, Master Frank, your eyes are too pretty to hide."

Tilting his head, Frank took a long look at Roberto as if seeing him for the very first time. "Monday night. Here, at 7:00 p.m." He grabbed Roberto and kissed him hard on the mouth before releasing the swaying man.

"Oh." Roberto blinked for several seconds. He brought his trembling hand to his mouth to touch his lips before giving Frank a big smile.

"Is it a date?" Frank asked while he eye-fucked the sub.

"Yes, Master Frank." Roberto blushed, glowed, and just about floated to his next task.

Tony laughed at him. "It's 1:00 a.m., people, let's move! Okay, is everyone ready?" Receiving various affirmatives, he lined up the angel-winged subs.

Zack slipped on his blindfold. How did he expect this to work?
Kneel.... Serve....

Maybe if he could just do one scene in the dark? He'd get his stupid fantasy out of his system.

"Imagine yourself as a flock of birds flying in formation onto the stage. Oh, um, your blindfold. Right, I forgot. Um, okay." Tony's tone suggested the eye covering didn't work in his world. He added, "Put Zack in the middle, and everyone link arms so he can walk straight."

Zack couldn't see a thing, but imagined the put-upon expression Tony wore.

"Sorry, Tony." This seemed like a good idea in theory, but in practice... not so much.

"No worries, Zack. Everyone needs accommodations. I think you said our limitations give us an opportunity to be creative."

Zack got an affectionate pat on the rump. Was that supposed to calm him? Did that ever soothe anyone's nerves in history?

"Guide him, people, and don't let him fall off the stage," Tony said as he clapped his hands.

The music cued, and the curtain must have risen. "Greetings! Welcome, Masters, subs, slaves, bottoms, switches, and Tops to Entwined's First Annual Charity Auction," Tony started the show.

Heat washed over Zack and his eyes registered a glow, so lights must be shining on them. With another pat to his ass, he walked forward, arms linked to a man on each side. What the hell? Were they playing sports? This had to be too much ass touching for a charity event.

Cheers rose up from the crowd. Zack didn't know how many members were in attendance, but it sounded like Entwined had a full house.

"Now, for legal purposes, we must make this clear. You're bidding to donate for the pleasure of a Master turned sub for the weekend. Scenes may be done within the new sub's limitations, but sex is not part of this arrangement. We're not running a prostitution ring here." Tony waited two beats before he added, "Apparently, the insurance was too high."

A drum rimshot rang out. Catcalls and hoots subsided, allowing Tony to finish. "If the Master and sub wish to take things there, everyone is an adult and free to do so, but Entwined is not advocating or in any way expecting that. So neither should any of you."

After a big inhale, Tony continued. "Masters turned subs, if you do not wish to be with the Master who wins you for the weekend, you simply pay his donation, and his money will be returned. The contract between you two will be null and void. Are we clear?"

"Spoilsport" and "Yeah" echoed through the room.

"Okay, then." Tony continued his spiel. "We have a lot of gorgeous, dominant males who think they are Dom enough to submit."

The crowd grew boisterous again.

Tony controlled and guided the crowd's reactions like a pro. Zack hadn't pegged Tony for a front man, but damn if he wasn't knocking the task out of the park.

"So, tell me, what do the subs and slaves of Entwined think? Can the Doms handle the challenge of being subs?"

Shouts and well wishes rang out.

"Let's meet the Doms, er, excuse me, *subs*, shall we?" Tony's pacing was perfect.

Tony's tone suggested he enjoyed the role of MC. A whoosh of air gusted past. Zack assumed Tony had rushed across the stage. "Here is Master—er, I mean, Bob. Why are you here?"

Bob grumbled but finally said, "Because I can be a better sub than Greg, and I'm going to prove it."

"Greg?" Tony asked, presumably to the man in question.

"Please! Bob is no better a sub than he is a Master."

The crowd laughed. Someone whistled and shouted, "Show us what you got."

Si, who stood next to Zack, whispered a play-by-play since the blindfold prevented Zack from watching the show. "Greg just turned around and bent over. He's wiggling his ass now. I have to say, boyfriend needs to hit the gym. And—" He started laughing. "Shit! Bob's knees hit the floor, and his hands are behind his head with his mouth open."

The crowd hooted.

Tony regained control. "Okay. Okay, you both have good potential. Let's hope you bring in a lot of money for charity. Here's something I never thought I would say. Get off your knees, Bob, and stop wiggling your ass, Greg."

A resounding slap rang out. Zack leaned into Si. "Did he just…."

"That's my baby!" Zack recognized the yell as Tony's Master. Tony's doctor must be front and center.

Si chuckled and confirmed, "Oh yeah. He popped him right on the ass. It was a real zinger. Greg is rubbing his butt like it's on fire. Damn, Tony's working this."

"And moving right along, we come to Carl." The applause showed how well liked he was in the club.

"Tony is playing with Carl's hair. You know, like Carl does to his sub, Mark, all the time," Si whispered.

"Tell us, Carl, why are you up here auctioning yourself off to the highest bidder?"

"To wish my sweet slave, Mark, a very happy birthday," Carl called out into the audience.

"Well, I guess someone's going to be getting a birthday spanking to remember. Slave Mark is a lucky, lucky man."

"Thank you, Master." Zack identified Mark's voice.

"Oh, not so fast. You must outbid everyone else," Tony teased.

The crowd whooped their approval. Carl and Mark would have prepared for the evening. Zack assumed Mark's lawyer salary wouldn't be outbid easily.

"And on this side." Tony hurried by, brushing past Zack. "Here, we have Frank Lopez." The MC waited for the applause to die. "You might not know that Frank is here because the Giants didn't make it to the playoffs. Even though I'm a Giants fan through and through, I have to admit, I didn't know which team to root for, because the Giants losing meant Frank's forfeit would be to get up on this stage."

Moving on, Tony introduced John. "John, it looks like you're ready to switch. How long has it been?"

John said in his soft voice, "I don't know. I guess about two years."

"Mmmmm, well, then. One of these men is in for a treat, huh?"

"Yes, Sir."

Purring, Tony moved down the line. "Si. He's *switching* it up too. Ready to submit?"

"Absolutely," Si said with enthusiasm. "Ready and able." His voice dripped with teasing lust, and the crowd devoured it.

Tony jokingly asked, "Is it hot in here?"

"Not as hot as your ass is gonna be later on." A shout from Tony's Master made Zack chuckle.

Si leaned in and said, "Wow, Tony's blushing now. Damn, he really is adorable."

"Promises, promises," Tony sassed back. He ignored the immature "uh-ohs" and "ahs" of the crowd. "Last, but not least, we have Sir Zack. He's just Zack tonight."

The crowd shouted their approval.

"This is an excellent opportunity for someone with some cash to see Zack in a very different light." The crowd broke out in applause and catcalls.

Zack had to do this. He would do this regardless of who won him.

Never. Not his.

"Before we start bidding, I need to let you know, Carl's back is still healing, so no heavy bondage and no suspension work. Zack wants his blindfold on, unless he takes it off. Si needs to leave his temporary Master by Sunday night at 5:00 p.m." The crowd rumbled, but Tony took control with a clap of his hands. "Now. Now. Okay, let's start the bidding on sub Frank."

"One thousand dollars," a tentative voice cried out from stage left. It sounded like Roberto.

"Well, well, well." Tony laughed. "Roberto. Roberto. Hmmm, it looks like we have a firm offer."

Zack whispered to Si, "Can Roberto afford that?" The young guy had only recently stopped couch surfing and got himself a decent paying job.

"I don't know, but he appears determined." Si bit off a snicker. "Hee-hee. Someone looked like he was going to bid, and the little guy actually gave him a pretty scary evil eye."

"Going once."

"He's sold. He's mine," Roberto exclaimed.

Zack couldn't stop the grin. Go little sub. He heard Roberto tell Frank, "I don't want to wait until Monday for a date."

Zack snickered. "That must have been some kiss backstage."

Si filled Zack in on the scene. "Roberto tossed the guy taking care of the money two credit cards and has led Frank out the back door." Si chortled. "Frank's going to have his hands full, but from his big smile, it looks like that's exactly what he's hoping for."

The bidding commenced.

Zack was pleased when Ms. Karma came back to bite Bob and Greg in the ass. A Master with a sub who Bob had been less than courteous to purchased him. Greg started a bidding war between two Masters who were convinced Greg needed to be taught how to be a better Master. They eventually agreed to share him, and the club gladly took both their large donations.

Poor Mark had to rescue his birthday present from the clutches of another Master, who wanted to bust their asses and make them donate more.

"John was sold to someone he's liked for a while. The guy isn't into the lifestyle 24/7, but neither is John," Si filled him in.

Tony walked over and pushed back Zack's hair. "Well, only two subs left." Tony's voice circled them. "Let's start the bidding on Si. How much for this pretty boy?"

Si's arm remained locked around Zack as he leaned over to speak into the microphone. "Just so y'all know, I spent my teenage years in the South, so I'm very polite and... *obedient*."

The crowd went wild.

Tony tittered at the bids rolling in. Finally, the bidding ended, and Si wished Zack luck before abandoning him onstage.

"That brings us to Zack. Keep in mind the blindfold is a nonnegotiable for the time being." A soft murmur rushed through the audience, but Tony didn't respond to it.

Without much conscious thought, Zack dropped to his knees, hands locked behind his back and his lips parted slightly. He removed the blindfold and opened his eyes. The light seared them. He was still unable to see who was there.

Tony pushed the button, and his wings whooshed out behind him.

Zack's feathered wings tickled the soles of his feet as he waited. The simple move made him hard, threatening the elasticity of the gold lamé.

Tony cleared his throat. "So with that, what is the opening bid?"

"Ten thousand," an unfamiliar voice called out. The bid was twice that of the highest of the evening.

The crowd grew silent.

Zack didn't recognize the voice. Maybe the bidder was a new member. God, he wished he could see past the glare for a moment to view the man who put up so much money for him. He gave up and retied the strip of silk over his eyes.

No, it was better without sight. Zack was proud to have brought in so much money for the children's research hospital, though he wished his stomach full of snakes would stop slithering. He waited, hoping against hope that Andrew's voice would cut through the crowd to claim him.

As he knelt, Tony asked for any other bids. When no one else increased the sizable amount, Tony went through the ritual. "Going once."

Zack swayed but willed himself steady.

"Going twice."

He held his breath and prayed for Drew's voice to cut in to bid.

"Sold, to the handsome man in the back," Tony shouted.

No. Never his.

He tried to push down the disappointment. Of course Andrew wouldn't buy him, even if he hadn't been sick.

Zack ignored the inappropriate guilt of allowing himself the illusion of Andrew buying him.

Tony steadied him as he stood to the thunderous applause, and led him off the stage. He guided Zack down to the man who would be his Master for the weekend.

One of the volunteer subs he didn't recognize said, "It's a shame to take off your wings, but I think bondage would be a little complex tying knots around them." The male chuckled as he unclipped the mechanism and took off Zack's wings. "Your Master is filling out the paperwork and dealing with the donation." The man pressed a kiss on his cheek. "A group of the subs were disappointed we were outbid immediately. We had plans for you." An unseen finger traced down his chest and followed the elastic of his waistband.

"Mine. Hands off," a dry, raspy voice demanded from Zack's left side.

The proclamation made Zack shiver a little, until self-reproach chased the thrill away. He'd done nothing that should make him feel bad.

Wasn't he betraying Drew and himself?

No. Never his.

There was no Drew. Zack pushed all the negativity away and focused on the present. Zack had a Master.

"Sorry, Sir," the pushy bottom said almost resentfully.

The sub leaned in and whispered in Zack's ear, "Maybe next week we can play and you can discipline me for being so forward?" The bold one gave him a quick peck on the cheek.

Another low growl came from the general direction of the man who'd donated a large sum for Zack's time.

His temporary Master remained a mystery. He had to be new or a member from a different club. The club vetted their members carefully, so Zack had nothing to be concerned about, right? Even though he couldn't see the man who bid on him, he was safe, but that didn't take away all of his worry.

Si whispered as he brushed past, "You're very lucky. Enjoy yourself."

Zack waited, trying to focus on his breathing. The anxiety coursing through him didn't eliminate the excitement of living out his fantasy. Now, someone would give him the weightlessness of submission for a little while even if it wasn't—

"I know you'll be very happy for the weekend. You can trust your new Master." Tony touched his arm.

Zack took the T-shirt and pants Tony handed him and pulled them on. He adjusted the eye covering and ran his fingers through his hair.

"Your shoes are at your feet," Tony informed him. "Are you really going to wear a blindfold all weekend?"

"Probably not." It wasn't practical, but fuck the world. Was it a crime that Zack wanted this first time, possibly his only time, to be what he wanted it to be?

Tony chuckled. "Okay. Um, do you need any more help, Sir—I mean, Zack."

"Nope. I got it. Thanks." Zack hadn't bothered with socks. He shoved his feet into the canvas slip-ons.

Tony whispered, "Don't look so worried. You're in good hands."

"Thank you." The repeated endorsement from Tony helped, allowing him to leave the blindfold on.

Before the little man could respond, Tony's Master's voice cut through the crowd. "Tony, you were very naughty on stage, and now it's time to pay the piper. I secured us room twelve."

Tony's happy giggle rang out on his departure.

Zack stood there alone. Blindfolded. He kept his eyes shut, leaving him in total darkness to maintain the fantasy for just a little longer.

Someone stood next to him and said, "Hello, my pet. You may call me Master for this weekend. My car is out back. Come."

"Yes... Master." Zack's heart thundered as his lips formed those words. They felt bittersweet on his tongue. He'd only wanted to use that title for one man, but.... What was done was done.

No. Never his.

The man helped Zack into some kind of low-to-the-ground sports car, protecting his head from the roof. His Master even reached across Zack's body and fastened the seat belt for him. Zack allowed himself to lean into the man's body heat.

Mmmmm, he inhaled leather and an unidentified spice. The man smelled delicious.

Fuck! He got hard from the scent of the guy. He tried to take another sniff, but the man moved back.

"Did you just smell me?" Amusement bled into the man's voice.

CHAPTER ELEVEN

"UM...." ZACK'S conversational skills were showing. *Not!*

The hoarse voice was laced with amusement, but still demanding, "Answer me. Did you smell me?"

"Yes, Master. I, um, inhaled your scent." Zack hoped the car's dark interior hid his embarrassment.

The man shut the door and went around to the driver's side. The car started up with a purr, and Zack was off to his weekend. His thoughts were cut off by the driver's question, "Why?"

Zack groaned. *Dammit!* How could he have been so lame? Smelling someone! What did he hope to gain by the man's scent?

"Zack, please answer the question. Why did you smell me?"

Would he be fumbling all weekend? Zack scrambled for an answer. "I... I can't see. It's natural to use the other senses when one is limited." There. That sounded good. It was a reasonable justification.

"Do you *like* how I smell?"

Zack opened his mouth, but nothing came out. How did he admit to such a crazy thing?

"If you don't want to answer, please state that and I won't press you, unless it's in regards to your safety or general welfare. But, unless you tell me you do not wish to answer me, I expect your truthful responses immediately. Clear?"

"Yes, Master." For years Zack had thought he'd make a good sub, but now that he finally had the opportunity, he couldn't even follow the simplest instructions. Honesty was one of the key points of a BDSM relationship, however temporary.

Zack needed to bring his truth to the forefront... even if he hated the reality of it. "You smelled like someone I know."

"I'm a Master in the same club network you're a member of. You realize there's a high degree of probability we've met."

"May I ask a question, Sir?"

"Of course, Zack."

Did Zack want the answer? Before he decided, the words tumbled out. "*Do* I know you?"

"I'd say there's a good probability."

Shit, he didn't need a genie Dom answer. What was he, a Magic 8 Ball? Should he ask again? Zack's heart hammered quicker as he tried to place the raspy voice, but was unable to do so. It frustrated him. The man gave him little time to ponder.

"Zack, why are you wearing the blindfold?"

Shit! Would a half-truth be enough? "This will be the first time I'm actually submitting and I thought it would be easier."

"Do you plan to hide from me and our activities the entire weekend?"

Yes. No. "Um...."

"It's okay if you don't know the answer, but you need to respond." The words were articulated slowly and evenly, as if Zack needed calming.

"I... um, I don't think that's realistic. But I'd like to wear it for now." Zack still longed to dance around reality and the truth.

"What will your safeword be?"

"Mushroom." Zack smiled. He'd thought of his safeword at fifteen when a pizza parlor had destroyed his dinner. This was the first time he'd ever shared the term with anyone. God, he despised the fungus, because few things were more disgusting than finding them hidden under something good.

Hoarse laughter, followed by coughing, rang through the car.

Zack asked, "Are you okay, Sir?"

"A touch of strep, but I've been on meds long enough that I'm no longer contagious. I've been cleared. Doc said my throat is in rough shape but nothing major. And it's Master, remember?"

"Oh, um, yes. Sorry... Master." Well, that explained not being able to place the scratchy voice. Zack should give up trying to figure out who this guy was and enjoy the fantasy of having a Master. A Master he'd pretend was whom he'd always wanted. Hell, this guy even smelled like—

Kneel. Serve. No. Never his.

"What are your hard limits?"

Zack needed to stop pining for what would never be reality. He was finally going to fully experience the other side of the collar. If he put himself in the excited place he was in prior to ever meeting Andrew, he could finally live out what his fantasies revolved around: submission.

"Zack?"

Fuck! Fuck! Fuck! He had been asked a question. "The usual limits of a new playmate: no scat, permanent marking, or piercings, no knife play, breath play, fire, etc. And condoms if we get that far."

"Got it. Nothing else you'd care to add?"

Shit, what did Zack know? He'd stopped thinking about himself in regards to submission that night, which now seemed forever ago but was never far from his thoughts. "I don't know my limits."

"What would you like to explore this weekend?" the soft voice asked as the car continued to their destination.

"Is my bag in the car?" It sucked not being able verify where things were visually.

"Excuse me?"

He blurted out the question again, "Is my bag in the car?" His computer, phone, and everything he needed to make it through the weekend resided in his bag.

The man chuckled. "My, you are a newbie when it comes to subbing."

Shit! He forgot to address the man properly. "I'm sorry, Master."

"Forgiven. Of course, your stuff is in the backseat. You're in my care. Though, I doubt you'll need the clothing."

Zack's cock hardened at the implied nudity.

The car rolled to a stop, and the man said, "Wait for me to help you."

The man put a protective hand on Zack's head as he helped him out of the car. Zack heard the guy lifting his bag out of the car. He allowed himself to be led into the house.

"You did well trusting me to get you inside," the man praised him.

Zack hadn't realized how difficult even the simplest activities became when he had to relinquish responsibility and rely on someone else. His respect for the subs at the club tripled.

"Let me get you some water." Mystery Man steered Zack onto a buttery-soft leather sofa. Footsteps told Zack the man had left the room. Within a minute, he returned and handed the cold bottle to Zack.

Zack opened the top and drank the liquid. Damn, he was parched.

"I like touching. If you want me to stop, safeword." A firm hand traced down Zack's arm, and he trembled in response. Damn, he must be hard up for caresses. "Ah, wonderful. It would seem you like to be petted. You're being very compliant."

Zack leaned into the enticing strokes. God, he wanted to be good. He wanted to be perfect. Though the last couple years had taught him that the glory in BDSM isn't in the perfection but in the attempt. He craved the surrender, the trust, and the bond that developed between Master and sub, which could fill the empty places in his soul.

"Sit on my lap." The demand was simple, but Zack had never felt more graceless. A "real" sub would've made an exquisite show of crawling into his Master's lap.

Zack tentatively put his hand out, and it landed on his Master's knee. The damned blindfold compounded his unsteady movements. His other hand slipped between the couch cushion and a leg. Zack had almost been seated, but he misjudged where his temporary Master's shoulder would be and almost fell.

His Master grabbed and steadied him.

Dammit! Zack didn't want to tumble off the sofa. He turned and slapped his hand on a tender location. "Sorry... Master."

Finally, he settled onto the man's lap.

It was difficult to assess in his current position, but his temporary Master seemed to be a little taller than Zack. Strong arms wrapped around him to adjust Zack's position. A hand guided his head down so he rested on the Dom's shoulder. The man's scent wrapped him in a sense of protection and security. Zack's tight muscles started to unwind.

Zack jumped when a hand caressed his face. "Shhhh, it's okay, pet."

"Sorry, Master." His only requirement was to just be.

"That's okay." A large hand stroked his hair. Fingers slipped through the strands, calming him. "You've cut and dyed your hair." The man picked up a piece of Zack's hair. He flipped the hunk back. What, was he examining him? "Ah, it's just temporary. Good, I love your natural color."

Lots of guys had complimented Zack's hair color but only one of them had ever declared to love it.

Can it be? No. Never his.

"I don't know what to say. Thank you... Master." The hand left his hair and trailed down his back to rub and soothe away tension Zack didn't even know he had.

A sense of peace Zack never experienced before came over him. God, he'd wanted to savor this forever. He'd waited a lifetime to live out this fantasy, and he deserved to have a little of what he'd never get. Maybe submitting to someone else would allow him to move on with his life. But God, the man smelled like....

No! Not his. Never.

Zack rested on his temporary Master's lap for a very long time as the man stroked him, allowing him to enjoy playing pretend. He absorbed the physical touches lavished on him. The gentle hand relaxed him. Fingers ran through his hair and massaged his scalp. Truthfully, Zack could have stayed there for hours, absorbing the attention.

"You are a needy one, aren't you?"

His eyelashes fluttered against the blindfold. Who was this man giving him such contentment? Should he give up his resolve to stay blindfolded and take a peek? What if it was—but it wasn't.

No, not knowing was better. It allowed him to keep the impossible alive.

"Since you didn't answer what you'd like to do, would you like to explore a little bondage?"

Zack's defenses were too far tranquil to stop the soft whimper that unleashed from deep inside of him. One of the desires he'd attempted to abandon long ago was to be put in bondage. He'd suppressed the yearning, but not his need to learn how to use ropes to give others the feeling he craved.

"I'll take that as interest. I'm not a *Kinbakushi* Master like you, but I'm passable."

Zack wasn't exactly an expert with Japanese rope, but he could boast being very close. He was set onto the sofa, assisted to his feet, and led down the carpeted stairs. A basement?

A quick slash of fear raced through him as every horror movie he'd ever watched flashed through his mind. He didn't know his Master—*Stop!* Everyone in the club knew where he was, and several of his friends thought he'd be happy with who'd won the bid.

Trust. Be. Let go.

"Zack, you can use your safeword at any time and everything will stop." The man's hoarse voice sounded close to his ear, making him want. Was the guy a mind reader or simply observant enough to guess what Zack's thoughts were?

"I'm ready, Sir."

"Very good, Zack. This is my basement. You can't see it, but I have a home theater setup down here. I'm taking you past that into a playroom. I'm going to start by putting you in a *Tejou Shibari*."

Zack could handle the simple handcuff restraint blindfolded. "Yes, Master."

The man guided him into another room and put Zack's hand on a wooden chair. "Remove your clothing."

Zack completed this basic request without question. He didn't need to be told each piece should be folded and placed on the chair. Then he was naked. There was no chill in the air, but he shivered a bit just the same.

Hearing the strike of a match, Zack turned his face in the direction of the sound and adjusted his blindfold. Please let his temporary Master not be a smoker. Soon the scent of light peach incense circled around him.

The man brushed against Zack. "Very good, pet."

Such praise should have been silly, but he gulped in the compliment. He even liked the nickname.

"Thank you, Master," he said as he held out his hands to accept his Master's decree like a good submissive should. God, he yearned to witness the ropes being twined from this perspective, but the cloth covering his eyes denied the wish.

This Master claimed not to be an expert in rope play, but he didn't cut corners when it came to supplies. Zack felt the good quality of the linen binding rope, probably from Japan. The twine was solid and didn't cut into his skin when tightened.

Zack's interest had led him to take classes with some of the top experts in the field. However, this man seemed to understand the Zen experience of binding and bondage. Zack was lulled into a further sense of serenity as the rope slid into place.

Oh yeah. He was safe and protected as the cords were fastened around his wrists. At the same time, he couldn't deny the erotic nature of his situation. The Master purposely flicked and glided the rope against his skin. Fuck, that sizzled his brain and forced his cock into full erection.

"Now that your hands are secured, I'm going to put you in a *Kikkou Shibari*."

A moan of pleasure fell from Zack's lips. *Fuck yes!* Oh, if only he could see the turtle-binding latticework as the rope secured him.

The diamond pattern pressed against his skin, making him quiver. His Japanese teachers used models to demonstrate, so he'd never been put into any type of bindings other than the ones he could tie and get out of himself. Dabbling in self-bondage had never prepared him for this heady experience.

His Master trailed the rope tail against his chest. The ends barely grazed his left nipple. The cotton skimmed over his other nipple, and he was unable to restrain a gasp. Knots were tied into place and pressed into his skin.

Bound and protected, all cares of the outside world vanished. For him, the slide of the ropes and his Master binding him were the only things that existed. All that mattered. A spiritual and emotional connection seemed to wind around him.

Finally, he was getting what he'd craved.

His Master's footsteps circled him. "You're a work of art in ropes, Zack."

He was laid back and secured to a semireclining bench.

The Master traced his fingers along the binding, which outlined Zack's body in a crisscross pattern. Fingers touched and fondled the knots, causing him to yearn for more.

Fingers teased down to Zack's thighs, raising goose bumps and need. "Look at you, pet. Your body is begging for me."

God yes! Zack arched his body to the maximum height the ropes would allow. A small stab of guilt washed over him. Was he being unfaithful? How could one be unfaithful to a man who'd never wanted him? He shoved the inappropriate thought away. He yearned to follow his body's need to its proper conclusion.

The man traced a finger along Zack's open mouth. The gesture was the closest thing he'd felt to a kiss in a long time.

Moaning, he licked at the digit.

"Ah, my sweet Zack. You're delicious as you struggle with your desire. As much as I want to give you pleasure, my pet, I need to see your struggle… all of it. In order for that to happen, you must take off the blindfold. Then I will bring you to your much-needed orgasm."

Zack groaned in disappointment. No way would he give up the pretense that this could be Drew, finally controlling his body and making him fly. Zack throbbed with the aspiration to climax; his arousal grew even though he had no intention of earning the pleasure.

"I can't. Please, Master." Oh hell, his begging cracked in the middle.

The man in control traced his hand down Zack's face to comfort him. "Just as you have some nonnegotiable issues, my sexy pet, so do I. I can't have you hiding from me." He traced his fingers over the edges of the silk covering Zack's eyes.

Fuck! Please! Fuck!

Zack was approaching the point where he wanted the blindfold removed. His body demanded this impending climax, but his mind refused to let go of the illusion. Right or wrong, he still wanted to have the fantasy.

"No, Master." His cock ached, regretting his words. "I can't."

"I understand. Though choices have consequences." His Master's arousing hands disappeared, and Zack heard a zipper being lowered. "Kiss me and this continues, or safeword." The demand made Zack's heart skip a beat before pounding out of control.

No way would he utter his safeword, not when he wanted this so badly. *Oh God!* Anything, even if it wasn't everything he desired. Something. He had to have more.

He tilted his head.

His Master knelt next to him, and his lips crashed down on Zack's to claim his mouth.

Yes! Kiss! More!

Zack's heart sang at the connection, and he parted his lips to welcome this dominant man's tongue inside. It had been forever since he'd kissed. He required so much more. Each talented thrust of the man's tongue reminded him of everything he denied himself.

Swish. Swish. Swish. Swish.

What was... oh God! Zack panted and struggled against his binding. The guy was taking matters into his own hands.

Fuck! It was Zack's decision that stopped his pleasure. His body trembled as the ropes held him firmly in place. He poured his unresolved lust into the passionate kisses, hoping to push his temporary Master closer to the edge of heaven.

The man took Zack's kisses and seemed to demand more.

Zack broke the kiss for a moment to suck in a bit of air and then pressed back for more.

His Master pulled back. Gasping breaths caressed Zack's face until the man grunted and recaptured his mouth. Their kiss deepened until the Dom's groans of passion evolved into a grunt of a cascading orgasm. His Master's kiss tantalized Zack with the gratification he wasn't obtaining.

The sated man pulled back, leaving Zack shaking and bereft of physical contact.

No, please. He arched his lower body off the surface he was on. His erection air-dried, making him shiver.

After a zip rasped, the man sighed in what sounded like contentment. He stroked Zack's face with his fingertips. "Oh, look at you, my poor, horny little pet."

The man sounded dismayed that Zack would be left in such a state.

Fuck! Fuck! Fuck! It was Zack's own damned fault that caused his suffering.

His Master's firm hands caressed Zack's body to bring him down. Slow, tender strokes of his Master's hands helped the trembling subside, if not his need.

"Let's get you untied and to bed."

The man took his time loosening each of the knots, which was almost as sexy as being tied up. The ropes dragged against Zack's skin as they were unknotted. As Zack was being unwrapped, his erection repeatedly got in the way of the ropes. The delicious glide of cotton linen over his heated shaft was almost enough for him to come.

His temporary Master was methodical and didn't rush, making sure Zack wasn't given enough friction. By the time the ropes were gone, Zack was left trying to capture a little air to draw into his lungs.

He ached for release.

"Just take off the blindfold, my sweet pet, and I'll make this all better," his Master promised as the man danced his fingers over Zack's cock. He used the pad of his finger to spread the liquid leaking from the tip along the entire top of his arousal.

Zack shook. He wanted to… he really did, but he dug in his heels. No, he craved the fantasy more than climax. Regardless of how badly he wanted orgasm, he refused. "No, thank you, Master."

The tantalizing finger stopped, halting Zack's torment. "As you wish." The man led him back upstairs and into another room. "I'll take you to the bathroom first."

He was guided to a bathroom counter. Both of Zack's hands were gathered up and kissed before they were placed flat on the surface. After hearing some rustling around, his Master said, "Here's a new toothbrush. I put paste on it."

Zack brushed his teeth, needing to bend low and feel around with his hand a bit so he didn't spit on the counter. He let his cock press into the coolness of the vanity, which helped reduce his erection to manageable proportions. When the man handed him a glass of water to rinse his mouth, his heart melted a bit. Zack should have felt silly, but he liked how the man was right there, anticipating his needs.

How many years had Zack longed to be seen? Finally, someone saw him.

"The toilet is behind you. I'll step out so you have privacy, but I'll leave the door open."

When Zack heard the footsteps retreating, he peeked under the blindfold, turned away from the faucet, and used the toilet, grateful the cold surface had allowed him to get soft enough to empty his bladder. Flushing, he glanced around the room. The bathroom was kind of fancy, all gleaming white marble and etched mirrors. He washed his hands and returned his eyes to total darkness.

The man encircled him with his arms and handed him a towel.

"Thank you, Master."

Zack couldn't help but relax back against the man. His first perception of his Master's height was incorrect. Based on how Zack's shoulders brushed against firm pectoral muscles, his Master had to be at least a good head taller than him. The man was toned. The most alluring thing was he still smelled so good.

Shit! That did nothing to prevent Zack's arousal from snapping back to full attention.

"Let's get you into bed, my pet." The Master managed him to a bed and tucked him in.

Zack forced down the disappointment as their evening drew to a close. He heard some noises, which sounded like clothing being dropped to the floor. Was the man naked? Was that a rustle of fabric and the opening and shutting of a hamper?

"Do you need any water, pet?"

"No, Master."

The opposite side of the bed dipped with his Master's weight. Zack turned toward the depression. The man answered his unasked question. "I can't leave you alone blindfolded. You might need to get up in the middle of the night, and I don't want your stubbornness to get you hurt."

He wouldn't be alone. A ridiculous level of happiness danced around inside Zack as his Master rearranged the covers. His temporary Master would watch over him whether he needed it or not. The concept floored him. Someone focusing and caring for *him* on this level stunned him.

"Are you comfortable, my pet?"

Except for his hard-on, which could be used as a battering ram, he was. Zack swallowed past the lump in his throat and whispered, "Yes, Master. Thank you, Sir."

Soft breathing was the only sound in the room.

Zack didn't know if the other man was asleep, so he tried not to toss and turn. *Oh God!* He hadn't been this horny since he had found his first BDSM magazine. If a stiff breeze blew across his cock, he'd come.

The ropes had really heated him. He tried not to focus on the delicious friction of the cover and how it caressed against his naked erection. The fact that he was actually in bed with a dominant male, who might or might not be naked, drove him crazy. He wanted to reach down and finish himself off. It would take all of thirty seconds.

He thrust into the blankets.

Shit! Stars burst behind his eyes. He pushed up again. *Oh God.* He clenched his ass. Zack couldn't decide if he should stop teasing himself or if he needed to continue.

As he contemplated such a breach in etiquette, his temporary Master cleared his throat. "It's dark. Take off your blindfold. I won't force you to look at me. Use your own discipline to keep your eyes closed. If you remove the blindfold, I'll put you out of your misery."

God yes! No! Wait!

The quiet voice continued, "It's the only way either of us is going to get any sleep. Unless you want to experience orgasm denial…."

The offer made Zack's heart race faster than the throbbing of his cock. Fuck, he had no willpower. He had to have some relief. "Okay, Master. Please help me."

Zack squeezed his eyes shut when he really wanted to open them wide to see who was allowing him to experience a whole new world. His fingers trembled as he removed the blindfold. He heard some shuffling.

What was his Master doing? He was dying, so he started to ask, "Should I just…?"

"I'll take care of you," the man answered, wrapping his hand around Zack's heated shaft and causing him to whimper. Holy fuck, this guy understood how to give a hand job.

A few seconds later, the Master's other hand parted Zack's thighs, and he felt a wet finger at his opening.

Fuck, yes!

In the dark, the Master's fist pumped and tightened around Zack's erection. He wanted the pleasure to go on and on but was only a few firm strokes away from bliss. Then the other man distracted him by removing his fingers.

What? No! More!

Zack heard a drawer slide open. After a short pause, something tapered and slippery slid between his asscheeks. "I think you need this plug inside of you, don't you?"

"God, yes!"

Moments later, a slick rounded hardness breached him. He groaned as he dug his heels in to tilt his hips and bend his legs to offer easier access.

"Do you like that?" his Master whispered in that deliciously husky voice.

It might have been a rhetorical question, but Zack was too far gone to tell, so he answered. "Yes, Master. I love it."

Zack grunted when the plug was fully seated. His mouth was captured in a breathless kiss. His attention returned to the delicious stroking along his cock. Pressure mounted, and soon it would be too much to contain.

"You have permission to come when you're ready."

Zack was beyond ready.

When his Master's talented tongue thrust between his parted lips, Zack came. Waves of bliss rushed through him. He squeezed his asscheeks around the small plug as he erupted. The hand pumped in perfect time with his pulses of release until he was empty.

Oh yeah! Fuck, yeah.

He collapsed back in satisfaction. His entire body was finally at peace, and it was fucking great. His Master had prepared, so all of his ejaculate was captured in a towel and swept away.

"Ahhhh, thank you." He snuggled down into the mattress, feeling incredibly grateful and sleepy.

Clearing his throat, the man asked, "Thank you, who?"

Not being able to help himself, he chuckled. "*Master*. Thank you, Master." Zack really did need to get into the sub mindset. He slipped his blindfold back on and rolled toward the man.

"I think the plug is small enough that you can wear it for a few hours. If you have any discomfort, wake me immediately." His Master deftly retied the blindfold.

"Yes, Master." His strong arms wrapped around Zack. A sense of protection descended, and he floated to sleep.

CHAPTER TWELVE

MORNING LIGHT streamed through the window, allowing Andrew to stare at the angel slumbering in his bed. A giddy happiness accompanied his perusal until the blindfold blocked the view.

Yawning, he stretched. He never slept until 8:00 a.m. on a Saturday morning, but since they had only gotten into bed three hours ago, maybe it was understandable. However, wasting the precious time he had with Zack wasn't an option.

How he wished his peaceful sub would remove the blindfold for good and acknowledge Andrew was his Master. He'd worn enough of his scent and dropped enough hints. How many Masters at Entwined had a basement home theater? Dusty had taken a great interest because he'd been planning to add one to their home. Was there anyone else at Entwined who would notice or care that Zack dyed his hair? Looking at the strands in daylight, the answer was anyone with eyes, but how many would know it was temporary versus permanent?

Zack's refusal to rip off the blindfold and look at what was between them had roused uncomfortable doubts.

There had to be a piece of Zack that realized it was Andrew who won him. Why was he hiding from that? Did Zack still want him?

Maybe Andrew deserved this ironic cosmic punishment. He had finally removed his blinders only to have Zack tie on a blindfold… literally!

Andrew found his center and grounded his fears. His pet belonged to him. He just needed to prove it to him.

Zack… jeez, the awkward kid he'd met years ago no longer existed. He'd grown into a gorgeous man with a honed, muscled body attained through his job.

A possessive thought went through him as he inspected Zack's hair. The stylist Zack had used was okay, but Andrew's fingers itched to once again recut Zack's gorgeous mop of hair into a style that highlighted his features to their best advantage. But until Zack was his, Andrew had no intention of making him any more irresistible. As it was, subs flocked to him, and Masters all voted him the man they would go vanilla for, just to have a taste of him.

He loved Zack's green eyes, not only for their beauty, but for the honesty that always shone through. Someone who knew him well could tell his every thought just by gazing into their depths. That was the main reason his blindfold needed to come off.

Andrew knew Zack possibly a little too well. He'd spent much of his time trying to make sure he wasn't hurt again. If it hadn't been against Zack's true nature, Andrew would've found it a relief that he'd never subbed for anyone.

It broke his heart to know Zack gave the subs exactly what they needed but he never got it himself. Not for the first time, rage at the pretend Master who took advantage of Zack ripped through Andrew. Bitter gratification slashed through him. The broken jaw Andrew had given him had taken the asshole out of circulation for a while.

Andrew refocused on the lovely sub in his bed. It had been ages since he had taken someone to bed. Usually he didn't bring his play partners past the front doors of Entwined. Here was the one man he wanted above everyone else, in his bed, waiting to do his bidding. All he needed was to ask, and he planned to, right after he convinced his tenacious but lovely sub to drop the blindfold and face reality.

Andrew pressed his lips against the lickable mouth of his bedmate. He snaked his tongue out and traced the outline of Zack's lips before sucking them into a kiss.

"Mmmm." Zack woke up midkiss and rolled into Andrew's arms. *Delectable!* He pushed against Andrew with a groan.

"The prince has awoken." Andrew sounded less like a frog today, and his throat hurt less.

Zack stiffened for a moment in his arms. He had to have recognized Andrew's voice!

Was he going to continue to pretend it wasn't Andrew? Would he leave when forced to admit the truth?

Pondering was cast aside by the aggressively needy sub in his arms. Zack slid their morning erections against each other. Damn, stars flashed behind his eyelids. He reached around to tap the part of the plug that protruded, causing Zack to shiver in his arms.

He had made sure to use a lot of his best long-lasting lube. Andrew checked the clock; they'd only slept a few hours. Zack appeared to have no pain or discomfort, but it was time to remove the toy.

Zack ground against him. His groans sounded like he was a few seconds away from orgasm. As nice as that would be, Andrew wasn't ready to allow bliss to swallow them yet. "Stop."

Zack whimpered but halted in grinding his cock against Andrew's flesh.

Dammit! Andrew wished he hadn't stopped him. He should have better control, but his entire being yearned to give in to what the trembling man wanted. Somehow he found his backbone to be the Dominant Zack needed.

"Time for a shower." His words were clipped even though he tried to keep them even. His voice might have been raspy, but he was sure Zack recognized it now.

Zack said a simple "Yes, Sir," and rolled off the bed. He stood and waited.

Andrew came around the bed and touched the blindfold. "Planning on wearing this in the shower?"

Pursing his lips, it was clear Zack hadn't counted on taking showers with the winning bidder. "I'd like my sub to wash me." Andrew shrugged, realizing Zack couldn't see it. "Though you can keep your eyes shut if that's what you decide."

Zack dropped his head forward and said, "Thank you, Master."

His pet removed the blindfold and handed the black velvet lined with silk to Andrew. It was one step closer, so he bit his tongue and willed Zack to tip his head up. He wished for acknowledgment, but Zack kept his head down and eyes squeezed shut.

By the time the shower water was hot, their erections had faded enough to use the toilet. They washed their hands and brushed their teeth.

Andrew guided Zack around the glass shower wall. "Here, pet." He placed a bar of soap in Zack's hand carried exclusively by his salon. It smelled of musk and sandalwood. Justin had told Andrew that Zack loved the smell, which was why Andrew made sure to always wear the scent.

Zack kept his eyes shut, but he reached out with the soap. "May I, Master?"

No way in hell Andrew would turn down an offer to get Zack's hands all over him. He swallowed down his excitement. In his übercontrolled voice, he granted the request as a boon.

"You may."

His pet took the soap and started running his callused hands along Andrew's body in long, bubbly lines. Zack's eyes were squeezed shut, but he paused. He leaned against Andrew's recently soaped arm and inhaled. All movements stopped as a strange, unreadable expression passed over Zack's face.

There could no longer be any doubt whom Zack had shared a bed with last night. The scent of Andrew's soap confirmed his identity. Would Zack run?

Zack's eyelids fluttered, and for a moment Andrew expected him to open his eyes, but the stubborn brat squeezed them shut tighter. Withholding his sigh of frustration, Andrew luxuriated in Zack's fingers massaging his body.

The slippery slide was electric. Andrew drank in the touch he'd waited so long to have, hungry, knowing he'd never get enough of those hands on him.

When the submissive of his dreams had soaped him up twice and looked to be ready to see if three times was a charm, Andrew said, "I'm clean, pet."

Zack bowed his head and shifted back, allowing Andrew to step under the water. Even with his pet's hair pasted against his skull, the man was exquisite.

Andrew indulged in something he'd been craving. He pumped some shampoo in his palm. Using all of his hairdressing talents, he washed Zack's poorly dyed strands. It would only take a few good washings to get back to the beautiful blond hair he'd tried to hide. Andrew focused on rubbing Zack's scalp in the relaxing, yet stimulating way he'd perfected over the years.

A soft moan escaped Zack as he bit his lip. His pet's cock brushed against Andrew's thigh a number of times. He continued the shampooing, but Zack's whimpers couldn't be concealed. After rinsing the suds away, Andrew methodically shampooed again, then applied conditioner.

Zack groaned long and low as Andrew worked his fingers down to the roots and rubbed small circles along his scalp. Still, the imp seemed determined to keep his eyes closed. His pet clearly needed someone to take him in hand, to help him overcome his stubbornness.

This was beyond foolish. Zack needed to deal with reality; pretending could no longer be an option. They were adults. Andrew asked, "What's my name?"

His pet inhaled sharply. He stepped forward and rested his head on Andrew's shoulder. Whispering, he said, "You're Master... your name is... Drew."

Yes! Mine! See me!

Andrew's heart hammered in his chest. "Open your eyes or safeword, Zack." It was the only command that came to his mind.

Those lovely dark green eyes fluttered open. Zack blinked in the bright light of the bathroom.

Andrew stepped in front of the intense stream of light coming through the window.

Zack stared at him as if it were the first time he'd seen him in years. Maybe it was.

Without waiting for another moment to pass, Andrew grabbed Zack's hair. Securing his head into position and tilting it to the right, Andrew pressed their lips together.

It was a kiss he didn't even know he had in him but had waited all his life to give. The slow sensual glide of his mouth against Zack's was enhanced when his pet's lips parted. Possession whipped through Andrew. With his mouth, he demanded Zack's surrender.

Zack gave his acquiescence with such passion Andrew almost didn't know what to do. The sub in his arms was no delicate flower; no, Zack ravished his lips with all the hunger and angst that had been locked up in both of them.

Zack moaned as their cocks pushed against each other.

"Please." Zack trembled against him.

"Anything, pet," Andrew said with a fierceness that surprised him.

"Master Drew, let me taste you." Zack panted.

Those words sent a shiver through Andrew. How many times had he gotten off to the fantasy of Zack begging to suck him off? *Damn.* The reality of his fantasy tapped into his Dominant side, and he readjusted his feet to shoulder's width apart.

"You may do so, but I expect you to swallow every drop, my pet." He was thrilled about the medical tests Entwined made their members get. He'd heard enough subs complain that Zack didn't usually take his scenes to sexual completion. Andrew hadn't ever been with anyone without protection, not even Charlie, which, considering all the lovers his ex-lover had taken, turned out to be a blessing.

With a broken moan, Zack's knees hit the white-tiled floor of Andrew's shower, and he presented himself with his hands clasped behind his back. His talented tongue turned Andrew inside out.

Zack flicked his tongue along the length of Andrew's cock. He ran his lips up and down Andrew's shaft. He grazed his tongue over every inch of him. Holy hell. His pet was too good at this.

He pushed down his jealousy as Zack demonstrated his impressive skill. Threading his fingers through Zack's wet hair, Andrew finger-combed the dark abomination of a dye job off his face. He didn't want to miss a second of this heated display of worship.

Andrew had never been quick to orgasm, but he fought back his desire to simply let go of his building climax and race toward the pleasure. Coming instantly would never do, so he bit back a moan when his exquisite pet started to lick the beads of precome as they emerged from his tip.

Drop. Lick. Drop. Lick. Drop.

Zack paused and tilted his head up to stare at Andrew. He swiped his tongue out. "Is this—" A quick lick of his tongue interrupted his words. "—good?" He twirled his wet tongue over the top before the kneeling man added, "Master Drew?"

Brat! His sparkling eyes told Andrew that Zack had to be aware of how good he was at this oral endeavor, and how he defiantly challenged Andrew.

Growling, Andrew threatened, "Bratty subs get spankings."

The imp moaned as he squirmed his lower half against Andrew's leg. "Mmmmm, I hope so," Zack muttered before he engulfed all of Andrew's length in his mouth, forcing the head of his cock to the back of his throat. He gagged a little, but instead of backing off, he moved forward, shivering.

Andrew froze, mesmerized as tears streamed down Zack's face. Blurry sight didn't stop his sub. No, Zack was a vision of determined devotion hell-bent on proving he'd suffer for his Master's bliss. The message satisfied Andrew's inner Dominant in ways he'd not indulged.

Remembering Zack's request for condoms, Andrew sought clarity. "Are you hoping to swallow?"

Zack nodded.

He grabbed Zack's hair on either side of his head and pushed in deep.

His pet turned up his lips in contentment, and that was all Andrew required to fuck his mouth.

"Yes, my slutty little Zack, suck me. Have you earned my come? Perhaps I'll just paint your face." The threat was futile because Andrew could never force himself to successfully pull out of heaven even for a moment....

Zack redoubled his efforts, as if to convince Andrew to let him swallow. Andrew's angle allowed him a view of the kneeling man's cock. Zack's erection begged for an orgasm. So delicious, so submissive, and he was all Andrew's.

Andrew was ready to come, so he guided Zack's head at the right speed to bring him to orgasm. "A little more, pet." He was done trying to hold out.

Zack's mouth was like a vacuum with a tongue. Big eyes gazed up at Andrew, and he fluttered his long eyelashes.

Andrew gave himself over to the pleasure of his beautiful sub and came hard.

KNEEL. SERVE... *swallow.*

His Master had orgasmed in his mouth. Zack quivered in pleasure. It was as if his body climaxed without his cock's involvement, and that was more than a little distressing, since his cock wanted active duty.

Zack ingested Drew's salty sperm and licked his dick clean, hoping for a little more before the water from the shower stole the remaining drops away.

He needed to keep perspective. This was a weekend thing. Drew wasn't his and never would be. Andrew had made that crystal clear. *Shit,* he needed to stay in the present and not think past the moment. Andrew—Drew, he'd allow himself this weekend with Drew as his Master.

Drew caressed his face and stared down at him with affection, making Zack's heart trip up with hope.

"You're skilled." Andrew's words caused Zack to want to do an end-zone dance. It was vital for him to keep a grip on his euphoria and keep perspective.

Master Drew pulled him from his knees and wrapped him in an embrace. Everything in Zack shouted with happiness. Drew grabbed the abandoned soap and washed Zack's back in long, slow strokes.

In a quick move, Zack found himself facing the wall. "Fuck." The word slipped out.

"Language." Drew patted his ass. He soaped him up. Drew's long fingers teased down the crease of his ass.

Zack wanted to bend over and wiggle, but he restrained his slutty desires, barely.

His Master spun him back around and danced his talented fingers over Zack's chest. When he got to Zack's nipples, he….

YES!

He pinched them at the same time. How would Zack's obituary read? Possibly, "Zack Davis died from prolonged sexual teasing."

Ah, again Drew pinched Zack's nipples.

He gasped and arched toward the pain. God, Drew must see how much Zack craved him.

Would he leave Zack trembling with lust?

Master Drew touched and caressed him everywhere. He owned him, just as Zack had always dreamed of being possessed by Drew.

"I'm going to get this black out of your hair," his Master growled.

What? Zack knew better than to whine.

Soapy, shampoo-filled hands went into his hair again. Fuck, Drew's hands were sex wrapped up in total relaxation. Zack lost himself in the luxurious attention Master lavished on him.

When he was rinsed and dried, Master Drew dragged him to the bed. He laid Zack down on his back. The plug shifted when his ass pressed into the bed. His insides were coiled tight. The toy now caused an itch that would only be satisfied by the appendage he'd sucked to satisfaction.

Drew's cock was back at full staff and would make a superior substitute. The man gathered the supplies needed.

Their gazes locked.

Damn! Zack bit his lower lip to stop the words that were threatening to spill out. This was it.

Master Drew broke the stare when Zack moved to get closer.

"Present your ass to me," Andrew demanded as he rolled on the condom, slicking it up with lube.

Obediently, Zack tugged back his knees to offer himself to his Master. Lust overrode any of the shyness he might have experienced. He pulled his legs apart to put himself on display. He swallowed hard and waited.

Master touched the plug, causing the silicone to nudge sensitive places inside of him. Zack's mouth dropped open, and the sound of a tortured animal came out.

"You want me inside, Zack?"

Yes! Yours! Yes!

Zack groaned out, "Yes, Drew... Master. Please." His head had jumbled all his words, but he hoped they fell out in the right order.

The butt plug was withdrawn from its hiding place. His Master poised at his entrance.

Please. Yours. Enter.

Drew slid in inch by inch until Zack was stretched full. He stared at the man he'd loved since his teenage hormones raged.

His! His! His!

Every emotion he'd ever experience paled in comparison to this complete joy. The Master of his heart and body interlaced their fingers. This single act slammed through the final remnants of the crumbling fortress Zack had erected to protect his heart. He'd need to rebuild, but that was later, not now.

His mind screamed with the knowledge, and his body built to a boiling point after only a few deep thrusts. His soul was nurtured by the connection, but the physical couldn't be discounted.

His! His! His!

Zack threw his head back and cried out, "Drew!"

He combusted. His shaft pulsed come all over his chest and stomach. His body synchronized with the man above him. Each deep thrust made his cock spurt a little until nothing was left. He sagged to the bed.

Time lost meaning. Minutes might have passed, or hours. Zack couldn't keep track of anything but the beating of his heart and the warmth of his Master's body next to him. The digital clock suggested he'd been out for about thirty minutes.

Drew smiled down at him.

As Zack caught his breath, he was surprised his cock, although drained, was still erect and trying to participate.

His Master held him.

It should have been too much, but it wasn't. He'd only just come, but his body struggled with a greedy need for more.

Zack never wasted gifts. He had the rest of today and tomorrow before all would return as it was before. Nothing would ever be the same again when their contract expired. He pushed the misery aside and allowed his body to take over.

Master Drew cleared his throat. "Well?"

Blinking, Zack blushed. He'd been caught chasing his own thoughts. "Master Drew?"

Andrew smirked at him. "I can't tell you how much I like the sound of that coming out of your mouth."

Jackass! Zack didn't say anything, but Andrew's laughter said the man read his thoughts quite clearly from the expressions he'd never been able to hide on his face. "I asked if you typically climax hands-free."

He shook his head. "No. That was a first."

Growling, Andrew kissed him. "Good. I want us to have a lot of firsts." He scooped up what remained of the cooled pool of come in his cupped palm and added lube to it.

The man wrapped his wet fist around Zack's cock and stroked him.

God! Zack squirmed as the less than warm stickiness coated his cock. "I'm, um, sensitive. I don't know if I can come again."

"Master." Andrew stared down at him and paused.

Huh? Oh! Zack was a god-awful excuse for a submissive. In all of his dreams of doing this, he had been technically a perfect slave, but in reality…. "Sorry, Drew. I mean Master. I don't know if I can come again." His face heated. Andrew's complete calm made his fumbling that much more pronounced. He spit out, "*Master.*"

Andrew slid back into him and pushed in and out. "Zack, what's the only thing you expected from the submissives when you played with them?"

"Um?" Damn good question. He usually had no expectations of them. "Nothing. I guess I want them to give up control to me."

"Why?"

"So I can make them feel and give them what they need." Zack was flustered, but remembered to add, "Master."

Andrew grinned at him. "Don't sweat the name thing. You know it's only a ritual to help get you into the mindset. This auction contract isn't the typical situation. But it gives us something to work on."

Zack gasped. He kept moving his lower body ever so slowly as Andrew's hand rolled his flesh up and down.

"I'll set the goals. Right now, yours is to feel, Zack."

"Yes, Master." He closed his eyes and surrendered to Master Drew. His Master would take care of things. He just had to let it happen.

A tingle of need started to build up in his balls. His Master's wet hand cupped them. They had tightened and readied. Drew rolled them between his fingers and squeezed them.

"That's um… good." He was on the cusp of being overstimulated, but Drew kept him on the right side of deliciousness.

"See how nice that is?"

"Yes, Master." Zack beamed like an idiot. He did what he was supposed to do as a sub. He gave himself over to his Master.

"You're going to come two more times," Drew stated.

Zack choked. "What?" That wasn't possible. Was the man insane?

Drew grinned down at him. "You heard me."

"I don't think…." Zack trailed off. He lost his fear in his Master's gaze. He'd do whatever his Master expected of him.

"Exactly. You don't have to think right now. You can just be and let me take care of you. You're trusting me to give you what you need." Andrew then demanded the only thing Zack wanted to give him. "Let me have all of you."

The words loosened something tight inside Zack he didn't even know was there. The relief that someone else would make sure everything didn't fall apart meant his soul could rest and be at peace, even if only for a little while.

"Yes, that's it," Master Drew purred. "Good boy. You are such a good pet."

Some people hated the use of the words "boy" or "pet" in a scene, but as silly as the terms might have sounded, it validated how Zack did what he was supposed to do. The praise made him want to do more. Give more. Surrender completely to his Master.

Damn, already he was close. The normal tingling in his balls, which signaled near-release, grew in intensity, slicing through his insides. His muscles quaked, and he flailed helplessly under Master Drew's expert touch.

Vulnerable, exposed, yet undeniably safe, Zack succumbed to the pleasure of overcharged nerve endings. The intensity spread, centering into a ball of energy in his groin. His legs quivered, he grasped the sheets, and sweat broke out along his body as he lay helpless to the onslaught of yet another release.

Andrew tightened his grip on Zack's cock and made him see stars.

Fuck! He really was going to come. Oh my God, he was going to… "Master! Master, I'm going to come. You're making me come."

"Yes, I am, *my* pet." Master Drew's acknowledgment and small smile pushed Zack to the top.

A zap of pleasure flashed through him, stealing his vision and leaving him in darkness. Only aware of sensations, the slick friction on his cock, and the cool breeze blowing against his soaked skin, he exploded.

Every muscle in his body clenched. His cock pumped streams of come onto his belly. Each pulse forced his ass to clench, although he remained full, Andrew's cock still lodged inside him.

When the waves subsided, so did his ability to focus. He drifted somewhere dark and peaceful, spent, needing time to recover.

ANDREW HAD been a little concerned when Zack appeared to pass out, until he confirmed it was only a light sleep. He took the pre-tied restraints out from their hiding place under the mattress at corners of the bed frame. He secured Zack's hands together with significant slack above his head. Beyond a soft snore, Zack barely made a sound.

Now that was a work of art! Finally he had Zack tied to his bed. Andrew drank in the vision of Zack's gorgeous body against his white sheets. The slender length of him, defined with muscles built helping his crew with the setup and breakdown of the stage and moving sound equipment, not from any gym workout, was sexy. His damp, dark hair was drying against the pillows, the blond starting to show through that awful color.

After sleeping for forty-five minutes, Zack roused. He blinked his eyes open and wrinkled his nose. Adorable.

"Well, I'm glad you're up from your *swoon*."

"Swoon?" Zack squinted his eyes and studied Andrew. He glanced around the room and gasped. "Fuck! I'm the worst sub ever! You didn't come."

Zack reached toward Andrew but didn't get far. He was held in place by a *Tejou Shibari*, a simple but effective handcuff tie. He tugged again. Was that a flash of excitement in his eyes?

"I put the restraints on while you slept."

Zack hummed. "I can't believe I passed out."

"I won't lie, you had me worried for a second, my pet, but your breathing remained even and you looked peaceful."

"Then why the restraints?"

Andrew shrugged. "Because I can."

"Ah."

"And you look incredible bound to *my* bed, but you can safeword or say 'Thank you, Master Drew.'"

A small smile appeared on Zack's slightly parted lips, and his erection was once again vying for Andrew's attention after years of neglect. *Nice!*

"Thank you, Master Drew."

Yes! Each time Zack called him *Master* it was as if he were admitting the truth: Zack belonged to him.

Zack absorbed everything Andrew gave him.

Andrew enjoyed the lust-driven show of his boy pulling at the ropes. He had his safeword, so he wasn't expecting freedom, only trying to test his Master's skill at fastening. The most erotic part was the sexy groan of happy defeat each time the binding held fast.

Andrew leaned down and huffed a stream of warm air over Zack's slick-tipped cock.

"No, Drew, I mean Master, I'm too tired. I can't," Zack complained.

His cock didn't seem as tired as Zack's protests would lead Andrew to believe. Andrew had witnessed Zack's cock harden when he realized he was held captive by the ropes. His pet's desire was as clear as the tip of his erection was wet.

"Master, I can't."

Andrew wasn't having that. He'd force the pleasure of orgasm on his new lover if he had to, at least until Zack used his safeword. There was just something he got off on by controlling the pace at which his subs were brought to the brink of orgasm, reveling in victory as they fell over that glorious precipice they claimed couldn't be reached so soon after the last climax.

"No, Master. I can't," Zack whined again.

Grinning, Andrew stated the facts. "You can. And you will. It's simply a matter of time." He let his tongue lick over the glistening tip of Zack's cock. "I." Andrew swirled his tongue in a long wet lick around Zack's cockhead. "Will." He blew a puff of air over his erection.

Zack tried to push off the bed.

"Make." Andrew teased his tongue along the slit before dipping in for a lick. "You."

"Argh!" Zack cried out as his body arched up, begging for Andrew's attention.

"Just be. Trust me to take you where you need to go." He blew another stream of moist air over the jutting appendage. Andrew swept his tongue out to capture the sweetness.

He bit back a moan of passion because he wanted to present a calm, dominant front. Zack was stunning. He gathered the sweetness over the tip with his tongue, and his pet whimpered. God, Zack craved with perfection.

Andrew licked around the crown of the prettiest penis he had ever seen. Dicks weren't supposed to be pretty, but damn it all to hell, Zack's dick was flawless in shape, just the right size, and a pleasing reddish pink.

He lavished long, slow licks all around the shaft.

Zack moaned but never uttered his safeword.

Andrew traveled up one side of Zack's cock and down the other. His pet would come. It was just a matter of how and when. The decision, not surprisingly, was made by his own cock, which throbbed anxiously, reminding Andrew it required attention too.

Andrew rolled on a condom and grabbed a tube of warming lubricant. He slicked the gel on his cock. Yeah, he definitely needed attention, and he pressed his wet fingers into Zack's opening and massaged his entrance with the slick.

His pet's eyes flew open, and he frowned. "I can't, Master," Zack complained.

Andrew hid the expression that revealed he was wrapped around Zack's finger and found his Master voice. "You can and will. Unless you use your safeword."

He studied Zack for a moment to make sure he read the situation correctly. Even though Andrew was satisfied Zack had understood, he said it again. "Safeword. Safeword or I'm going to slide inside of you and make you come."

Zack pursed his lips at Andrew's promise and closed his eyes in a sign of submission. "I'm not going to safeword."

Andrew glided into his pet's willing body. "You're going to come."

"No." Zack whispered his denial.

"Are you defying me? You know what happens to boys who defy their Masters?"

Zack opened his big green eyes to stare at Andrew. His pupils were huge. His breathing hitched and came faster now.

Ah. His pet needed boundaries and consequences. Unless Andrew misread him, Zack was begging for a proper discipline session. "Bad boys get spanked. Are you a bad pet?"

Zack opened his mouth, but only a whimper came out. He tried to move his arms but couldn't.

Andrew slipped Zack's ankles free from the loops. Immediately, Zack wrapped his legs tightly around Andrew and thrust up, drawing more of Andrew's cock inside.

"Mmmmm, you feel good wrapped around me, but I think you're a good boy who's been bad," Andrew stated. He glided his hand over the rounded cheek. "I'll be spanking this sweet ass. Not only have you been naughty, playing with other subs and taunting me, but...." He squeezed and gave Zack a small smack. Experience told him the impact, while not hard enough to even sting, would pull Zack back from subspace a little.

Zack whimpered.

He captured a piece of Zack's formerly blond hair and tugged. "You took away your golden hair, replacing its gloriousness with flat emo black... and now you've tried to lie to me. Saying you wouldn't come when we both know you most certainly will."

Andrew leaned back and gave himself a little room to connect his palm with Zack's asscheek.

Zack cried out, "Drew!"

Encouraged, Andrew slapped his hand down again.

Zack moaned and shook his head.

Andrew didn't need a picture drawn for him.

Slap, slap, slap.

"Drew," Zack called out.

Smack. Slap. Whap.

"Master Drew to you," Andrew corrected.

Zack's eyes were dazed and unfocused.

Ah good, his pet was heading deep into subspace.

Zack squeezed rhythmically around Andrew's cock as he continued to thrust in and out. "Yes, yes. Master Drew. Yes. God."

Bloody hell. This was something they needed to explore, but Andrew had a problem. He'd reached his limit, but he had to get Zack there first.

He swatted Zack's ass harder, giving him some real stingers.

Smack. Slap. Swat.

Andrew tried to refocus the ecstasy circulating through his body, beginning at his cock, and launching it to redefine Zack's reactions. His patience and endurance were coming to an end. He wrapped a hand around his pet and stroked him.

His sore throat gave his voice a raspy quality Zack seemed to appreciate. "I'm gonna spank your sweet little bottom for each and every sub you've played with."

"Definitely. You should," Zack murmured in agreement as he writhed under Andrew.

Spank. Spank. Spank.

"You're going to remember me punishing you every single time you sit down for the next week," Andrew promised him.

Zack's moans told him the guy liked a bit of humiliation. Again, Andrew filed the information away. He tugged on Zack's erection. "I'm going to smack your butt. You'll go right over my knee, and I'll spank you until I know you're really sorry for being such a brat."

"Yes, yes. Spank me." Zack was muttering, in a world of his own. "Yeah. Punish me. I deserve it."

"Maybe I shouldn't let you come."

Zack gave a guttural groan.

Andrew gave him one more loud, sharp smack to his ass.

"Coming," Zack cried out as he spilled.

As Andrew's fist was coated, he gave a small prayer of thanks before he let go. He thrust in deep and let Zack milk him. He came hard, shuddering into Zack's body, filling the condom with his well-earned climax. The pleasure was intensified by the long delay. He sagged when he stopped shooting his stored frustration.

Zack stared up at him with a dreamy, sated, well-loved expression. Andrew took care of the condom and did a quick cleanup of both of them. He nestled down next to Zack, who softly snored as Andrew untied him. A nap did seem to be a good idea.

CHAPTER THIRTEEN

ZACK AWAKENED to Drew hacking up a lung. "You okay?" He rolled toward the man hunched over the side of the bed.

"Yeah, sorry I woke you." Drew tucked a long hank of hair behind Zack's ear. The man's voice was shot, and he appeared a bit flushed.

"You don't look good." Zack checked the time on Drew's digital clock. Wow, it was late afternoon.

"Neither do you with your passive-aggressive poorly dyed black hair." Andrew frowned and stood. He shot a hand out to catch the nightstand for support.

Zack scooted across the bed and bounced up behind to steady him. "Let me help you."

Drew exhaled loudly. "I'm fine." He straightened up slowly.

Zack put his wrist to Drew's head. "You feel warm."

"I'll take my temperature. Thermometer is in the bathroom."

Smirking, Zack bit back a laugh.

Drew glared at him. "No, it's not a rectal thermometer, but if you're into medical play, I can work something out."

Zack lost it and burst out laughing. "Let me get it. Sit. Where is it?"

"Third cabinet on the left-hand side, in the blue box marked Medical Supplies."

Zack's laughter died as he stared at the compulsively organized man.

"What? It's good to know where your things are…." Drew raised his chin at him. "What?"

"No, um…." *Shit!* Zack tripped into the bathroom, more to hide his erection than to fetch the item. He opened the third cherrywood cabinet under the double sink, and sure enough, on the left-hand side was the item in question.

Fuck! That was hot. Wow. Zack's cock throbbed as he tried to get a grip on himself. He'd known Andrew practiced restraint and control, but seeing it in action flipped major switches.

Drew called out, "You found it?"

Zack sat the device on the counter. "Yeah."

He stared at his reflection in the mirror. Damn, his hair was fucked up, his lips were swollen, and he had a big hickey on his neck, but fuck if there wasn't a happy glow about him.

Jeez! He splashed some cold water on his face as he thought about terrible things like cute animals getting smushed by Mack trucks and being force-fed mushrooms to eliminate his arousal.

Mission accomplished, he trotted to where Drew sat on the king bed, swathed in white satin and cotton.

Drew gestured with his head. "You're going to let me help you strip that horrid color out of your beautiful hair."

Zack stuck the thermometer in Andrew's ear. "Yes, Sir."

Drew raised his head.

The scrutiny made Zack squirm. His Master's gaze seemed to touch him physically as it trailed over his naked body. Fuck, his willful cock jutted out proudly, failing to respond to anything but the gleam in Drew's eyes.

In a quick move, Drew pinned Zack underneath him. Did the thermometer beep, registering Drew's temperature? "But you might have a fever." He gestured to the device still in his hand but no longer in Drew's ear.

Drew was naked, aroused, and that knowledge did nothing to steady Zack's hand as he guided the thermometer toward an ear.

"I'm definitely hot." Drew rutted against Zack.

"Just let me stick this in…."

Drew growled.

Fucking Christ! Was he meant to play out all his wet dreams at once? Barely able to hold the medical tool in Drew's ear, he was relieved when it beeped.

Focusing on the digital display, Zack reported the results. "It's 98.6. But you should still rest."

"I will." Drew took the mechanism and set the device aside.

"We need to stop." Zack locked his ankles around the back of Drew's knees and rolled over into the superior position.

"Oh ho! The hell we do." Drew fondled Zack's erection before snuggling the arousal next to his own. He slid his fist over both cocks.

God, that was good. No, Zack had to bring this to a halt. "Drew. Come on, we have to stop. You're not feeling well. Let me take care of you." He needed to take control of the situation.

Drew groaned. "You *are* taking… care of me." He writhed against Zack. "You're making me feel much better. Now kiss me."

Kiss. Love. His.

Oh fuck. He was helpless to do anything other than obey. He leaned over Drew and started to thrust his hips in time with his Master's hand.

"Good pet. Now give me your lips," Master Drew ordered.

Zack whimpered, unable to resist. He merged his lips with Drew's in a hot, wet caress. He opened to give access to his Master's questing tongue.

They pressed their erections against each other. Slick, hot friction pushed Zack closer to the edge. Drew cupped his ass, guiding his movements to a quicker cadence. He slid his body in time with Drew's as their lips locked together, tongues battling for more contact.

Drew groaned as his hips stuttered.

Zack pulled back to watch his lover's body twist and contort against him. It thrilled him to feel his Master's heated orgasm roll over his cock.

Drew purred as he stroked out the last of his pleasure, making Zack spill over the edge, adding to the wetness.

Zack collapsed, drained, until he remembered Drew was sick. He tried to bolt up, but an arm locked him in a vise. Zack said, "You're sick. We shouldn't have done that."

Drew opened his eyes and smirked at Zack. "But I feel so much better."

Annoyed at his own lack of restraint, he broke free of Drew and grabbed a washcloth. He cleaned them both as Drew stretched out, sighing with a big smile on his face. Aliens had apparently stolen the strict Dom and replaced him with a very cooperative lover.

The many facets of Andrew didn't exactly confuse Zack; he had memorized the complexity long ago. Though he really didn't quite know how to react to him either. He opted for retreat.

"I'm going to make you some dinner. Do you want to stay here or come downstairs?" Zack asked on his way back from putting the damp cloth in the bathroom hamper.

"Downstairs. I need to keep my eye on you."

Mmmmm, yes please. "Okay, but you'll do so lying down."

Drew saluted as he marched past Zack, carrying a pillow.

Once Zack settled him on the couch with a thick blanket, he asked, "What should I make you?"

"You can put the tray of baked ziti in the oven to reheat it. The salad is on the second shelf on the right-hand side."

Zack tottered across the cold wood floor and was impressed, but not surprised. He found the salad components not only where Drew said they'd be, but each was stored in separate sealed plastic containers on the second shelf, each one labeled. On closer inspection, the entire interior of the refrigerator was identified with tags. Each shelf and drawer had a designated label: dairy, cheese, vegetables, fruit, and meat… there was even a place dedicated to leftovers.

Zack peeked into a drawer. Even inside the drawers items were in neat little clear plastic bins… labeled.

Holy fuck! He had always craved this level of organization in his life, but he'd never been able to make it work with his brothers and their chaos. He traced his fingers over each tag, identifying where the item was located. He'd traipsed into an obsessive-compulsive daydream.

Drew called out, "The salad dressings are in the right-hand door." The bottles were lined up in the holder marked Salad Dressings. Zack grabbed one he'd seen Drew order in a restaurant.

"I can't have any alcohol because of the antibiotics, but if you'd like, you can open a bottle. I picked up some ice wine. I'd love your opinion on the taste. It's chilled in the wine refrigerator. The top row has a selection I thought you might like. The corkscrews are in the drawer above the fridge."

"I don't want to drink alone."

Drew laughed. "I'll be here with you, and you can give me some sparkling cider."

"Well, okay." Zack had never had ice wine before.

"The glasses are in the cabinet directly above the same refrigerator. The flutes will work well given the luscious sweet quality of the wine. They retain carbonation and capture and distribute the aroma to your nose and mouth." Drew's assertive nature and explanation settled Zack.

Zack left the paradise of labeled salad items where they were, grabbed the pan of ziti, and slid it in the oven. Before he could ask, Drew called out, "Three hundred degrees should warm it up."

Kneel. Serve. His.

Having Drew anticipate Zack's every need was erotic. It only took one round of imagining being force-fed mushrooms to regain his focus. A soft melody drifted into the kitchen from the living room as he stepped over to the small wine refrigerator. Drew must really appreciate wine if he had one of these babies, or maybe it was his need for precision. The alcohol was kept at the correct temperature.

Zack found the right bottle, then shut the chiller. He grabbed a corkscrew from a drawer above the wine refrigerator and opened the cabinet. Fuck, Drew lived an organizer's wet dream. Damn him if the glasses weren't all suspended in perfect rows. Each glass section was labeled with the type of glass it held. Zack's cock tried to harden.

Mushrooms! Mushrooms! Mushrooms!

Temporary, his time with Drew was just temporary. Well, that thought worked much better than any of the other horrible things he'd come up with, but Zack worried the thought would kill his erections forever.

He reached back down to pull the sparkling cider out of the refrigerator as he tried to get a grip on his runaway emotions. He shouldn't enjoy playing house as much as he did. This was only for the weekend. He needed to stop mentally inserting himself in Drew's perfectly organized life.

He trudged back to the gorgeous male reclining on the couch. Did Drew have to be so fucking hot?

"Thanks, Zack." Drew reached for the bottles and opener.

"For what?" Zack asked as he watched the efficient movements used to open the Inniskillin with no cork broken off inside the neck of the bottle.

"Making us dinner." Drew peered at the bottle. "Ah, good choice. The 2007." Drew opened and poured Zack a flute of the sparkling wine, which made Zack's heart clench at the gesture of being served first. Drew focused on opening the sparkling cider Zack had brought him.

Drew was the Master of Zack's dreams, always seeing to his needs before his own, which in his fantasy world allowed Zack to focus on Master Drew.

Not his.

"You had everything already prepared. All I needed to do is move the dishes around and throw the salad together. Shouldn't I do the work?" He was supposed to be the sub here.

"Why?" Drew sniffed Zack's wineglass before handing the flute over. "This is nice. Smell it."

He begrudgingly sniffed the liquid and admitted, "Smells delicious." Zack huffed. "I'm supposed to take care of you." He needed to get some distance and reality into this situation.

"We'll take care of each other… or I mean…. Wait. Is that what you want? You want to be in more of a slave relationship?" Drew scrutinized him a little too closely for comfort.

"What, 24/7? Nah, I wouldn't want to be micromanaged like that." Or did he?

Drew nodded.

Thinking of nothing more to say on the subject, Zack raised his glass to make a toast. "To health."

"To you." Drew lifted his sparkling cider and clinked their glasses.

Zack savored the sip. The cold liquid burst sweetness over his tongue. "That's really good."

"Glad you like it. I love the stuff. I'm happy to have someone to share this with." Zack tried not to give more meaning to Andrew's words. "But you do like D/s outside of constructed scenes?"

"Dominance and submission? I guess… never really thought about it…." Zack certainly found the organized lifestyle sexy. He'd relish boundaries being set so he could decide to step over them or not. Defined lines made the world clear. The elimination of the gray shit that littered one's daily life was heaven. Of course, someone skilled enough who understood his triggers and used them to put him in an erotic tailspin when the time came was all the better.

"How do you see a BDSM and/or a domestic discipline relationship working?" Sipping his drink didn't lessen the intensity of Drew's aura.

"If I were to ever do this, I'd want it to be private. Having never experimented beyond the club, I'd have to do some exploring as to how much I would like it to be a part of my everyday life." That sounded like a safe, measured response.

It didn't indicate how Zack's heart screamed for Drew to be asking him for real. This was simple curiosity, right?

"So, not 24/7?" Drew pushed Zack to clarify his own thoughts.

"I don't know. I guess I'd want a normal relationship."

Drew held up his hand and asked, "What do you mean by *normal*? Do you think BDSM is abnormal?"

Shit. Did he? No… though having his mother toss him out of his home for having BDSM magazines certainly didn't imply the practice was typical or widely accepted. He'd learned to hide this part of himself from others, but he didn't have to with Drew. "I guess that's not the right word."

Drew touched his cheek for a moment. "Sometimes we hear we're different like it's a bad thing. And we can believe it."

"And it comes right out of our mouths." Jordon's therapist would be pleased. Score one for Zack's self-awareness.

Drew nodded. "Yes, exactly. So please continue what you were saying. You're looking for a relationship...."

Somehow stomping around wording as opposed to the actual words was safer than the truth. Zack took a deep breath and released it. "I'd like equal partnership, someone who's willing to explore aspects of D/s, in and out of the bedroom and find something that works for...."

Andrew leaned toward him as if it mattered. "So not BDSM all the time?"

"Well, no, more like friends with ownership. There are times I might be in the mood to top." Zack stated his versatility to gain a bit of distance from this hypothetical conversation.

Drew widened his eyes. "You'd still want to top?"

"Yeah, I mean sometimes." He was grateful Drew hadn't questioned his desire to sub. Though he tried to backpedal, his mouth seemed to be on automatic pilot, trudging forward. "Sometimes, I think I'd want vanilla sex too, you know?" Exactly like they'd shared. He almost pretended Drew loved him back and they needed to be together without the trappings of a scene.

Drew smiled. "Good old-fashioned vanilla sex." The man sat upright to pour a little more bubbling liquid into Zack's glass.

"Yup." Zack drank as he imagined the bubbles loosening his tongue, one pop at a time. He scrunched down on the couch and watched the gas flames in the fireplace dance.

Drew relaxed into the couch. Their bodies were touching shoulder to knee.

"How about you?" Zack couldn't contain the pointless question, and it twisted the knife still embedded in his heart.

"I could do the same, easily." Drew brushed his fingers over the top of Zack's hand.

"Is that how you and Charlie—?" What in the hell was wrong with him?

Drew didn't hesitate to answer. "No. Charlie.... Charlie wasn't sure what he wanted and blamed me for not giving it to him."

His sofa partner shifted, but not before Zack witnessed the faraway expression of… what? Was that regret? Was he still mourning the loss of that asshole?

Drew shook his head. "We were so young when we started dating, and instead of growing together, we grew apart. Instead of including me in his life, Charlie simply cut me out, and if I'm honest, I let it happen. I held on for as long as I could, certainly longer than he wanted me to…. Sorry."

"It's fine." Zack finished the rest of the wine and tried to block out Drew's longing for another man. He'd needed a good reminder that this was just a weekend dream.

Fantasy or not, Zack refused to waste a second. When Drew opened his arms offering an embrace, Zack set their glasses down and settled back onto his Master's warm body. He was determined to drink in every caress and absorb every interaction, because it would never be repeated. Being in Drew's arms was a wish come true. Zack planned to push his luck until his blessings or their time ran out.

Turning his body, Zack dragged the blanket off the back of the couch and tucked it around Drew as he snuggled against his chest. He reached out, combing his fingers through Drew's perfect hairstyle.

God, how many times had he wanted the freedom to simply touch the man he loved? Zack listened to the heartbeat close to his ear but closed his eyes to avoid Drew's stare.

"Mmmm, that's nice." Clearly, the man didn't mind Zack's roaming fingers.

Once he'd determined the guy's hair really was afraid to stay out of place, Zack ran his fingers down the side of Andrew's face. Stubble from a sexy five o'clock shadow rasped against his fingertips.

Drew's body relaxed further.

Zack peeked up at him. His eyes were closed, and his breathing slowed. Drew was on meds and needed sleep. The scenes they had done were physically taxing, and Zack was sure Drew should have more rest.

The smell of cheese, basil, and tomato sauce woke Zack. Drew murmured before he snored softly. *Oh wow!* Was there anything cuter than this?

Zack carefully unwound himself from the sleeping man he was tangled around and tiptoed to the open kitchen. As quietly as he could manage, he set the table with Drew's fancy white china rimmed in silver, crystal stemware, and what Justin had described as his grandmother's silverware.

ANDREW WOKE up from a deep, relaxing sleep. "Zack?"

"Here. I finished setting the table."

Andrew ambled over. "Wow. You've set the table perfectly." He sat down, gazed across the candlelit surface, and pictured their happy future.

He wasn't quite sure when his lustful crush on Dusty's kid brother had gone from spark to blaze, from affection to love. But at some point his feelings had shifted. They were meant for each other.

Zack moaned. "My God! This is delicious."

Andrew nodded. "Mom taught me. She believed everyone should be able to cook seven dishes." He imagined them spending nights like this one, laughing and eating in front of the fire. It was a shame Zack insisted on clothing because of Andrew's illness. Aw, pushy subs made loving spouses.

Pointing the remote at the stereo, he started a slow love song playing. "Shall we?" He held out his hand, hoping like hell Zack didn't think two guys dancing together was dumb the way Charlie had.

"Oh." Zack did a double take but took his offered hand.

Andrew swung Zack into his arms to lead him into a simple box step. He added a number of turns. Zack followed him effortlessly, carrying himself in perfect form.

Zack asked, "Where did you learn to dance?"

"My brother wanted to learn, and he wouldn't go to class. So Justin and I practiced from videos online." Andrew executed more intricate footwork, but instead of stepping on his feet, Zack glided with him. "Who taught you?"

A smile lit up Zack's handsome face. "Dusty." They shared a chuckle. "He wanted to impress Justin and needed a partner."

"Damn, where would we be without our brothers?" Andrew really considered Dusty and Jordon family.

"Right! When Jordon saw Justin and Dust dancing, he begged to learn. Justin was a very patient teacher with Jordon, because I can tell you, I don't think the kid knows how to count. The steps were too limiting for him." Zack chuckled.

"I bet you picked it up immediately. You like the boundaries of knowing where to step." Andrew enjoyed the light pink that brightened Zack's cheeks with a heartfelt compliment. "Do you Lindy?" Could Zack do his favorite dance?

On a quick nod from Zack, Andrew clicked the remote and "Johnny B. Good" wailed through the room. His pet kept in time without a glitch. Andrew did a swing out with an inside turn into a rag doll drag.

Ah, yes. Zack leaned into him, following with a blind trust that usually took years to develop. They even did a *Texas tommy jump turn*. He'd have attempted a between-the-legs slide, but they were on carpet.

He executed a turnup and dropped Zack into a low dip. His breath came in pants, but he wasn't sure if it was from excitement or the exercise.

"You can dance."

Zack grinned as Andrew hauled him up into a standing position. "So can you."

"Ever want to take dance lessons?" Once the question tumbled out of Andrew, he realized that was putting the cart before the horse.

Zack's face lost all expression. "I've never thought about it."

Andrew refused to let Zack's lackluster response bother him… much. "We should clean up."

They gathered the dishes, Andrew making light conversion until Zack laughed and relaxed again. There wasn't much to clean up, so it was accomplished quickly.

Andrew wanted to know everything about Zack. "When did you know?"

"About?"

"That you liked BDSM."

Zack paused. "I was about eight or nine. I saw a suggestion of sex while someone was tied up on television and became enthralled. Then I saw *The Secretary* and…. You?"

"Yeah, I was a bit older. Though I knew I was into BDSM before I realized I was gay." Andrew really wanted to ask how Zack spent the last few years doing something so counter to his inner workings, but instead he asked, "You want more ice wine?"

"Yeah, that'd be good." Zack wandered toward the fireplace.

"There are extra pillows and blankets in the carved wooden trunk."

Zack squatted down and ran his fingers over the intricate pattern.

"It came from Thailand."

Zack opened the storage unit and adjusted himself. Not for the first time, Andrew noticed Zack seemed turned on by organization and clarity. Andrew filed the observation away to revisit later.

Andrew uncorked the wine, poured a glass of it and more sparkling cider. On a whim, he went to the cabinet above the wine cooler. He pulled out the canister of candied rose petals and dropped two in each glass, giving the liquid a romantic pink blush. He hurried out to the pile of pillows and blankets Zack had assembled, making the floor fit for a sultan.

Andrew handed him a glass, and Zack inspected the contents with curiosity. "What are those?"

"Candied rose petals from Brussels."

"Ah, the European part of the last tour. I spent most of my time working or with Jordon at the museums and chocolate shops."

"Jordon on caffeine? You're a brave man."

Zack snorted. "Or foolish."

This was all Andrew wanted. He and Zack fit. They were friends, and the passion between them was quick to flare.

After they toasted and took a sip, Zack took the fluted glass from Andrew's hands and set both on the marble shelf above the fireplace. Then Zack grabbed and toppled Andrew to the floor.

Interesting. Andrew's pet landed on him as they sank deep into the cushioned pile of colorful pillows and blankets.

Zack drew him in and pressed his lips to Andrew's.

God, Andrew had missed kissing. They exchanged wet kisses while they let their hands explore. Andrew had never made out with someone so totally into the sensual glide of lips. Zack had it down to an art. Andrew's mouth began to feel tired, though he'd die before stopping.

Time ceased to exist.

Zack rolled on top and trailed his lips over Andrew's throat, the slight graze of his teeth evoking tingling shudders. Damn, how long had it been since anyone attended to him? Why had he said no to this?

Groaning, Andrew gripped Zack's poorly dyed hair and guided those talented lips against the base of his throat.

Mother of God! He'd have a ring of hickeys. Zack sucked on more skin under the collar of Andrew's T-shirt. Was his fever spiking? Did he care?

Zack sat back, and his cock pressed against his cotton briefs, making an enticing bulge. He drew off the borrowed T-shirt and tossed the material to the floor, then toyed with the hem of Andrew's tee before he made the shirt fly across the room to join the other.

There was no submissiveness in Zack when he fell forward to reclaim Andrew's mouth for his own. He caressed his lips over Andrew's chin, back down his neck, and licked across his chest. Heavenly hell, why in the world had he waited to take Zack?

Zack massaged Andrew's arm before he restrained him.

Hmmm, intriguing. Andrew was supposed to be the one in control. Maybe it was okay to hand the reins over to Zack?

He enjoyed seeing Zack become a little more direct with his approach. His pet certainly seemed anxious to have him, if the way he flicked his eager tongue was any indication.

Long, wet licks were traced across his pecs and down his torso. Zack gave a soft moan of gratitude as he worshiped Andrew with his mouth and tongue. Maybe he should…. He tried to move again, and Zack's head tilted.

"Please, Drew."

God, he loved when Zack called him Drew. How he'd missed it. Zack was the only person to ever use a nickname for him.

Andrew usually stayed in tune with everyone around him and read between the lines, but the lust and affection coursing through him made it difficult to understand what Zack was asking. He fell back against the pillows and let his pet do whatever he wanted.

Pressure on his shoulder made him open his eyes, tearing him from the indulgent dreamy place he was in. "Roll over."

A nip on his shoulder delighted Andrew when he didn't move fast enough to satisfy the demand. He tried to force some dominance into his voice, but he failed miserably. "Excuse you? Aren't I the one who gives the orders?"

Zack grinned. "Unless you safeword, you're mine right now."

"I don't need a safeword since we aren't doing a scene." Andrew closed his eyes so he didn't have to witness Zack's grin turn into a gloating smirk. He rolled over, pushing his face into the pillows. "Do your worst."

Zack's strong hands kneaded all the way down Andrew's back. Each vertebra loosened, releasing tension he wasn't aware he carried.

His back was sore from coughing, so Zack's hands were heaven on his stiff muscles.

He floated in a relaxing sphere until Zack skimmed his hands down to the waistband of his sweats. With one pull, Andrew's ass was exposed. Another tug and the pants were gone.

When nothing happened, he peered over his shoulder to find Zack practically drooling. His hands hovered over Andrew's ass, but he seemed to be afraid to touch. Okay, the awed expression was appreciated, since Andrew worked long and hard at the gym, but not having those hands on his butt was driving him mad with need. He shoved his rump upward.

An intake of breath was the only reaction, so he wriggled his backside like a slutty bottom looking for action. Was that where this was headed?

He contemplated the motionless man. Andrew read Zack's expression: he wanted inside. As much as he needed air, Andrew wanted to feel the stretch and burn of Zack's cock sliding into him.

Coherent thoughts evaporated as Zack palmed both of Andrew's asscheeks, spreading them wide to expose him. Zack circled his hands around the mounds of tight flesh.

His pet appeared to be in a trance as he worshiped Andrew's ass. The weight of his lean body pressed down on Andrew. Kisses and licks rained down his spine.

Kiss. Lick. Kiss. Lick. Kiss.

Zack was insatiable until he got to Andrew's opening, then all action stuttered to a stop. Was he uncertain as to whether Andrew wanted this?

Did he want this? How long had he gone without a partner he trusted to share this part of himself?

Andrew arched his back, pushing his ass out in answer to the unspoken question. The invite appeared to be all his pet needed.

Zack tentatively licked Andrew's asscheeks. Long, wet strokes of an eager tongue bathed him.

A very undominant whimper escaped Andrew. Incredible. He was too much of a hedonist not to enjoy the hell out of this devotion.

Charlie had always been more interested in receiving foreplay than bestowing attention. Andrew had grown used to a selfish partner, and when he did scenes at Entwined, his focus was on the subs, what they needed and his own control. Being vulnerable was a unique experience, but with Zack… it was safe to do a bit of a role reversal.

Ah, yeah. Zack painted moisture across his backside with agile flicks of his tongue, making Andrew anticipate the main course.

Andrew adjusted his erection. Damn, he couldn't believe he'd hardened already but was shocked to have to worry about shooting off between the silk and satin surrounding his cock. Pleasure zinged through him and telegraphed a readiness to his cock. His control slipped with Zack.

Hell, his worry wasn't allayed but doubled when Zack gained enough confidence to slip his tongue into the seam of Andrew's ass.

Oh God! Andrew face-planted. The wet probe was a transcendental experience and forced a moan from him. He parted his thighs to give Zack more access.

A more insistent pressure teased his opening. Zack pressed his tongue in deeper.

"Yes, Zack. Yeah."

Never disappointing him, Zack tongued and laved his entrance, making his need more desperate.

Andrew reached back to spread his own ass so there was no question of what he wanted. God, it had been years since he'd had anything besides a dildo back there.

Zack pushed his tongue in deep, then pulled back and traced one shy digit around his entrance. The slow circles were maddening.

Andrew was panting, sweating, and restless. His body empty and wanted… needed to be full of Zack.

Finally, Zack slid a spit-wet finger into him.

"Yes." Andrew squeezed his eyes shut.

More. Give me more. He grew impatient waiting, so he pushed back, only to hear a strangled sound coming from his lover.

Peeking back over his shoulder, Andrew asked, "What?"

"Tight. You. You're so tight." Zack's voice dropped into a lower-than-usual range.

Andrew wasn't sure if he should be insulted. Did the guy think he'd be gapingly loose? No, there was something…. Good God!

Zack gently probed his finger in and out. His movements were hesitant yet fascinated.

If Andrew had to guess, he'd say Zack might be inexperienced. Had he never…? He was only twenty-one. Maybe…. *Jesus!* The thought was almost enough to make him come.

Grip. Inhale. Exhale. Find center. Inhale. Exhale. Okay.

He was in better shape now and asked, "Zack, have you never topped before?"

"What? You know I've played with subs before."

Growling at the unwanted thought, Andrew said, "Don't remind me." He did seriously plan to spank him for each and every man he'd ever played with. "Answer me," Andrew demanded in his best alpha voice.

A whimper escaped Zack. "No."

Joy coursed through Andrew. Call him wrong and archaic, but the thought of being Zack's first and hopefully last piece of ass made him want to take a victory lap.

"Add another finger." Andrew forced himself to relax.

Zack followed the instructions without question.

Getting fingered and allowing his Dom out to play was an unexpected combination that revved Andrew's engine further. If he wasn't careful, he'd orgasm before Zack got inside of him.

"One more." Yup, that should be enough. He wanted Zack to still feel the tight friction surround him. He arched back onto the fingers. "That's right. Open me up for you."

"Open? You? What?" Zack sputtered.

"Mmmmm, pet. Don't you want to fuck me?" Andrew swiveled his hips against the bed of pillows to entice Zack and demonstrate how ready he was for the experience.

"Y-yes." Zack choked on the word.

Andrew shifted away, forcing Zack's fingers to slide out of him. He reached under to squeeze his cock in consolation. "Lie down."

In the future, he might give Zack a little more control of the pace, but not right now. Andrew needed to ensure his pet gained the right memories of this experience.

Zack lay among the pillows, unmoving, staring up at Andrew with his big emerald eyes. His cock, still in the game, tried to jut out of the jockeys.

Andrew reached out and caressed him through the fabric.

Writhing against the cushions, Zack thrust his hips forward.

Sliding the fabric off, Andrew freed Zack's cock. It gave a satisfying slap against his sub's lower belly. Aw, poor thing looked lonely. Andrew covered the shaft with his mouth.

Zack trembled and groaned. Truly amazing considering all they'd done earlier today, Zack was still ready for more. Ah, to be twenty-one again.

Blindly reaching for his sweatpants, Andrew found the little packet of lube and condoms he'd stashed in the pocket. Always being prepared had served him well. He shifted to cover Zack's throbbing cock in a condom.

Andrew squeezed the lube onto Zack's fingers. "Finish preparing me, Zack." When he didn't move to obey, Andrew put a bit of steel in his voice. "Do it, pet. I'm going to ride you." He grazed his finger over Zack's protected cock.

Zack did as he was told. But his slick fingers weren't enough.

"You ready?" Andrew didn't wait for an answer. He required more.

Zack dropped his mouth open in a silent scream as Andrew straddled him.

Andrew's entire focus honed in on Zack's shaft. He craved the connection. The erection poked him in between the asscheeks a couple of times before everything lined up properly.

A thrill, both physical and mental, whipped through Andrew. He'd damn well give Zack a first to remember. He shifted back and slid down Zack's shaft.

A broken cry emerged, half surprise, half whimper, from Zack.

The stretching and the slight burn were delicious reminders Andrew hadn't done this in forever. He pushed down on Zack's cock.

Zack filled him.

Oh God! Andrew gritted his teeth. He drew in slow, even breaths, reaching down deep for control. *Mustn't come. Not right now!*

Andrew focused on the man staring at him like he was everything. Tonight he'd meet all of Zack's expectations, even the ones the man didn't know he had.

"Feel that? You're inside me." Andrew rotated his hips in a slow circle, working Zack's cock inside him so he pressed more against one side of Andrew's internal walls than the other. "Right where you belong."

Zack tried to form words, but only sounds came out.

Andrew rocked forward and sat back down on the hardness. Yeah, Zack's dick hit spots too long ignored.

Inhale. Focus. Exhale. Control.

Andrew shoved his own sensuality aside and concentrated on his lover.

Zack clawed at the pillows, digging his fingers into the foam, his muscles taut. "Ah, ah, ah!"

Forward. Back.

Pleasure and pride slashed through Andrew.

Zack panted and groaned. He gripped his hands around Andrew's thighs, squeezing and lifting. The man wanted faster?

Ha, only on Andrew's terms.

Forward. Back.

Andrew was in control.

Zack started to thrust up, pushing with his hands to increase the speed.

"Forget who runs this show?" Andrew couldn't allow Zack to fly headfirst into an orgasm while bypassing the anticipation.

Stilling his movement, Zack choked.

Andrew refused to let his lover squander a milestone event the way he'd wasted his own. His pet only had one first time; besides, they'd only just started.

He held down Zack's hips and communicated with nothing but his eyes.

Pitifully, his pet whined, but Andrew wouldn't yet grant him mercy. He'd get what he needed, not what he believed he wanted.

Andrew rocked and maintained a rhythm too slow to bring either of them to completion.

Zack trembled and built to an animalistic crescendo. He gasped as if he drew his last breath. "Drew! So close...."

It appeared as if Zack had gotten to the end of his endurance. Acting fast, Andrew reached back between Zack's legs and applied three fingers of pressure to block the eruption.

Zack's eyes and mouth opened wide.

Andrew froze. He could make out the pulsations of Zack's cock but no eruption.

His lover relaxed until only confusion remained on his scrunched-up face. "What did you do? How did you...?"

Andrew was never so grateful for his sexual experience as he was in that moment. "Simply closed your urethra so you couldn't ejaculate."

"I've read about that, but never tried it." His lover exhaled and kept shifting and trying to thrust. "You feel good."

Smiling down, Andrew began to ride him again. "I wanted to give you a chance to appreciate your first time."

Zack's cock was thick, hard, and perfect in Andrew's ass. Previously, lovers he'd allow to top him had been too big or too rough or too small, but Zack fit him to perfection.

His attention shifted inward.

It might have been Zack's first time, but his natural rhythm synched to Andrew's.

"Sublime." Andrew moaned in absolute ecstasy. He wasn't one of those Doms who always pretended to be in control and didn't acknowledge pleasure. He wanted to share how Zack made him feel.

God, various shades of gratification swept over him. He wrapped his hand around his dick so Zack could focus on his own world of sensation. "You like that?"

"Yeah, Drew." Apparently Zack's conversational skills were maxed out.

Andrew rocked a little quicker as he held out his hand to Zack, who promptly kissed and licked the palm.

He didn't stifle the moan of delight as he returned his wet fist to his cock and stroked. That's what he needed. "Keep thrusting, Zack. You're going to make me come."

A smile adorned Zack's face. His teeth gleamed, and he moistened his lips. His squinting eyes and furrowed brow painted a picture of the torturous bliss of near release, hovering a breath away from the final surge of completion. He was sex incarnate.

Zack's priceless expression nearly drove Andrew over the edge. He had to slow his hand for fear of ending things too soon.

Yeah, Andrew had succeeded in pushing all the right buttons. "Gonna come with you inside of me. Do you wanna come?"

Zack's mouth hung open. A strangled moan was the only affirmative answer Andrew could expect, so he wasn't in a place to split hairs.

Andrew stroked himself and moved his ass quicker. "Come inside of me."

"Yes," Zack hissed out as the condom began to pulse.

Andrew's fist was a blur as he rubbed out his own climax. He went over the edge and made sure to tighten his muscles around Zack's eruption to intensify the bliss.

His orgasm marked Zack's lean body. Damn, he even got some in his lover's hair.

Andrew was drained but at the same time complete. He fell forward to hastily kiss Zack.

They disconnected.

Andrew hated that part. He rolled so he lay pressed up flush against Zack.

Zack lay there with a hand over his eyes and an unreadable expression on the part of his face that was visible. Did Andrew break him? "Zack?"

After a minute, worry started to creep in until Zack finally said, "Yeah?"

Andrew pulled the arm off his pet's face. He had no idea if he'd hurt him somehow. "Are you okay?"

"Yeah, fine." Zack's voice cracked, and he rolled into Andrew and held on as if he were a life preserver.

The quivering suggested the opposite of fine, but Andrew remained silent. He rubbed Zack's back, and the shaking turned into an earthquake.

Andrew rubbed his back. "Shhhh, it's okay. You were amazing. It's a little much, right?"

He held and reassured him until Zack fell asleep in his arms. The condom hung precariously off Zack's flaccid cock. If it weren't dealt with immediately, come would be everywhere.

Andrew untangled himself and received a disgruntled groan, but Zack continued to sleep.

He dealt with the condom and then stretched. Was he sore from the romp or lying on the ground? When had he gotten so old? His younger lover would exhaust him in a lot of ways, and he'd love every single minute. He tottered down the hall to the bathroom and took care of the unsexy part of sex.

When he returned, he couldn't resist studying Zack. The flawless skin, the terrible hair color, poor haircut, the long lashes, the gentle face all made him laugh. How had he ever expected to stay away from this kind of perfection?

It wasn't just Zack's physical beauty. There were lots of pretty boys out there, but none understood all the sides to Andrew. Others expected things of him because he was a Dom. Zack expected things of him because of the person Andrew was... not as part of a constant scene. He'd missed their friendship and easy conversation. No one had ever danced like he'd been born to be Andrew's partner, except Zack.

Lying back down within the welcoming cushions, he pulled the blankets up around them.

In his sleep, Zack reached out and pulled him close, then sighed contentedly.

Andrew found what he'd been seeking. He wasn't giving Zack up.

Still, Zack's reaction after they'd climaxed had Andrew worried. He'd said he was all right, but then why the trembling? Sleep took time to claim Andrew as he wondered whether he'd opened up to Zack a little too late.

CHAPTER FOURTEEN

TIME CEASED to have meaning.

Zack's world shrank to Master Drew, the ropes, and the slick hand that skimmed far too loosely up and down his shaft. Sunday morning, their last full day together, his Master gave him the choice of what he wanted to explore.

"Oh God!" *Fuck!* Why had he chosen to explore orgasm denial? He could have picked anything else. But no, this insane, desperate hell was his own damned creation. He loved the feeling of dying to orgasm... as he had for hours... days... forever.

Even during his rest periods, he was tormented with dreams when he escaped into sleep. Visions of being collared by Master Drew, being fucked on stage at Entwined for all to see, and hot vanilla sex, dipped in love, filled his head.

Sometime in the middle of the night—or was it day, impossible to tell with Drew's blackout curtains—a friendly hand teased Zack. The quiet manipulation left him breathless and panting but without satisfaction.

He shuddered, frantic for relief. His Master had dragged him to the precipice where each stroke made him dance maddeningly close to giving up and letting go.

His Master's knowledge of his body was once again used against him as the fist tightened and set up a rhythm to bring him off.

Shit! God, why did Master Drew have to stroke him perfectly?

The speed increased by a fraction.

Fuck! Zack might have been tempted not to confess the orgasm he edged. All he needed to do was remain silent, and he could so easily slip over into the bliss that beckoned him. But deep inside, even more than the transcendent feeling of orgasm, it was vitally important to him to be Drew's perfect sub. That accomplishment meant more to him than any release.

Kneel. Serve. His.

Fuck! He tightened his grip on the damp sheets. When the weekend ended, Zack wanted to be the one Drew would regret never having again.

He choked out the words through a groan. "Close. Um, oh so close."

The delicious pressure vanished, leaving his cock to pulsate in the cool air. Was this the eighth time or eightieth? Zack had lost track of the number of orgasms he hadn't been allowed to have.

"Such a good pet," Master Drew purred to him as he traced his hands down Zack's quivering body.

He tried to speak, but only a whimper came out.

His Master licked the palm of his hand and traced wetness over the length of Zack's cock. When he reached the tip, he pressed the shaft down, stretching Zack's cock toward his thighs. The turgid member held there, pointing at his toes for a moment before Master Drew released the staff and allowed the length to snap up, slapping Zack in the lower belly.

"Oh." Zack breathed out a groan at the tingling. He was in the zone. Every sensation his Master gave him became a precious gift he wanted to savor.

His Master danced his fingers along Zack's body to stroke his face. Drew pressed a soft kiss on Zack's lips, which made his heart sing. "You love this, don't you, pet?"

Yes. No. Zack managed an affirmative grunt.

Master Drew wrapped his hand around Zack's cock and pulled upward on the shaft. "Can you answer me, pet?"

Oh fuck! He did adore the overwhelming feeling and unidentified emotions. Totally focused on his body, finding words to answer the question proved difficult. He wanted to suffer for Drew and prove himself worthy of being Drew's.

Master Drew tipped a bottle of oil over his cock.

Zack held his breath as the line of lubricant hit his oversensitive flesh, making him keen with tormented pleasure as the liquid slid down his shaft. The sensation was almost enough to make him come, and then Master Drew massaged the oil all over to force Zack even closer to the edge.

His cock dripped with the glistening substance.

Master Drew cupped Zack's full balls and squeezed.

Mmmm.

His Master pulled his sac down and held him. Any stimulation was amplified. Zack shook his head to deny the irresistible pleasure trying to defeat him.

No! Oh God. No!

His Master's fist glided up and down, easier with the lubricant. Resistance to his ministrations was futile. The pressure increased slightly, pushing the stimulation closer to the threshold of pain. "Answer." The clipped word demanded Zack's attention and respect as his Master tightened his grip.

Answer? Answer what? Oh, he'd asked something.

Zack forced past the torturous stimulation in order to obey his Master's command. What was the question he asked? Oh yeah: *You love this?*

The answer was easy. "Yes, Master Drew. I love...." A groan prevented him from answering completely.

Thank God! To admit such a bold truth would surely make any sense of normalcy in their future impossible. He wouldn't share how deep his affection ran or he'd push Drew away completely.

Zack panicked and changed his words to something completely obvious. "I love what you're doing to me."

The squeezing discomfort ended, and a loving stroke was given to his cock. Zack's mind and body responded to the simple black-and-white world of reward and consequence. If he succeeded in his task, he'd be rewarded, so it stood to reason if his attempt failed, he would be punished. Although Master Drew enjoyed blurring the lines, punishment became pleasure and reward a torment. Trust was the only thing Zack could do.

Kneel. Serve... his.

Zack panted as Master Drew pumped him slowly from the root to the tip of his erection. "You love it but at the same time hate it. You want me to stop?"

Stop? Yes! No! He'd die if his Master didn't continue. Zack tried to thrust up against the maddening ecstasy and torture to get a little more of the friction he craved.

Not enough! More! Never enough!

Ropes held him in place, however. He was grateful Master Drew made him secure against Zack's own selfish actions. His Master helped him succeed in achieving his gift of submission.

It was a deceptively simple bondage structure but completely effective. His thighs and above his elbows were wrapped with three inches of cotton bands. The bands were attached to a lead of rope that disappeared under the bed, secured to his other side. There was only enough play in the rope to allow him to squirm.

"Don't stop, Master" sounded more like a sob than a response.

Master Drew wrapped one hand around Zack's balls and tugged them lightly while teasing around the crown of Zack's penis with the fingertips from his other hand. Zack leaked so much precome he didn't know what he was wetter from, the lubricant or his own fluids.

His Master's attention to his body couldn't have been more complete. He rubbed each droplet of fluid exiting his slit along Zack's flesh.

When Master Drew wrapped his fist around Zack's erection again, he almost shouted his demand to orgasm. The strokes started out light and unhurried. The caresses built up in strength and speed. He was paralyzed; all he could do was lay there and endure for his Master.

Trust. Serve. His.

He was there as a toy to be played with or ignored as Master Drew deemed fit.

Surrender. Trust. His.

"That's right, my little sub. Relinquish your control. Believe in me to give you what you need. You're doing well," his Master praised him.

His. Submit. Always.

Zack no longer struggled against achieving his own satisfaction. He'd given Master Drew everything he had and everything he was.

His Master gave him a deep, approving growl. "That's right. Surrender to me, my pet. Just be." The cadence of his Master's words was hypnotic.

The request was a balm soothing Zack's soul. He'd wanted this for so long, and he could do nothing but grab his submissiveness with two hands and see where this ended. His needs didn't vanish, but they were reorganized into the background as he flew higher than he'd ever imagined possible.

Physical desire mounted in Zack, but he separated from the excitement to focus on his Master's actions. He'd do his Master's bidding regardless of the toll it took on him.

Zack required his Master to make him pay a price, to make his submission worthy of his Master. His balls constricted, and he tried to push the need to ejaculate away, but he couldn't.

He whined, hoping to be saved. "Master!"

"Do not come." The command brokered no room for confusion.

The words froze Zack's orgasm within his trembling body and stopped his imminent eruption.

Master Drew didn't give him any relief but tightened his grip, causing Zack to shake with the added tension. His cock jerked angrily at the denial as the strokes continued to force him to ride the razor's edge.

"You're so good, Zack." His Master sounded pleased with him and made the accomplishment worth the painful struggle.

Sweat dripped off Zack's body as he strained against his need.

Master Drew stroked him at the perfect tempo as if he dared Zack to come.

"Now, I'm going to pull out your plug, and I'm going to fuck myself inside of you until I come." He wiped some of Zack's sweaty hair out of his face. "Will you enjoy me taking my pleasure inside you?"

Zack croaked out something he hoped might be passable for a yes.

His Master stared down at him. "You won't come. Understood?"

Impossible! A whimper escaped as Zack contemplated the task in front of him. He squeezed his eyes shut for a brief moment. He wanted to please his Master, but his body didn't seem up to the continued deprivation. He'd never attempted sex without orgasm. Was he capable of succeeding in this task?

Failing his Master was unacceptable.

Kneel. Serve. His.

"Do you understand?"

Zack recognized the concept, but setting it into practice was another matter. "Yes, Master."

Drew paused and smiled at him. He grabbed Zack's hand and kissed the palm. "You're incredible. You know that, right?"

Zack's love for Drew expanded the seams of his heart a bit more. He'd do anything asked of him.

Drew caressed the side of Zack's face and then slipped back into the Master role. He retied Zack's legs with impressive efficiency so they were bent at the knees to accommodate having a pillow tucked under his ass. The angle put his opening in perfect position for Master Drew's cock to enter him.

The slick plug was twisted out of Zack's ass, leaving behind an empty void. Master Drew rolled on a condom, traced a palm covered in lube over his jutting cock, and pushed into Zack. The head of Drew's cock moved past the tight ring of muscles on a slow glide until Zack was full of his Master.

"Yes." Zack hissed at being filled.

Joined. Connected. Heaven.

At that moment, his orgasm no longer mattered. His whole being now focused on pleasing this man he loved.

Master Drew trembled against him when he was fully seated. A zap of power coursed through Zack. He wanted to cause this magnificent, dominant man to lose his tightly held control.

In. Out. In. Out.

The rhythm remained leisurely, his Master's breath was coming in pants, his eyes squeezed closed.

Zack's muscles strained with the lack of orgasm, but his mind rejoiced at having an opportunity to satisfy his Master. He dug his heels into the mattress to eliminate the give. He not only held still for his Master's gratification, but he thrust as much as the ropes allowed, helping his Master achieve greater heights.

Master Drew's eyes widened as he sighed with appreciation of the unrequested change. Zack was probably topping from the bottom, but he wanted his Master to feel as good as he did. He squeezed his ass muscles.

Drew gasped out a moan. His name fell from Master Drew's lips like an accusation and exaltation all at once.

Zack throbbed for release. His total concentration was on bringing his Master to orgasm. Master Drew gripped Zack's thighs as he sped up his thrusts.

He continued to welcome his Master's invading cock, as much as being tied down granted. The angle was perfect for hitting him in exactly the right spot. He could have easily enjoyed a powerful hands-free orgasm, but Zack wouldn't fail.

No. Zack pushed away his need and focused on Master Drew's impending climax.

Again and again his Master thrust into him and withdrew. He leaned down to crash against Zack's lips to claim a hard, passionate kiss. Drew snapped his hips forward and back, continuing to fuck Zack hard and fast.

Master Drew's grunts turned into a long groan, and he held himself deep inside of Zack.

A thrill raced through Zack when he imagined he felt the heat fill the condom. When the peak of his orgasm passed, Master Drew fucked into Zack to extend the last few seconds of bliss.

His Master collapsed on top of him, pinning Zack's aroused cock down to his stomach. The pressure was delicious. His cock was positioned in a way that if he rocked a little, he'd be capable of climax.

Don't come. Don't come. Don't come.

His body trembled with his pent-up lust. He remained still, awaiting permission, concentrating on the feeling of his neck being nibbled and teased.

His Master pulled his head back to smile down at Zack, causing butterflies to dance and flutter about. "Your restraint was admirable." Master stroked Zack's wet hair off his neck and face. "You need beautifully."

Tears pricked the back of his eyes. Fuck, Zack's control over his emotions vanished with a few choice words of praise. "Thank you, Master."

"Shall I untie you?" Master Drew slid out of him and tossed the condom into the waste bin near the bed.

Disappointment washed over him. Was the scene over? Was Master Drew going to make him continue to experience orgasm denial? He quivered with the concept. What had seemed like a very exciting idea hours ago sucked in his current reality.

Zack decided he rather liked orgasm delay, but orgasm denial, not so much.

By Master Drew's smirk, Zack realized his face broadcast his thoughts. "Or should I continue?"

"Continue," Zack blurted out. He quickly added, "Master." Frankly, he didn't care what Master Drew meant by continuing, just as long as he didn't stop. He wasn't ready to leave this place.

"Zack, I'm thirsty."

What? Now? A stab of desire passed through him at the idea of tending to his Master's simpler wants. Anything Drew needed, Zack wanted to provide. "Um, if you untie me, I can get you something." Though bottles of water were in the mini fridge in a nightstand cabinet only a few feet away from the bed.

A sexy smile crawled over his Master's lips. "I need *you* to quench my thirst."

What?

As the man slid down his body, he teased every part of Zack with his sexy slither. "I need to taste my pet's completion."

"Oh." The word squeaked out as if Zack had turned into a mouse. He only hoped his lust-addled brain was right about where his Master was going with this discussion.

Drew dipped his dark head of perfectly styled hair toward Zack's aroused cock. "You've done incredible today. You've earned the right to satisfy my need to drink you. Would you like to quench my thirst?"

Zack's cock was more than ready. "God, yeah. Please!"

His Master grinned. "Yes, that's what I want. I want you to beg me as I suck you off."

Hell yeah! He could do that. "Master Drew, please suck me off," Zack choked out, totally ready for the sweetest death ever.

"Try to hold back, so you can enjoy a little more buildup." After saying that, he lowered his head and licked the trail of wetness that seeped from the tip of Zack's cock. He backed off to add, "You've made me very happy. Come when you want, my sweet little sub."

My. Aw, that word touched Zack's empty places inside and filled them. He'd made Drew happy. That's all he'd ever wanted out of life. His cock pulsed, reminding him of something else he wanted at this moment.

"Yessssss," Zack hissed from a desperate place only hours of denial could locate.

His Master covered Zack's cock with his mouth. Slurping pulls of suction teased him. He slid his mouth farther down to envelop more of Zack's shaft.

Zack wanted to beg in a sexy way, but his brain was fried.

His Master started bobbing his head with purpose. No matter how manfully Zack tried to hold out, he couldn't stop the floodgates Drew opened with his sucking.

"Please." Zack's arousal had built into an inferno that Drew had stoked and ignited countless times. This time Zack wasn't going to be stopped. His Master was thirsty, and Zack's duty was to quench his Master's thirst.

Zack reached for his climax. It was impossible to catch his breath as his balls drew up tighter. His core started to tingle. The trembling sensations radiated through his belly and thighs.

The feeling no longer could be contained. Ecstasy chased up his body, and with thrusts of his hips, come shot out of his cock. Long waves of pleasure rocked him as his Master swallowed around him. Again and again his cock pulsated with spurts of his delayed climax that seemed to shake him forever.

He lay there in a daze.

Drew released the knots one at a time. The sliding of rope loosened up and freed Zack in a way he never wished to be liberated.

He drank from the bottle of water his Master held for him.

His Master. No never his.

Zack closed his eyes as Drew wrapped the covers around him.

Why couldn't he stay here forever? He wanted to remain locked at Master Drew's side.

Their forever was about to end all too soon. This was only a fantasy, not a key to the future.

CHAPTER FIFTEEN

ZACK PACED under the diner's awning a half hour before dawn in the drizzling rain. He glanced at his phone. How was it Tuesday?

Over. Devastated. Alone.

After he had left Andrew's condo on Monday morning, he'd wandered around, numb. Monday had slipped away into the night. Here he was at a diner in not the best part of town.

At least the weather was kind enough to match his mood. He dialed Jordon's cell.

"Zack? Where the hell have you been?" Jordon growled into the phone.

"Good morning to you, grumpy one!" Zack injected some happy into his voice.

"I'm not grumpy. I can't make the exact color I need…. Wait, where are you? What time is it?"

Zack pushed sweet into his voice. "Almost time for breakfast. I'm outside a diner. You're up working anyway. Meet me."

"Why can't we have breakfast here at home?"

He'd stoop to bribery. "I'll buy you breakfast."

"What's going on?" Jordon demanded.

"I need you to bring me some clothing." The request wouldn't allay worry or suspicion, but there was nothing to be done about it. He couldn't stand the idea of the weekend being over. If he could just avoid it a little longer, he could deal with the sinking feeling of loss threatening to overwhelm him.

"Why do you need clothing? Just come home and change. Can't we do lunch? I'm having trouble with this piece…."

"Jordy, please. I'm not going home yet and I need you to bring me some clothing and a few other things."

"Why? Why don't you come get them yourself?" With barely a breath, Jordon's questioning turned into conclusion-jumping. "Wait! Are you in trouble? You're in trouble? Oh my God! What did you do? Did you kill someone? Christ on a cupcake! My own brother on the lam, a fugitive from the law."

"What? No." Jesus, his brother's imagination scared him. Chuckling, he shook his head to try to follow Jordon's line of reasoning, getting lost quickly. "Insane much? I just need you to bring me a few things."

"Like your passport, right?"

"No! I don't need my passport." Zack checked his pocket to make sure he had his wallet. All he needed was his driver's license for ID. "Meet me."

"This piece is really…." Jordon became silent, and what sounded like paint being slapped onto canvas became louder.

No. No. No. Strangling him was out of the question because it would make Dusty even more pissed. Plus, a dead Jordon wouldn't be able to do his bidding. He couldn't lose his accomplice to his brother's art.

Zack groaned. "Jordy, please. I need your help."

His younger brother grumbled, "Fine. Why do I have a feeling you don't want me to mention our breakfast plans to Dusty?"

"'Cause you're the brightest crayon in the entire box."

"Dusty's going to kick my ass for this, isn't he?" The excitement that tinged the kid's voice was distressing. Damn, any little bit of intrigue…. Jordon needed more friends.

Zack rolled his eyes. "He won't. If he finds out, I'll tell him I swore you to secrecy."

Jordon muttered, signaling he'd caved to Zack's demands, "Well, he's gonna be pissed. See *I* knew you were fine, but *he* was worried."

Jordon believed his own faulty logic, which was scary, but Zack didn't have the energy to address it. "Yeah, sorry I worried anyone. Meet me."

"We expected you home yesterday. Where were you?"

He'd walked out of Drew's before dawn and into the city. He had spent some time in a coffeehouse and then went to several movies, back to back, at an all-night theater. Fuck if he remembered what he'd seen.

"I was around, Jordy. Please bring me a couple pairs of jeans, some T-shirts, and my chargers." He added, "And some aspirin."

"Sure." There was a slight pause. "Um…. Asshole came to the house yesterday."

"Don't call him that." Zack instantly defended Drew. What was he doing at the house? Fuck, he shouldn't ask. Ha, like he had a choice. "What happened?"

"That asshole barged into my room, demanding to know where *you* were." Jordon's infrequently used mean streak bled into his voice. "I told the fucker I wouldn't tell him even if I *did* know. The moron was covered in hickeys. What is he, twelve?"

Oops, Zack had left love bites on Andrew's neck, among other places, and no, he most certainly wasn't twelve.

Kneel—no! Not his.

"Please meet me," Zack pleaded again and gave Jordon the address. "I'll be there in thirty minutes."

Dammit. Jordon disconnected before Zack extracted any more information.

He wasn't going to worry if Master Drew—no, Andrew. Now and forever, he was back to Andrew, Justin's brother, not the Master of Zack's heart.

No, Zack wouldn't give two shits about Andrew being mad. He couldn't. *Fuck.* He yanked the finger he was gnawing on out of his mouth.

He stalked into the diner, sat down, and stared at the rain coming down in a steady drizzle. Must be a change of shift, because no one came over for quite a while. Finally he got a cup of bitter coffee.

His attention was drawn to two parking spots down from the front of the diner where a car barreled into the spot and parked halfway up on the sidewalk. Ah, good, Jordon had arrived.

Zack hugged Jordon when he ambled over and sagged back down into the ripped red patent-leather booth, which hadn't been renovated since the old run-down diner had opened. "So, tell me what happened."

"With what?" Jordon wrinkled his nose as he assessed their booth.

He handed Zack a filled duffel bag as he took three napkins out of the dented dispenser, sitting off center near the dirty window, and fastidiously wiped the crumbs off his side of the table. With a look of disgust, he tidied up Zack's side too. Probably the first time anyone had attempted to clean the table in hours, maybe days.

"You know *what*! Why did you piss *him* off?" Zack lowered his voice, but he didn't remove the growl.

Jordon snorted. "Ha, he was already pissed. Why is he looking for you? You look like shit."

Zack shrugged.

His brother wasn't stupid and wouldn't be distracted. "What the hell did he want with you?"

Zack sighed. "Nothing."

"Couldn't you pick anyplace else?" Jordon scanned the diner as if he were trying to figure out if they were about to get jumped by the man in the trench coat sitting at the corner table or the working girl flirting with the cook at the counter.

The kid pushed down a hood with little cat ears. Zack had given him the hoodie as a joke.

"What? This place is classic." Zack didn't really feel the need to defend the shit hole, but he hoped it might distract Jordon enough so he wouldn't ask about all the bullshit.

Jordon glanced around with a grimace. "Classic what?"

He gestured at Jordon's getup. "You do realize I didn't give you the hoodie to actually wear, right?"

Zack had seen the stupid brown hooded sweatshirt with the artistically drawn lines mimicking fur in a teenybopper shop at the mall. The damned cat hoodie came complete with tail and paw mittens. The tail hanging off the back was a mix of white and brown faux fur. The hood was the most comical part of all with its little kitty-cat ears.

"What? I adore this hoodie." Jordon smirked as he unzipped his cat jacket, exposing a black shirt with a big rainbow on it. The lettering under it spelled out *It's okay. I'm Gay.* Zack should know better by now. Every joke present he'd ever given Jordon, his kid brother actually found a use for and enjoyed every one of them to spite Zack. There was a string of bass holiday lights strung around his room year-round, adding even more quirkiness to his artist space. The kid actually used the noodle-cooling fan whenever he ate wonton soup. He used every one of those bacon-scented Band-Aids. Zack didn't want to think of what Jordon had done with the umbrellas that attached to shoes.

"So, come on, enough stalling. Tell me what the hell happened." Damn, the kid wasn't taking the bait. It was impressive how Jordon appeared solemn in a cat hoodie. He leaned back with his arms folded.

"Nothing." Zack inhaled and slowly exhaled. An ice pick stabbed him in the gut.

When Jordon didn't make a sound or a move, Zack mistakenly glanced at his brother. *Fuck.* The kid had the same stubborn streak peeking through as he had when the time had come for bratty seven-year-old brothers to be in bed. Dusty had always been able to deal with the kid, but Zack was defenseless.

The seventy-year-old waitress strolled over in her faded uniform, holding a pot of burned coffee. "What can I get you boys?"

"May I have hot chocolate, please?" Jordon requested in a soft, sugary voice.

"Aw, of course, honey, and since you're so polite, I'll give you extra whipped cream."

Zack almost laughed when Jordon bounced happily in his seat. The imp vibrated with excitement about getting a treat for behaving. "Thank you, ma'am."

Jordon's charm won Zack a refill of the mud that passed for coffee before she tottered away.

"What's with the collar?"

Zack ran his fingers up to the circle of leather. He'd left it on. *Not his.*

Zack wanted to feel taken and possessed just a little longer by Drew. Yeah, it was an unhealthy thing, but fuck it. He shut his eyes for a moment and savored the feel of smooth leather.

"Just fucking spit it out. Does any of this have to do with *that* club?"

"What club?" *Shit!* How did Jordon know about Entwined?

The kid huffed out his breath and then lowered his voice. "You know, that sex club you go to." Jordon smirked. "Didn't think I knew, huh?"

"I, um…." Zack had confessed his interests to Dusty on the night his mother kicked him out, but he'd never talked about it to Jordon. Hell, he'd successfully avoided any and all other conversations when Dusty tried to discuss the subject with him. There were certain things he refused to share with his brothers.

With a wave of his hand, Jordon demanded, "Save it. I don't care what you do to get off as long as you don't get hurt." Immediately, he leaned forward across the semi-crumb-free table. "Did he hurt you? You know, in like a bad way?"

Zack shook his head. "He wouldn't do that."

"So, he hurt you like…." Blushing, Jordon struggled to get the words out. He twirled the cat tail that was attached to the hoodie. "Like… you know, how you want to be hurt?"

How the hell could he explain this to his little brother? "It's not like I want to…."

Jordon slapped his tail on the table with the conversation. "I don't need the details, Zack."

The waitress returned with a mug of hot chocolate with a huge head of whipped cream.

Jordon batted his eyelashes. "Thank you." Once she shuffled back to the counter and was out of earshot, he hissed, "Well…?"

"Okay. So what the hell do you want me to say?" When was the last time he'd slept? Not since he curled up around his… around Drew—Andrew. He was too exhausted to sleep.

"I want you to tell me why the fuck you're in love with him?"

Well, that cut right to the heart of the matter. It wasn't as if there had been a choice. Zack loving Andrew was as essential as breathing.

Zack didn't meet his brother's eyes and tried to swallow the bitter swill. How to explain something he didn't understand himself? "It's everything about him. I can't… not." Fuck it all. That was as close as he'd ever come to admitting the depth of his emotion. "I've tried."

Jordon remained silent. He stared off into space, then with a nod, he asked, "So what happened? You look horrible."

"Thanks." Zack tried to make light, but his voice cracked, killing the attempt at humor on the vine. He pulled a napkin from the dispenser and started ripping the cheap paper into strips as he summed up his trauma in as few words and as vague of details as possible. "I spent the weekend with him."

Jordon's green eyes appeared as if they were going to pop out of his head. "What? OMG! How was it?"

Great. Amazing. Incredible. "Fine."

Jordon snorted, then nodded. "So the weekend was wonderful, but Monday came, and you were like, 'Later, dude'?"

Zack shook his head. "No, of course not."

"Fuckhead asked you to leave?" Jordon demanded, and he appeared to self-soothe with a sip of his hot chocolate.

"Um, no."

Jordon growled, "He told you he doesn't want to see you again?"

"Well, no…."

"No? If you love the asshole and he didn't tell you to go, then why…?" Jordon stopped talking and his mouth dropped open, then he shook his head, trying to piece together the puzzle of Zack's love life. "You did it with him and then left? Hit it and quit it? Oh! Was he that *bad*?" Jordon sounded somehow pleased with the concept of Andrew being a lousy lover. He picked up his cat tail and caressed the end over his face.

"No! Argh! If you must know, I left before he woke up."

"You *what*?" Jordon slapped the tail down on the table like a gavel.

Zack folded his arms and said, "I didn't want to hear him tell me that since the weekend was over—"

"So you left before he told you anything?" Jordon's words made what he did sound bad.

"Well...."

His brother fell back against his side of the booth. "You're an idiot. No wonder he's pissed."

"I, um...." Zack needed sleep, and then maybe he could think of a defense or, hell, even just have a coherent thought.

Jordon slapped the hoodie tail on the table again. "He's not the fuckhead—you are."

"Hey. We agreed to the weekend. I stuck to the contract the club had us sign." Zack certainly hadn't signed up to have his dreams crushed again. If anyone was going to shatter the illusion he'd allowed himself for the weekend, it was going to be him.

"Contract? Club? I don't wanna know. You don't think he wanted more?" Jordon tilted his head and squinted at him.

No. Maybe? No, of course not.

Zack shook his head. "Doubt it. I didn't want to deal with his rejection." *Again* went unsaid.

"Jesus, you fucked him, then fled the scene. Did you drop a hundred on the nightstand before you left?" Jordon didn't wait for a response before he drew his cell out of his front pocket to start dialing.

Zack's heart pounded and demanded, "Who are you calling?"

The kid put up an index finger to silence him. "May I have a reservation for Jordon Davis. Thank you. Checking in today and checking out...." Jordon met Zack's eyes for the answer.

"Wednesday," Zack mouthed.

"Wednesday. Yes, one night." Jordon took care of the rest of the details, including giving his credit card information so Zack couldn't be traced by anyone.

He owed the kid for his creative thinking. "Thank you."

"You're welcome. You know my therapist would call this avoidance but I'm hoping that it will give you enough time to pull your head out of your ass. But, you should talk to the asshole and deal with this bullshittery once and for all." Jordon grabbed a napkin and began to doodle with his multicolored pen.

Why did that idea make him feel like he was staring into an abyss? Admitting it was done… there'd be nothing left. He couldn't.

Zack shook his head. "I can't. Not yet, Jordy." He didn't know how to explain his desire to hold on to the dream that somehow Andrew wanted him for a bit longer. It was childish, but the weekend had been so much more than even he'd imagined—he just couldn't let go yet.

"One of the things I do is assume the worst. After all, Mom kicked me out. My therapist said I would rather deny myself happiness than risk rejection. Maybe it's like that for you?"

Running his fingers through his hair, Zack shook his head. Though his mom threw him out too and Andrew rejected him once before and…. "No. It doesn't sound… I don't know. Maybe…." He tugged on his hair, wishing it would help him think.

"Okay, fine, enough therapy for today. Please text Dusty and tell him you're okay," Jordon commanded, then ignored him in favor of his drawing.

Zack texted Dusty and Justin. *Sorry. I'm fine.*

Immediately, texts came in from both of them. *R U OK?*

I'm not doing anything crazy. Just needed some time to get my head on straight, he texted back.

His brother jumped and gathered his pen. He leaned forward and whispered, "Let's get breakfast at the hotel."

"Why?"

"I think I just saw a roach." Jordon slid out from the booth slowly, grimacing at the floor under the table.

This place might be less of a hideout and more of a dump than Zack originally thought. "Sure. Let's go."

Jordon left the napkin he drew on under the ten Zack put on the table. Examining the napkin made Zack's breath catch. The picture was beyond perfect.

On the square was a dragon with a long twining tail, and a master padlock dangled in one talon. Even though the drawing had been done as a pen sketch, Zack easily imagined the blues and greens of the scales shining in iridescence and the gold lock with the word MASTER embossed on it. With a few alterations, this would make the perfect tattoo. He slipped the napkin into his pocket.

Jordon shifted from foot to foot impatiently at the door. "I don't see your car."

"Left it at the club."

"Is that safe? You want me to swing by so you can pick it up?"

No! His heart couldn't handle being at Entwined. He didn't want to go anywhere near that side of town. "Nah, you can drive us to the hotel. I'll leave the car in the lot. There's round-the-clock security in the parking lot."

Jordon frowned with a scrunched-up face but shrugged and didn't question him further.

Zack folded himself into Jordon's toy car and couldn't stop the complaint wrapped in a suggestion. "Next time you should get a four-door."

Jordon turned the key, and music exploded from the speakers.

Zack turned down the volume. Latching on to safe conversation, he asked, "Who's this?" His brother always found obscure groups from all over the world. Zack tried to discern if it was a male or female singing. Jordon's bootleg copy was terrible.

"It's a new group. They're freaking awesome. Wait, wait… listen." Jordon pointed to the stereo control panel as if he cued the singer's voice to tremble and rise dramatically, then fall to low notes. Jordon navigated from the curb with a minimum of scrapeage to his Volkswagen Beetle.

"She's good." Zack made sure his seat belt was fastened.

"The singer's a he. And oh my God, he's beautiful, gorgeous, sexy, a bit androgynous, but he's all he." Jordon's little gush made his cheeks go pink.

This deserved some brotherly attention. "Jordon's got a boyfriend. Jordon's got a boyfriend," Zack teased in a singsong voice.

"Stop it." Jordon shook his head, glaring at the road in front of him.

When he stopped singing, Zack was impressed. He didn't want to admit it, but the music was good if you got past the poor audio quality.

He had to ask, "So, where'd you find these guys?"

"Well, I watched some videos on Youku and…."

"You what?" Zack chuckled.

"Shut up!" Jordon reached over to whack him on the arm. "It's China's version of something like a censored YouTube."

"What's the band your new boyfriend sings with?"

"Stop! He is not my boyfriend," Jordon insisted, getting a tad pissy.

Finding some energy, Zack rolled his eyes. "Touchy little thing, ain't you?"

"Well, you know I don't have a boyfriend." The kid's laughter had a brittle and bitter quality that worried Zack as he continued his little rant. "I've never had a boyfriend! And I probably never freaking will…. Okay? So, he's not my damned boyfriend."

"Hey, easy there, baby kitty." Zack reached out and squeezed Jordon's shoulder.

"I'm not a pussy." Jordon giggled, chasing away most of the upset. "Just 'cause I have a tail and cat ears doesn't mean you have the right to label me."

Zack snorted out a laugh as the song ended. Another replaced it with a different style but just as catchy. "They're good."

"They're in Suzhou, China. They don't even have a demo yet. Apparently, some high school kid doing a school project uploaded a music video he made with them. It went viral."

"Why didn't I hear about it?" Zack tried to stay on top of musical trends.

Jordon shrugged. "Fine, it was more of a localized fever than viral. But they're great."

Zack listened to another song. They were good.

Jordon pointed to the radio. "Listen to the drum solo on this track."

"Damn. He'd give Dusty a run for his money."

Jordon grinned. "I don't think we should point out that the drummer's around your age." The kid returned to mouthing the words. He stopped to gesture wildly to the stereo to ensure the end of the song had Zack's attention. "You hear the voice? Did you hear how he vibrates the end of his notes? It's awesome."

"How long have these guys been around?"

"I don't know. I've been digging for information, but it's like searching a cyber void. Did you know China doesn't even allow Facebook?"

"That sucks." Zack hoped he said it with enough vehemence to make Jordon feel validated, but right now he didn't give a shit.

Jordon turned into the hotel parking lot. Once the kid checked him in, they sat down to breakfast. He sipped his black coffee while Jordon tucked into a big stack of pancakes, sausage patties—not links because the kid refused to eat the sausage skin—and a big glass of milk. Jordon even charmed the waitress into giving him a glass of half and half: half orange juice and half cranberry juice.

"It's good. You want some?" Jordon held out a fork to try to tempt him.

"Nah."

"You got to eat."

"I will. Later." When the kid's eyes widened—*oh shit*, he was definitely gearing up to lecture—Zack cut him off. "I promise. I'll eat later. I don't feel like it now."

He barely held himself together. Christ, he wanted to sleep for a week.

Jordon surveyed him and shoveled a "perfect bite" into his mouth. The perfect bite was developed and now defined as two pancake triangles with the right amount of syrup and a bit of sausage on the top.

Jordon chewed and swallowed before stating the obvious. "You miss him?"

The loss would have to subside at some point. Staring at Jordon was the only answer Zack mustered up.

"So what the hell are you going to do?"

"Sleep for a year. Focus on work." Zack shrugged.

Jordon continued to construct perfect bites. On a better day, Zack might have enjoyed watching Jordon's careful rationing of the sausage patties so he'd have enough for each mouthful.

Enough? Zack would never have enough of Andrew. He picked up his coffee and gulped some down. *Ow!* He wasn't paying attention. When did the waitress refill his cup? He didn't really need his taste buds.

"So, what's it like?"

Zack shook his head to clear thoughts of his Master. "What's what like?"

"Being with someone?" Jordon's light skin betrayed him by tinting his cheeks a deep pink. "You've been with other people, not only him, right?"

"Yeah." Staring at his brother, Zack realized he wasn't really a little kid. Jordon was an adult. Zack and Dusty should stop treating him like a preteen.

"How many?"

He rolled his eyes. "I don't know. Some."

"If you use more than one hand, that's a lot." Jordon pinned him with a stare. "Do you, you know, take them to the dungeon?"

"Mostly." *All*, except....

Jordon gasped and fanned a hand in front of his face, doing a good imitation of a horrified maiden about to swoon with the vapors.

Zack dismissed the idea with a wave of his hand. "It's not a big deal."

"Not a big deal?" The expression of shock reminded him that his brother didn't have much, if any, experience, and Zack shouldn't be callous.

"Okay, look, I don't mean it like that. It's a big deal. Usually the scene doesn't go that far."

Jordon pushed his plate away from him. "I mean, what do you do?"

"Do you want to know?" Praying the answer would be no, Zack waited.

"No. Yes." Jordon paused and shook his head. "No." He picked up his cat tail and played with it. "Tell me, was it different with him?"

His. Love. Forever.

A memory whip-sliced Zack open. "Yeah. It was… very different. With him… I don't know. I was able to just be me."

Kneel. Serve. Love.

Jordon pursed his lips. If Zack listened closely, he could probably hear a sucking sound of the kid's brain absorbing the information. "So, with the others, you weren't yourself?"

"I focused on their needs. With him… I could just let everything happen."

How was he ever going to let Drew go now? Fuck, he'd been an idiot. There was nothing to let go.

"So, he just did what he wanted to you?"

"No. He did what *I* wanted. He gave me what I craved." Zack dropped his face into his hands. "I don't know what I'm going to do, Jordy."

There was silence. Jordon slid to sit beside him in the booth. The kid wrapped an arm around Zack's shoulder and hugged him tight. "You know what you're going to do?"

"What?" The serious determination on his brother's face was a little disconcerting from someone Zack had viewed as too young to know how to impart advice.

"First, you're gonna get your head out of your ass. Get some sleep, because you look like shit. Then eat and man the hell up, find Andrew, and apologize. Beg if you have to. Because *you* screwed up."

His brother's words were like a slap to the head. "What if he doesn't want me?"

"Then at least you'll know."

That was the point. He didn't want to know.

CHAPTER SIXTEEN

SHIT! THE kid had been right. After no sleep for almost thirty-six hours, Zack collapsed into the hotel bed and slept. He slumbered through the afternoon and into the next morning.

Dreams had plagued him with what he'd in all likelihood never have again.

The weekend had changed him. He could never go back. He needed to keep the experience with him. It was vital he cherish the moments of when he'd had the Master he'd always wanted.

Zack pulled out the napkin Jordon had drawn on and studied the picture. He shouldn't go and get a tattoo. Perhaps doing it could be seen as a tad psycho.

Fuck it! His whole world had tipped upside down. He needed to do this for himself. But first, he required a shower and food.

The tattoo parlor his buddy worked at was only a few blocks from the hotel. He called Marcus and made an appointment.

On the walk over, Zack tried to enjoy the sunshine, but his head was too full of what-ifs to fully appreciate the break in the frigid weather.

"Hey, Marcus." He waved to the tall man in blue jeans and a T-shirt that said *You Say Sadist Like It's a Bad Thing*. The guy's face lit up as he made his way through the obstacle course of the tattoo parlor's lobby to give Zack a big bear hug. "How are you doing, man?"

"Fine. Fine. You?" Marcus's deep baritone soothed Zack's nerves.

"Okay. Thanks for coming in early for me."

"No problem. Soooooo?" Marcus examined him closely. "Well? How did the weekend go? I saw who won you."

"It was...." What could he say? It had been everything, and he wasn't able to let it go.

"Holy fuck! Really?" The jackass had always been way too perceptive.

"What?" Not hiding his defensiveness, Zack dared him to verbalize the shit going on in his head.

Marcus shook his head. "How did I not know this about you? I thought we were friends."

"What are you going on about?" Zack meandered over to the binders of tattoos.

"I don't know why I didn't see your nature when we played together."

Marcus was always a safe bet when subs wanted to play with two Doms. They balanced each other well. Being a sadist, Marcus handled the more pain-oriented part of the scenes, and Zack focused on the lighter aspects.

When the scenes ended and the subs had all returned to earth, he and Marcus usually would go get a bite to eat. Their place of choice was an all-night diner near Entwined. The eatery was far enough away that other members weren't there to bear witness as they indulged in greasy foods no one would go near unless courting a heart attack.

The artist followed him to the binders. "So, whatcha thinking about getting on your virgin skin?"

"I'm looking for something like this." He handed Marcus the white scrap. The man specialized in small, intricate designs.

Marcus stared at the rough sketch. "Your brother's work?" His fingers traced the lines with such reverence. He was likely memorizing the details of each stroke.

"Yeah."

"The kid's got flare." Marcus lifted his eyes from the art. "Where'd you want this?"

Zack held out his right arm and traced a space on the inside of his forearm, just above his wrist. "Right about here."

Nodding, Marcus asked, "Any adjustments you want?"

"Yeah. I want the dragon's body and tail to be curled around the letters *D*, *R*, *E*, and *W*. I want the letters to be somewhat hidden." He paused before adding, "But if you look closely, you'll be able to see them." He'd keep the finished design covered mostly.

"Okay. Here's the consent form."

Zack read the basic release and signed at the bottom.

"Have a seat." Marcus resketched the picture with the additions of the letters for Zack's approval. "How's this?"

"Yes, exactly. That's great."

Marcus busied himself with the tattooing tools and inks. He flipped on some new age shit. Zack supposed the music helped to relax the clients.

Settling into the leather chair, Zack stared at the textured black walls before tilting his head back to study the patterns of the vivid tie-dye painted ceiling.

"The dragon will be about this size and will go from here to here. Not much hair, so I don't have to shave it." Marcus traced the pattern with his finger. He washed the area with a green soap. "So, Andrew must be pretty amazing…." Marcus held Zack's arm and strapped it down to the armrest.

Zack bit back a moan as Marcus pulled on the leather strap, securing it with a buckle. Closing his eyes against the memory of Drew's restraints, he rested his head against the cushioned chair back and tried to get a grip on the emotions threatening to overwhelm him. Affection, joy, need, and arousal all vied for top position in Zack's head.

"You like that?" Marcus asked with an amused smile.

"Fuck you." Zack tried to mask his embarrassment with what he hoped was an annoyed expression. There was no escaping the fact. He was being secured to mark himself with the symbol of the Master of his heart.

"Ha! We never did that. No need to ruin a good friendship with a messy exchange of fluids. Though…." Marcus fiddled with the leather, pulled, and then refastened the strap to make it a tad tighter.

"Sadist," Zack complained. Bastard probably did it to hear Zack moan.

"Yup, with a streak of masochism," Marcus snarked. He turned back to finish preparing the machine and inks before giving him an arched eyebrow as he snapped on purple surgical gloves. "Had I known you were just behaviorally a Dom…." The man cleaned the area and started the outline of the dragon.

Zack gave him an expression of mock horror. "What? You'd have tried to turn me into your own personal pincushion with play piercings?"

Marcus grinned. "Definitely and maybe we could have played with—"

"No." The word squeaked out, and it had nothing to do with the process of ink being poked into his skin. He couldn't let there be any misunderstanding. "Only with him…. Drew's the only one. He's…." *Everything*. The soft hum of the machine was calming, and the little needle jabs were enticing. He stared at his friend, hoping he'd fill in the blanks.

"Only for Andrew, hmmm. Well, the plot doth thicken, my friend. Tell me what happened. And let's skip the part where you tell me 'nothing'...." Marcus wiped a medicinal-smelling solution over the beginnings of the design cut into Zack's arm.

Zack closed his eyes to defocus and settle into the pain. Needle sticks, swipes of the cloth, and the whir of the machine allowed him to pour out the details of his weekend to his friend. The pain seemed to operate his mouth and spill out his innermost secrets. Maybe there was something to needle play.

Marcus pulled the tattoo machine back to wipe the soft cloth against Zack's skin. "How long did he keep you on edge?"

A flush of heat spread over Zack's body as he relived the hours of torture and ecstasy. Drew had edged him without mercy.

The memory made him achy. Why couldn't his cock have responded as it usually did in his morning shower? Now was not the time to get hot and bothered.

"Mmmmm." The delicious agony took him by surprise as Marcus continued his work. His wrist caught on fire before the burn turned into something else entirely. "He kept me on the cusp for hours, I guess...." He recalled the sexy torture Andrew had put him through. "Most of the day and into the evening."

"You lost track of time?" Marcus's envy bled into his voice.

"Yeah."

The whir of the needle pricks blended together, making the pain morph into deliciousness as it merged. The pain turned into a sensual throb.

"So, where'd you guys leave it?"

Zack's ears were still ringing from Jordon's tirade. He refused to give someone else the excuse to call him all kinds of stupid. He needed a little space to figure out what he should be doing. "It was only a weekend thing. You know, the auction was for a temporary contract... nothing more."

"Just a weekend thing. Right. Yeah, after a hookup, this is the sane thing to do?"

Zack opened his eyes. "What?"

"Dude, you're getting his name inked on your body! Well, don't worry if you want to change this in the future, the design allows for that."

Zack bit back that he'd never want to change the tattoo. He changed the subject. "So why are you panting as you torment me?"

"I enjoy my job." He pointed to his T-shirt. "Need I say more?"

Zack chuckled and switched subjects again. "How's Hunter?"

"*Fine*." The tough tattooed man sighed like an eighth grader, rolling eyes and all. Marcus and Hunter had been in an open relationship with each other for almost six years. They were the poster couple of BDSM happiness.

"But…?" Zack hoped there wasn't trouble in paradise.

"As you know, he isn't into pain or needle play, and as masochistic as I am, I don't play sub all that well." Marcus stopped tattooing to wipe the droplets of blood away. "How's that look to you?"

The dragon's tail scrolled perfectly around Drew's name. The details of the lock were amazing in spite of the size of the tattoo, but the word *Master* could be clearly read.

"Fantastic."

"I should color the dragon with blues, purples, and a hint of green. The lock will be gold and the letters a muted red, almost pink. I want to make sure all the colors of the rainbow will be represented. Needs to be balanced."

"You sound like Jordon." Zack regarded his friend with the same tenderness he afforded his brother. Marcus was a lot like Jordon. Huh. Wonder why he hadn't noticed that before? Diligently prepping the colors, Marcus's attention seemed divided between his task and something else. "So, Hunter's not willing to try needle play?"

"Yeah. Oh, the man's prepared to do whatever makes me happy, but he's a paramedic. His work life gives needles a different definition than mine. And you know there's a difference between having a craving and wanting to make your lover happy."

Kneel. Serve. His.

A shiver of that kind of yearning stole through Zack as his longing to give Drew everything flooded him. He'd gladly suffer for him. "But that's one of the reasons you two have an open relationship."

"Look, he'll do anything, but he's dominant. He wants to orchestrate the scene. Boyfriend's just a bossy boss who needs someone craving his guidance and instructions." Marcus kept up the slow, steady pace of coloring the iridescent scales of the dragon. "He doesn't find many play partners. I think we should find a third to bridge the gap." He pulled the gun back to soothe the abused skin with the cloth.

"You'd be comfortable with a permanent third?" Zack tried to keep judgment out of his voice. He wouldn't condemn. The concept of sharing didn't bother him, but adding another partner *permanently*, that was some serious shit. A third had appeal, but not on a regular basis.

"I don't know. It feels like we both have part of ourselves that is shut off. I want someone to ache to accept the pain I want to share with them. That's hard to find with random play partners. I want someone who needs to serve Hunter and I the way you clearly need to give yourself to Andrew."

"I—"

"Oh, for fuck's sake, you can say it was a weekend-stand, but here I am tattooing his name on you. Are you delusional or just an idiot?"

"Fuck you." Avoiding the topic, Zack returned to his friend's drama. "Would Hunter want a third?" The lull of the machine as the needle danced over his skin started to feel good. His endorphins must be kicking into high gear. He closed his eyes to enjoy the rush.

"Hunt says no, but I know I'm not meeting his needs, and with his schedule, it's harder for him to find play partners. I love him and want him happy." Marcus's stare saw far too much. "Fuck, you really have the potential to be a pain slut."

Unable to deny the pleasure he found in pain, Zack cracked open one eye and asked, "Your point?"

On a quick inhale, Marcus shook his head and focused on his work. Zack shut his eyes and relaxed into the soft burn. Certain areas on his wrist were more sensitive, so the sensation was sharper, giving him more direct stimulation. Crazy as it was, each needle seemed like a caress on his cock. He endured the pain so he might wear a reminder of all that would never be.

Fuck, he was horny? Again and again the needle pricked him. All this insertion aroused him. He needed to come. His cock throbbed in time with the ticks of the wall clock, counterbalanced by the needle pricks.

Marcus wiped the colorful image again and stared at the dragon, as if it was telling him something. "Sub drop? That's what happened, huh?"

"What?"

"Waking up from the intense weekend, you crashed in a major way, freaked, and I bet you took off."

Shaking his head, Zack wanted to deny the explanation.

"I didn't run. I simply left."

"You were sad and depressed, so instead of turning to him, you escaped into a dark melancholy of bad decisions." Marcus continued to work more shadows and color into the tiny masterpiece. "How many times have you been there to help a sub find equal footing after you've played with them? It's part of your role as a Dominant, but by cutting bait the way you did, you denied him his responsibility."

Zack dropped his head forward. "I'd be a lousy sub in every sense of the word. If Drew—Andrew *had* ever wanted me... my inferior display would have turned him off."

"Dramatic much? You'd be a fine sub," Marcus commented, drawing Zack back from the land of self-pity to give Marcus a doubtful snort. "Think about it. As a Master, you aren't looking for perfection but for someone you can help grow and whom you can grow with...."

"He rejected me once already. I don't want to go through that humiliation again." To answer Marcus's unasked question, he finished, "Said I was too young."

"When was this?" Marcus looked up from his work.

No one from Entwined was aware of Zack's embarrassing habit of crushing hard on Andrew. He tried not to smile, but he lost the battle. "When I was too young."

Marcus snorted out a laugh. "Asshole, you're not too young now." The artist kept the pricks of color moving across the image. "You're marking yourself as his."

Zack inspected the picture that did exactly that. His heart would shatter further if Andrew rejected him again, but he did have to know. Sub drop or not, he'd behaved poorly by running away.

Master Drew should spank him. God, he hoped he'd spank him. Hard.

A particularly sensitive area was being colored in, the pain compounding his need to accept a punishment.

Marcus's raised eyebrow meant he'd noticed Zack's reaction. The fucker slowed the process. Again and again, darts of torturous pleasure shot through his wrist. Christ, the sensation landed as the pain transformed into a suck on his cock. He shifted in the chair, trying to be subtle, but Marcus's knowing smirk confirmed his failure. *Bastard!*

"Oh." He couldn't hold in the gasp or the shiver that followed.

"Hurts, huh?" Marcus stared at him with interest. "You want it to hurt, don't you? You want to suffer for him."

"Yes." If it weren't for the leather straps holding his arm secure, Zack would have pushed toward the pain. An insane need, but he wanted to experience every bite of agony as deeply as possible.

Pain. Deserve. His.

The torment linked him to his Master, his yearning to submit, and his hope that Andrew would want him. Now, even if Andrew didn't want him, he'd always have a memento of their time together. No one could take his declaration away from him.

"More." Zack breathed through his nose, trying to get a grip.

"Imagine his reaction to your tat. Although, it's the ultimate in topping from the bottom, huh?" Marcus chuckled at Zack squirming against the leather. "Glad I have you strapped down. You'd have made me fuck up for sure." The man glided the cloth over the picture. "You really need a Master to control your unruly behavior."

Zack closed his eyes and tried not to let a whimper escape.

"Andrew should punish you." Marcus's voice remained light and teasing, but his tone suggested he purposefully fed Zack's need.

"Don't." Zack sounded pathetic and whiny, and he didn't care.

"I'm not the one three strokes away from coming."

"Fuck you. You know you're getting off on making me hurt."

Marcus stopped, grinned, and pointed to his T-shirt again. He ducked back down under the light to work on some shading and highlights. "Question is, would Master Andrew let his horny little sub get his slut on in an ink shop?"

If Master Drew was there, he'd bend Zack over the table to take his ass, or even better, he'd spank him, then have him. He'd take full advantage of the endorphins moving through his sub. They'd have to be quiet because there might be people in the lobby and only a thin door separating them from exposure.

Zack groaned. *Cocksucker!* Damn, he needed release; he barely stopped from wiggling in the chair. Marcus was almost done. Zack wanted what he was sure his Master would give him. He tried not to squirm in his seat and waited for the process to end.

Finally Marcus disinfected the inked area and covered it with a clear wrap. "This needs to stay on for an hour."

"Can I... um." Fuck, was Zack really going to ask to do this here? His cock throbbed angrily, leaving him no choice. He gestured to his tented jeans.

Marcus folded his arms and smirked. "Sure, no one else is here…
if you think Andrew would *let* you.…" He adjusted the front of his
pants. "Afterward, I've got no other appointments, so if you want to grab
something to eat.…"

"Yeah."

"I'll get you some after-care instructions and cream to keep it
moist." Marcus's words were professional but the tone mocked the hell
out of Zack. If he wasn't so horny, maybe he might have cared. Maybe
this was the best treatment available for sub drop…

As soon as the door was shut and locked, Zack plopped back in the
chair. With shaking fingers he unzipped to allow his cock the space he
craved. He spit into his hand and captured his dick. Clamping his mouth
shut to silence the moan of relief, he stroked himself. The movement
pulled at the bandage, but it was incredible. Fuck, this wasn't going to
take long.

He imagined Master Drew praising him for enduring the pain of
his mark so well. Oh, he had. Drew's imaginary fingers combed through
Zack's hair, and his other hand caressed Zack's stomach.

Zack fantasized about his Master running a hand up and down his
torso as he stroked himself to paradise. Drew toyed with Zack's nipples
and squeezed. His Master's breath teased Zack's ear.

"Come," the memory of Andrew's voice commanded him.

Fuck, yeah! Ecstasy rolled through him as he tugged on his
throbbing cock. He erupted all over his T-shirt, but the release was a
necessity, so he didn't even give a shit.

In Zack's mind, Andrew whispered praise for his performance in
following directions, as if he could have done anything else.

He grabbed one of Marcus's clean cloths and wiped away the
sticky mess he'd made. Hmmm, would Drew have allowed him to come?
Where was his Master? What was he doing?

CHAPTER SEVENTEEN

WHY THE hell did Zack take off? Maybe once Zack had had Andrew, he was done. Or perhaps something bad had happened to him. Andrew should check the hospitals again. Possibly Zack didn't feel the same. Or maybe his brat simply ran away. Maybe he was scared. Was he lying hurt in a ditch?

Why the fuck hadn't Andrew followed his instincts and talked to him Sunday night? He should have woken Zack, but he lay there smiling and lightly snoring. He'd worked his pet hard, and the poor thing had been wrung out.

Andrew had done that. He'd flown high on Zack's total trust and surrender. Even sick, he could meet all of Zack's needs.

If that was the case, where was his pet? "Fuck!"

"Come out, come out wherever you are, my sweet little pet." Andrew circled back through the circuit of Zack's usual hangouts, but once again, no Zack.

What if Zack hadn't wanted more? Maybe he left to avoid a scene. That would explain him not answering his cell.

"Fuck!" Andrew pounded the steering wheel several times, as if that had the power to make Zack appear. Gripping his abused hand, he shouted again, "Dammit! That hurt."

He hadn't slept since he'd woken up late on Monday morning to a deserted bed and an empty home. All the sex combined with medications had put him into a deep sleep.

It was Tuesday now and close to midnight, but he found himself back at his brother's gated community. He punched his brother's number into the security callbox.

"Hello?" Justin yawned.

"Hey."

"You okay?"

"No." Andrew was honest to a fault at times.

"You didn't answer your phone!"

"What?" He pulled out a completely discharged phone. "Goddammit! It's dead."

"Meet me in the kitchen. I'll make you some tea."

"Okay." The black wrought iron gate swung open, and he drove to the house Justin shared with his lover, Jordon, and Zack. The modern design of the house cast creepy shadows across the driveway.

He got out of his car and stretched. *Ow!* Damn, he'd been sitting for a while. Trudging through the wet grass, he kicked a few misplaced stones back into the rock beds. Marching around the side of the house and up the back stairs, he used the sparkly tie-dyed key Justin had given him and opened the kitchen door.

His brother turned away from the sink, holding two mugs of tea. "You let your cell discharge? How is that even possible?"

"I don't know." He really didn't. Nothing made sense and everything was out of order.

"You look like shit."

"Thank you and you need a haircut." Guilt swamped Andrew as his brother self-consciously touched his hair. "Sorry, I can trim it tomorrow."

"It's fine." Justin asked, "So what's going on?"

"Have you heard from him yet?" Andrew trailed his brother into the morning room. The room was filled with sunshine-loving fern and ivy, which Zack tended. Hands down, during the day, this was his favorite room of his brother's weirdly angled house. But now only the Murano glass fixture lit the room. He sagged into the padded chair Justin kicked out to him.

"I left a message right after he called this morning. You didn't get the message? Zack's okay."

"What? He is?" Andrew was on his feet. "Where is he? He's okay? Is he here?"

"Sit. Zack's fine. No, he's not here, and we don't know where he is. Dusty even tried to track him through his credit cards, but that's not legal to do. He texted us."

"But he's okay?"

"Yes."

He pushed away the disappointment that Zack had contacted his brothers but not him. Or maybe he did? Glaring at his cell, he wondered if he even wanted confirmation. He didn't know when his phone died because he was pretty sure he never turned the alerts and ringer back on.

Focus! The important thing was Zack was fine… or at least was at the time of the phone call. "Can I use your landline?"

"Of course. But his phone must be powered off."

Andrew dialed and when his call went directly to voice mail, he didn't leave a message. He needed to—

"Have some tea." His brother pushed a cup closer to him.

Sipping his herbal tea, he stared at the darkened windows covered almost entirely by the jungle of green.

"Have you slept?"

Andrew could lie, but what would be the point? He shook his head and drank more tea.

"So you going to tell me what happened?"

"Where's Dusty?" Andrew opted for stalling.

"The band had practice, and then they needed to go to dinner with some investors." Turning toward the clock, Justin smiled. "Chances are, he became the designated driver. Jordon and I have a deadline coming up, so I stayed here to finish the storyline." Taking a sip of tea, he returned to the original question. "What happened?"

"I told you I'd win him at the auction. I did. We had an amazing weekend, and then he vanished come Monday."

Justin set down his mug, which depicted one of his romance novels. Andrew studied his mug and realized it was a depiction of one of the Dark Angels' manga. "What did he say?"

"Nothing, he left before I got up." Andrew sipped more tea and avoided Justin's eyes.

His brother scratched his head. "That doesn't make sense. He's been in love with you for years."

"Yeah right." Andrew couldn't keep the disbelief out of his voice. Justin didn't know how many admirers Zack had.

Justin scoffed, waving him off, and sipped his tea. "So, what did he say when you told him you were ready to stop being the instrument of your own misery?"

"Keep the Yaoi in your manga." Andrew glared. The cosmos continued to laugh at his expense.

Justin gestured for him to talk. "Seriously, what did he say when you told him how you feel?"

"I didn't get a chance to tell him." Andrew added quickly, trying to justify, "As I said, he wasn't there on Monday."

"Zack was in your home for the entire weekend, and you didn't find the opportunity to talk things out with him?"

No, he'd been too busy proving his prowess as a Dominant. "I know."

Frustration ate at him. Exhaustion swamped him. He stood, then dragged himself over to the sink to rinse his cup and put it in the dishwasher. He pulled his car keys out of his pocket.

"Nope." His brother was quick in snatching the car keys out of his hand. "You'll sleep for a while."

"I need to go back out and look for him." Andrew stifled a yawn.

"You will, after you sleep. You're too tired to drive anymore. I can make up a guest room."

Defeated, Andrew blew out a loud exhale. "Okay, but I'll stay in his room. Perhaps he'll come home." To find his bed filled with his Master. Andrew hoped Zack wouldn't mind.

He weaved a little as he trudged up the stairs. *Damn!* He reached out to grab the railing.

Justin turned on the light and went to the unmade bed. "I can change the sheets."

No! He wanted to be in the sheets that had touched Zack. Wanted to smell him. "Nah, don't bother."

"And bro, take a shower. Hand me out your clothing, and I'll wash them for you."

"You don't have to do that, Justin." Now that his brother had mentioned it, Andrew did smell rather ripe. Sweat, fear, and regret were not alluring scents.

"Trust me, I do have to do this," Justin teased. "Give me your cell. I'll charge it for you. Take a shower and go to bed. I'll leave them outside the door when they've dried."

"Thanks." Stepping into Zack's large dark green bathroom, he turned on the shower before handing out his smelly clothing.

"Commando, huh?" His brother chuckled before Andrew heard the bedroom door close.

He shampooed, rinsed, and shampooed again, because it really did make a difference. Looking around, he only found a cheap conditioner. How did Zack's hair stay healthy if he was only using this inferior product? Not having a choice, he palmed the strawberry-smelling cream and applied it to his hair. He found a razor and changed the head before taking care of his heavy stubble. Damn, almost a beard. He soaped up, rinsed, tugged a fluffy light green towel from the cabinet, and dried off.

In the bottom drawer, he found Zack's stockpile of items in clearly labeled containers. He pushed aside the bins of razors, extra bottles of the cheap shampoo, conditioner, and body rinse, toothpaste tubes, and finally, he grabbed a new toothbrush. He brushed, rinsed, and put the new neon green toothbrush in the holder next to Zack's. He liked that.

He straightened the sheets and comforter before he sank down into the bed. Wow, he couldn't actually remember when lying horizontal felt so good. He pulled off the towel and set it above his head.

Andrew turned his face into the pillow. He inhaled and exhaled and, oh, inhaled again. Delicious. Zack's scent was faint, but present. Not caring that he might be acting like a cat with catnip, Andrew rolled his face in Zack's sheets.

Zack was okay, and when Andrew saw him again, he'd make him understand what should be happening between the two of them. He promised all the gods and goddesses of every known religion and the cosmos he'd take it at whatever pace Zack needed to go. Andrew wouldn't rush him.

Yeah. It could be good with them. Maybe he'd wake to find Zack cuddled next to him.

Hmmmm, wonder if Zack had any…. Reaching under the pillow, then the mattress, then under the bed, his hand came into contact with a cardboard box. He dragged the stash out. Did Zack keep BDSM porn mags? How retro.

Absent was the guilt he should have experienced at snooping, so he opened the box. Inside there were pictures. The first photo showed Andrew at Safari West. The next one had been taken of him at one of the Dark Angels' concerts. The third was a picture of Andrew at the beach. There were dozens more, all of him.

What the hell? He'd had no idea. Zack had been collecting his image and article clippings about him. He flipped through the stack. It was a "this is your life" captured in snapshots. Under the pictures were newspaper and magazine clippings of when Andrew had been interviewed about his business or about being a stylist to a rock band. Several he didn't even remember doing, but here they were in this box.

Dammit. Either Zack was a stalker or he cared about him. He'd take it as slow as Zack wanted to go so he didn't scare him off again.

They belonged together, and Andrew planned to make that happen as soon as he got a little bit of sleep and found his wayward pet. His cock protested with an angry throb.

Ah, what's this? Score! A bottle of lube was in one corner of the box. Maybe he'd put it to use. As he wrapped his hand around his cock, he heaved a grateful sigh. He shut his eyes after the first stroke.

His fogged mind tried to relive the events of his weekend with Zack but couldn't. He conjured Zack in the bathroom he'd just left, in the big bathtub taking a bubble bath. The cheap peach body wash would make a lot of suds.

Andrew's beautiful blond-haired, green-eyed sub beckoned him. "Join me, Master Drew." His little sex kitten tempted him, drawing out his name.

He stroked a bit faster. In his mind he stepped into the hot water. Zack kneeled up while bubbles skated down his body, dripping with water. He wet his parted lips in silent invitation.

Stepping forward, Andrew almost felt the heated breath brush past on the way to his destination. His pet's mouth tightened around him in heated suction. He whispered to the vision, "Such a good pet."

The imaginary Zack drank in the praise and sucked deeper.

The erotic image and perceived feelings created by Zack's skilled mouth tossed Andrew over into a sharp orgasm.

He bit off his moan of pleasure so it didn't echo down the hallway, alerting his brother he'd whacked off.

Grabbing the towel he'd used after his shower, he wiped off his stomach and chest. He gathered the pictures and put them back in the box, shoving the secret box back into its hiding place.

His gaze landed above Zack's desk. Several pictures, all signed by Jordon, were displayed. One in particular caught his interest.

Shit! It was a set of skeleton keys with a chain that went off the canvas. He'd bet, if the holiday painting Jordon made for him were placed beside this one, the paintings would combine to make a complete image.

Sleep must have stolen his consciousness because he dreamed of keys and locks. He was padlocked away from life. Zack strolled by his cell, swinging Andrew's freedom around his finger.

"Want something," his pet teased him.

Andrew growled. "Yes, I want a lot of things."

"Imagine that. You know what I want?"

"What?"

"I want a kiss from my Master." His sensual pet sighed. "If only I had one."

Andrew grabbed him through the bars of his prison, pressed their mouths together, and delivered a fiery kiss.

Zack went slack in his arms when their lips touched, and the locks of Andrew's jail popped open.

The bars melted as Andrew kept kissing Zack until a door slamming down the hall woke him.

"What?" His arms were empty. He surveyed the room and remembered Zack was missing. He grabbed for his phone on the nightstand. *Wait, where is it? Oh, right, Justin took it to charge it.* Jesus, he'd actually slept for eight hours.

He needed to get back to having some control in his life, so he showered and shaved again. Morning routine reestablished, he was feeling ready to accomplish the task of getting Zack back.

Taking a deep breath to find his center, he left Zack's room and headed downstairs to find everyone. They were in the dining room.

As soon as he entered, Justin hugged him. "Good, I'm glad you slept." Then felt his head. "No fever. Did you even take your medication?"

"Yes, Mother. The antibiotic was a Z-Pack, so it was done in five days." Andrew wasn't taking the other shit that had knocked him out, letting Zack escape without an opportunity to talk.

"Sit. Here's your phone and a car charger for your phone. I'm making you scrambled eggs." His brother dashed away before Andrew said anything.

He pocketed the charger and turned to Jordon, who sat on the other side of the dining room table with his arms folded. The kid gave him his best attempt at a sneer.

"Mind if I sit?" Andrew asked the question and then wondered if he'd get a denial.

Jordon flicked his glance to the kitchen where Justin hustled around like a stylish version of Betty Crocker. "Does it matter if I did care? Does it?"

Andrew sighed and crumpled into the chair. "I want to be with him."

"You've hurt him."

No denying that. They'd hurt each other. "Never my intention."

Jordon snorted but didn't give him an inch. "No kidding."

Dusty moseyed down the steps and into the dining room, twirling drumsticks between his fingertips. "Hey."

Andrew dipped his head. "I have something to talk to both of you about." Jordon continued to glare at him but didn't leave. "All three of you, actually."

Justin kissed Dusty on his way to park a plate filled with scrambled eggs, wheat toast with what looked like their mom's peach jam, ham, and a steaming mug of tea in front of Andrew. "Thanks, Just."

His brother sat next to him, and Dusty sat across the table with a plate of three hard-boiled eggs, one piece of toast, and coffee.

"Is this about Zack?" Leaning forward, Dusty pushed the hair trying to fall onto the table over his shoulder.

"It is. I know the whole dynamic between Zack and I hasn't been easy on everyone."

Jordon snorted again and muttered something under his breath that might have included a number of swear words.

Dusty pointed a finger at the kid, causing him to snicker.

Justin bumped into Andrew's side. "Well, you know I think you handled everything poorly."

Dusty shook his head. "I disagree with that. I appreciate that you waited. He was… hell, he still is a kid."

Andrew didn't see Zack that way now. He cleared his throat. "I appreciate that. I honestly don't know if I made the right decisions, but he'd only turned eighteen when we met—"

Jordon waved dismissively. "Yeah, yeah, yeah. So spit out what you wanted to tell us," he demanded before he gulped his chocolate milk.

"This weekend, things…." Andrew searched for the right word. "Things have changed."

"We know he was with you all weekend, but when you were here looking for him, *you* didn't say what happened," Jordon pointed out.

The smugness in Jordon's demeanor gave Andrew pause, but hell, he needed to apologize. "Look, I'm sorry about running around your home out of control like—"

"A fuckhead? An idiot? A dickwad? A jackass?" Jordon supplied the insults with joyful glee, and only ground to a halt when Justin glanced at him.

"Yes, Jordon, I was all those things and more." Andrew had to find Zack. He wanted to hug him, spank him, kiss him, fuck him, dance with him, shower him, change the color of his hair back to his natural gorgeous blond, but most of all, he wanted to explore what was between them.

Jordon scoffed and glared at him over his glass.

Andrew cleared his throat until all eyes were on him. "I want to see him."

Jordon choked on the liquid. "You're going to hurt him."

"I really care about him." Perhaps he should have led with that.

"Finally!" Justin squealed and hugged him as he eyed the two Davis brothers.

"So what are you asking?" Jordon scoffed and leaned his chair back onto two legs.

For everything.... "Zack and I need to see what's between us."

"Awww." Justin sniffed. "I know you guys will make each other happy." Justin squeezed Andrew tight.

Dusty turned toward Jordon.

The kid sighed and shrugged in a "whatever the fuck does it matter" kind of a way.

Dusty stood up and held out his hand. "I don't know if you need our blessing to date Zack, but as long as it's what Zack wants, we're happy."

Andrew released his brother and stood to shake the eldest Davis's hand. Dusty stepped around the table. After some manly whacks on Andrew's back, which seemed more like a warning, Andrew turned toward Jordon.

"I ain't hugging you. We'll see what Zack says." He abruptly grabbed his plate and glass and stomped out to the kitchen.

Dusty rested a hand on Andrew's shoulder. "Give him time."

Glancing at his brother, Andrew got a nod of reassurance from Justin.

He gathered his plate of uneaten food and hurried to the kitchen, wanting to catch Jordon alone. He needed to make amends, and the youngest Davis might know something.

Ignoring the scowl he received for his effort, he spoke. "Jordon, I care about him... a lot. It was very difficult not being with him, but it wasn't the right time." Shaking his head, he exhaled, frustrated, wanting this kid to understand. "He was young. I didn't want to be his regret. I had just gotten out of a long-term relationship—"

Jordon glanced at the Roman-numeral wall clock and back to Andrew. "He'll have already checked out of the hotel he stayed at. But he'll need to go pick up his car at Entwined."

Andrew reasoned out loud, "He'll head there first."

"Genius."

It was the kid's olive branch, and if he wanted to beat Andrew with it, so be it.

"Thank you, Jordon. Really." He stuck his hand out and hung his palm in midair. He almost gave up, but Jordon clutched his hand.

"Don't hurt him… except in whatever kinky way he likes. 'Cause if you harm him the wrong way, I will take you out."

Andrew didn't laugh, because the cold expression and dead eyes the kid wore worried him a little.

Chapter Eighteen

ZACK RUSHED into Entwined. He welcomed the strict technology-free zone today, because the policy prevented him from dealing with reality. Zack tossed his powered-off phone in a personal lockbox at the main entrance.

He'd charged it but hadn't turned the thing on since he'd had breakfast with Jordon. Even then he hadn't checked his messages when he texted Dusty. He should have, but what if there were no messages? What if there were? He wouldn't have been able to avoid responding to Drew—Andrew! No more Drew! A message would have forced him to face reality. He hadn't been ready. Maybe Marcus was right and he had been dealing with a case of sub drop.

Zack didn't know where else to go. He didn't want to go home. He wanted Andrew, but well… he needed a little more time to figure out what to say. Entwined had always been a place he'd come to find his center, and he was already here.

It was early, so the club wasn't crowded. A few people were having lunch. Zack meandered over to the bar, ordered a juice, and grabbed a gilded table in the corner. Tony must have seen him since he made a beeline over to his table.

"Hey, Sir."

"Just Zack, Tony." His fingers automatically touched his collar. There was no way he could pretend anymore. He might never do a BDSM scene again, but he no longer wanted to play a part.

The guy's eyes went big. "It's so good to, um, uh, see you here. Usually you don't… well, you don't come here for lunch. And… um, so, like how was your weekend?" He twittered like a nervous bird.

Zack asked, "Please sit down with me, Tony."

"Oh, Sir. I couldn't." Tony shifted from foot to foot.

"It's just Zack… from now on." Zack glanced away from Tony's shocked expression as a peace settled over him. The relief of a burden that always weighed him down had finally been lifted.

Several other subs who hadn't been to the auction glided over to the table. Tony filled them in on his take of the situation. "Sir Andrew bid and won him. It was a huge sum, and now Zack says he's no longer a Sir. He's just Zack. It's so romantic."

Ross and Joey Junior plopped down in available chairs. "So you don't want to be called Sir? Are you no longer a Dom?" Ross spoke slowly as he clarified the story.

Zack had played with most of them, so he understood the shock of him rejecting the Dom title and wearing a collar. Hell, he had to ignore the pang of loss that went through him at the thought of never helping someone explore that side most buried deep. He'd miss it. Maybe in the future he could….

"Zack is fine."

"You were won by Sir Andrew, right?" Joey Junior pointed out, as if the others might have missed that fact.

"Yup." Zack nodded and took a sip of juice.

Kneel. Serve. Always his.

Ross giggled more than a man his age should, but with his baby face, he got away with the cuteness. "Is he so good at being a Master that you gave up being a Dom?"

Yes! If Zack didn't laugh, he'd cry. "I had a wonderful time with Master Drew."

"Master? Oh, is that what he let you call him? He never let me call him anything but Sir. Right, Al?" Ross's best friend waved to Zack as he joined the crowd.

"Who?" Al asked, glancing around the group he'd just joined.

"Sir Andrew never let us address him as Master in a scene, right?"

"Nope, never… only Sir." Al's eyes widened as he touched the leather encircling Zack's neck.

Mine. Mine. No.

"You okay, Sir—I mean, Zack?" Al inquired.

No, he'd never be okay again. "Yeah, it's just, I don't know. Auction's over…."

"And you're still wearing a collar." Clapping excitedly, Ross asked, "Did he collar you?"

Zack stared at him. The longing in his heart made a verbal response impossible. He shook his head.

"No, but you wish he had. Right, Sir, I mean Zack?" Tony answered for him.

Zack dropped his head for a moment. Fuck, of course he did. How could he not?

Kneel. Serve. Only him.

He nodded once before he took another sip of juice and almost choked on the swallow. When Zack glanced around, he realized he was in the center of a much larger group of subs.

"What's going on?"

Ross gestured to the seated crowd of about twenty-five men, most of whom Zack recognized. "Oh, this is Entwined's male sub's meeting. We meet to talk about our issues, get support, ask questions, and—"

His lover added, "Gossip," interrupting Ross's explanation.

Zack didn't belong there.

He tried to stand, but Joey Junior gripped his shoulder, stilling him. "Stay. You're part of this group now... Zack."

"No. Yeah, maybe, but...." He turned to see all the curious faces. "I should go."

Chatter cascaded through the group to explain what Ross had meant. Zack caught snippets of "Zack's a sub," "Zack's a switch," "I knew it," and "Aw, sweet."

"Oh no. You should definitely stay. It's like having a double agent in the group," someone new, whose name he didn't remember, chirped.

"Yes, our secret weapon to understanding the minds of the Doms." Ross winked and teased him.

"All in favor of Zack staying with us." The club filled with calls of "Aye." "So you have to stay, Zack."

He had nowhere else to hurry off to, so Zack stayed put. This was part of being who he was meant to be. He'd taught several of them to submit. Fuck, perhaps they'd teach him to be a good sub.

Tony clapped his hands. "Everyone take your seats."

Everyone rearranged chairs and tables into a loose circle and sat.

"Who's going to start?" Ross asked.

There was a brief silence, which Tony broke. "I want to continue discussing abuse versus discipline." Everyone glanced around them until all gazes fell on Orion Gordon.

Zack had never played much with the researcher because he couldn't meet Orion's need for pain. Though they'd had plenty of discussions about the progress being made in cancer research.

Fuck, no. Zack did recall he'd noticed Orion with more than one blackened eye; the guy had said it was a work-related injury. *Shit!* Today the guy sported two black eyes, a swollen cheek, and a split lip. How had he missed the way Orion flinched when someone made quick movements around him?

Orion shrugged but wouldn't meet anyone's stare. "I don't see the big deal. They're mostly the same thing."

What? He couldn't be serious. Zack had to say something. "Discipline is what a submissive submits to in order to learn, grow, make atonement, or find subspace. Abuse is nonconsensual and serves no purpose other than to vent anger or torment another in a non-agreed-upon way."

When Orion didn't look at Zack, he continued, "Even if you agreed to discipline, you didn't agree to the willful disregard of your personal welfare."

There was silence until someone across the room said, "Safe, sane, and consensual, right?"

"Or RACK." Zack threw the term out there.

Someone new asked, "What's RACK?"

Joey Junior cleared his throat and got everyone's attention. "Risk-Awareness and Consensual Kink. Nothing is completely safe. Driving a car isn't completely safe, but we have seat belts and airbags. It's about being aware of the risks and trying to minimize the potential issues."

Tony asked, "I never understood why consensual kink instead of sane?"

"Well, think about it. Do you want someone not in the lifestyle telling you what sane is? Because I'd bet their definition is different than ours. If I give consent to explore breath play, I don't want someone telling me that I'm insane. That's between me and my Master." Joey Junior glanced around the group.

Many gazes drifted back to the man who had everyone's worry.

Orion peered up with a glint of defiance. "What if the play was consensual?"

"Was it?" Zack doubted Orion had given consent.

Orion folded his arms and pressed his lips together, which reopened his lip.

Xander, Orion's best friend, pulled a tissue from his pocket and dabbed at the blood.

Orion grabbed the tissue and snarled, "Don't. I've got this."

Zack shook his head. "I find it difficult to imagine a contract or a discussion between a Master and sub, or even a slave, requesting consent to beat someone in the face."

Tears sprang to Orion's eyes, and he glanced away from the group.

Zack surveyed the other subs. *Shit.* Entwined was meant as a safe haven, but it happened even here. He'd never wanted anyone to experience the betrayal and violation he had. "Is this something that happens frequently?"

No one would answer until Sam said, "On occasion. Even with all the members being vetted, a couple Doms who don't understand power exchange make it through."

"What happens?" *Jesus!* Zack dug his fingernails into the chair, but he kept his voice even.

"Usually word gets out, and no one will scene with them, so they vanish."

"Who did this to you, Orion?" Zack demanded, but the guy stubbornly refused to speak. Well, fuck no. Not happening again. "Do you want that to happen to someone else? Do you want this guy to hook up with Xander? Or anyone else?" Zack wanted to wring the guy's neck for protecting someone who needed his ass kicked.

"You know I like it rough." Orion's admission dared those around him to say something about it.

"There's a difference between rough and out of control. A Dom should never be out of control. No one should be abused under the guise of BDSM play."

Xander said, "Orion, don't make me. You should say who, or I will." He stroked his friend's hair.

Orion pressed his lips together into a frown, but ultimately he coughed up the name. "Dom Henry."

"That fucking bastard," one of the subs three seats away from Zack yelled out. "I'd like to explain the difference between discipline and abuse to him."

He signaled the bartender, who allowed Zack to use the emergency contact phone. Zack danced his fingers over the keys and texted the owners about this poor excuse for a Dominant. "It's done. Remember the agreement we signed as part of the understanding of being a member? A single word stops the action here, but a thousand words won't stop abuse. Everyone stay away from the asshole until the owners remove him from the entry list." Zack didn't voice his wish that Orion would press charges, but the owners would try to get him to file.

Orion appeared miserable but accepted a hug from Xander. Others went over to him to offer hugs and their numbers if he wanted to talk. The owners would also follow up and make sure Orion met with a therapist in their community. Zack would recommend a seminar on the subject to the owners.

God, he missed Drew. He longed for the security and safety of being near him. Had he screwed it up?

When everyone returned to their seats, Tony said, "Okay, on a happier note, I want to hear from those of you who won an auction."

Someone Zack didn't recognize asked, "Roberto, how was Sir Frank as a sub?"

The adorable man stood up and untied a multicolored scarf to show off his collar. "My Master."

Everyone clapped. "Details!"

Roberto took a big inhale and began his story. "Well, I took him back to my place, and you know, I had no clue what the hell to do as a Master. By the way, it's a lot of stinking work."

Zack chuckled with everyone else. Indeed it was.

Roberto pointed to himself. "Well, I'm no dummy. I commanded him to get naked right away."

After the *oohs* and *aahs* and dirty chuckles died down, Roberto continued. "Then I made him give me a bath." He dramatically fanned himself. "Let's just say I needed a shower to get clean from my bath. And honeys, I hate to break it to you since he's off the market, but my man can suck the chrome off a fender."

"Congratulations! Make sure you put ample blowjobs in your contract. I did with the doctor," Tony called out.

Roberto giggled. "Trust me, I most definitely will add it in when we create the official contract. One a day at least!"

Glancing around the room, Ross lowered his voice. "So, um, how did Master Bob and Master Greg fare?"

Sammy responded in a low voice, "I heard not well." Hoots of glee broke out in small pockets among the group. "Apparently, *Bob* can't take what he likes to dish out, and *Greg,* from what I heard, did even worse and left before the weekend was over."

"Really? Imagine that! The wimp." Timmy vented his venom. Sam quieted him down when he tucked him under his arm and hugged him close.

"What about Si? I really like playing with him." One of the quieter subs, Zack thought was named Perkins, inquired after the man.

Si and Tony were good friends. Tony answered, "He had a nice time, though I don't know how long he'll stay on this side of the collar."

"Why do you say that?" Perkins asked, blushing red, probably from the attention the question raised.

Tony shrugged. "Just a feeling. Should I tell him you asked about him?"

"No! I mean… no." He paused with his mouth opened, frowned, and waved a hand at Tony, then said, "Well, yeah, I guess you can tell him I said hi. I mean you can tell him that *we* all said hi."

Hmmm, okay, all that for a "hi"? If Zack's life wasn't such a hot mess, he'd try to fix Perkins and Si up. They'd make a good match.

Tony chuckled. "I'll do that." He turned to Sam to mouth, "See? I told you so."

A collared sub by the name of Paul asked, "How about John? How'd he do?"

"He had a good time." The sub who answered sighed. "He's a good one too."

"Any general comments, topics for next week, or reminders for the group?" Sam asked.

"How to say 'no' without safewording," Perkins called out.

"'Sub' doesn't mean checking your self-esteem at the door. If anything, we're more than most, because of our ability to submit. We're more, because we're willing enough to put our trust in someone else, and"—Xander skimmed his hand down Orion's shoulder—"that trust should never be violated."

A quiet man in a suit said, "Nullification shouldn't be taken lightly."

Fuck! Zack hoped not. A few men lowered their heads. Dear God!

"It's okay to have limits pushed, but boundaries should never be violated," someone new commented. Zack didn't remember his name.

"Sane doesn't mean you can't get a little crazy." Roberto laughed.

Just then, the door opened and shut. Boots clicked on the floor. Every sub in the room turned to the figure striding toward them in black leather.

A hushed "oh" went through the crowd.

Andrew strutted across to the circle of subs, stopped dead in front of Zack, and stared into his eyes until Zack's insides melted.

Kneel. Serve. Love.

"We need to talk." Andrew signaled the keeper behind the bar and said, "Room thirteen, please."

CHAPTER NINETEEN

MINE. WANT. Need.

Fuck, his Master was a wet dream.

The barkeep simply threw Andrew a key with a red ribbon attached to the brass. He turned on his heel and strutted down the damned hall like he owned the club.

"Go," Sam hissed. The hands of the various subs Zack had dominated pushed him in the general direction his feet were reluctant to drag him.

Roberto pulled him aside. "Zack, don't be afraid to get what you want."

Want. Kneel. Serve.

"Go!" Tony whacked Zack on the ass.

What the fuck? Zack stared at Tony.

The guy shrugged. "I always wanted to do that. But enough about me... don't make him wait, Zack."

Whatever. Zack shook his head. He spun to the eager faces around him. It was impossible to convey what their support meant to him, so he went with a simple "Thank you."

He trudged down to the room. *Shit!* His world was about to change. He didn't know *how* it would be modified and Andrew's face gave him no indication.

Zack was viewing his life from a hundred feet away. The surreal quality intensified. Andrew had come. What did that mean? Was he here for closure? An explanation? Was this the beginning or the end? Questions swirled until Zack stepped through the open door of number thirteen.

Andrew was sprawled on the abstract muted-colored love seat. His wide stance took up the entire piece. He didn't turn his head when the door shut and Zack clicked the lock into place.

Silence.

The quiet hurt Zack's heart. He waited. Nothing. Should he undress like a sub as expected?

Just as Zack touched the hem of his T-shirt to raise it up, Andrew barked out, "Don't."

Fuck! He doesn't want me. This is going to be another rejection. Run. Fucking get out of here! Why wouldn't Zack's goddamned feet move?

"Come to me," Andrew commanded.

Lagging with the speed of someone heading to the electric chair, Zack shuffled to fulfill the instruction. He stood in front of the man he loved with his gaze on the floor, pressing his lips together because he wasn't going to lose his composure.

Zack had never really expected to have a weekend with Drew, let alone anything more. Fuck the hope he allowed to grow in his heart! Fuck the man who'd encouraged him to wish for something that never was.

He'd crushed the fucking dream himself by fleeing Andrew's condo like a prime suspect from a crime scene, so he could avoid this exact scene. When Andrew strutted into Entwined, the seed containing his dearest wish was replanted in his heart.

Dumb. Stupid. Idiot.

Andrew cleared his throat, which prompted Zack to meet his gaze. He finally spoke. "Why did I wake up to an empty bed?"

Anger flared within Zack. Much better than the pathetic need that tried to overwhelm his dignity. He'd hide behind fury as the abyss threatened to swallow him. "Why the hell do you care?"

"I'd appreciate if you would answer my question. Why. Did. I. Wake. Up. Alone?" Andrew enunciated each syllable, as if that would assist Zack in spitting out an answer.

Fuck! Zack needed an escape, but first he'd find the words, so this little unavoidable event could end as quickly as possible.

"Zack?" Andrew said his name like it was a question.

This time Zack wasn't letting go of his pride. Fuck if this go-round he'd not give up his dignity without a fight. "It was Monday, *Andrew*. The auction contract was complete."

Andrew's silence made Zack more surly and defiant.

The man hadn't given him any indication Zack should stick around past the weekend, and he hadn't planned to wait around to be tossed out. Maybe he did avoid rejection even at the cost of his happiness, but fuck it! "Should I have made you breakfast? Probably. But you already know I'm a terrible sub."

Andrew cocked his head and studied him. The close scrutiny was unnerving. "Let's try a different question. Why did you leave?"

Why the hell did Andrew need to dissect his explanation? What did it matter? Why had Zack put himself in this position again?

Leave. Run. Escape.

Zack clenched his hands into fists at his side, and he narrowed his eyes at the man who seemed hell-bent on not only breaking his heart again but wanting to step on it too. He channeled all of his younger brother's sarcasm and said, "Oh, I'm sorry. Should I have waited around for you to kick me out?"

He ignored Andrew's tilted head and screwed-up expression. Zack was fucking done. Finished with feeling like shit, he stomped to the door.

"Stop." The word was voiced with reinforced iron.

Obey. Stop. Wait.

Unable to do anything but submit, Zack froze in his tracks. He paused, his hand halfway to the knob and escape. He slid his eyes shut for a moment as hope battled with bewilderment.

"Breathe." Andrew's unique scent surrounded him. *Inhale.* His Master embraced him.

Exhale. Zack relaxed into the warmth behind him.

"Sit with me." Andrew didn't wait for an answer as he guided Zack back to the love seat. He sat and pulled Zack right into his lap.

Oh! Zack tried to keep his body stiff, but remaining board-like while perched on Andrew's legs proved impossible.

"Why did you go?" Andrew ran his fingers through Zack's hair.

Mine. Melt. Merge.

No. Stop. Still.

Zack's traitorous body liquefied from the inside out. No, he wouldn't fall apart. "Because...."

Andrew's voice was gentle as he asked, "Didn't you want more?"

His Master's talented fingers wandered over Zack's back, which allowed his body to relax against his Master's—Drew's—Andrew's lap. "Yes, *I* wanted more."

"Did you leave because you thought I didn't want more?"

The scene of his mother throwing him out of the house yelling for him to remove his perverted self from her home skated through his head. It was easier to leave than to get rejected... again. But fuck if his heart bothered to follow any of the rules Zack tried to live by.

Zack frowned. "We didn't talk about… more."

"For that, I take full responsibility. You aren't a mind reader and especially with our history…."

"Our history…," Zack repeated as if he could make sense of where Andrew was going with this conversation. The dynamic between the two of them seemed to always be off course. "You thought I was too young…."

Andrew stroked down his back. "I didn't want to be your regret. It killed me not to have you."

"You were still getting over Charlie." Zack hated to say that out loud. But he'd wanted too much of Andrew and pushed too fast. If given the chance, Zack wouldn't make the same mistake again.

"It was more that I'd never gotten to explore who I was before becoming serious with Charlie, and I didn't want to do that to you."

"You thought we'd become… serious?" Joy leapt through Zack, followed by regret.

"I've never liked spending time with someone as much as I enjoyed our time together at the salon."

"Me too." He managed to keep his voice even.

"But you were young." Andrew combed his fingers through Zack's hair.

Old anger crawled through Zack's system. "I was legal."

Somehow Andrew read the tension. "Don't be angry."

Zack shrugged. Damn, Andrew raked his talented fingers through his hair and it was hard to stay pissed. "I wasn't young, and I've always known what I wanted."

"You were only eighteen," Andrew pointed out.

His shrug was not much of a defense. Andrew opened his mouth, but before he said anything, Zack decided to end the fruitless discussion. "Can we agree that age is no longer an issue?"

Andrew stared into his eyes long enough to make Zack worry. When he nodded, Zack released the breath he'd been holding.

Andrew threw out, "Justin told me to stop using him as an excuse."

Dusty dating Andrew's brother simply put a crimp in the idea of pursuing him until Zack got to know Andrew—Drew. Then Zack simply mowed down all barriers between them and waited.

He asked, "Were you?"

"I don't know, but maybe it turned into an excuse." Andrew put his head back on the love seat and rested a hand on Zack's thigh. "But after the attack, I was terrified. He tried to commit suicide, and I focused a lot of energy on his happiness. I didn't want to lose him. So, when he finally got in a good place with your brother, I was afraid to do anything to screw it up."

"So if we got together and things didn't work out...." Zack didn't have nearly the worry Andrew did, but he didn't want to ruin his own brother's happiness either.

Andrew caressed Zack's thigh, easing the tension his words caused. "But Justin told me in no uncertain terms I couldn't screw anything up because he and Dusty were solid."

"Yeah, they are. I've never seen my brother so content and thrilled with life," Zack confirmed.

"Good."

Zack understood talking things out was important, but he wanted to skip to the end to find out if Andrew would be kissing him anytime soon.

Andrew raised Zack's chin, forcing his eyes away from Andrew's pink lips and asked, "Since we're strolling down stumbling-block lane, what about Safari West?"

"I didn't want to be a second choice." Zack hated to admit that. He sounded like he was whining, but in this one aspect of his life, he'd not be a consolation prize.

Andrew gazed into Zack's eyes. "You weren't. Never. Charlie getting married had no impact on me wanting to kiss you."

The band that had tightened around Zack's heart loosened. He shared some blame in the debacle. "I should have listened and not overreacted."

"Well, I shouldn't have left without trying to make you understand."

"It surprised me you'd actually left." It had been horrible when he found out he'd chased Andrew away. But that's what he got when he pushed too hard. He really needed to change the way he interacted with Andrew or he'd lose him again. Wait! Was he actually getting him?

"I went to San Francisco and hung out with Robin and Josh. They were with Jack and Sean. Watching Sean being a dope and not go after who he wanted... well, I realized it was exactly what I was doing. I allowed so many things to stop me from what I wanted...."

Zack needed it spelled out for him so he asked, "And what did you want?"

"You."

Fuck yes! He was getting a chance with him!

Turning, Zack melted in Andrew's embrace. He peeked up in time to see Andrew's mouth a moment before it was pressed against his own.

Happiness exploded around him, but he didn't let go completely. He would need to avoid pushing if he wanted to keep Andrew.

Andrew pulled back. "I've missed you."

"Me too." Zack's heart was sore from the Drew-shaped empty place. He spun around and straddled Andrew's lap to pepper tiny kisses across his cheek.

"I missed you. I missed our friendship," Andrew said before Zack's lips reached their destination, and he groaned into his mouth.

Zack should say something, but Andrew's mouth stole all his words. He'd settle for friendship with ropes.

Between kisses, Andrew said, "I want more. Our weekend together gave me a taste of everything I've craved."

Rainbows and sunshine of everything Zack desired was laid out in front of him. He wasn't going to screw this up by becoming desperate. He put the affection-confirming words threatening to bubble up out of his mouth under lock and key.

He didn't speak. He tilted his head to give Andrew and his talented tongue total access to his neck to lick wet trails in long lines.

Yes. Yes. Yes.

"I'm going to 'use my words,' as my brother reminds me I need to do more often." Andrew kissed Zack on the nose and halted his hips.

Holy fuck, that was embarrassing. Zack hadn't even realized he was lap dancing on Andrew like a horny stripper. Horny stripper…. He could do a horny stripper for Andrew. He could…. *Shit! Focus!*

Andrew said, "I talked to our brothers. I told them I want to see you and figure out where this goes."

He couldn't imagine what they'd said, but Zack was glad he hadn't been there to witness it. "And?"

"They gave us… their blessing."

Odd choice of words, but Zack wasn't going to read more into it than Andrew meant. He reached up to scratch his neck.

Andrew caught his hand.

"I have an itch on my neck," Zack complained before he realized why Andrew examined his wrist.

Absentmindedly, Andrew ran his perfectly manicured nails over Zack's neck to tame the itch.

"When did you do this?" Andrew traced over the image still coated in gel.

Shit, so much for not being desperate. Was Andrew going to be angry? Well, it wasn't his arm. "Um, on Wednesday. Marcus did it."

"Jordon's design?" Still Andrew gave no indication of how he felt about Zack doing such an impulsive thing that might be seen as a bit stalkeresque.

Talk about being overly eager. "Yeah. The damn kid doodled it on a napkin after he called me an idiot for leaving you."

"I'd never call you an idiot, but you shouldn't have left."

Wanting to change the subject, Zack asked, "Do you like it?"

"It's incredible. I love it. I can't believe you did this…," Andrew said. "Does it hurt?"

"A bit. Marcus gave me cream to keep it moist."

"We'll make sure you use it. You marked yourself for me even after you left me?"

Not wanting to admit his anguish-filled desire to be claimed by Andrew, Zack said, "I couldn't let go of what we shared without having a reminder." *Of who I'd always belong to….*

Andrew shifted Zack off his lap and steadied him as he stood Zack upright. "Undress, pet."

"Yes, Sir." Zack started to pull off his clothing.

"No. *Master* Drew." Andrew swatted his ass as he corrected Zack.

"Oh hell yes! Um, Master Drew." Life was sometimes too perfect.

Drew chuckled and winked at him. His expression grew serious, and he morphed into the Master of Zack's dreams.

Master Drew meandered over to his bag and pulled out a crop. Mmmm, yes. Crop well applied equated to erection city.

"Kneel." This command accompanied the crop skimming over his bare skin.

Naked, Zack hit the floor with his knees spread, hands on thighs, head down, and cock up. Anticipation ate at him.

"My pet needs to be tamed." His Master purred the statement.

Biting his lip didn't hold back the whimper.

His. His. His.

Master Drew set a purple velvet pillow in front of him. "Head to floor and ass up, pet."

The words sent shivers through him. Zack rested his head on the purple velvet and presented his butt. To ensure he was totally exposed, he parted his knees farther.

Drew tickled the crop over his balls, and then the stimulation disappeared.

Snap! The leather kissed his backside. There was a slight pause before the sharp painful bite. The crop trailed off his butt.

Pause. *Snap!*

His Master traced the little leather flap around to the other cheek.

Circle. *Slap!*

There was no rushing through this discipline to get to the good stuff. Besides, the pain morphed into euphoria. Fuck, this *was* the good stuff!

Every nip of the crop was affirmation his Master cared for him. Zack needed to suffer in celebration. He wanted the loneliness taken from him.

Snap!

He pushed back to receive as much correction as his Master believed he should receive. Fuck, he could come just from this attention.

Love. Pain. Pleasure.

The next strike rang out.

Zack's grunts followed each slap. Pain increased and accumulated to the point of almost being too much to handle. With less of a pause, the crop struck again.

Many times the flappy leather bit into Zack until he was lost in a calm, beautiful place where nothing else existed except his Master and the sensations he was given to experience.

Mine. His. Complete.

Zack was free, unrestrained by the world.

An exquisite peace encompassed him. The leather kissed him, but any and all pain translated into elation. His Master attended to all his needs. His soul was fed. The discipline converted into pure... love.

He rode the sea of sensation, free from everything except Master Drew. He was the only thing that kept Zack tethered so he could soar like he wanted without fear. Master Drew would ensure his safe return.

The flashes of heat that kept him liberated in the stratosphere slowed and came to a halt.

No. Not yet. More.

All too soon, firm hands applied a cooling cream. The rubbing of his backside demanded that he return to his body. Zack came back down to earth.

Sadness tried to creep in, but his Master slipped his creamed fingers inside him and returned him to the happy place of superb sensation in consolation.

His. Surrender. Mine.

Patience was difficult, but he waited. Master Drew opened Zack's entrance and made his cock throb with impatience. He thrust back and moaned, trying to convey his deep desire to be joined and filled by the love of his life.

Smack!

Zack groaned. The whack might have been humiliating if it hadn't sent delight racing through him. His insides clenched, wanting more.

An empty foil package floated to the floor. Drew sleeved his cock. Inch by inch, Drew pushed into him, giving Zack everything he'd begged for, balls deep.

Mine. His. Complete.

Master Drew grasped Zack's hips with his strong hands and held him motionless when he'd have bucked forward and back, regardless of the discomfort.

Zack groaned. What was the use of being given everything you wanted and not being able to use it? Before an answer rose to the forefront of Zack's lust-addled mind, his Master, as always, gave him exactly what he required.

Drew withdrew his cock an inch at a time before he advanced the length again, a little deeper each time. Dear God, each withdrawal and thrust sent Zack into orbit.

Zack squeezed his eyes shut. The thought of his Master filling him so entirely combined with the tormenting delicious stretch of his insides had Zack panting, desperate to stave off his rising orgasm.

"Master?" Control. He had none.

"Almost, my sweet pet, but for now, wait." His Master petted him on the ass, reawakening the sore flesh and sending desire crashing through him.

Groaning, Zack clenched his jaw and curled his toes. His Master nudged his prostate. The impact made him tremble with need. He stiffened every muscle in his body to try to hold on against the fiery pleasure.

The speed of Drew's thrusts increased, his pounding assault on Zack's ass accompanied by guttural groans. His Master tightened his fingers around Zack's hips and nails bit into Zack's skin... all signs that meant Drew was close to climax. His hips spanked into Zack's sore ass, making his wait even harder.

His Master wrapped a hand around his cock and stroked his shaft. "Come."

Zack obeyed.

God, the connection with Drew made his completion stronger. His ass muscles milked his Master. Intense pleasure radiated through him as he came.

Satisfied. Sated. Peaceful.

Zack fell forward.

Drew caught and wrapped him up in his arms. He clung as his Master half carried and half walked him to the horizontal padded surface that often doubled as a bed. Drew kept a hand on him when he settled into the blankets and joined Zack.

Master Drew massaged Zack's ass. Was this an apology for the treatment of his backside? Zack sure the hell hoped not, because he loved the cropping.

Zack was a little cold, so he shifted closer to the warmth. Drew tucked the blanket around him and tightened his arms around Zack, making him sigh with the memory of the entire afternoon. He might have fallen asleep. There were no windows or clocks to mark the passage of time.

Lifting his head, Zack peeked at the warm body next to him. His heart soared. Drew. "It wasn't a dream?"

Drew chuckled.

Zack needed to put his sappy side on lockdown. He nuzzled against his Master's chest. "How long did I sleep?"

"Not long. About two hours."

"You held me for all that time?" When his day started, he'd never imagined in his wildest dreams this would happen.

"I figured I'd get in some practice." Andrew skimmed his hands down Zack's chest. "Are you still cold?"

Cozy. Happy. Content.

Zack kept it simple. "Nope."

"Are you thirsty?"

A bottle of water appeared at Zack's mouth, so he took a sip. "Thanks."

"How are you feeling?"

Ah, Zack recognized a sub inventory of feelings and emotions. "I'm good... *Drew*." Damn, he'd never flown that high. Ah, he stretched out over Andrew's incredible body and utilized him as a body pillow.

"Looks like you're back on the ground with me."

Zack might be grinning like an idiot. "Yeah, when I start thinking of you as Drew and not Master, I know I'm back. Do you mind if I start calling you Drew again?"

Holding out Zack's wrist to display his dragon, Drew said, "I'd prefer it."

Drew ran his index finger above and below the design. "We need to get some ointment on this."

"I have some in my pocket." Zack frowned as his body pillow went to fetch it.

Drew sanitized his hands with a wipe from near the platform and, with sure gentle touches, applied the healing gel. "I really love the tattoo. Do you think Jordon would design one for me?"

"Sure... once he stops hating you."

CHAPTER TWENTY

ANDREW PROMISED himself he wouldn't make Zack feel pressured about their relationship. He'd take his cues from Zack and not rush.

Zack spent most nights at Andrew's. About a month after their "talk," Andrew added a bright green spinning head toothbrush to the medicine cabinet next to his. It screamed of permanence and put Andrew's heart at ease.

When he saw Zack examining it, he said, "I was at the market and picked you up a decent toothbrush."

Zack's smile disappeared into a wide-eyed expression void of emotion. "Um, thanks."

Did he see a toothbrush as a shove? It wasn't.

"You know it seemed wasteful to throw toothbrushes away each time you were home for a night or two." Not that Andrew had to do that but it gave him an excuse for buying Zack a real "I'm almost living here" toothbrush. "Besides this one will help fight plaque."

"Um, I appreciate it. Thanks." Zack frowned and then nodded.

Later that night when they got ready for bed, Andrew didn't miss the little smile Zack wore as he got his brush out. Perhaps it was a good nudge.

Hmmm, maybe next he'd offer a drawer and space in the closet. It might be rude not to, but he'd wait a while on that.

AFTER TWO months of seeing each other, Andrew said, "I reorganized my dresser and closets."

"Oh, did you finally space-bag your clothing, leaving only the current season out?"

"I did. I can't believe the extra room I have. So if you wanted to leave stuff here… you know, to have some of your things in the closet and in the drawers, you could."

Zack stilled, and that damned mask of indifference slid into place.

Andrew threw open his walk-in closet. "See? I even have no-slip hangers."

A slow smile brightened Zack's face. "I love—"

Elation ripped through Andrew.

Zack slammed his mouth shut and pressed his lips together. Finally he said, "Um, yeah. I'd love that. Um, it would be great not to lug around a duffel."

Well that cancelled Andrew's celebration dance. He settled for reminding Zack of their bond by tying him to the bed until pleas for release echoed off the bedroom walls. He'd be patient and wait until Zack was ready to admit his feelings.

A COUPLE weeks before the summer tour, the doorbell rang.

Andrew pushed the basted chicken back into the oven.

He hurried to the door and opened it.

Zack launched himself into Andrew's arms.

Mmmm, he adored having his arms full of Zack. "Well, hello to you too." Andrew took his lips in a welcome-home kiss that reassured his heart.

A light pink blush colored Zack's cheeks when he untwined himself. "Hey. Sorry I'm late. Traffic was horrible."

Andrew tugged his pet into the kitchen. "No worries, I got your text. Dinner's not ready yet. How did the band meeting go?"

"Eh, nothing major. Megan is still ironing out the final details for the last leg of the tour."

Andrew handed Zack a glass of ice water. "Good. Oh, I was, um, at the hardware store."

Zack stopped midsip, and excitement lit his eyes. "Yeah? You get those chains?"

He didn't bother to hide his smirk at Zack's anticipation. His pet had admitted he wanted to mix chains in with ropes for a bondage scene. Andrew already changed the configuration of their pre-tied ropes that were kept under the bed. Zack would respond well to the rattle of chains. "Yes, we can try them after dinner."

Zack hooted.

Andrew's heart soared, but he proceeded with caution. He took Zack's hand and kissed the palm. "I also had this made for you while I was there." He pulled the key from his pocket and placed it in Zack's hand.

Zack's face flashed with an emotion Andrew hadn't been able to read. Was that distress? Happiness? Concern? Did he feel pressure? It felt like Andrew was tiptoeing around their relationship, but with all the shit they'd gone through to be together, he would be patient. This wasn't about a short sprint but the long haul.

"Zack, I figured you should have a key. That way you don't have to ring the bell or fish for the extra key hidden in the plant if you get home before me." Hopefully that would seem rational and not like Andrew was forcing him into this next level.

"Oh… okay." Zack jerked his head around, searching the kitchen. "I, um… thanks. I… yeah. Um, how can I help with dinner?"

The abrupt subject change meant Zack needed to process so Andrew went with it. "Chicken's in the oven for another hour. The salad is already made."

Zack stalked over to him. "Then maybe we could take a look at those chains."

And if his submissive wanted to hide in their world built for two, Andrew would just use the time to tie them tighter together.

TIME SEEMED to melt. He and Zack were on tour with the Dark Angels. The road crew and style crew didn't bunk together. Andrew roomed with the new makeup artist, so opportunity for Master and pet to have *alone* time was close to nonexistent. The "it'll work out" method of spending time with Zack was an epic fail. Three times the previous week, one of their roommates walked in on them at inopportune times.

Andrew set his phone aside. "The closest Entwined club is four hundred miles away."

"That's only a few hours." Zack skimmed a hand over his.

He might be desperate too, but he wasn't going to allow Zack to go without sleep. "Try five hours and twenty minutes. By the time we get there, it will be closed."

Zack dropped his head into his hands. "Are there any other clubs?"

"Not doing that." No way would he let Zack go into one of those back rooms.

"Um, other hotels?" Zack pulled out his phone.

"I already checked. Everyone is sold out due to the Dark Angels concert."

Zack eyed the restroom. His face contorted with all the dirty possibilities before he said, "You know, I bet no one uses the men's room in this lobby all that much."

"I have nothing against public sex, but getting arrested for indecent exposure is not on my to-do list."

"Shit, Drew, I can't take this!" Zack growled and pulled at his hand.

"Language. Just 'cause we have no privacy, doesn't mean I can't punish you," Andrew reminded Zack. Oh, but to have some privacy would be heaven.

"Promises, promises," his pet grumbled.

Maybe Andrew could book a room for them to share in the next hotel. It would start rumors, but no more than their roommates catching them together.

"I'm done with this." Zack dialed his cell.

"Who are you calling?"

Zack put up a finger to request he wait. "Hi, Ellen. Fine, you?" Zack nodded. "You're in charge of logistics, right?" After a slight pause, he continued. "Good. Listen, I've got a favor to ask. As of tonight, I want to room with Andrew Nikeman." There was a pause. "I know it's not how it normally works." Zack was quiet. "Okay, great. Yes, until further notice. You'll take care of telling our current roommates? Thanks."

Andrew was more than a little turned on by how Zack handled it.

"Yup… let's go to the front desk and get our keys."

His pet deserved a reward.

Zack grinned and asked, "Now about that punishment…."

THE DARK Angels' summer tour was drawing to a close. Time had flown by. It had been great to have Zack in his arms every night. Andrew believed these last few months proved he and Zack made a good team, in and out of bed. It wasn't pushing that Andrew wanted to ensure it continued, was it?

Zack snuggled closer to him. "I can't believe the tour is over next week."

"I've enjoyed rooming with you." Andrew tucked the blanket up around Zack's neck.

"Yeah, you're a good roomie, even in tight quarters."

Andrew asked, "Is it my organizational talents or the blowjobs?"

His pet fairly purred. "Wait. I don't have to decide, do I?"

They both laughed.

Hmm, Andrew needed to go for it. It wasn't shoving; it could be seen as more like advocating and planning. Besides, most of Zack's stuff was in Andrew's condo. He cleared his throat. "Maybe after the tour, you'd like to continue."

The sleepy sated Zack vanished, replaced by an alert Zack who sat ramrod straight in bed, staring at Andrew. "Continue what? The blowjobs... yes, I believe I would."

Andrew swallowed the worry. "I mean living together."

"Oh." A hundred expressions crossed Zack's face. It made Andrew nuts not to be able to interpret them.

Because that's what they were doing, but maybe Zack wasn't ready to name their cohabitation. "Unless you don't want to, and then well, we can just—"

"Er... um." Zack fumbled with the blanket, and his gaze darted around the room, trying to find a place to land other than on Andrew.

Maybe a small push wouldn't be a bad thing. It could fit under guiding. "I mean, we basically have been living together for months. I'm suggesting we make it more official, unless you don't want that. If you don't, we can—"

"No! I mean no, I think, um, it's a good idea. We should definitely live together." Zack fussed with the blankets.

A weight lifted off Andrew but he didn't take a victory lap. "Really?"

Zack's peridot-colored eyes were huge as he nodded and burrowed back under the covers to snuggle against Andrew's side.

Neither of them said more about it. Andrew didn't like walking on eggshells, but controlled methodical moving forward was working, so he wasn't going to rock the proverbial boat.

The day they arrived home from the tour, Andrew tried to remain low-key as they finished unpacking their clean clothing. "So when should I take off time to help move you in?"

Zack poked his head out of their now shared walk-in closet. "Um, I guess sooner might make more sense. I think most of my stuff is already here."

Glancing around Andrew grinned. It was true! He tried to keep the excitement out of his voice but it was a big step in the direction he wanted them to be. "Great! I'll stop by the shop for an hour in the morning then we can get you moved in by tomorrow midday."

Zack nodded and bit his lower lip. "So I should stay the night?"

Yes! Don't push! "I'd like that… unless you have packing or whatever."

"No! I mean nah. I can get my shit—I mean stuff tomorrow morning."

A PINCH on his ass made Andrew squawk. "Zack!"

"What?" The innocent expression Zack wore belied the hand that cupped Andrew's ass and squeezed.

Of course the door swung open at that moment. "Happy New Year!" Dusty shouted, pulling him and Zack into the warmth of a hug.

Andrew smacked Dusty on the back and beat him to saying more by shouting, "It's going to be a great year!"

"It is!" Dusty took their coats and hung them in the closet.

Zack sniggered as he toed off his boots. He kneeled to slip them onto the boot tray, shook his head, and gathered up the half a dozen pairs of boots and sneakers and straightened them into a neat row.

While his pet was down on his knees, Zack turned toward Andrew and untied his boots and slipped them off. He stared at Andrew from his submissive position, as if awaiting an instruction, and then licked his lips. If that didn't make Andrew wish they were home, nothing else would.

"Dinner's almost ready." Dusty hurried off to the kitchen.

"Thank you, pet," Andrew said for Zack's ears only and reached a hand down to help him off the floor.

Zack popped up, readjusted his pants, and gave Andrew a smile of wicked promise. His pet trailed after Dusty and turned to grin at Andrew before disappearing into the chaos.

Andrew snapped out of his daydreams of wanting everything with Zack. He followed Zack and Dusty into the mayhem that was the Davis kitchen.

Zack whispered, "Glad our house isn't this confusing."

His use of the word "our" should not have made Andrew euphoric, but it did. He floated through the final prep for the meal and was still happy when they sat down to eat.

When seconds were passed around, Jordon cleared his throat. "So now that you and Andrew are officially living together, will you be getting married like Dusty and Justin?"

Leave it to Jordon to ask a pertinent but difficult question.

Dusty and Justin had gotten engaged at Christmas. Andrew was thrilled for his baby brother. They hadn't set a date, but their commitment highlighted the gray area he found himself in with Zack.

Andrew wanted to say yes they would, but Zack spoke first. "We don't need to fit in a heteronormative tradition." He stopped and looked at Justin, "I mean not that there's anything wrong with that, but...."

What the hell? Did Zack believe that? Is that why he'd avoided conversations about their future and distracted Andrew in delightful and varied ways whenever the conversation leaned in that direction? Or maybe he didn't want to go any further?

Jordon rolled his eyes, resembling one of the characters he drew, and said, "It's only heteronormative because not everyone had freedom to do it before now. In this country there are over eleven hundred protections married couples get that cohabitating couples don't get. Besides, people were in the closet before, so to even have a relationship was a feat, but now with marriage equality, it's a possibility—"

"Life isn't like one of your Yaoi novels," Zack pointed out with far too much skepticism for Andrew's liking.

"It should be! Not everyone may want to get married, but we should have the opportunity and not toss it away because it's a societal norm. All kids should grow up knowing they can have a happily ever after, which could include marriage if they want it," Jordon insisted and fist-bumped Justin. "And why shouldn't life be like Yaoi? Insta-love, hot sex, and happy endings... *both* kinds for all."

Justin chuckled.

Jordon glanced back and forth between Andrew and Zack. He shrugged. "I don't know, but I figured with you two shacking up during the tour and Zack living in your condo, I thought that would be next."

Zack's face appeared devoid of emotion. It was the same mask his pet had worn before the auction. He simply asked, "Please pass the green beans."

Jordon stared at Andrew. "What? Oh, have you like collared him? Hey, Zack, does that require any kind of a license?"

Dusty growled, "Jordon."

"What? I'm not talking about a dog license, but…." Jordon snickered.

Andrew found his center. He ignored the irritation he had in having to wait to collar Zack. Again, he didn't want to pressure his pet. This line of questioning didn't help. "Not yet, Jordon, and no, it doesn't."

Justin asked, "Isn't there a ceremony?" His brother knew the answer because Justin had gushed to Andrew about Robin and Josh's red-rose ceremony pictures.

"Yes, there is." Andrew hoped his glare communicated a knock-it-off vibe.

Zack cleared his throat and asked Jordon, "Are you and Justin hitting your next deadline?"

The rest of the dinner conversation revolved around Jordon and Justin's work.

Andrew tried to listen, but his mind kept circling back to the fact that he and Zack should talk. This avoidance needed to stop.

After dinner cleanup, the Davis brothers disappeared, leaving Andrew with his own brother. They sat in front of the windows with tea, watching a cardinal hop around from feeder to feeder. Eventually the bird's mate came, and they flew off together.

Justin cleared his throat and asked, "So, aren't you supposed to have a contract or something with Zack?"

Yes. Why had he let it go on this long? "It's unwritten."

"Shouldn't it be written down? Wouldn't that make *it* more official?"

Yes. "Not everyone needs to do that. He clearly doesn't want traditional things." The heteronormative comment still ate at him.

Justin snorted. "Are you sure about that?"

Andrew wasn't sure of anything, so he shook his head. He should have guided them better but he needed to be careful not to drive Zack away by moving too fast. "I don't know. I thought I'd wait until he settled into the condo."

"He moved in months ago. I think he's established your place as home. Don't you want commitment?"

"Yes!" Andrew lowered his voice to a more controlled volume. "Yes. I want us on solid ground."

"What are you doing to move the relationship to firmer ground? Other than making him walk funny?"

Laughter barked out from Andrew. "Wow." Granted every milestone in his relationship with Zack seemed to happen with way too much forethought. The progress had been achingly slow. "I don't want to push him." He left off his fear of shoving equating to losing Zack.

Justin shook his head. "Seriously, I don't get it. You define everything, why not this?"

"Clarity is not a bad thing." The pronouncement might have been a stalling technique. Andrew never understood how people thrived in chaos.

"And Zack refuses to give you clarity?"

Yes! Well, no… "I didn't say that."

"You didn't say what?" Zack slipped into the room and massaged Andrew's shoulders.

"Mmmm, that's good."

"Anything else you need help with, Just?" Zack kneaded the tension out of Andrew as he spoke.

"Nah, we're good."

He and Zack were *good*, but they could be better. It was a new year, and Andrew was tired of settling for less than they should have.

Once they said their good-byes and got into the car, Andrew said, "I want to stop at the salon, okay?"

"Okay." A very amorous Zack teased his fingers up and down Andrew's thigh, testing his resolve.

As Andrew pulled into the salon's lot, Zack attached his mouth to the erogenous spot on the base of his throat.

He groaned and tried to stop Zack from doing exactly what he wanted. "Come on, let's go inside."

Zack zipped his coat and followed Andrew into the building after the alarm was turned off.

"You know we've never done it on the front desk before." Zack ran a hand along the polished wood and began to push the appointment book aside.

Andrew chuckled, snatched Zack's hand, and pulled him toward his office. "Zack, we need to talk."

His pet froze like he'd been doused with cold water. "About?"

"Nothing bad." Andrew unlocked his office door and flicked on the light.

Zack had changed his office for the better. He'd gathered the arts-and-crafts hairstylists into a congregation of crazy on the bookshelf, which made the figurines take on an artsy look. Though when he sat behind his desk, he no longer saw them. The garden was hidden in shadows now, but they had turned the small space into Eden last spring, and they'd made love under the stars the night before the tour.

Andrew sat on the couch and patted the seat next to him.

All color appeared leeched from Zack's complexion. "What?"

"It's nothing bad... I don't think." Anxiety crept along Andrew's spine as he tried to reassure himself that they loved each other.... Granted they just hadn't said the words, but that was because they were going slowly... *too slowly!*

Zack rubbed the back of his neck and stared at Andrew. Finally his pet plopped onto the couch.

Had Andrew been afraid of going too fast for Zack or was he terrified of repeating his own past? And whatever he was doing, was that screwing up his present? "We've been together for over ten months. Most of that time was on tour, so I haven't pushed."

"Pushed?" Zack repeated the word.

"We've taken things slow."

Zack asked, "Slow?"

Andrew needed something other than Zack repeating back what he said. He needed to take the lead. "Do you know how I feel about you?"

Zack glanced around the office. "Um...."

The hesitation was like a slap in Andrew's face. "It's not a trick question."

Shifting next to him, Zack seemed to be at a loss. "Well, I mean... you know...."

Clearly, his pet didn't know or wasn't completely sure, and it was Andrew's fault. He should have said the words, even if Zack didn't say them back. Honesty was essential. "I love you."

"What?" Zack asked as if he might have misheard.

"You have to know I love you." Andrew said it louder, pronouncing each word with care.

"Oh my God! What?" Zack studied him with his huge eyes and asked with heartbreaking uncertainty, "You love me?"

"Yes. I love you."

Zack tipped his head closer, nudging Andrew's nose. As much as he wanted Zack's kiss, he needed him to understand. "I love you."

"Kiss me," Zack demanded and pressed their lips together.

Andrew groaned as his pet shifted, crawled over him and ended by straddling Andrew's leg.

Lips glided over lips, Zack started a slow grind. Fabric was in the way, but damn, it was too good.

No. Control. "Stop."

By the confused expression on his face, Zack's body followed sooner than his brain was able to process "no means no" or "stop means stop."

"Why are you flagging me with a vanilla safeword?" Annoyance bled through in Zack's words.

Some Doms would be irritated by Zack's lack of continuous submission. But each time Zack surrendered and exchanged power with him meant more to Andrew because it was a conscious gift.

Zack sat back on his lap and folded his arms.

Andrew dragged his fingers through Zack's hair and tucked an unruly section behind Zack's ears.

"How do you feel about me?" Was that a strain of doubt in his tone?

Zack half choked when he asked, "Are you serious? I've loved you since the moment I met you. You must know that!"

That might be a bit of an exaggeration, but now wasn't the time to split hairs. "Why haven't you told me?"

"Remember the first time I told you how I felt and how that went?"

"Yes, but—" For God's sake, they both needed to check their past baggage.

"I pattern quickly. I chased you away once with my intensity…."

It wasn't that but Andrew could see how someone not in his head could see that. "Were you ever planning to tell me?"

Zack shrugged. "Were you?"

"Well, I…. Okay. Point taken. I was trying very hard not to rush you."

"Can we, and by *we* I mean *you*, stop acting like I don't know what I want?"

"Well, I didn't know how you felt or what you wanted." Andrew needed to stop tiptoeing around and acting like Zack would shatter if Andrew pressed him for answers. In the hopes of doing better, he asked, "What *do* you want?"

"You. I don't know how many ways I can show it." Zack raised his arm to show his tattoo. "Always you."

Andrew kissed each letter of his own name colored into Zack's skin.

Zack took Andrew's hand and skimmed his fingers along the symbolic collar encircling Zack's throat.

Now it was time to ask the question. Andrew got up and rushed to his bottom desk drawer. Pulling out the golden box he'd gotten months ago, he kneeled in front of Zack. He opened the hinged box and asked, "Will you wear my collar?"

Zack fingers hovered over the intricately etched leather collar Andrew had had specially made for him. His smile lit up his whole face, and he said, "You have always been my Master, and you always will be, so yes. Drew, yes, a trillion times yes!"

CHAPTER TWENTY-ONE

"Do we really have to do *this* now?" Damn, Zack could think of so many other things they should be doing on their sofa. And it was *theirs*. Zack had found one that matched Andrew's current furniture, and this one had heat, massage, and reclined. All of the glorious things he'd like to do involved Drew with much less clothing, and none of the activities involved the revision of a standard consensual BDSM contract.

"Zack, pet, we need to make amendments to this document so it will represent and meet both our needs." Drew picked up and handed Zack a copy of the contract he'd set on the coffee table for a third time.

"You don't need a contract to meet my needs. I can give you a list verbally right now and—"

"We've put this off far too long." Drew gave him *that* look. The stare that said Zack needed to toe the line, not because Drew wanted him to, but because it was in his best interests to do so.

So another night wouldn't make much of a difference? He sighed. "I know."

"Do you have any issue with the contract beginning immediately when I slip your new collar on? This document refers to a start time of midnight on the eve of the collaring."

"No issue. I'd like it to begin immediately." His nervous angst about the ceremony seemed light-years away. "If we have to wait until the collaring when it's fastened on, I think it would be the best symbolic starting point." Zack fondled Drew's thigh.

Hmmm, his pants were definitely tightening. Yes, Master wanted playtime too.

"Okay, as lovely as that is, stop, pet. So, with the provisions of the contract, what do you think?" Drew appeared determined to do this now.

Fine. Work now. Play later.

Zack pointed to the first section. "I'm not crazy about the wording of 'renouncing all rights to my pleasure.' I'm good with the devoting myself to your pleasure and desires, but by the very nature of that, it means I'm not renouncing my pleasure."

Drew reread that section out loud and took a few notes on the yellow legal pad he had on the arm of the sofa. "All right, I see what you mean. Okay. Let's focus on the do's of it, instead of the don'ts."

"Good." There, that was easy enough.

"I'd like my devotion to you, as your Master, in this contract. I want it on paper that I intend to put your needs before my own. Let's work on the wording here and here." Drew tapped his finger on the contract. "So we can make the document more about dedication and love."

"Agreed." Someone else must have written something more positive. Zack scanned to the next section. "Oh, hey. I don't like this part about you taking full responsibility for me."

"How about we replace that line with something about 'your submission won't extinguish your responsibilities in meeting your full potential'?" Drew suggested as he wrote down the possibility.

"Hmmm, yeah, that's better. I'd also limit the contract to BDSM play and revisit this in the future in case we decide on an expansion of that."

Drew nodded. "I agree. We can ease into something 24/7 if we decide that's what we want."

Zack wanted to ensure he took care of his Master too. "Oh, not for this document, but we should both have a living will. I want to make sure that it will allow me to take responsibility for you if any accidents or shit happen."

Andrew made a note on a different page entitled: Living Wills. "Thank you, my pet. Um, you do trust me in that regard for you as well, or will you name Dusty as the responsible party?" Drew regarded Zack, raising one brow.

"No, I trust you. I just don't want to be a kept man." Drew's financial stability didn't mean Zack had to relinquish self-sufficiency. No way would he be comfortable with that.

Drew purred, "Unless I'm keeping you in bed for my wickedness?"

"Or kitchen or bathroom or backstage or this sofa, anywhere my Master decides he needs his way with me. Again to restate… *this sofa* is an option…." *Take me now, dammit!*

Drew's mouth landed on his, giving him a small taste of what he needed. He pulled back and said, "I like your thoughts on that. But let's finish this."

Fuck Drew's single-mindedness. Zack sighed as his lover turned the page of the document without really appreciating the possibilities of what they might be doing instead of hammering out a contract.

For example, Zack, bent over the couch and being fucked senseless with the massage function on high.

Drew pointed at the first item on the top. "This one I must insist upon."

Zack read the stipulation and laughed. Of course, Drew would have more demands than the average Dominant in the area of his submissive's appearance. "As hairdresser, elevated to stylist of rock stars, I'm sure you have strong feelings on this topic. You just want to make sure I don't dye my hair again."

Drew pointed at him. "That's a given. Hiding this beautiful color is a sin against nature." His Master ran his fingers through Zack's lush mop, murmuring approval at the condition of the strands. "Pet, I want to clothe you in what will make you shine. Lots of green, less writing on your T-shirts, and much less bagginess in your jeans."

Jesus, Zack was beginning to get a sense of what a dress-up doll must feel like. Why couldn't Drew want to play "strip the sub" right now? "Fine, but I want veto power on work clothing."

"I'd never ask you to wear anything inappropriate or allow you to appear less than professional."

He wouldn't. Zack was sure of that. "I know, but I want a bit of control."

"That's why you have a safeword." His Master pointed that fact out before starting every scene and playtime escapade.

Zack sighed. "Right, I'm going to safeword over clothing?"

"I don't know, but the option is there," Andrew challenged.

He growled. This again, so Zack possibly had a small issue. "I know using my safeword isn't a bad thing."

Drew shook his head. "I believe you understand the concept in your head but not in your heart. I've seen you struggle with it and your discomfort with using an out. Using your safeword is something we need to work on." Drew kissed his cheek before reviewing the contract some more. He glanced up from the agreement. "Are you sticking with your safeword of *mushroom*?"

Zack hadn't thought about changing his safeword. "Hmmm, I guess so."

Drew made a note. "I'd also like to begin using the word *yellow* when we're getting close to you using *mushroom*."

"So a safeword leading up to a safeword?" Wonderful, another word he wouldn't want to say. Though maybe he'd be more comfortable giving the warning before the possibility of tapping out.

"I want to be able to know if I'm skirting the edge of too far. This will help us both identify your boundaries and maybe help *us* accept that safewording isn't a negative reflection on the part of the submissive."

"By *us*, you mean *me*."

Drew shrugged. "I think it'll build more trust between us and can be very positive. We, meaning *me*, might want to force us, meaning *you*, to use your safeword."

Zack scoffed. "Nice."

"I want to ensure you'll use it when we are in unchartered territory, where we have no idea what your limits are going to be." Reading further, Drew added, "We should keep this bit about there never being any punishment for safewording, and I would like to retain the right to stop the scene all together."

"Of course." The "stop completely clause" was always the Dom's unwritten safeword.

"This section is another nonnegotiable for me," Drew said when they reached the section on emotional and physical well-being of the sub.

"You have a lot of nonnegotiables." Zack gave him an eye roll, attempting to lighten the mood.

Andrew remained serious. "As you entrust yourself into my care, I must trust that you'll provide me with complete disclosure on your physical and emotional state when we're doing a scene. I also expect that in the rest of our relationship as well."

He was right.

"I will if you will. I don't want to be in the dark." Fair was fair. Zack wanted information to be a two-way street.

Drew nodded. "I'll share with you everything outside of our BDSM relationship. I do reserve the right to discuss certain matters with other Doms and not you."

Zack didn't like people knowing their business, but there might be a need for Drew to ask questions or confide in others. "Okay, I trust your discretion."

They moved on to the next section of the document regarding toys. Drew stated, "I want any and all of your current sex toys disposed of."

"Um, I have some specially made pieces and gifts from mentors," Zack hedged. He didn't want to give up some of those things he might want to—

"If they've been used on others…." Drew's words trailed off as he stared at Zack.

"But…." *Shit!* How did he bring this up? "Are you planning on playing with anyone else in—"

"No, this will not be an open relationship," Drew snapped.

Fuck, he wasn't asking for that.

Drew stared at him and leaned toward him. "Wait… do you want that?"

God, Zack loved his man, who would backpedal on his own trigger subject. Zack didn't want an open relationship, but possible future wiggle room. "No… I… look, I know Charlie cheated. I don't want an open relationship."

"He went behind my back. I can't have that done to me ever again, Zack." Drew's gaze remained focused on the document.

"Of course not."

Fuckety, fuck, fuck.

"Okay, so you wouldn't cheat on me, but you'd like to occasionally play with another…." Andrew assessed Zack and the situation possibly a bit too well, until he questioned, "Without me?"

"*No!* Never alone."

Drew stared deeply into Zack's eyes. "But, you'd like to explore other people with me involved?"

Zack's heart pounded hard. He swallowed. "I don't know. Maybe?"

"Now is the time to discuss this." Drew's expression remained devoid of emotion.

Fine! Zack would throw his feelings out there. "I've always had this fantasy, and it's really okay if it never happens, but I would get off on serving you with another sub."

"And…."

"And, okay, I've thought about dominating *with* you." A raised eyebrow got Zack to add, "I'd still be serving you, though. So you'd be in charge of the scene."

"Explain," Drew demanded.

Zack tried to run after the right words to chase down his feelings on the subject. He still struggled to wrap his head around the sacrifice of never dominating someone again. "Yeah, you know, double-teaming some sweet little sub, training them or helping to heal damage.... You know, together."

"Ah, I see. You don't want to give up your fan club?" Drew folded his arms in front of him and stared Zack down.

He sighed and shook his head. "It's not about that.... Okay, maybe a little, but that isn't the main reason. There's a joy in bringing someone to subspace, and I'd regret never experiencing that again. To do it with you...."

"Your fantasies are not without—" Andrew seemed to riffle for the right word. "—appeal. I'd love to see you in action. You in leather, in complete control of a sub, helping them find subspace... working with me... incredibly arousing."

Zack was good on both sides of the knots. "Making a sub fly and turning my Master on at the same time would be beyond mind-blowing."

"No penetration for either of us. That's nonnegotiable for me... at this time." Drew continued to add notes to his long list.

Zack nodded. "I agree. We should both have veto power on who we play with."

"Never behind each other's back. In the last scenario, where you'd be acting with me as the Dominant, we would draw up the scene together, but I'd want to have the final say. In addition of a sub to serve with you, I'd want to be clear on your expectations and needs on how that would play out. I'd want to define what you're looking to achieve."

Even though Drew didn't sound like he expected an immediate answer, words seemed to fall out of Zack's mouth. "To know that even though you could have anyone, it's me that you chose."

"Always, Zack. Always." Drew pressed his lips against Zack's, taking his breath and doubts away. "Would you want to do that often?"

"No."

Drew made some more notes. "*Often* should be defined, so we need to think about that. After any such play, I expect full disclosure on your feelings and what you've gained from the experience."

Zack nodded. Wow, the matter was out there, and lightning didn't strike.

Drew glanced at the contract and shook his head in mock despair. "Well, we both know you're going to have trouble with this next one."

"Hey, come on now. I'm much better at using the right terms." Zack purposefully paused before adding, "*Master*."

"I'd like it if you continue to call me Drew when we are in public to remind us both that you are mine, even when we aren't formally in our BDSM roles."

"I'm definitely, undeniably yours." Zack scanned the section since they were getting close to the end of the sheaf of papers. "We should move this section up to where clothing is discussed. Anyway, since I've given you control over my style, I have no issue with this section."

Drew grinned and rubbed his hands together. "I'm looking forward to getting rid of all those baggy jeans."

Zack scoffed. "That's my signature look."

"No longer. I want to see your ass—correction, *my* ass, 'cause you belong to me—encased in tight jeans."

"Not too tight for work," Zack reminded him, because having the circulation constricted in his balls was no fun.

"You have veto over work attire but not the style."

Zack rolled his eyes. "Yes, Master, but I can still safeword."

Drew set the papers aside and took Zack's hand. "I want to be clear that if you *ever* feel like I'm asking you to do something you really don't want, I expect you to safeword so we can discuss the issue. Okay?"

"Yes, Master." Zack batted his eyelashes, hoping to lighten Drew's mood.

"Wow, why do I feel I should savor you giving in so easily?" Drew's eyes sparkled with mirth.

Zack swallowed back a retort.

Drew grabbed the pages and pointed to the *Punishment* section. Just reading the title set Zack's insides on broil. Oh, how he loved most kinds of discipline. They set him free. However, he couldn't be too easy. "I don't want long-term denial. That's my nonnegotiable."

"How about short-term?" Andrew's smirk and nod told him the man was too observant.

Oh fuck! As exciting as that type of torment might be, it could be agony. Delicious, delightful agony. The thought of orgasm denial made him squirm against the cushions. "Orgasm delay. Yeah, but I want a maximum limit."

"Three days," Andrew tossed out.

"What? No way!" Was he insane?

Andrew barely kept a straight face. Oh, Drew was teasing. "Funny, Master, funny."

"How about a maximum of thirty hours?" Andrew suggested the outward limit that some would argue headed more in the orgasm denial territory.

Zack could handle a day and change. "And not to be done more than once a month."

"Up to twice a month. If I choose and you require the pleasure of that kind of discipline."

Purr. Submit. Yum.

Zack growled. "Fine." He attempted a glare, but he had a feeling it appeared more like a leer.

"Any other punishments off the table?" Drew asked.

"The usual, no cock and ball torture, scarring, maiming, or scat." Zack figured he'd go with basics.

"Of course, I'd never do that—not my thing—but I'll add it. When we adjust the wording, we can have this notarized at Entwined. I believe the manager is a notary."

"Good. I'd also like the owners to review the contract to see if there's anything we need to address."

Drew nodded. "Good idea. We should both reserve the right to revisit the contract any time we desire. But we must both review the entire document prior to our collaring anniversary."

"Makes sense."

"Now about those pants." Drew pushed his index fingers through the belt loops of Zack's jeans.

"What? I love these jeans." Zack shifted in place and hiked them up.

"I think they'd look better off." Drew tugged, and the material slid off Zack's hips.

"Oh, well, you are the Master."

CHAPTER TWENTY-TWO

ZACK PACED, wearing the floor down with his back-and-forth circuit. He stared at the clock on the wall. Damn, only two minutes from the last time he'd checked. He wanted Drew.

Anxious knocks sounded at the door. "Zack? Zack! Are you in there? Let me in."

What the...? "It's open."

Jordon almost fell into the room. The kid panted and tried to catch his breath. He gestured wildly toward the door. "Zack, oh my God. There are people out there barely dressed."

Why bother? Their kid brother was twenty. Jordon's immaturity was Zack and Dusty's fault. This was a prime example of them having overprotected Jordon. "Entwined is a BDSM club, Jordy. Relax, it really is no big deal. It's, um, think of it like a dress code."

Jordon shook his head, and his expression deemed Zack insane. He shut the door and pressed on it. "So, are you nervous?"

Zack wasn't. "No, is that weird?"

His brother shook his head. "Nah, it means you're doing the right thing. God, I can't believe it."

Bam! Zack hit the wall when Jordon slammed against him in a hard hug. *Ow, that did not feel good.* Jordon almost crushed the life out of him.

A quick knock on the door drew his attention. He called out with the little breath he had left in his body, "Come in," hoping for a rescue.

Dusty and Justin hurried in with big smiles on their faces.

Justin made a beeline to Zack and Jordon. "Aw, look at you guys. You two look so handsome in your leather."

Dusty adjusted Jordon's long jacket so it hung better. "I like this shirt." The kid wore one of his original paint-spattered T-shirts, which worked perfectly.

Dusty shook his hand. "I can't believe this is happening." The handshake turned into a hug with a broken "Congratulations, Zack. I'm so happy for you."

No, Zack wasn't going to test the waterproof mascara that Drew suggested he wear for the pictures. "Oh hell, Dust. Don't get all choked up."

Jordon jumped onto Dusty from behind. He wrapped his legs around him, gave him a huge embrace, and kicked his heels into Dusty's thighs. "Piggyback ride. Piggyback ride," Jordon shouted.

Zack snorted. "Not usually what that means around here."

Dusty belly-laughed, and Jordon groaned. He jumped off Dusty and couldn't seem to wipe the grimace off his face. "Not enough brain bleach to wash away the images flashing through my mind right now."

Dusty whispered something to his leather-kilted fiancé, making him laugh.

"Shhhh, Dust. Later." Justin gripped Dusty's butt before slapping it. The smack echoed off the walls, which experienced the reverberation of leather on flesh daily. "Oh, I like the sound of that," Justin growled. He must have, too, because he did it again.

He'd have done it a third time, but Dusty caught his hand and kissed the palm. "As you said, love, later."

Grinning, Justin grabbed Zack and squealed. "I'm so happy for you and my brother. You both deserve love and happiness." He stepped back from the hug. "You look handsome. I'm glad you went with Robin's recommendations on color. I should go check on Andrew."

Jordon grabbed a program and skimmed it. He snapped his head up from the page. "Oh my God! You exchange blood? That's gross." As an afterthought, he added, "And dangerous."

Sighing, Zack answered, "We've been tested; it's symbolic."

"What the hell are you, a BDSM vampire? You know, come to think of it, I've not seen you in the sunshine in years. Do you sparkle when he spanks you? I bet you do," Jordon teased.

Dusty cleared his throat and, in that uncomfortable way of his, hid behind sharing knowledge. "Jordon, it's only a small amount, and it's dripped on the white rose, which signifies losing virginity…."

Jordon snorted. "That ship sailed long ago, right, Zack?"

Dusty pinched the bridge of his nose and slid his eyes shut.

Can't laugh. It's not funny. The sad way Dusty shook his head and Jordon's perky tone really taxed Zack's ability to deny the snort.

"What? Just 'cause I'm going to die a virgin doesn't mean Zack will." The kid swiveled his head, glaring from one to the other.

Damn! What could Zack say? He dragged the kid in close. Everything would be all right. Jordon should shut up now.

Dusty wrapped his arms around both of them. They stood there for a moment. It had always been the three of them against the world. Zack didn't want that to change.

The oldest Davis, as always, seemed to be hardwired into his and Jordon's brains and appeared to read Zack's mind. "Hey, no worries. Justin joined us, and Andrew will do the same. But this"—he squeezed Jordon and Zack—"this is still what it is, yes?"

Jordon sniffled and held on tighter. "Yeah."

Zack carefully wiped under his eyes. "Dammit, stop. I'll get misty and ruin my makeup."

Jordon pulled back, staring at him like he would be breaking the law. "No, don't do that. Your eyes look so good. Not as stunning as mine, of course, but better than usual."

Zack tried to ruffle Jordon's carefully structured, height-defying manga hair, but the kid bobbed out of reach. "Hey, don't mess with your man's work. I found out Andrew does have his uses...."

Zack rolled his eyes, and Dusty tossed his long mane over his shoulder.

Turning to the mirror, Zack had trouble believing this was his image. He wore tight, butter-soft white leather pants and a pair of white boots. Josh called them "erection friendly" pants, though luckily Dusty hadn't been within earshot at the time. Robin had talked him through how to get the most out of the haircut Drew had given him and insisted Zack line his eyes in the same dark green liner his little brother used on occasion. He had to admit that between the clothes, guyliner, and the mascara, he looked rather attractive.

"Something borrowed." Jordon handed him white hand warmers. "'Cause I want those back."

Zack frowned as he put them on. "It's not a wedding." He had to admit, though, they looked pretty sexy since he was shirtless, so he shut up. *Thank you for the new exercise routine.* Zack wasn't ripped but much more toned than he used to be.

His younger brother turned his hand over and pointed to the perfectly placed cutout. "See? They don't cover your wrist tat."

Dusty stared.

Zack shrugged. "I know you don't like ink."

"No, it's not that. I wondered if you guys think I should get one…
you know, for Justin."

Jordon squealed. "Oh my God! I know just what I could make
you." He paused and stared off into space, probably visualizing some
fantastic design. "I have several things in mind…." He drew to a halt.
The kid got quiet. "Sorry, Zack. So, um, you signed your paperwork
and shit?"

"I'M SO glad you guys made it." Andrew hugged Robin and Josh. Damn,
it was good to see them again.

Robin sighed and untied Andrew's white silky poet's shirt. "Leave
it open."

"You sure I shouldn't wear the pirate shirt?" He held up the other
option for Robin's final judgment.

Andrew didn't acknowledge Josh's eye roll, which his friend
stopped rooting around the toy closet to give.

Robin whisked the silk out of Andrew's hand. "Positive. Johnny
Depp has left the building." The blue-green-haired keyboard player and
full-time fashionista hung the silk on the hook. "Besides, you wouldn't
be able to show off your chest."

"True." Andrew skated a finger over the image covering his heart.

Josh swung a cat-o'-nine-tails, catching Robin on his blue-green
leather-covered ass. Impressive. He hit dead center.

Robin stiffened, closed his eyes, and shivered. He spun toward
Josh with an evil smile and said, "I like all the little leather tails. We
don't have one of those."

"On it." Josh pulled out a phone hidden in the waistband of his
skintight brown leather pants.

Andrew turned toward the door as Justin entered.

His brother did look good in the black leather kilt, fishnets, and
leather combat boots, but he had to ask, "Are you playing bagpipes?"

"Would you like me to?"

"We'll leave you two alone." Josh twirled the cat-o'-nine through
his fingers, not even looking in their direction. All the man's focus was
on his lover.

"Um, how long until you start?" Robin's face tinted to a lovely
shade of pink.

Andrew laughed. "You have time, but don't dally. And Josh? Don't give him the cat as hard as he wants, or he'll be walking with a limp."

Robin sniffed. "I fully expect to be limping, but not because of the kitty cat."

Andrew stared at them. Damn, how hard did they play? He originally would have bet on light play, but Robin's reaction to the cat suggested they were far from novice.

"We'll return *this* after we're done." Josh grabbed Robin by the hand and dragged the excited man out of the room, presumably into one of the empty rooms set aside for Andrew and Zack's use.

When Andrew met Justin's gaze, they simply burst into peals of laughter. "Oh my. That's priceless." He carefully blotted the tears of amusement that escaped.

"They are a mix of sweet and kink."

"I bet Josh has his hands full." Andrew stared at his reflection in the mirror.

Justin fussed a bit with the silky poet's shirt as he peered at the skin beneath the shirt.

"Stop trying to peek." He pushed his brother's hands away as Justin tried to pretend to do something other than uncover Andrew's gift to Zack. "I spent the last week and a half with a T-shirt on. You're not seeing the tattoo before Zack."

Justin rolled his eyes as a flush brightened his cheeks at being caught. He stopped. "Fine." He grinned up at Andrew. "So, how are you doing? You ready for this?"

"Absolutely. I can't wait to make him officially mine." Andrew had been counting down the weeks, then the days, the hours, and now the minutes.

"He's always been yours," Justin pointed out.

"No." *Possibly.* "You think he's ready?"

"I think Zack was ready the second he met you."

Andrew pushed away regret at the time lost with the knowledge they were both in a place to move forward as life partners. This was forever.

He turned to fuss with Justin's dark hair. Andrew had convinced his brother the severe black hair color would benefit from some blue-black highlights. "This cut and color looks so great on you. Damn, I'm good."

Snorting, Justin laughed. "Yeah, you are. You really aren't nervous?"

"For what? I'm looking past the celebrations, getting back on the road with the band, and exploring all the new places with Zack."

"Yeah, the tour should be awesome. Angel talked Megan into giving the band some slack time. We won't be rushing from one city to the next at breakneck speed. It'll cost more, but the guys want to enjoy the ride a bit."

"I can't wait to spend more time in Europe, China, Japan, and Thailand."

There was a knock, and Robin popped his head into the room. "It's time now."

"Um, are you limping?" Justin asked before laughing.

Running fingers through his blue-green hair, he stepped over to the mirror and swiped a finger under both eyes. A hint of a smile formed. "Just a little."

"Let's go." Andrew wanted to see Zack.

Robin thrust a red rose at him. The bloom was open a little past the bud stage. "Don't forget your rose."

"Thank you, Robin." Andrew took the flower. It was supposed to be fully opened, while the white one Zack intended to hold was to be a bud, but he didn't like the connation of inequality, so Robin had assured him their flowers would be opened as identically as possible. He wanted a representation of them growing and loving together.

Andrew opened the door and allowed Justin to walk through.

Justin nearly skipped up to the stage area. Halfway up the makeshift aisle scattered with white rose petals, his brother squealed and threw an arm around Andrew to tug him close.

He and Justin weaved up the aisle with gleeful satisfaction. Andrew's kid brother only unwound his arms when they approached the stairs to the stage and needed to climb them single file.

The seated members of the club mixed in with some of their closest friends. Almost everyone he knew attended. Some of the members Andrew had known for years, others he barely knew, but all were here in support of him and Zack joining in a bond most in this room believed fused people together stronger than marriage.

INSIDE ZACK'S room, Jordon had turned into a worrywart.

"Yeah, Jordon. Of course I signed my *paperwork* and shit." Zack chuckled at having his contract with his Master referred to as "paperwork." Ah, the vanilla among them. May the Goddess bless them and keep them safe from the reality of BDSM. "You'll take the document to Andrew and bring it back to me?"

"Yes, sort of like a dog playing fetch. Can I be Toto?" The kid shimmied. "'Cause I'm all about the rainbows."

Dusty and Zack laughed.

"Here. This is from Jordon and me." Dusty thrust a velvet box at Zack.

"Oh, thank you." He opened the package. A fingernail-sized emerald earring caught the light. He removed the new starter earring that was recently pierced in his right ear.

"I picked out the stone," Jordon bragged. "I figured the color brought out my eyes, so I believed it might make yours look nicer than usual."

Smiling, he opted not to let the thinly veiled insult annoy him. "It's perfect." He stepped back in front of the mirror to make sure he wasn't making a new hole. "How's it look?"

Dusty put a hand over Jordon's open mouth and stopped the snarky comment that was sure to spew forth. "Andrew's very lucky."

As if on cue, Robin knocked before poking his head in. "He's up there. Jordy…."

The youngest Davis grabbed the rolled contract Zack signed, not only with his signature but also with a lip-glossed kiss, and ran out the door.

ANDREW STOOD at the foot of Entwined's stage. Someone had decorated the chains hanging from the ceiling with twinkle lights. There were several large arrangements of red roses in black vases dressing up the tables lining the walls. The stage curtains had garlands of red roses and white statice draped over them. The chairs were parted to create an aisle, which was littered with rose petals.

Jordon hurried down the aisle as if on urgent business from a king. He handed Andrew the rolled page secured with a red ribbon.

Andrew unrolled the page and reviewed the document. He cleared his throat and turned toward the crowd. "Today, Zack and I officially begin our contract. We will reevaluate the terms yearly on this date, but there is no end date. Zack is mine and I am his for this lifetime and beyond."

Andrew stopped and took a moment. He hadn't expected the rush of love and affection for Zack to nearly overwhelm him. He centered himself and continued. "Thank you for being here and playing witness to our commitment to each other. Today my signature will join my love's, binding us with more than just ropes."

Andrew had decided not to read the entire contract aloud, only certain parts they were willing to share. He traced a finger over Zack's signature and lip prints.

He signed the document with flare and kissed near his signature, with love. His clear lip balm left the outline of his lips next to Zack's. When he turned to hand the form back to Jordon, he chuckled.

Poor Jordon stared openmouthed at the guests.

DUSTY SNICKERED. "Well, Jordon may finally be coming around."

"Drew, I mean, Andrew has been working on him." Zack paced to the mirror and back.

With a serious look, Dusty studied him. "This is what *you* want, right? You know all of *it*—"

"It's more than I dreamed I could have, Dusty."

"Truly?"

"Honestly. I swear I knew he was mine when I met him. He's *the One*."

Dusty sighed and nodded.

Zack's BDSM interest worried and might have even scared his big brother, but Dusty had never reproached Zack. "He gives me what I need, Dust. He understands me."

"He's good to you?"

"Of course. When he…." Zack stopped his words as Dusty paled. "Sorry. TMI. Rest assured, he's amazing at things other than hair."

Chuckling, Dusty held up a hand. "Good to know." He shook his head. "I only want the best for you. You deserve to be happy."

Jordon dashed in with the signed contract in hand. "Your man actually read parts of the contract to the crowd. Are you sure about all that?"

"Yes, Jordon, very sure." His kid brother eyed the room.

He meandered over to the wooden cabinet.

"You don't want to open that," Zack warned, not needing his brother swooning.

Jordon nodded. "Did you know some of your guests were kneeling on the floor, and others were almost nude? I saw the guy with a cage on his junk, and he was with two other guys locked up. I think a few of them were having sex right there in the crowd. One of the women had a chain between her nipples."

Zack shrugged. "Welcome to a BDSM club. Entwined is a *safe* place for people to be themselves with *no one* judging them. Don't be like Mom, okay?" Pain at her absence in their lives still stung. He pushed the hurt away.

"Of course not."

"Did the woman with the nipple chain have long red hair?"

Jordon nodded.

"That's Julie and her partners. I'm so glad she made it." Miracles never ceased. She'd beaten her disease and found not one but two partners to adore and cherish her.

True to form, curious Jordon opened the cabinet he had been told not to. He peered inside for half a second before squealing and slamming the door shut. "What the hell?" He stared at Zack with accusation in his eyes.

"Jordon." Dusty's tone demanded silence.

The kid, as if drawn by some magnetic force, reopened the door and poked around in the cabinet.

Their older brother stomped over with clear intention of shutting the door but froze in front of the cabinet, staring into it.

Zack went over and closed the cabinet. "Stop screwing around. It's time."

"Oh, don't forget your virginity symbol." Jordon carefully handed him a perfect white rose, sporting very sharp thorns. He leaned in and said, "Now I know what's meant when they say 'screw the roses, give me the thorns.'"

"Who says that?" Dusty folded his arms over his black leather vest.

Jordon gestured to the closed door. "Those people out there do."

Zack shook his head. "Let's go."

THERE HE is! Drew! Zack floated up the aisle toward his Master. The only thing that seemed to keep his feet on the ground was the weight of his brothers' hands on his shoulders. They also forced him to put one foot in front of the other, not dash to be with Drew.

Once Zack finally got to the bottom of the stage, his Master clasped both Zack's hands and interlocked their fingers. A complete calm fell over him as Drew guided him onto the stage.

Marcus officiated. The smug bastard kept smirking at him.

Focusing on his Master took his breath away. He looked extraordinary in white leather pants and a silk shirt. The white candles flickering on the stage painted Drew's face in shadow and light, turning him into a sexy demon. Hard to believe this man was his now and would be for the rest of his life.

Zack made himself listen to Marcus.

"I am honored these men have given me this great privilege." Marcus addressed Zack and Drew directly. "Your journey to each other has been full of twists and turns, but you've reached your destination… each other. We, your friends and all of your brothers, stand with you today. You both have our support to succeed in binding yourself together in a way stronger than the laws of the land."

Damn, Marcus loved attention. He took the opportunity to employ a sense of drama and torment Zack just a little. The officiant touched each of their three brothers and Robin, who stood up as the fourth witness, on the shoulder. "You will bear witness to Zack's commitment to Master Andrew and Master Andrew's commitment to our Zack."

Half the people in the audience sighed. Marcus raised his hands. "Do not mourn the loss of a Dom, rejoice in the addition of a worthy submissive."

Zack would kill the man, or possibly just his younger brother, who snickered at the word "submissive." Drew cleared his throat, and instantly the murmuring stopped, including Jordon's.

Ah, that was better. Zack squeezed Drew's hand in thanks.

"Master Andrew." Marcus gestured to the Dom, who dropped one of his hands to reach behind to Robin.

Zack accepted the gold box his Master handed him. They had agreed on getting him a new collar to begin their new life together. He opened the lid and touched the heavy silver necklace they would be using in the everyday world.

He met his Master's gaze, and their connection eliminated all else around them. His Master removed the necklace while he handed the box to Dusty.

Drew passed the chain briefly through a candle flame. "With fire I purify. You've signed your acceptance, now it's time you wear the other symbol of your commitment to me and to us."

Zack dropped to his knees so the thick silver necklace that would symbolize his collar could be placed. When they played, his Master would change the necklace to his leather play collar he'd given him when he asked Zack to be collared. The tiny padlock made a loud click when it was shut.

He was finally locked to his Master.

Master Drew helped him stand and gave him a soft kiss on the lips. Romantic sighs echoed through the room. "You wear my collar, and you have marked yourself as mine."

"I do and I have," Zack stated.

Drew kissed Zack's tattoo and opened his shirt to display his ink. "I can do no less for you. You are my love and my key."

Zack immediately touched the almost healed dragon key over his lover's heart. He traced his name, which was colored onto the key's shaft. The beautiful art got a little blurry as the power of love and affection overwhelmed Zack.

Marcus spoke for Zack's ears only. "I believe he's now marked as taken, as are you, my friend."

"With Jordon's help, I have this, a symbol of our bond. You are beyond my partner in life. You are the missing part of my soul." His Master's voice cracked just a little.

Love. Kneel. Mine. His. Happy. Serve. Love.

"And now, the Ceremony of the Rose." Marcus interrupted their moment to finish their binding. "The two of you together have reformed this ceremony to suit your individual needs. Proceed."

Master Drew held Zack's index finger to his lips. He kissed the tip and pressed Zack's flesh into the thorn on the red rose. A hiss of sexual pleasure escaped Zack's lips. He held Zack's finger over two white roses until two drops stained the petals.

Zack held his finger up to Andrew's mouth. His Master kissed and licked Zack's digit briefly. He sighed in disappointment when the display ended but was reminded their brothers were standing right there by Jordon's quiet gagging noises.

His Master didn't like pain and winced a little as he opened his own finger to sacrifice two bubbles of blood. Oh, poor Drew. The droplets hit the roses, merging together.

His Master pressed his and Zack's fingers together and said his vow: "I will be yours, as you are mine."

"I will be yours, as you are mine," Zack repeated. As soon as the last word left Zack's mouth, Drew pressed their lips together and demanded a kiss unparalleled to any other they'd ever shared.

Marcus handed their brothers and Robin a chain that had been purified by the candle's flame, and they wound the length around Zack and Drew.

Zack barely heard Marcus claim they were bound for eternity because his Master didn't seem intent on breaking the kiss any time soon. Finally Andrew led Zack down the stairs of the stage and out of the main room.

Their lives were fully entwined. Zack had locked himself to Drew and given him the key.

Chapter Twenty-Three

SOMEHOW ONE of the guys must have run ahead of them, because their white roses were together in a bud vase on a table. The chain used to bind them for all eternity had been placed in a black silk bag with an embroidered *A* and *Z* on it.

Zack tried to calm his breathing, but his heart raced. It had been far too long since he'd spent time with Drew. He hadn't been denied orgasms. There just seemed to be little time to arrange to have them with all the last-minute planning for the next Dark Angels tour and collaring celebration prep.

"You're finally mine, pet."

"Always have been." Regretting lost time only wasted more moments, so Zack refused to dwell on the pointless past. Instead he'd focus on his future with Drew.

He tugged Drew down into a kiss and walked him backward to the bed someone had thoughtfully made up of the padded platform. When the backs of Drew's knees hit the cushion, he sat and Zack crawled on top of him.

"Mine. All mine." Zack growled and marked Drew's neck with a love bite. When Zack got to a ticklish spot, he received a rumbling belly laugh.

"Yes. Yes. All yours, without a doubt." Drew did a quick ninja flip.

Zack landed on his back, attempting not to purr at the dominance but failing.

"Mine." His Master rumbled as he raised Zack's hand and licked his dragon tattoo.

"Let me try." Zack ducked his head and ran a tongue across Andrew's colorful key. "I wanna see if the colors taste different."

"What? They don't...." Drew gasped and suggested, "Keep checking."

Zack wanted him without any barriers because neither of them had done that with anyone. He wasn't fighting the ghost of his lover's past relationship, not really, but he wanted Drew inside him without a condom. They knew it was safe to do so. He wanted that *first* for himself.

"I want you inside me."

"I see you're still trying to top from the bottom, my pet."

Shit! "I'm sorry, Drew. We haven't been together in forever; I feel like a virgin." Zack even batted his eyelashes. Perhaps he'd overdone the flirting, because his lover burst out laughing.

"Did you follow my instructions?"

"To the letter, *Master*." Zack completed the entire list as thoroughly as possible. He wiggled, and the butt plug, which he'd lodged inside himself, nudged against him in an erection-building way. "Should I take off... um, sorry. Right."

"Let's just be."

Zack was collared. Shouldn't he be taken like a sub? "Um...."

Drew undid Zack's snap and eased the leather past his erection. "Umphf." His lover took Zack's cock in his mouth and sucked.

Stars burst behind his eyelids. Damn, the suction was perfect. Maybe scenes were overrated; vanilla sex was fine with him. He didn't need ropes... all the time. Drew took him to the root and licked his way back up until Zack's cock was drying in the air.

Andrew hauled Zack's pants the rest of the way down his legs. He stripped out of his own shirt and danced out of his pants. His lover stared at him for a moment and must have come to a decision.

"Zack?" Andrew tapped the butt plug, bumping the end against Zack's prostate.

Zack's voice cracked. "Yeah, Drew?"

"Are you mine?"

He swallowed and said with as much conviction as he could manage, "Completely."

Drew twisted the butt plug.

"Fuck!"

"I'm glad we still need to work on your swearing." Drew chuckled.

It wasn't funny, and Zack might go insane with the light little taps and turns Drew gave the device. He needed more and he begged, "Come on."

His impatience earned him several swats from the palm of his lover's hand to his ass, though Drew must have known that would do absolutely nothing to cool his ardor.

Zack shoved his ass back, seeking more of the delicious attention.

His lover adjusted his position, so Zack wound up flat on his back. The butt plug was withdrawn, leaving Zack feeling empty. God, he wasn't above begging. "Please?"

"Patience, my love." Drew slicked lube onto his fingers and pushed two into Zack's eager hole.

Impatient, he grabbed his knees and pulled them back, offering his entrance in submission. "Yours, Drew."

Andrew's eyes slid closed. "Mine."

Zack cried out as his true love pushed in deep. He bit his lip. He required the burn as it skirted the line between agony and "got to have more now." Zack wiggled, trying to adjust to the cock stuffed inside him.

Master Drew froze and studied him. The pain morphed into something pleasurable, and his face must have communicated it was time to thrust. And thrust his Master did.

Damn, the man had a cock direct from heaven. Zack's toes curled as enduring the strokes merged into wanting them. He nudged his ass against his Master's thighs, begging for more.

"You want this, don't you?"

"Forever. I want you forever." Zack's voice cracked a little.

"I'm yours, and you are mine." Drew punctuated each word with a forward stroke. "You're mine to take care of. Mine to love. Mine to be with, always."

Zack tilted his hips just a little, ensuring maximum stimulation against his gland. He gasped as his cock throbbed. "Yes, I'm all yours."

"You want it all."

"Yes, Drew." His voice was only a whisper, yet carried all the need swirling within him.

Drew lifted him and pulled his hips higher so Zack rested on his Master's powerful thighs. Though still on his back, gravity helped Drew impale him in the most erotic way. Drew talked, so Zack tried to pay attention and make sense of the words.

"Who do you want right now? Me as your lover or your Master?"

"Huh?" Confusion clouded the question.

"Do you want me to be your Master or your lover?"

Concerted effort allowed him to focus and find an answer. "You're one and the same." Zack whimpered.

"Who do you need right now?"

"Today, Master Drew collared me," Zack reasoned and touched his new circlet. Drew wasn't only his Master; he was Zack's everything.

His Master used Zack's precome as lubricant, gliding his fist in smooth strokes. Each pass of his rough hands drove Zack closer to orgasm... closer, but never over the edge.

Drew was still embedded inside him when Zack tipped his head back and spread his arms out on the blankets. He hoped to present the picture of complete submission. "Whatever you want, it is yours to have. Deny me. Make me come. As long as I'm pleasing to you, Master."

A groan from above told Zack that he'd said the right thing. His Master pushed into him quickly and with more purpose. He loved his Master's hand stroking him. He tilted his hips, and the angle made his prostate a target for Drew's insertion.

"Tell me what you want."

"Please." Gazing up at his Master, he was lost in a rush of emotion. "Give me what you want me to have. Please, Master, I'm yours. Truly yours."

"Does my Zack want to come?"

"God yes, Drew... Master, please let me come."

Drew captured Zack's lips with his own as he thrust faster.... Zack barely hung on to the edge when warm wetness filled him.

Holy fuck! Drew's essence was inside him. He'd never been so connected to anyone.

His Master choked out in a hoarse voice, "Come."

Zack didn't need to be told twice. Drew was inside him. Zack was pumped to a glorious orgasm. Ecstasy hit strong and rolled on for so long, he wasn't sure when the climax ended and the aftershocks of pleasure kicked in.

His Master glowed and smiled at Zack.

Zack tugged Drew down on top of him. Fuck, that was amazing. "I love you, Master." He mused out loud, "I love you, Drew."

"I love you too." His Master laughed. "Who do you love more?"

Hard question, because while they were one and the same man, they were very different and fulfilled different needs for Zack. "Does it matter?"

"Curious." Drew grabbed an alcohol-free towelette from the dispenser near the platform. He cleaned Zack's opening with teasing swipes, which were more tantalizing than feeling Drew leak out from him. Master Drew took another towelette, cleaned himself off, and then tossed it away in the trashcan.

Andrew interlocked Zack's fingers with his, which made a wave of happiness dance through him. He studied the long, talented fingers of his Master, lover, and friend. "I love all of you. I love my Drew and my Master Drew the same amount but in different ways. You fit into many categories."

"So, I'm versatile?"

Zack shrugged, and he might have been smirking. "You proved that."

Andrew snorted.

He wanted to articulate his feelings, but he was still euphoric about being collared by the man he'd loved for years. No more pretending. "I want to explore my limits and be pushed past them within an equal relationship."

Andrew nodded. "Friends with ownership?"

Laughing, Zack agreed. "Exactly."

"You know I'm yours as much as you're mine, right?"

That was a surreal concept for Zack. "Getting there."

Andrew huffed. "It will take time." He pointed to the vase with the two roses. "Hey, you want to pluck the petals and make our wishes?"

"Aren't we supposed to wait until tomorrow?"

"My interpretation is after our bond is consummated." Andrew rolled on top of him and proceeded to tickle him. "I think you've been consummated. Haven't you?"

"Don't you mean consumed?"

Andrew dug into his armpits.

Zack laughed hysterically and squealed, "Stop. Stop. No."

"Maybe not? Maybe I should consume and consummate you again?" Drew pressed his advantage.

"Yeah, maybe just to make sure." Struggling between fits of laughter, Zack planted his feet on the flat surface of the makeshift bed and tried to buck Drew off him. "Stop. I can't stop laughing. Drew! Come on."

Minutes later, when his erection began poking against Drew's asscheek, Zack was released from the tickle torture.

Drew swung his leg off so he fell to the side of him. "Seems like tickling is also something we should explore in the future."

Zack opened his mouth to deny his interest, but the evidence stacked up against him. Drew gestured with his head toward Zack's jutting erection.

Zack glanced down and shrugged. "Yeah, I guess."

"Bet you'd like to be tied down and tickled."

A gasp of desire escaped Zack.

"Me, in total control of you." Drew caressed Zack's face tenderly as he tormented him with his words. "You helpless, begging, as I prove to you I own you."

"Yes, Drew... Master.... Anything you want." Zack would provide.

"I'll fulfill every fantasy and every sexy thought you've ever had, and I'll keep looking for more."

A surge of love washed over him. He wrapped his arms around his perfect man and held on tight. It was overwhelming to get everything he'd ever wanted, and at the same time, he'd always be greedy when it came to Andrew. He'd always want more.

A weird question popped into his mind. "How did you know I was ticklish under the arms?" Drew had gone straight for the kill zone. There hadn't been a moment of hesitation, no trying to figure out what was ticklish. To top it off, Zack wasn't ticklish unless his arm was held down, how did Andrew figure out the key?

Andrew snorted. "A wise man never reveals his source."

"That little pecker-head! Jordon squealed, huh?" He rolled into Drew's embrace.

Holding his right hand up and the left over his heart, Drew solemnly told him, "I was sworn to secrecy."

"So, you're telling me Jordon didn't do it?" Zack asked, totally sure the loose lips belonged to his kid brother.

Hands still in place, Drew nodded enthusiastically. "I cannot verbally agree or disagree. I promised not to say a word."

Music drifted into their room. He hated to suggest leaving their haven, but he did. "We should get out there. Shouldn't we?"

"We will, but first things first." Drew's eyes sparkled. He captured Zack's mouth with his own and wrapped his warm hand around Zack's erection.

This was a good *first* thing. Zack pushed his hips up, thrusting into Andrew's palm.

"Are you going to be a good little pet and quench my thirst?" Drew turned and trapped Zack's cock between both hands. He glanced over his shoulder and gave Zack a look that almost made him lose control before the good stuff happened, because the last time Drew was "thirsty," Zack got a mighty fine blowjob, and he definitely didn't want to miss out.

"Um, yeah. It's my duty as your sub to fulfill all your needs. God yes—" His words stalled when Drew's talented mouth swallowed around his cock. Through his moans, he begged for the one thing to make this experience even better. "Want to taste you—" He craved his lover's dick in his mouth as he was sucked off. Perhaps he did have the sub mindset: always needing to give to be truly satisfied.

Drew swung a knee over Zack's head and straddled his face. Zack inhaled the clean scent left by the towelette mixed with Andrew's maleness. His mouth watered when he saw a drop at the tip of his man's cock.

Zack opened his mouth but stopped himself. "Please?"

"Please, what?" Cool air rushed across his cock before Drew used his hot mouth to take Zack back in.

"Please, may I suck on you?" Zack whimpered. Drew was almost fully hard and so close to Zack's mouth.

"Hell, yes!" Drew returned his attention to Zack's cock, swallowing him once again.

Fuck, Drew gave superior head.

Dammit. Zack wanted to give him some head. "Want you." He yearned to lick the fluid drop to taste him.

Again, Drew pulled off of Zack's excited erection to chuckle. "Really? I couldn't tell."

"Don't talk with your mouth full, it's rude." Zack helped Drew to stop speaking with a thrust of his hips.

Drew pulled back and laughed. "Do you think you'll taste me before I taste you?"

Fuck! He'd try, but he didn't know if he could accomplish the feat. "I'll try."

"There is no *try*, only *do*. I have faith in you." Drew stopped talking and used his mouth for a higher purpose.

Zack groaned. Fuck, he sounded like he'd been shot instead of sucked.

When Drew shifted and resettled over his face, Zack slurped the dangling treat into his mouth. His only hope was strong suction and speed.

He grabbed Drew's well-formed ass and guided his lean hips. Experience had taught Zack that his lover enjoyed a well-placed finger. He shoved one into his mouth alongside Drew's cock and wet it. Concentrating on his Master helped him gain control over his unruly body, which only screamed for release.

Zack teased along his crease and circled Drew's entrance with his wet finger before entering him a fraction. Good thing his Master wasn't a rigid top who never wanted anal play, or wouldn't… oh God….

His Master groaned around his cock, giving him a buzzing in his balls, which drew Zack's impending orgasm threateningly close to the surface.

Acting fast, Zack pulled the round asscheeks in his grip down, forcing his Master's dick to the back of his throat.

Zack gagged a little.

Drew groaned. His body trembled under the onslaught of Zack's mouth, signaling he was close.

God! Zack dug deep into his reserves and hollowed his cheeks until they hurt.

Swallow, suck, swallow, and suck.

He could handle being treated to a supreme tongue-lashing, but Drew increased the suction he provided.

Fuck! Zack was defeated.

In the same moment, his Master moaned around him as essence pulsed into Zack's mouth.

Yes! Success! Mine!

Zack groaned and allowed the full pleasure of his orgasm to wash over him. Waves of bliss shook him. He swallowed everything Drew gave to him.

Eventually Drew rolled off him, turned around, and placed a loving kiss on his mouth. He sagged onto the platform and held Zack close. His lover's heart thumped fast, matching his own. Their breathing and bodies returned to normal.

The Dark Angels' music drifted in from outside. Damn, they had to get out there. There was no escaping their friends, let alone their brothers.

"Come on. We can take a quick shower and head out there." Drew was right.

Zack only sighed.

"Hey." Drew turned to grin at him. "I love you, Zack."

"And I love you, Drew, Master Drew, and even Andrew."

Drew chuckled but didn't debate; he led Zack into the tiny attached bathroom. They showered quickly.

Damn! Zack would have much preferred to hide in this haven, having sex in a variety of ways....

They entered the main part of the club. Everyone danced to the song while laughing and having fun.

Angel saw them, and the music turned to a soft, romantic song.

Without his usual need to hide, Zack didn't mind being the center of attention. Drew twirled him around the floor. He didn't even care if he appeared like Cinder-fucking-fellow, because life could be amazing.

Zack lost himself to the music.

Drew led him through intricate steps, turns, and spins.

He followed flawlessly, anticipating Drew's every move and expectation of him. He might not have been the perfect sub, but he was perfect for Drew.

Their dance came to an end with a twirl into a low dip and a hot kiss. *Man!* His Master knew how to use his lips, mouth, and tongue....

A collective sigh penetrated his mind. *Oh.* Opening his eyes, he realized they were surrounded, and now everyone applauded.

Drew scooped him to his feet and led him into a stylish turn as the applause drew to a close. Angel regained the focus of the crowd and said, "Okay, pretty ones in leather. Let's see what you got."

The band started a fast song. Zack was content to simply hold and be held as he watched the crowd dance along with them.

Zack twirled without being led into the spin. He ignored Drew's arched brow and grinned mischievously at his lover/Master. "Hey, if I wanna to swirl around the dance floor, I damned well can."

"You're adorable at times." This proclaimed, Drew kissed him on the nose. "But sometimes, you're just plain naughty. I love you, though."

Zack got ready to give a disgruntled response, but he shrugged and said the only thing that mattered. "I love you too."

After another song, the DJ took over for the band members. They finally made it through the gauntlet of fanboys and girls who crowded them as soon as they came off the stage.

"Hey, thanks so much for playing, guys." Zack hadn't expected it when they'd invited the band but wouldn't turn down the generous offer.

"We wouldn't have missed your collaring for the world." Josh wrapped an arm around Robin, who nodded.

"The Dark Angels in a BDSM club. It was like a no-brainer," Angel joked as he adjusted his tight red leather outfit, as if it needed adjusting.

Darius hugged Zack. "It was a beautiful ceremony. The rose part was really... I don't know... moving."

"Thanks. We merged several different ceremonies and made one that worked for us."

Darius smiled a bit sadly and said, "It's stunning to see this kind of commitment between two people. You're both very lucky. Congratulations."

MUCH LATER, Zack lay sprawled over Drew in their own bed, and they were finally plucking petals and making wishes.

"I wish for us to have a long, healthy, happy life together." He pulled off a delicate white petal and let it float into the glass jar that sat between them.

"Well, that's gathering a bunch of wishes together," Drew teased. "But I think it's all right." He pulled off a petal and let it drop. "My wish is for us to grow together."

"I wish to make you happy." *Pluck.* Zack dropped the flower petal into the jar.

Drew shook his head. "The psychiatric society would shake their finger at you because no one can be responsible for another's happiness. Although I've always been of the mindset that codependence would be a very happy way to live, as long as both parties put the other person's needs in front of their own. I wish and sincerely hope I will always make you happy, in all things." *Pluck*, and the petal floated to the bottom of the jar.

A petal came off in Zack's fingertips. "I wish for us to be able to explore and continue to discover wonderful things together."

"Good one." Drew plucked one and stared for a moment at the white-stained-with-red-petal. "I wish to grow old together." He grinned wickedly at Zack. "You're the man I want to have erectile dysfunction with."

Zack grimaced but couldn't stop a chuckle. "You're a sick camper. I need to counteract that horrible wish. I wish neither of us experience ED or prostate issues." He shook his head and dropped the rose petal into the jar. He plucked another to be safe and dropped it into the jar. "You better hope that worked."

"My wish is that we explore the world together." Drew's petal drifted into the jar.

"Well, considering we're leaving for an overseas tour with the band, that one will happen sooner rather than later."

"Oh, Zack, did you do the paperwork for our visas for Vietnam and China? Megan said she sent it over. I completely forgot."

"Yeah, I filled out both of ours. You just need to sign it. It's on your desk."

"Awww, thanks. I like that." Drew leaned over and gave Zack a soft kiss.

Zack asked, "Yeah?" The love Zack saw in Drew's eyes, his Master's eyes, was reflected in his heart. "You are my everything."

"As you are mine. You are the key to my heart." Drew pressed another wet kiss onto Zack's lips and then another as they began making all their wishes come true.

Kneel. Love. Forever.

Z. ALLORA believes in happily ever afters for everyone. She met her own true love through the personals and has traveled to over thirty countries with him. She's lived in Singapore, Israel, and China. Now back home in the USA, she's an active member of PFLAG and a strong supporter of those on the rainbow in her community. She wants to promote understanding and acceptance through her actions and words. Writing rainbow romance allows her words to open hearts and change minds.

E-mail: Z.AlloraHappyEndings@gmail.com
Facebook: www.facebook.com/Z.Allora
Blog: zallora.blogspot.com
Website: www.zallorabooks.com

Z. ALLORA

Illusions & Dreams

THAILAND'S #1 LADYBOY SHOW

After Randy Camster failed at marriage, his life centered around work, TV sports, and listening to his friend Jake complain about how Randy's lack of a sex life will be the downfall of mankind. Not true! Well, not totally. Randy has just never understood the fascination with sex... until ladyboy performer Lalana Dulyarat shimmies into his world via an Internet ad for Thailand tourism. After that, it doesn't take much for Jake to convince Randy to take a Bang Cock vacation.

Finding an adorable little imp named Boon-nam wasn't on Jake O'Neil's itinerary. Gay, straight, and undecided, Jake has had 'em all, but never a virgin aching to explore her new body after successful affirmation surgery. Talk about pressure. And what's with everyone warning him not to break Boon-nam's heart? His is the one in danger.

Jake's openness about sexuality has always made Randy wonder if he is too focused on gender. Lalana is even more beautiful in real life than he'd hoped, but she's keeping her "male parts" and has no intention of ever having surgery. Does it really matter? A return ticket to reality awaits. The clock is ticking on the two couples' hopes for love, unless they can find a way to span gender, culture, and half a world.

www.dreamspinnerpress.com

Also from Dreamspinner Press

DEBT

K.C. Wells

www.dreamspinnerpress.com

Also from Dreamspinner Press

reckless

caitlin ricci

www.dreamspinnerpress.com

Also from Dreamspinner Press

WHAT
ABOUT
NOW

Grace R. Duncan

www.dreamspinnerpress.com

www.ingramcontent.com/pod-product-compliance
Lightning Source LLC
Chambersburg PA
CBHW070056030726
47506CB00002B/492